Charlaine Harris is the internationally bestselling author of several supernatural and mystery series, including the *Sunday Times* Number One bestselling *Sookie Stackhouse* books, filmed as the award-winning HBO® television series *True Blood*. She lives in a small town in southern Arkansas.

Toni L.P. Kelner is the Agatha Award-winning author of the *Where Are They Now?* and the *Laura Fleming* mysteries. She was awarded a Romantic Times Career Achievement Award, and her short stories have been nominated for the Agatha, the Anthony, the Macavity and the Derringer Awards. She lives in Massachusetts with her husband, fellow author Stephen P. Kelner, Jr. and their two daughters.

HOME IMPROVEMENT
UNDEAD EDITION
Edited by

CHARLAINE
HARRIS
& TONI L.P.
KELNER

Jo Fletcher
BOOKS

First published by The Berkley Publishing Group (USA) in 2011
This edition published in 2011 by

Jo Fletcher Books
an imprint of Quercus
55 Baker Street
7th Floor, South Block
London
W1U 8EW

To the third member of the FP Clan,
DANA CAMERON,
who can float like a butterfly and write like a dream

CONTENTS

INTRODUCTION

We tried writing an introduction using a labored analogy between building a house and assembling an anthology, but it just felt wrong. This is our fourth collaboration, and the process of collecting and editing an amazing assortment of stories is still great fun. We love making up our "dream team," sending out our invitations, and seeing who accepts and who has a previous engagement.

When we first began working together—on *Many Bloody Returns*—we didn't know how successful these books would come to be. We were nervous about asking a strange mixture of mystery and urban fantasy writers to take a leap of faith and send in stories that combined two random elements. In that case, it was vampires and birthdays. Since then, we have dreamed up some more combinations that seemed interesting and fun to us: *Wolfsbane and Mistletoe*, about werewolves and the holidays, and *Death's Excellent Vacation*, about creatures out of their normal habitat.

Home Improvement: Undead Edition came about when we both had teeth-gritting, jaw-clenching experiences arranging for mundane repairs around our own homes. After an orgy of consumer hand-wringing, we began to wonder how a supernatural creature would handle the same problem.

Each story we received is a unique vision of a situation that has arisen since the first mud hut sprung a leak in the rainy season, or the first cave needed a level floor. We've all been there. We hope you enjoy the creative ways writers have found to solve some common problems: fencing, housing inspectors, kitchen flow, water in the basement, security systems, vandalism, and, oh yes, resident ghosts.

CHARLAINE HARRIS
TONI L. P. KELNER

If I Had a Hammer

CHARLAINE HARRIS

"If I had a hammer," I sang, as I used the measuring tape and a pencil to mark where I needed to drill.

From the next room, Tara called, "I'm going to leave if you're going to sing."

"I'm not *that* bad," I said with mock indignation.

"Oh yes, you are!" She was changing one of the twins in the next room.

We'd been friends forever. Tara's husband, JB du Rone, was part of that friendship. We'd formed a little group of misfits at our high school in Bon Temps, Louisiana. What had saved us from utter outcast-dom was that we each had a redeeming talent. I could play softball, Tara was a great manager (yearbook, softball team), and JB was incredibly handsome and could play football, given good and patient coaching.

What put us on the fringes, you ask? I was telepathic; Tara's parents were embarrassing, abusive, poor, and public in their drunkenness; and JB was as dumb as a stump.

Yet here we were in our later twenties, reasonably happy human beings. JB and Tara had married and very recently produced twins. I had a good job and a life that was more exciting than I wanted it to be.

JB and Tara had been surprised—amazed—when they had discovered they were going to be parents, and even more startled to find they were having twins. Many children had grown up in this little house—it was around eighty years old—but modern families want more space. Though cozy and comfortable for two, the house began to creak at the seams after Robbie and Sara—Robert Thornton du Rone and Sara Sookie du Rone—were born, but buying a larger place wasn't a possibility. That they owned this snug bungalow on Magnolia Street was something of a miracle.

Tara had gotten the house years before when Tara's Togs started making some money. After careful consideration, she'd chosen the old Summerlin place, a bungalow built in the late twenties or early thirties. I'd always loved Magnolia Street, lined with houses from that same era, shaded by huge trees and enhanced with bright flower beds.

Tara's one-floor house had two bedrooms (one large and one tiny), one bathroom, a kitchen, a living room, a dining room, and a sunroom. The sunroom, which faced the front of the house and lay through an arch to the right of the living room, was becoming the babies' room because it was actually much larger than the second bedroom. And the closet that served that bedroom backed onto the sunroom.

After a summit meeting the week before, attended by me; my boss, Sam Merlotte; and Tara's babysitter, Quiana Wong, Tara and JB had made a plan. With our help, they'd knock out the wall at the back of the little bedroom's closet, which was between that room and the sunroom. Then we'd block in the closet from the bedroom side so the opening would be on the sunroom side. We'd frame that opening and hang louvered doors. The sunroom would become the new baby bedroom, and it would have a closet and shelves on the walls for storage. We'd paint the sunroom and the little bedroom. And the job would be done. Just a little home improvement project, but it would make a big difference.

The very next day, Tara had gone to Sew Right in Shreveport to pick out material, and she'd begun making new curtains to cover the bank of windows that flooded the sunroom with light.

Sam had agreed to perform the wall removal, but he was pretty anxious. "I know it can be done," he said, "but I've never tried to do it." JB and Tara had assured him they had the utmost faith in him, and with some tips from all-purpose handyman Terry Bellefleur, Sam had assembled the tools he'd need.

Tara, Quiana, the twins, and I had assembled in the sunroom to watch for the exciting moment when Sam cut through the old wall. We could hear a lot of cutting and sawing and general whamming going on, along with the occasional curse. JB was dragging the bits of drywall outside as Sam removed them.

It was kind of exciting in a low-key way.

Then I heard Sam say, "Huh. Look at that, JB."

"What is that?" JB sounded surprised and taken aback.

"This piece of board has been cut out and replaced."

"[*mumble mumble mumble*] . . . electric wires?"

"No, shouldn't be. It's kind of an amateur [*mumble mumble*] . . . Here, I can open it. Let me slide this screwdriver in . . ."

Even from our side of the wall, I could hear the creak as Sam pried the panel out from between the studs. But then there was silence.

Unable to contain my curiosity, I left the sunroom and zoomed through the living room to round the wall into the current nursery. Sam was all the way in the closet, and JB was standing at his shoulder. Both were looking at whatever Sam had uncovered.

"It's a hammer," Sam said quietly.

"Can I see?" I said, and Sam turned and held the hammer out to me.

I took it automatically, but I was sorry when I understood what I was holding. It was a hammer, all right. And it was covered with dark stains.

Sam said, "It smells like old blood."

"This must be the hammer that killed Isaiah Wechsler," JB said, as if that were the first thing that would pop into anyone's mind.

"Isaiah Wechsler?" Sam said. He hadn't grown up in Bon Temps like the rest of us.

"Let's go sit in the living room, and I'll tell you about it," I said. The little room suddenly felt hostile and confined, and I wanted to leave it.

The living room was pretty crowded with five adults and two babies. Tara was nursing Sara, a shawl thrown discreetly across her shoulder. Quiana was holding baby Robbie, rocking him to keep him content until his turn came.

"Back in the early thirties, Jacob and Sarah Jane Wechsler lived next door," Tara told Sam. "In the house Andy and Halleigh Bellefleur live in now. The Summerlins, Daisy and Hiram, built this house. The Wechslers had a son, Isaiah, who was about fifteen. The Summerlins had two sons, one a little older than Isaiah, and one younger, I think thirteen. You would have thought the boys would be friends, but for some reason Isaiah, a big bull of a boy, got into a fight with the older Summerlin boy, whose name was . . ." She paused, looking doubtful.

"Albert," I said. "Albert was a year older than Isaiah Wechsler, a husky kid with red hair and freckles, Gran told me. Albert's little brother was Carter, and he was thirteen, I think. He was quiet, lots of curly red hair."

"Surely your grandmother didn't remember this," Sam said. He'd been doing math in his head.

"No, she was too young when it all happened. But her mom knew both families. The fight and the estrangement caused a town scandal because the Wechslers and the Summerlins couldn't get Isaiah and Albert to shake hands and make up. The boys wouldn't tell anyone what the fight was about."

Tara reached under the shawl to detach Sara, extricated her, and began burping her. Sara was a champion burper. I could feel the sadness in Tara's thoughts. I figured the old story was rousing memories of her contentious family. "Anyway," I said with energy, "the two Summerlin boys slept in the room in there." I pointed to the wall Sam had just breached. "The parents had the bigger bedroom, and there was a baby; they kept the baby in with them. In the house across the driveway, Isaiah Wechsler slept in a bedroom whose window faced this house." I pointed to the sunroom's north window. "I think Andy and Halleigh use it as a den now. One summer night, two weeks after the big fight between Isaiah and Albert, someone went through Isaiah's open window and killed him in his sleep. Beat him to death."

"Ugh." Sam looked a little sick, and I knew he was thinking of the dark-stained hammer.

Quiana's slanting dark eyes were squinted almost shut with distress, disgust, some unpleasant emotion. She left the room with Sara to change her after handing Robbie to Tara.

I said, "The poor Wechslers found him in the morning in the bed, all bloody, and they sent for the police. There was one policeman in Bon Temps then, and he came right away. Back then, that meant within an hour."

"You won't believe who the policeman was, Sam," Tara said. "It was a man named Fuller Compton, one of Bill's descendants."

I didn't want to start talking about Bill, who was an ex of mine. I hastened on with the sad story. "The Wechslers told Fuller Compton that the Summerlins had killed their son. What could Fuller do but go next door? Of course, the Summerlins denied it, said their son Albert had been sleeping and hadn't left the house. Fuller didn't see anything bloody, and Carter Summerlin told the policeman that his brother had been in the bed the whole night."

"No CSI then," JB said wisely.

"That's just sad," Quiana said, returning with Sara, who was waving her arms in a sleepy way.

"So nothing happened? No one was arrested?" Sam asked.

"Well, I think Fuller arrested a vagrant and held him for a while in the jail, but there wasn't any evidence against him, and Fuller finally let him go. The Summerlins sent Carter out of town the next week to stay with relatives. He was so young. They must have wanted to protect him from the backlash. Albert Summerlin was regarded with lots of suspicion by the whole town, but there wasn't any evidence against him. And afterward, Albert never showed signs of a hot temper. He kept on going to church. People began speaking to Daisy and Hiram and Albert again. Albert never got into another fight." I shook my head. "People were sure the Wechslers would move, but they said they weren't gonna. They were going to stay and be a reminder to the Summerlins every day of their lives."

"Are there Wechslers still here in Bon Temps?" Sam asked.

"Cathy Wechsler is about seventy, and she lives in a little house over close to Clarice," JB said. "She's nice. She's the widow of the last Wechsler."

"What happened to Albert?" Quiana asked. "And the baby?"

"Not much," I said. "The older Summerlins passed away. Carter decided not to come back. The baby died of scarlet fever. Albert married and had kids. Raised them here in this house. Tara bought the house from Bucky Summerlin, right, Tara?"

"Yep," she said. She was patting Robbie on the back now. Robbie was goggling around at everyone with that goofy baby look. Sara was asleep in Quiana's arms, and I checked on the nanny automatically. Her thoughts were all about the baby, and I relaxed. Though I'd checked out Quiana thoroughly when Tara had told me she was thinking of hiring her, I still felt I didn't know her well.

If JB, Tara, and I had been considered odd ducks, Quiana had received a double whammy of misfit mojo. Her mother had been half Chinese, half African American. Her dad, Coop Woods, had been all redneck. When Quiana was sixteen, they'd both been killed when their car stalled on the train tracks one night. Alcohol had been involved. There'd been rumors that Coop had planned a murder-suicide. Now Quiana was eighteen, staying with whatever relative would have her. I felt sorry for her precarious situation . . . and I knew there was something different about the girl. I'd given Tara the green light to hire her, though, because whatever her quirk was, it was not malignant.

Now Sam said, "You think we ought to call the police? After all, there's a detective right next door."

I noticed none of us hopped in to say *Yes, that's the ticket.*

Sure, the hammer had stains, and Sam's nose was telling him the stains were old blood.

Sure, the hammer had been concealed in the wall.

Sure, a murder had taken place next door. But there might not be any connection.

Right.

"I don't think we have to," Tara said, and JB nodded, relieved. It was their say as the homeowners, I figured. I looked at the hammer as it lay on an old newspaper on the coffee table. Hammers hadn't changed much over the decades. The handle was worn, and when I picked it up and turned it over, I saw that the writing on it read FIRESTONE SUPREME. With the dark stains on it, the tool looked remarkably ugly in the sunny room. It could never be just a tool again.

Tara picked it up by folding the paper around it, and she carried it out of the room.

Tara's action jogged us all into motion. We split in different directions to go to work: JB to the fitness club, where he cleaned and trained; Sam and I to Merlotte's Bar; and Tara to check on her assistant, McKenna, who was running the store while Tara was on maternity leave. As I called good-bye, Quiana was putting the twins down for their nap on Tara and JB's bed since the babies' room was full of dust.

I FORCED MYSELF to go to Tara's by nine in the morning the next day. I had to fight a deep reluctance. For the first time, the pretty little house with its neat front yard seemed gloomy. Even the sky was overcast. I tapped on the front door, opened it, and called, "Woo-hoo! I'm here!"

Quiana was already at work folding laundry, but her full mouth was turned down in a sullen pout and she only nodded when I spoke to her. JB was nowhere in sight. Of course, he could be at the fitness club already, but normally he worked in the afternoon and evening. Tara, too, didn't show her face.

Sam trailed in right on my heels, and we got mugs of coffee in the kitchen. Quiana didn't respond to our attempts at conversation, and she fixed a bottle for one of the twins in silence. Tara was having to supplement, apparently.

JB emerged from the bedroom looking groggy. My old friend was usually the most cheerful guy around, but this morning he had circles under his eyes and looked five years older. "Babies cried all night," he said wearily. "I don't know what got into them. They're in the bed with Tara right now." He downed his coffee in record time. Gradually he began to perk up, and when we set our mugs in the sink we all looked a little brighter.

I began to worry. This was a funny kind of day—in an ominous way.

Sam and JB went back into the little bedroom to finish cutting out the doorway. I climbed a folding stool to mount some brackets for shelving, which would be right above where the changing table would be placed. The tracks for the adjustable brackets were already up. (I had learned how to use an electric drill to mount them, and I was justly proud of myself.) I began counting holes on the tracks so the brackets would be even.

"And there you have it, a solid brace," I said with some satisfaction. They were mounted too high for the twins to be tempted to climb on them, when they got bigger. They were designed to hold things Tara would need when she was changing the babies, and on the higher shelves would be the knickknacks people had given her: a china baby shoe with a plant in it, a cute picture frame with a photo of the twins, their baby books.

"Good job, Sook," Sam said behind me.

I jumped, and he laughed. "You were thinking too hard to hear me come through the new closet door," he said. "I tried to walk heavy."

"You are evil," I said, climbing down. "I don't think I'll work for you anymore."

"Don't tell me that," he said. "What would I do without you?"

I grinned at him. "I expect you'd find a way to carry on. This economy, there are plenty of women who need a job, even working for a slave driver like you."

He snorted. "You mean a pushover like me. Besides, you have your own financial interest in the bar now. Where are the shelves? I can hand 'em to you."

"JB cut them yesterday, and he was going to paint them when he got in from work last night."

Sam shrugged. "Haven't seen 'em."

"Tara," I called. "You up yet?"

"Yeah," she called. I followed her voice to the current baby room. Tara was changing Robbie. She was smiling down at the baby, but she looked haggard.

"He wants to know where his sis is," Tara said, freely interpreting Robbie's googly stare. "I think JB's got Sara."

"I'll track 'em down," I offered. I stepped into the kitchen, where Quiana was at the stove cooking . . . spaghetti sauce, from the smell. "You seen JB and Sara?" I asked. She was thinking that she didn't like the idea that someone could read her thoughts. I could hardly blame her for that. I didn't like the fact that I could, either. I sensed more strongly than ever that there was something different about Quiana, something that chimed in with my own peculiarity. It wasn't the time to tax her with it, though.

"They went outside," she murmured, her bony little figure hunched over the stove like a junior witch's. I crossed behind her to go out the back door.

"JB?" At first glance the fenced-in yard with its minute patio and lone water oak looked empty.

The shelf boards were there, and they were painted, which I was glad to see. But where was JB? And more important, where was baby Sara?

"JB!" I called again. "Where are you?" Maybe because of the high fence, there was not a bit of breeze in the backyard. The lawn furniture sat dusty and baking on the bricks. It was hot enough to make my skin prickle. I closed my eyes and took a deep breath, inhaling the scents of town: asphalt, cooking, vehicles, dogs. I searched for a living brain in the area and had just found two when a subdued voice said, "Here."

I circled the water oak close to the west corner of the yard to find JB sitting on the ground. I closed my eyes in relief when I saw that he was holding Sara, who was making those cute little baby noises and waving her arms.

"What's the matter?" I asked, trying to sound gentle and relaxed.

JB had let his hair grow, and he pulled it back with a ponytail holder. If you had to compare him to a movie star—yes, he was that handsome— he was pretty much in the fair-haired Jason Lewis mold. Physically. "There's something angry and sad in the house," he said, sounding way more serious and troubled than I'd ever heard him. "When we opened the wall and touched the hammer, it got out."

If I hadn't had such a strange life, I might have laughed. I might have tried to convince JB it was his imagination. But my friend was anything but imaginative, and he'd never shown a taste for the dark side before. JB had always been sunny, optimistic, and generally along for the ride.

"So, when did you . . . notice this?" I said.

Sam had approached us quietly. Now he knelt by JB. With a finger, he stroked the line of Sara's plump little cheek.

"I noticed it last night," JB said. "It was walking around the house."

"Did Tara see it, too?" Sam asked. He didn't look directly at JB. The sun set his strawberry-blond hair on fire as he knelt in the yard.

"No, she didn't." JB shook his head. "But I know it's there. Don't tell me I'm making it up or that I'm dreaming or something. That's bullshit."

"I believe you," I said.

"I believe you, too," Sam said.

"Good," said JB, looking down at his daughter. "Then let's find out how to get rid of it."

"Who'm I gonna call for that?" I wondered out loud.

"Ghostbusters," Sam said automatically. Then he looked embarrassed.

"Me," said a new voice, and we all rotated to look at Quiana. She still had the spoon in her hand, and it was dripping red.

There was what you might call a significant pause.

"I know stuff," she said, sounding pretty unhappy about it. "I get pictures in my head."

The pause extended to an uncomfortable length. I had to say something. She was already full of regret at revealing herself, and I could see *that* clearly, anyway. "How long have you been psychic?" I asked, which was like saying, *Do you come here often?* But I was clean out of ideas.

"Since I was little," she said. "But with my parents, you know, I knew not to say anything after the first time . . . they got spooked."

That was probably an understatement, and I could completely sympathize with Quiana. I'd had the same problem. Having a little girl living with you who could read your mind had been tough on both my mother and my father, and consequently tough on me.

"How does it happen?" I said, since Sam and JB were still floundering through their thoughts. "I mean, do you get clear pictures? What triggers them?"

She shrugged, but I could tell she was relieved that I was taking her seriously. "It's touch, mostly. I mean, I don't have visions when I'm driving or anything like that."

"That's so interesting," I said, and I was totally sincere. It was kind of neat to know someone else who was completely human but also wasn't normal.

She felt the same way.

"So when you touch the babies," JB said abruptly, "what do you see?"

"They're little," Quiana said with surprising gentleness. "I ain't going to see nothing with them this little."

Since that wasn't true, I had to applaud her for keeping her mouth shut. And I was grateful that she didn't spell out whatever she had seen in her own head, that I didn't have to see it with her. If anything was worse than reading people's minds, it would be knowing their future—especially when there wasn't anything you could do about it.

"Can you . . . You can't change anything?" I asked. "When you see something that's going to happen?"

"I cannot," she said, with absolute finality. "I don't have a bit of responsibility. But people make decisions, and that can change what I've seen." Quiana's golden skin flushed as we all stared at her.

"Right now," said Sam, getting from the bigger picture to the smaller, "do you think you can help us with the problems in this house?"

Quiana looked down. "I don't know how, but I'm going to try," she said. "When I figure out what to do." She looked at each of us questioningly. None of us had a helpful idea, at least not at the moment.

I said, "I'm hoping that the funny feeling in the house will sort of wear away, myself. Sam opened the wall, we've found the hammer, so we know Albert did kill Isaiah. Surely that should set it all to rest."

JB said, "Is that the way it works?" He didn't seem to have a doubt in the world that I would know the answer.

"Friend, I don't know," I said. "If it doesn't work that way, maybe we should call the Catholic priest." One came to Bon Temps's little church from a nearby town.

"But this isn't a demon that needs to be exorcised," Quiana said, outraged. "It's not a devil. It's just real unhappy."

"It has to go be unhappy somewhere else," JB said. "This is our house. These are our babies. They can't go on crying all the time."

As if he'd pressed a cue button, we could hear Robbie start to wail in the house. We all sighed simultaneously, which would have been funny if we'd had a clue what to do. But further conversation didn't trigger any plan, so we figured we might as well go back to the job that had brought us there.

Sam and I picked up the painted shelves and went inside to put them up. Quiana followed, and she returned to the stove to stir the spaghetti sauce, her face tense with distress, her brain concentrating on fighting the unhappiness that flowed through the house like invisible water.

Sam brought in the paint. While I painted the doorframe, the men put up the drywall to close up where the old closet door had been. Once that was done, Sam very carefully painted the new wall on the old babies' room side while I painted the interior of the closet from the new babies' room side. It was odd to hear his brushstrokes just a few millimeters away from mine. We were working on the same thing, but invisible to each other.

It didn't take long to finish my task. JB planned to put up two hanger rods for the twins' tiny clothes, and shelving above them, but he'd left a few minutes before to run errands before going to work. JB had been moving slowly. When he'd gotten into his car he'd sat for a moment, his head resting on the steering wheel. But before he'd reached the corner he was smiling, and I felt my shoulders relax with relief.

After cleaning his brushes and drop cloths, Sam left for Merlotte's. It was my day off and I needed to take care of some bills. I could hardly wait to get out of the house. I offered to take Tara with me while I drove around town, and to my surprise she agreed to go. She sat quietly in the car the whole time, and I couldn't tell if she was depressed or exhausted, or maybe both. She grew more talkative the longer we were away.

"We can't leave our house," she said. "I can't afford to buy another one, and we can't live with JB's folks. Besides, no one would buy it unless we can make it a regular home again."

Since I hadn't been in the house as long as Tara, I recovered my spirits more quickly. "Maybe we're just being silly, Tara. Maybe we're making a mountain out of a molehill."

"Or a haunting out of a hammer," she said, and we both managed to laugh.

We returned to eat Quiana's spaghetti and garlic bread in a much more grounded frame of mind. I can't tell you how cheered I was by our little excursion . . . or how bleak I felt after we'd been back in the house only ten minutes. The exhausted babies slept for a while, and lunch was at least tolerable, but always at the back of our conversation was the feeling that any moment one of us would burst into tears.

There wasn't a mind I could read to get any information on what was happening in this house. There wasn't an action I could take, a deed I could perform, that could help. I had a few friends who were witches, but Amelia Broadway, the only one I trusted, was in Europe for a month. I felt oddly stymied.

LATER THAT EVENING, we met back in the living room, even Sam and JB. No one had arranged it—it was like we were all drawn back to the house by whatever unhappy thing we'd disturbed.

Tara had slipcovered the love seat and couch recently, and she'd hung some pretty pictures of the Thomas Kinkade school: lots of cute cottages with flowers, or lofty trees with the sun grazing the tops. This was the kind of house Tara wanted: peaceful, bright, happy.

The house on Magnolia Street was not like that any longer.

Tara was holding Sara, and JB was holding Robbie. Both babies were fussy—again, still—which upped the tension in the room. Tara, uncharacteristically, had decided to turn away from reality. She was blaming JB for the misery in the house.

"He watches *Ghost Hunters* too often," she said, for maybe the tenth time. "I've lived here for four years and I've never felt a thing wrong!"

"Tara, there's something wrong now," I said, as quietly as I could. "You know there is. Quiana knows there is. We all know there is."

"Oh, for God's sake!" Tara said impatiently, and she jiggled Sara so hard that Sara started crying. Tara looked shocked, and for a moment I read her impulse to hand Sara to someone else, anyone. Instead, she took a deep breath and rocked Sara with exaggerated gentleness. (She was terrified of turning into her mother. I think that says it all about Mama Thornton.)

Quiana stood, and there was something desperately brave about the way she went into the sunroom and approached the closet. Her thick black hair pulled back in a band, her thin shoulders squared, her golden face determined. With great courage, Quiana stepped into the space where the hammer had been stowed for so long.

I rose hastily, covering the few steps without a thought. I stood outside the closet looking in. Quiana turned a muddy white and her eyes rolled up. I sort of expected her to fall to the floor and convulse, but she stayed on her feet. Her small hands shot out in my direction. Without thinking, I grabbed them. They were freezing cold. I felt a charge of stinging electricity passing from her to me, and I made my own little shocked noise.

"Sookie?" Sam was just about to put his hand on my shoulder when I stopped him with a sharp shake of my head. I could just see us forming a chain of shaking, grunting victims of whatever had entered Quiana Wong. I could see a shape in her brain, something that wasn't Quiana. Someone else inhabited her for a few awful seconds.

And then it was over. I had my arms around Quiana and her head on my shoulder. I was patting her a little desperately, saying, "Hey, you okay? You need to go to the hospital?"

Quiana straightened, shaking her head as if she had cobwebs caught in her hair. She said, "Step back so I can get out of this fucking closet."

I did so very promptly.

"What happened?" Sam said. The hairs on his arms were standing on end.

Quiana was understandably freaked, but she was also excited. Her skin glowed with it. I'd never seen her look so lively.

The babies were as quiet and big-eyed as fawns when a predator is near. JB looked scared and Tara looked angry, both pretty typical reactions.

By an exchange of half-finished sentences, we agreed to adjourn to the backyard. Though it was hot, the heat was better than whatever had been in the closet.

Tara brought all of us sweating cans of soda from the refrigerator, and we sat in the darkness, the area lit only by the light coming from the house windows. I wondered what the neighbors would think of our silent, somber party if they could see over Tara's fence.

"So, what was it?" I asked Quiana when she looked a little more collected.

"It was a ghost," she said promptly.

"So it must have been the boy Isaiah," I said. "Since he was the murder victim. But why would his ghost be in this house? He was killed next door, right? Andy and Halleigh haven't had any problems, because Andy would have told me." (On purpose or by accident—Andy was a clear broadcaster.)

"There weren't any bones or anything," Tara objected. "Just the hammer." Quiana leaned over to take one of the twins from Tara, and Tara hesitated before letting Quiana take the baby. I could feel Quiana's sadness, but she didn't blame Tara. "Shouldn't there be remains of a body if there's a ghost here?"

"Ghosts don't have to be where their physical remains are laid," Quiana said, her voice weary. "They're stuck where the emotion . . . grabbed them up."

"Huh?" Tara said.

"It's the strong emotion that imprints them on the place," Quiana told us. "It's the trauma."

Now that she'd decided to tell us she was a psychic, Quiana was just full of information.

"What kind of trauma?" JB said.

"Usually the death trauma," Quiana said, a little impatiently. "If a person dies real scared, real angry, he leaves his imprint on the space where that emotion took over. Or sometimes the person gets fixed on an object that played a part in the traumatic event. Like a bloody hammer? And after he dies, that's where his ghost manifests. In this case, the hammer and the closet are the objects."

"Huh," Sam said. He didn't sound like he was automatically signing up for the Ghost Hunters Club, but he didn't sound skeptical, either. More like he was chewing these new ideas over. That was kind of the way I felt. My world had not included this before now. "So you're saying he—is it a guy?—could be buried anywhere."

"In the movies, when you find the bones, the ghost is laid," JB said unexpectedly.

"The murder victim was Isaiah Wechsler, and his headstone is out in the cemetery by my house," I said.

"But someone's not resting easy," JB said, sounding just as reasonable. "You know that, Sookie."

Suddenly I felt tired and depressed, more depressed than I'd ever been in my life. And that just wasn't me. I'm not saying I'm Pollyanna, but this sudden misery simply wasn't my normal style.

"Sam," I said, "do you think you could change to your bloodhound form? And maybe go over the yard? If there was a burial that had to do with the murder, it would be really old, and hard to scent." I shrugged. "But it's worth a try."

"This is real life," Tara said, not exactly as if she were angry, but simply protesting that none of this should be happening.

Real life? I almost laughed. Experiencing a ghost secondhand and looking for a corpse weren't what I wanted from my real life. On the other hand, worse things had happened to me.

"All right," Sam said grudgingly. "But not tonight. It's nowhere near the full moon, so it won't be as easy to change. I need a full night's sleep first." *I wouldn't do this for anyone but her,* Sam thought, feeling ashamed that he was dragging his feet.

I could only be grateful I had such a friend.

THE NEXT DAY I was at Tara's house by midafternoon. Sam pulled up just as I got out of my car.

I was startled to see JB and Tara on their way out, in workout clothes. "I got called in to substitute for another trainer," JB explained.

I looked at Tara, my eyebrows raised. She said, "I have to get the hell out of this house. Quiana just got here. She's in charge of the twins." In truth, Tara looked awful, and JB not much better. I nodded. "We'll keep on with the plan, then," I said, and they were out the door before I could say good-bye.

When Sam and I went in the kitchen, Quiana was bathing Robbie, while Sara sat in her infant seat. The babysitter looked determined to do her job. Robbie was whimpering, and I picked up Sara from her infant seat and patted her back, hoping she'd stay quiet. But she didn't. She began to cry. It looked as if Quiana needed some help for a while.

Since there wasn't a third baby for Sam to hold, he went to work on the hardware for the new closet doors. I walked Sara around the house, trying to make her happier, and when I went through the sunroom I helped by handing Sam whatever he needed. Sometimes being a telepath can be handy.

"Do you feel as lousy as I do?" he asked, as both babies escalated to full Defcon Five. I chickened out and put Sara in her infant seat in the kitchen while Quiana dressed Robbie.

"At least that lousy," I said.

"I wonder if hauntings are all like this."

"I hope I never experience another one to find out," I said. "I wonder . . ." I dropped my voice to a whisper. "I wonder if any of this would have happened if Quiana hadn't been here. If a psychic hadn't been around, would we have had the same experience? Would the hammer have been a haunted hammer, or just a bloody hammer?"

Sam shrugged and laid down his tools. "Who knows?" He took a deep breath. "Come on. If I'm going to turn, I want to get it over with. Kennedy is watching the bar, but I want to get back sooner rather than later." The atmosphere of the house was having its way with Sam.

I followed him through the house. Quiana watched us pass through the kitchen, her face dark with unhappiness, her eyes shadowed. The babies had finally gotten quiet in their infant seats, watching their nanny clean up from the bathing ordeal. I looked into her brain to be sure that Quiana was herself and that she was alert; Robbie and Sara were safe.

Though I'd seen Sam change before, I could never get jaded about watching a human turn into an animal. I'd overheard some college kids in the bar talking about the physics of shapeshifting, and they'd seemed to think that the transformation was *impossible*. So much for their impossibilities. It was happening before me: a full-sized man changed into a bloodhound. Sam liked to turn into dogs, because humans weren't as likely to shoot him by mistake. As a true shapeshifter, he had an advantage over wereanimals, who had to transform to one thing—werewolf, of course, or weretiger, werewombat—whatever their genetic makeup was. Sam enjoyed the variety. Sam, who normally had a smooth and swift transition, was panting on the ground when I got a scare.

"Smooth move," Quiana said from right behind me. I jumped about a mile. "I wish I could do that," she added.

"Hell in a handbasket, Quiana! Why didn't you say something?"

"I was making plenty of noise," she said casually. "You were just too interested in watching."

I opened the back door and threw Sam's clothes on one of the dinette chairs. "Aren't you supposed to be with the twins?"

She unclipped a device from the waistband of her shorts. "I got the monitor right here. They're both asleep in their cribs. Finally."

Sam rolled to his feet and ambled over to me. I never knew exactly how much he understood human speech while he was in animal form, but he was looking at the house and his chest was rumbling. "I'm going to check on them," I said. If that sounded distrustful, I didn't care.

The atmosphere in the house seemed somewhat easier, more peaceful. I wondered if the bad influence was wearing away—or was it because we three were out in the yard? That was a disturbing idea. I made myself put it aside, and I looked at the sleeping Robbie, hardly daring to breathe loud. The baby seemed perfectly all right. So did Sara, in her own crib. I put my hand gently on Sara's back. The inchoate dreams of an infant flowed into my head. I thought of putting both of them in the stroller and taking them with me into the backyard, but the house was so pleasant and cool, and it was so hot outside. We had the monitor.

I went back to the yard. Sam was scouting around, examining the space with his nose. His floppy ears were hanging forward. I'd read that this pushed the scent up to a bloodhound's nose. Amazing. I personally thought he was very cute as a bloodhound, but that got into kind of queasy territory, so it was a thought I had to banish.

"He's working hard," Quiana remarked. She'd perched on the edge of one of the yard chairs, her hands tucked between her bare knees. Her thick dark hair was twisted and secured on top of her head with a clip or two, because it was too hot for long hair. My own was piled up in much the same way.

"You two have been friends a long time," she said, when I didn't respond to her last comment.

"Yes," I said. "A few years, now."

"You have a lot of friends."

"I have a lot of friendly acquaintances. It's hard to have close friends, when you have a mental thing like mine."

"Tell me about it." Quiana shuddered delicately.

Frankly, I didn't know if I wanted to be Quiana's friend or not. There was something in her that put me off. I realized this was pretty damn ironic, since that was the way people often felt about me, but I didn't think Quiana made me uneasy simply because she had an unusual ability. She made me anxious because for a few minutes the day before she hadn't been alone in her skin. Someone else had been there with her.

I turned my eyes away from the girl. I didn't want her wondering what I was thinking about. I watched Sam instead. He was sniffing the ground with the efficiency of a vacuum cleaner.

The lot was long and narrow, with the house leaving very little room on either side. On the north side of the house, there were maybe five feet between the air conditioner sticking out of the kitchen window and the fence that surrounded the yard from the front wall of the house to the rear property line. Naturally, it was in that narrow strip that Sam found a promising scent. He went over it anxiously, and then he raised his head and bayed.

I hoped all the neighbors really were at work. At least the fence blocked the view.

Sam's doleful bloodhound face swung toward me, and he pawed at the ground at his feet. "Awwwrrrrhr," he said.

I got the shovel from the tool shed. This was not going to be pretty. I was trickling with sweat after the first few shovelfuls, and I was maybe a little peeved that Quiana didn't ask to take a turn digging. She looked down into the gradually increasing hole with an unnerving and unswerving fascination.

I looked at Sam, who was licking one of his paws. "You better go inside and change back," I said. "Thanks, Sam." He started ambling toward the steps and paused, stymied. I pitched a shovelful of dirt at Quiana's feet. "Quiana," I said sharply, "You need to open the back door for him."

It was like I'd stuck a pin in her, she looked so startled. "Sure," she said. "Sure, I'll do it."

I watched her go over to the door, and it seemed to me she stumbled a little, was a bit shaky on her feet. Her mind was blurry, foggy, with strong impressions coming from God knows where. After Sam was in the house, I resumed digging. The faster I went, the sooner we'd know if Sam had found an old turkey carcass or human remains.

After another five minutes I had to pause. Quiana had returned to her place at the edge of the hole. Her stance was rigid and her eyes were fixed on the upturned earth.

I heard a couple of slamming car doors. JB and Tara had returned. I felt a surprising amount of relief.

I was leaning on my shovel when they all came into the backyard—all the adults, that is. The twins were still sleeping. Sam had resumed his human form, and he was in his cutoff jeans again. His Hawaiian shirt looked cool with its loose drape around his torso. I envied him. My tank top felt wet and clingy.

JB and Tara were still wearing their workout clothes, so they were as sweaty as I was, but they both looked more relaxed.

"So, there something in there?" Tara asked, peering down at the hole I'd made.

"Sam thinks so," I replied. "JB, you want to shovel for a while?"

"Sure, Sook," he said amiably, and he grabbed the shovel. I sank to my haunches and watched him work.

Sam squatted by me. He never wavered in his expectant posture.

And with a terrible predictability, the shovel hit something that scraped instead of crunched. Without being told, JB started to scratch at the dirt with the shovel blade instead of sinking it in.

We didn't need the monitor to hear the babies begin to wail.

Quiana tore herself away to go in to them. Tara seemed relieved to leave it to her.

JB uncovered a femur.

We regarded the bone in silence.

"Well, we got us a body," Sam said. "Now we need to know who it belonged to."

"How are we gonna explain what we were doing?" Tara asked.

"We could say you were going to plant some beans," I said. "I know it's late for beans, but a cop would believe that." I left unspoken the fact that Andy would believe that if we said it was JB's idea. "We can say we were digging the holes for the runner poles."

"So they'll come get the bones out, and then what? Will things get better in our house?" Tara's eyes were bright with anger. "Will we stop being miserable? What about the babies? I think we have to find out who this guy was."

"It's not Isaiah Wechsler, and we know Albert lived, and we know Carter was sent away after the murder. So who could this be?" I looked around, hoping someone would look as though he had had a revelation, but everyone looked blank.

JB, shovel in hand, was standing by the crouching Sam. They were silently regarding the hole that was a grave. Sam was scowling.

"Tara, we can't ignore this," I said, as gently as I could. I was fighting a rising wave of irritation.

"I know that," she snapped. "I never said we could, Sookie. But I got to figure out what's best for me and my family."

Quiana had been gone a handful of minutes by now. I could still hear the babies crying. Why hadn't she found out what was wrong and fixed it?

The normally placid JB nudged Sam to make him move away from the grave. Sam's jaw set in a way I knew meant he was barely holding on to his temper.

I didn't trust any emotion I felt.

Tara was angry with me, which wasn't normal. Sam and JB were glaring at each other. The anger in the air was affecting all of us. I made myself run into the house to find out why the babies were weeping. Tara should be doing this! I followed the sobs to their little room.

Quiana was sitting in the rocking chair crammed in beside the cribs, and she was crying, too.

"Oh, for God's sake," I said. "Snap out of it."

Her tear-stained face looked at me with resentment written all over it. "I have a right to grieve for what I've lost. Only my brother knows the real me," she said bitterly.

Uh-oh.

"Quiana," I said, suddenly feeling a lot calmer and a lot more nervous, "you don't have a brother."

"Of course I do." But she looked confused.

"You're being haunted," I said, trying to sound matter-of-fact. I didn't want to say the word *possessed*, but it was definitely hovering in the air.

"Sure, that's right, blame me because I'm the one who's different," she snarled in a complete emotional about-face.

I flinched, but I had to pass her to get to the babies, whose cries had redoubled. I decided to take a chance. "You want to go outside?" I said. Then I made a guess. "You can see your bones." I watched her carefully, since I had no idea what she'd do next.

There was someone else behind Quiana's face, someone both anguished and angry. All I could think about was getting her out of the room.

And then Quiana got up and left the room, her face blank. She wasn't even walking like herself.

I scooped up Sara, who was shrieking like a banshee.

"Sara," I said. "Please stop crying." To my amazement, she did. The baby looked up at me, her face red and tearful, panting with exhaustion. "Let's get your brother," I said, since Robbie's wails continued unabated. "We'll make him happy, too." Robbie also responded to my touch, and in a moment I was walking slowly holding the two babies. It was awkward and terrifying.

What would have happened if Quiana had been utterly overrun by the ghost while she was here alone with the twins?

Now that the bones had been uncovered, the emotional miasma in the house was intensifying, without any doubt. It was a struggle to get out of the house, aside from the difficulty of carrying two children. Though I wanted to leave more than anything, I stopped in the kitchen to put them in their child seats. I opened the back door and passed Sara to JB. I went down the back steps with Robbie, moving very carefully. Sam, Tara, and Quiana were in the corner of the yard farthest from the bones, and JB and I joined them there.

In sharp contrast to the lighthearted meeting we'd had when we were planning the renovation, our conference in the backyard was grim. The late-afternoon sun slanted across the bricks of the patio, and the heat of them radiated upward. Even the heat was preferable to the haunted house.

We waited. Nothing happened. Finally, Tara sat in a lawn chair and started feeding Sara after JB fetched her nursing shawl. Robbie made squeaky noises until it was his turn. They, at least, were content.

Sam said, "I dug some more, and I think it's a complete skeleton. We don't know whose bones, whose ghost, or why it's angry."

An accurate and depressing summary.

"The only neat stories are the ones made up," Tara said.

Quiana, who seemed to be herself at the moment, sat slumped forward, her elbows on her knees. She said, "There's a reason all this is happening. There's a reason the haunting started when the hammer came out of the wall. There's a reason there's a body buried in the backyard. We just have to figure it out. And I'm the psychic. And it's trying to live through me. So I got to try to take care of this."

I looked at Quiana with some respect. What she was saying made sense.

"It's tied to the hammer," Quiana said.

"So, okay, if we want to know what happened so we can fix it," I said, "and since I can read minds, and since the ghost can get into Quiana's mind . . . I'm wondering if maybe Quiana and I can do something with the bones and find out who the spirit—the ghost—is."

Quiana nodded. "Let's do it," she said. "Let's get this bitch settled." She reached over to the old patio table and took the hammer.

We stood, full of purpose.

JB and Sam shot out of their chairs. Sam said, "You don't need to do this, Sookie."

Wild horses couldn't have held me back from this experience. I stepped away from Sam and took Quiana's left hand, bony and strong and cold. We went over to the excavated skeleton. Its skull gaped up at us from its grave. Quiana was holding the hammer in her free hand. Then she gasped and jerked, and suddenly I was holding the hand of someone completely different.

And I was seeing what Quiana saw, but not through Quiana's eyes. I was seeing . . . faces. A round-faced woman working over a kitchen table. I recognized what she was doing; she was making piecrust. She was looking up, bewildered and sad. *Mama.* A burly man bending over something on a tool bench, with the same air of worry about him. *Father.* And looking at a boy—older than me, but still a boy with an open, honest, freckled face, a face that was serious and full of doubt. *Albert.* I would have done anything to remove the anxiety from their faces, anything to silence the cruel words that had caused that unhappiness.

Words spoken by that devil, Isaiah Wechsler.

Part of me could still be only Sookie, and that part felt the growing resolution, the horrible resolve, as the entity in Quiana played out his plan.

The night, the darkness, only streetlights in the distance where town lay. (That almost threw me out of Quiana's mind. Since when had Magnolia Street been out of town?) *Running silently across the short distance between the windows, from my window to his, and his was open in the warm night . . . through it quietly enough not to wake him Father's hammer in my hand and . . .* then he raised his hand, oh . . . oh, no. In the moonlight the blood looked black.

Back out the window, breathing hard, and over to the one *in my house, safe now, back home hide the hammer under the bed* but Albert woke up, Albert beloved brother, and Albert said *what did you do?* And I said *I shut his foul mouth.*

And there was more, but it was too much for me, Sookie. I had to pull Quiana out of this, but that was impossible until we saw the end.

Then we did. We saw the end.

I gasped and choked, and Quiana folded silently to the dirt as if her strings had been cut.

Sam caught me, braced me, as JB supported Quiana.

JB said, "What happened? Why were you all holding hands, Sookie?"

Tara said, "They'll tell us, honey. Wait a minute." The twins were silent, and when I could see I realized they were back in their infant seats, at the base of the tree. The evening was closing in. The shadows had gotten so long they almost covered the yard. I could hear a car door closing next door. Andy had gotten home. Should I call out, get him to come look?

"Do you know who it is?" Sam asked, keeping his voice low, pointing at the open grave.

I went over to it. "This boy killed Isaiah Wechsler. This boy is Carter Summerlin."

"But you said his folks sent him away," Sam said.

"In a way, they did," Quiana said weakly. Tara had propped her up against the fence and was giving her a bottle of water. Quiana looked as if she'd survived a death march. "This boy killed himself because he couldn't stand what he did. He climbed through the window at night—the window of the house next door—with the hammer he took from his dad's toolbox. Came back in his own bedroom window, blood all over."

I shuddered. The others stared at us, their mouths open.

"But his big brother saw? Is that right, Sookie?" Quiana asked.

I nodded. "Albert took Carter's nightshirt and burned it in the backyard in the middle of the night, and hid the hammer in the closet wall. Later on, he closed it in. The fight he'd had with the Wechsler boy, it was because—well, Isaiah had made fun of the, what he thought was the effeminate ways of Albert's little brother. And to Carter it was so terrible, so unthinkable a slur, that he had to wipe out the one who'd voiced it. Albert believed he should have protected Carter better; he thought he should have shown Carter how to behave in a more manly way."

"But I felt terrible about killing Isaiah. And about how people thought Albert was to blame. The next week, I killed myself," Quiana said. She was unaware she was saying anything odd. "I hanged myself in that same closet, from a hook. I figured that would make things better for Albert. When they found me, Albert started crying. He told them what the fight had been about and how he'd helped cover up for me. They had one son dead, so to protect Albert and the family's good name, my folks buried me in the yard in the dead of night and told everyone they'd sent me off to live with relatives."

"And Carter haunted them?" I said, not liking how shaky my voice was.

"He haunted his parents, because they were ashamed of him." Quiana said, and I welcomed her return to perspective with huge relief. "But not Albert. Albert had tried to keep faith with Carter, but he must have felt terribly guilty himself every time he saw the Wechslers."

"So Carter started making his presence known again now because . . ."

"Of the hammer. When you found the hammer, that was the trigger for his . . . activation." Quiana shrugged. "I don't know much about ghosts, but I got that from him. He was full of anger—well, we all got that. He was confused, and agitated."

"What can we do? To get rid of him? He can't stay here," JB said, his mouth set in an uncharacteristically hard line.

"We can call the police," I said. "They'd come get the bones and take them away for evaluation and burial. They'll take the hammer, too. The closet has been reconfigured, so it's no longer the place where Carter died." I wondered, if we sent the bones *and* the hammer to the police, would the ghost manifest at the police station? I tried to imagine Detective Andy Bellefleur's face.

"Will that do it? End his presence?" Tara asked.

"Ought to." Quiana looked at me.

I shrugged. "Maybe."

There was a doubtful silence.

I cleared my throat. "Or we could just take everything, bones and hammer, and bury the whole kit 'n' kaboodle in the cemetery. By ourselves. And no one would ever need to know, which was what the whole Summerlin family wanted."

They all thought about my proposition for a few seconds.

"I'm for that," JB said. "I don't want people coming around to see where the body was buried. The babies wouldn't like that. People might not let their kids come over to play with Robbie and Sara."

Tara looked at her husband in surprise. "I didn't think about that, JB. Sookie, since your house is right by the cemetery . . . can you and Sam . . . ?"

"This isn't a usual best-friends job," I said, maybe a little tartly. "But okay, I'll do it. You got an old sheet?"

She vanished into the house and came back with a white percale double fitted. Quiana laid it out by the grave, and Sam and JB disinterred the bones. Wearing rubber dishwashing gloves, they transferred the remains of poor Carter Summerlin to the sheet. The ground was so shadowed by the side of the house, I needed the help of a flashlight to sift the earth, searching for anything they might have missed. I came up with two teeth and a few little finger bones. After a while, we were reasonably sure the entire skeleton had been harvested from the soil. Tara put the hammer on top of the bones, gathered up the sheet corners, and tied them in knots.

There was a pause when Sam picked up the grotesque bundle.

"Oh, all right, we'll go, too," Tara said angrily, as though I'd accused her of being callous.

There was a little car caravan out to my house: me, Sam in his pickup, JB and Tara and the twins in their car, and Quiana in her old Ford.

We tromped through my woods to the cemetery. The dark was closing in around us when we came to my family plot. I was going to be late for work—but somehow I didn't think Sam would dock my pay for it. The space at the back of my family headstone was unusually large, and since it lay at the edge of the graveyard there wasn't another family plot abutting it from the north. We took turns digging—again—by the light of the lantern-sized flashlights I'd snatched from my tool shed.

JB lowered the bundle of bones and hammer into the makeshift grave. We shoveled the dirt back in, a much quicker job, and the men stamped down the new patch with their boots so it wouldn't look so raw. Maybe

I'd come back tomorrow and stick a potted plant in the dirt to kind of explain the digging.

When that was done, there was an odd moment, when the night around us seemed to catch its breath.

Her dark head bowed, Quiana said, "The Lord is my shepherd . . ." and we all joined in.

"God bless this poor soul and send him on his way," I said, when the prayer was finished.

Then the night exhaled, and the air was empty.

We trudged back to my house in silence, Quiana stumbling with exhaustion from time to time.

There was an awkward pause as everyone tried to figure out how to cap off the experience.

Finally, JB said, "Y'all gonna come help finish the closet tomorrow?"

I laughed. I couldn't help it.

"Sure," Sam said. "We'll be there, and we'll finish."

And tomorrow, it would just be us in the house. Us living people.

Wizard Home Security

VICTOR GISCHLER

"Did the burglar hit any other rooms?"

Broahm shook his head, standing in front of the nearly empty cupboard, absently stroking his beard, which was only just now starting to form some respectable gray streaks. Clients wanted wizards with a little experience. Nothing said experience and wisdom like a bit of gray. He'd even known some journeymen spellcasters who'd used minor glamours to make themselves look older.

Broahm blinked. His mind was wandering again.

He turned to the young mage who'd asked the question. "What?"

"Anything else stolen?"

"A silver mixing bowl from my workshop and a few other minor items," Broahm said. "Mostly it was the supply cupboard. I'll be a year replacing those ingredients. More."

The mage *tsked*, shaking his head. Broahm found him infuriatingly handsome and trendy. He was clean shaven, a fancy gold earring in one ear, hair cut short and spiky in the way that was fashionable among the young gentry. Trendy breeches and a loose shirt open at the neck. Unlike Broahm in his conservative burgundy robes, this young mage—Sulton was his name, Broahm now remembered—didn't have to conform to conventional wizard fashions, since his clientele were other wizards and not the public at large.

Broahm had sent a message to Wizard Home Security, and Sulton had shown up the next morning.

"What security did you have on the cupboard?" Sulton asked.

Broahm shuffled his feet. "Well, I'd rather not give away any secrets."

"Come now, sir. We need to know every detail if we're to provide the best possible service."

A sigh. "A rather expensive padlock," Broahm said. "And the usual wards."

"There's your problem," Sulton said. "Not good enough. Not by a long shot."

Broahm bristled. "That's self-evident."

Sulton smiled in a way Broahm was sure was meant to be disarming but only irritated him. "No disrespect intended. I feel sure you took the appropriate precautions against your run-of-the-mill thieves. But if run-of-the-mill thieves were all you had to deal with, you wouldn't have needed to consult Wizard Home Security, eh?"

"Get on with it."

"The cupboard was full of valuable items, and any decent thief could have pawned them around the city for a nice bit of silver," Sulton said. "But ask yourself, who needs those items the most? Don't bother, I'll answer for you. Other wizards, that's who. You're in the Wizard's Quarter. You can't swing a dead weasel or toss a stone over your shoulder without hitting a pointy hat. And with so many wizards in one place, all of whom are vying for the same ingredients to concoct the same spells, well, a few bad eggs are bound to resort to pilfering from their neighbors rather than paying the inflated prices."

Broahm sighed, then pinched the bridge of his nose. That just figured. Nine years ago, when he'd finished his apprenticeship with Hemley, his old master had given him some advice. *Try the edge of the Northern Waste. Ice City is the sort of place a young wizard can earn a good living.* Twenty years ago this had been true. On the edge of the Great Frozen Sea, a wizard could get rich guiding ships through the seasonal storms or spelling fire stones to warm a hearth when fuel was short. But word must have gotten out, because Ice City had become simply lousy with wizards over the next two decades, all looking to score some quick silver.

Ice City—the place had some long, multisyllable name in the Old Empire tongue—was a bitter, frozen, miserable place nine months out of the year, and Broahm could not believe he'd spent nine years of his life here. And now his fellow wizards were *robbing* him.

It had been just three days ago that his neighbor Bortz, a fellow wizard Broahm spent time with occasionally, had complained bitterly about so much competition for wizarding business in the city. Bortz had reported at least half a dozen young mages of his acquaintance who'd tossed it in, packed up, and left the city. Bortz and Broahm had begun their commiserations over tea and had ended deep into a bottle of tawny port.

Broahm wondered idly why the robbers hadn't hit Bortz's house. Maybe because of the house maiden, a sort of ghostly servant who wandered about the place. She wasn't exactly equivalent to a security system, but she could at least shout at the first signs of an intruder.

"What do you suggest?" Broahm asked.

"What I always suggest in these situations," Sulton said. "That you completely mageproof your household."

"What will that cost me?"

"Sixty gold."

Broahm admired the way Sulton said *Sixty gold* with a completely straight face. It took a lot of nerve and a lot of self-control.

"Please leave my home," Broahm said.

Sulton lifted his hands, palms out, and attempted a soothing, placating gesture. "Your reaction is quite understandable."

"I think you should be flogged."

"Now let's not get hostile."

If Broahm worked hard all year, not taking any days off, he might— *might*—be able to accumulate sixty gold. It was a minor fortune. There were kitchen workers in middle-class homes who might slave over hot stoves all their lives and never *see* a single gold coin.

Relatively speaking, Broahm considered himself a moderately wealthy individual. He lived in a comfortable home at the better end of the Wizard's Quarter. Hidden within the stone wall in his top room, guarded by his most powerful spells of warding and concealment, was a small locked chest. Inside were exactly one hundred sixty-nine gold pieces—his entire savings from nine years of work in this frozen city on the edge of the wasteland. He would have to pay much of that to replace his lost wizarding supplies. Another sixty to Sulton would put him almost back at square one.

"I see by your expression that you are displeased with the price," Sulton said.

"How observant."

"Consider how valuable this security could be to you," Sulton said. "The ingredients you've lost surely cost more than sixty gold."

Broahm opened his mouth to spit a curse at the young mage, then paused, tugging anxiously at the end of his beard. "Go on."

"A single wise, albeit somewhat painful, investment now would keep your valuables safe for the entire time you remain at this residence. You are, without a doubt, a capable spellcaster in your own right. But how long would it take you to prepare such spells from scratch? And this is only after hours of painstaking research. We at Wizard Home Security have done this tedious preliminary work for you."

Broahm opened his mouth to get a word in, but Sulton pressed on quickly with his sales pitch.

"And we can customize the tone of your package to enhance whatever sort of reputation you've been cultivating. A wizard's public image is everything, after all."

Broahm raised an eyebrow. It had not occurred to him to have any sort of public image other than professional wizard. "How do you mean?"

"For example, if you want to perpetuate a sort of kinder, gentler image, we can fix you up with a capture gem to take intruders prisoner. If you'd like your potential clientele to see you as a bit more sinister, we can incinerate intruders. No problem. Nothing tells the public better that a badass powerful wizard lives here than dumping a pile of bone ash into the gutter where everyone can see. Burglars will think twice."

"Seems a bit harsh."

"Consider your empty cupboard," Sulton reminded him.

"Good point."

"Others prefer a guardian option."

"You mean like a vicious dog or something?"

Sulton shook his head. "Nothing so mundane."

"A vicious bear?"

"You'd have to feed and take care of a bear," Sulton said. "I usually suggest a zombie. Or a skeleton."

"I'm not paying for a zombie."

"A zombie will simply stand there until it's activated," Sulton said. "No fuss. No muss. Stick it in a closet. I know one guy, he makes the zombie stand in a corner holding a candle in each hand, makes a nice lamp while waiting to repel intruders."

"I said I'm not paying to animate a zombie. Those can be tricky, expensive spells."

"Ah, but that's the beauty of the zombie, sir," Sulton said. "We can get you one secondhand."

"Oh, come on!"

"It's true," insisted Sulton. "A wizard or priest raises one to perform a task—usually murder some chap—and then when the task is complete there's still this perfectly good zombie cluttering up the place. No extra charge to you, sir. All part of the service."

Broahm tugged at his beard again. He'd already made up his mind and was just deciding how to begin the bargaining. "Well . . . sixty is outrageous. Thirty."

Sulton *tsked* and shook his head. "Sir, for that price I'd have to cut too many corners, and I don't dare risk my reputation on a shoddy job. But it is my slow season, so I'm willing to make you an incredible bargain at fifty."

"I do need some additional protection," Broahm admitted. "That much is obvious. But it's not like the Titans of the Underworld are coming to knock down my door. Surely we could do it for forty."

"Forty-five," Sulton said.

"Deal." Broahm grinned.

They shook hands and discussed the details.

THREE MONTHS WENT by, and in the middle of a particularly bitter night, during a howling snowstorm, another intruder woke Broahm out of a deep sleep.

Technically, the house maiden had awoken Broahm, not the intruder himself.

"There is someone downstairs," she said in a soft voice. The house maiden hovered over his bed, ghostly and glowing.

The maiden was a fake consciousness modeled to look like a house servant. She floated around Broahm's five-story home, keeping an eye on things. Broahm had admired Bortz's house maiden enough to add her as a supplement to the security measures Sulton had installed.

Broahm's residence was an octagonal tower on the edge of the Wizard's Quarter, a stone's throw from the city wall. He'd picked it up for a reasonable price when the elderly former resident had decided to chuck it in and head for a warmer climate.

"What?" Broahm rubbed his eyes as he kicked off the multiple layers of quilts and furs. "Who is downstairs?"

"I've never seen him before, milord," the house maiden said. "An intruder."

"Go see what he's doing, then come back." In cold weather like this, Broahm slept in his robe and socks, so he had only to pull on his short boots to be dressed. "Hurry."

"Yes, milord." The house maiden disappeared through the floor.

Damn it! Broahm had scoured the town and the outlying areas, every little obscure market he could find, to replace the stolen wizarding ingredients in his cupboard, and now here was another burglar already—

In a flash, it came to him. Prying eyes and keen ears had been keeping tabs on Broahm, watching as he replenished his precious materials. Some sly villain *knew* he now had a full cupboard again and had been waiting to strike. And to add insult to injury, Broahm had not activated the security system.

In a mere two weeks, the security system had become a cumbersome nuisance. Clients coming and going during business hours meant he either had to go through the tedious ritual ten times a day, or leave the system off during business hours—which was what he eventually started doing. It didn't take long for Broahm to become complacent, and it wasn't long after that he started to forget to activate it after closing. Often, he would already be in bed, warm under the covers, when he would remember, and more often than not he was simply too cold and lazy to get out of bed again.

The house maiden, at least, was a part of the system that could be left in operation all the time. If not for her, Broahm would have slept right through the second burglary.

He grabbed the twelve-inch dagger from his bedside table and slipped it into his belt. No time to consult his spell book. He'd have to go into action with the half-dozen spells already clunking around in his brain.

The house maiden drifted up through the floor again. "He's standing in the foyer, milord, looking at the hallway through a glass circle he's holding up to his eye."

A wizard's loupe. Broahm muttered a curse. If the burglar had as rare an item as a wizard's loupe, then that meant he was a spellcaster himself, or, at the very least, highly familiar with the ways of wizards. He would have to engage this prowler with caution.

Broahm felt like such a lazy fool. If only he'd taken the three minutes to perform the ritual over the small, silver wolf's head nailed to the front doorframe downstairs. The wolf's head was the size of a peach, with small garnets for eyes, a wide-open mouth, and sharp fangs within. In an emergency situation, Sulton had explained, Broahm could simply prick his finger on one of the wolf's teeth to activate the magical protections. His blood would identify him as the rightful resident while all others would fall victim to the dwelling's defenses.

It was too bad Broahm had cheaped out. For an additional fee, he could have had an identical wolf's head affixed to the doorpost in his bedroom. But noooooooo. He had to save four gold pieces and was now screwing up his courage to do battle with an intruder.

He sighed. No time to cry about it now. He had to man up and deal with the problem. He mumbled the syllables to his first spell, and they flew out of his mouth as an unintelligible garble. He took an experimental step. No sound. No squeak of floorboards. Good, the silence spell was working perfectly. Too bad an invisibility spell was so complex and hard to memorize, but being able to move silently would be some advantage.

"Keep an eye on him," he told the house maiden. "Tell me immediately if he moves beyond the first floor."

"Yes, milord." She dissolved back through the floor.

Broahm drew his dagger and eased down the stairs. The floor below his bedchamber was his workshop. He kept going to the floor below that—a sitting room, storage, a guest chamber. He passed by another

floor—sitting room, dining room, places to entertain clients and guests—
and started down the final flight of stairs to the first floor.

The first floor consisted of a generous entranceway, the kitchens, and
a servant's quarters should Broahm one day be able to afford a corporeal
servant.

The nervous wizard slowly descended the circular staircase to the first
floor, then stopped abruptly when he saw the burglar in the foyer. Broahm
pressed his back to the wall, clinging to the shadows. Moonlight streamed
in from the small round window in the front door, barely illuminating the
crouched figure. The burglar's head was wrapped to hide his identity, only
a narrow slit in the fabric for the eyes. Soft leather boots. A short, fat
sword on his belt.

The burglar had yet to move beyond the foyer. He kept looking through
the loupe, scanning the floor, looking up at the ceiling. What was he looking for?

The eldritch lines, Broahm realized. The burglar *knew* there was a
security system, and the fact that he couldn't see the eldritch lines was
confounding him. Soon the burglar would stumble upon the truth. The
stupid homeowner had simply not activated the security. And when the
burglar figured this out, he would move into the rest of Broahm's home
and loot all of the rare and expensive items Broahm had just spent a small
fortune replacing.

Unless Broahm acted fast.

He began uttering the words to a flame spell. *Fry the son of a bitch.*

He bit his tongue.

No. It was a common offensive spell. A burglar with a wizard's loupe
would know what he was up against. Likely he had some protective shielding. There was no way to *know* this, naturally, but Broahm would have
one chance at surprise, and he needed to make the most of it. The dagger
suddenly felt very heavy in his hand.

Broahm was not accustomed to wet work. One of the distinct perks of
being a wizard was that in combat situations, at least in the very few
battles in which he'd participated, he could cast his spells from a distance,
far from sword points and bone-crushing maces. But Broahm's dagger, in
this situation, might be the best bet. He'd had it for years, and it was spelled
against armor and eldritch shields and had the best chance to penetrate.

The burglar turned his back, examining the front door with the wizard's loupe.

Now! While his back is turned! Go! Now!

Broahm flew down the stairs, the silence spell muting his footfalls. He nearly tangled himself in his robes, righted himself, and hit the first-floor landing at a full run, dagger in front of him ready to strike.

The burglar turned and saw Broahm running flat-out toward him. His eyes went big in the fabric slit of his mask as his hand fell to his sword.

Broahm swept the dagger forward with everything he had. The tip sliced through the burglar's throat. A garbled yell died in the rush of blood. The blood—

—sprayed—

—drops landing in the open mouth of the silver wolf's head on the door.

Panic flashed up Broahm's spine. *No!*

Intelligence. One had to have the right sort of brain to be a wizard. Intelligence, yes, but not just any ordinary sort of intelligence would do. A wizard needed to take in a situation, appraise, analyze, decide, all in an instant. Broahm was at least above average with this sort of intelligence, and so he saw immediately what had happened and what it meant. The blood had sprayed, droplets scattering in an arc. Droplets landing in the mouth of the wolf's head.

Not Broahm's blood.

The burglar clutched his throat, blood oozing between his fingers as he went down, flopping on the ground, kicking, trying to stop the blood flow coming from his open throat, but it just kept coming, and he was on the floor of the foyer, the blood pooling and flowing out like it might never stop.

But all Broahm could see were the few drops that had sprayed into the wolf's mouth, the droplets that would activate the house's security system. The blood of the person who'd be safe. *Not Broahm's blood.*

Broahm was screwed.

He panicked, went for the front door, grabbed the knob. It burned his hand, and he jerked back. Just like that, the security system had been activated.

His house. Against him.

Not thinking, he walked backward into the foyer, backing away fast from the front door, hand going up to his mouth. He sucked the burn, wincing, and even in that split second remembered the house's defenses, the security he'd paid big gold for only a few months ago.

He wrenched his hand from his mouth and spat the syllables for the iron skin spell a split second before the poison darts launched. The darts bounced off his face and arms with metallic *tinks*, his skin turning iron just in the nick of time.

Flustered, he stumbled into the kitchen and thrust his burned hand into a bucket of cold water. Relief brought clarity. The house. What was next? It would detect that he'd survived the darts and activate the—

"Grrrrrraaaaaaaaarrrrr . . ."

Broahm spun to see the zombie lurching toward him.

Broahm had thought it funny at the time. What were the odds? A zombie bear. The hulking beast came at him, claws out, eyes vacant, mouth and fangs ready to rip him to shreds.

Broahm dove to the floor as the claws raked the counter where he'd been a moment before, splitting the bucket in two, splashing water all over the kitchen floor.

Now Broahm did cast the flame spell, hand extended toward the zombie animal, flames shooting from his fingertips, curling around the creature, the patchy fur that remained on its body catching fire. The zombie bear roared but turned on Broahm and kept coming.

Broahm ran from the kitchen, back through the foyer and up the stairs.

Two things. The zombie bear behind him, and whatever the security system would do to him on the second floor.

The zombie bear came after him slowly. As Sulton had promised, it had been purchased secondhand and was almost worn out to begin with. Broahm paused on the staircase to look back at the creature. It lumbered up after him, patches of mangy fur smoldering. It was, frankly, a pathetic sight, but if it got hold of him, it would tear his arms and legs and head off.

What spells were left? The thing had survived the flame cast, and in other circumstances, Broahm would have been glad to get his money's worth. As it was, the wizard sort of wished the thing had gone down a bit easier. He went through the list of the remaining spells in his head.

Sleep? No, you couldn't put a zombie to sleep. The undead do not slumber. He had three other spells to choose from: Voice. Light. Shatter.

Shatter might do the trick. It was meant to destroy armor and swords, but maybe it would do the same to the bear's patchy skin and dried bones. The more Broahm thought about it, the more he thought it would work. He turned, mouth falling open to utter the words, hands raised to weave arcane symbols in the air.

Slam!

The zombie bear was already upon him, barreling into him headfirst, butting the wizard backward, arms flailing into the main area of the second level. The iron skin spell kept his ribs from cracking.

The zombie bear knocked Broahm over a plush divan. "Shit!"

Broahm scrambled to his feet just in time to see the undead animal knock the furniture aside to get at him again. In a thousandth of a second, this minor debate unfolded in Broahm's brain: *I can cast the shatter spell now. He's coming right at me. It's a point-blank shot. Or I can take a deep breath. There's no time for both.*

He took a deep breath.

At the same moment the four brown ceramic toads placed around the room began to belch a thick, pea-green fog. It filled the room at alarming speed. Broahm turned and sprinted for the next staircase leading to the level above. He had to stay ahead of the fog. Breathing in any of it would send him instantly into a deep coma.

A distant part of his brain registered that the iron skin spell had worn off.

Broahm hit the stairs hard, turned his ankle, and yelled in pain. He made himself go on, every other step upward sending a shock of agony lancing up his leg past his knee. His lungs were already burning for air. Broahm was no kind of athlete, neither particularly strong nor fast, but he pushed through the jagged fire in his ankle.

He reached the top step and turned, dagger out, ready to fend off the undead guardian.

Nothing.

Broahm cocked his head, listening for pursuit, but no sound came up from the level below. He stood frozen, panting, waiting.

A zombie bear, Broahm thought. *How fucking clever. And what will people say about you in the guild meetings? Stupid old Broahm was eaten by his own zombie guardian. I told you that fellow wasn't the brightest candle on the altar.*

The dark green fog had climbed two-thirds of the way up the stairs, then floated there like some ugly pond of dirty smoke, but it came no farther. The fog was too thick and dark to see anything below, and Broahm had no idea at all how to disperse the fog. He realized he'd neglected to ask Sulton a number of important questions about his security system. Did the fog fail to rise any farther because it was so thick and heavy, or was it spelled to keep to its own level so it didn't conflict with the house's other defenses? And if he *had* breathed any of the fog and fallen into a coma, what, if anything, would bring him out of it again? Another half-dozen questions sprang to mind, but Broahm dismissed them. Right now he needed to focus on getting out of this mess.

"House maiden!" Broahm shouted. Perhaps he could send her to scout the situation. Sooner or later he'd have to go downstairs again, and he wasn't eager to tangle with the bear. Maybe the thing had a limited life span. It might already have tumbled over into a docile heap. "House maiden, where are—"

The zombie bear rose through the fog and leaped for Broahm, eyes vacant and dead, claws swiping at the wizard, ripping through robes and slicing three thin, shallow cuts across Broahm's chest. He fell back, tripping in his own robes, the cuts stinging and cold, the bear still coming.

The shatter spell flew from Broahm's lips.

The zombie bear's skin shredded like dry paper, the bones beneath splintering and flying in every direction, chips and dust raining down on Broahm and over the room, but Broahm had already stepped onto the upper floor.

A blinding bright flash of blue light.

Sudden silence.

Then everything went dark.

BROAHM GROANED AND sat up in the grass, holding his head.

The world around him was blue. He blinked at it but wasn't quite ready for it, so he closed his eyes again. He reached into his robes, his hand and chest sticky and warm with his own blood, but the claw marks weren't deep. The wound would keep for now.

Broahm had bigger problems.

He opened his eyes again slowly, looked around, and sighed.

He sat on a slight rise in a blue world of blue sky and blue grass, a vast open plain in one direction. A hundred yards in the opposite direction was a wall of blue quartz that stretched out of sight to the horizon in both directions and went up into the sky until it disappeared.

In the center of Broahm's workshop was a small pedestal on which sat a pyramid of rough blue quartz. Broahm was now *inside* that piece of quartz.

How to escape from a capture gem was another question Broahm had neglected to ask Sulton. It wasn't really a gem. Just quartz. Capture gems were little artificial worlds unto themselves, and nobles often purchased such items fashioned of emerald or sapphire, but a wizard knew any old hunk of quartz would do, so there was no point wasting money. Oh, there were subtle beneficial reasons for using a more expensive stone, but all Broahm was interested in was capturing an intruder.

Well. He'd captured himself instead. *Bravo, idiot.*

He stood and hobbled slowly to the quartz wall. He looked it up and down, then reached out and rubbed the cold quartz. He tapped it with his dagger. The wall was thick, solid. Even if Broahm hadn't already expended his shatter spell, he doubted it would so much as scratch the quartz.

Brute force wasn't going to get him out of this one.

A quick, mental inventory: a voice spell and a light spell. Not much left in his addled noggin.

Broahm had known very old wizards who could keep thirty-five or forty spells in their heads, ready for use at the click of a tongue. It took years of study and discipline to accomplish such a thing. Most wizards kept secret how many spells they could hold, but Broahm suspected his old master, Hemley, could hold as many as fifteen comfortably. *Comfortably* was the key. Broahm could jam eight spells in his mind in a pinch, but the buzz in his brain proved too distracting to cope with. Once he'd tried nine spells, but it had almost driven him mad. He'd had to run outside to launch a lightning bolt into the sky to make room in his head.

Anyway, someday he would study and work and be able to hold nine spells. Then if he was disciplined and worked hard, ten. But not today.

Today he was trapped in a world of blue with two nearly useless spells.

What Broahm *really* needed was to be rescued. If he'd bothered to memorize some kind of simple communication spell, maybe he could have called for help.

Hmmmmmm. Broahm scratched his chin. Maybe there *was* a way he could call for help. The point of being a wizard was not simply to know spells, but also how to be clever about using them.

So . . . be clever, moron.

THE HOUSE MAIDEN lingered over the burglar's body long enough to make sure it wasn't her master's. Relief. It wasn't Broahm. The pool of blood spread out from the body left little doubt. He was very, very dead.

She drifted up to the next level. "Milord?"

Where could he be? The intruder had obviously been vanquished, so where was her master?

She drifted though a sea of dark green fog, up the stairs past an explosion of dust and bone and old fur. Something was not right. Not right at all. She entered the master's workshop and started suddenly at the misshapen shadow on the wall. It was huge, waving its arms like some deranged creature. She floated in a circle, looking all around at anything that could possibly cast such a shadow.

A bright glow radiated from the quartz in the center of the workshop.

This wasn't right at all. She had to find her master, had to tell him something was amiss. She turned and floated back toward the stairs.

And stopped.

Had she just heard . . . her name?

She cast glances into every corner of the room. Nobody.

Was her imagination playing tricks on her? Since she was barely a ghost, a thing artificial, a puff of magic herself, she had to wonder if she even had an imagination. And anyway, *house maiden* wasn't technically her "name."

She hovered, waiting to see if she heard it again.

"IN HERE, YOU stupid cow!" Broahm screamed.

His magically amplified voice shook the interior of the capture gem like an earthquake.

He jumped up and down, waved his arms, and tried to imagine how it must look inside his workshop. He could see the shimmering figure of the house maiden blurred through the quartz. "Pay attention, you dumb ghostly transparent bitch!"

Broahm had used both his remaining spells.

First, the light spell. He'd taken twenty steps back from the quartz wall and had jabbed his dagger into the ground among the blades of thick blue grass. Then he'd focused on the hilt, casting the light spell with all the intensity he could muster. When he was finished casting the light spell on the dagger, he couldn't look at it, had to turn away. The blinding light scorched his eyes, and he'd turned back toward the quartz wall, hoping it would act as a lens and project his shadow where the house maiden could see it.

Then the voice spell. Broahm liked this spell a lot. It could do various things depending on how you cast it. It could make Broahm's voice seem appealing to others, not a bad trick when trying to make an argument and convince someone. It could also throw his voice up to half a mile away, a magically charged ventriloquism. It this case, Broahm had simply gone for volume. The spell made his voice boom like a Titan's, but though it was ear-shatteringly loud within the capture gem, Broahm could only hope it made it to the outside.

"House maiden! I'm trapped in the quartz! Damn it! HOUSE MAIDEN!"

It wasn't working. A leaden feeling crept into Broahm's gut. What if she couldn't hear him? What if she wasn't able to go for help? House maidens were the simplest sorts of servants, not terribly bright. She would simply go dormant until her master called for her. It might be weeks before anyone was curious enough to come looking for Broahm. Months? Years? Broahm did not like the idea of being trapped forever in the blue world.

A sudden panic gripped him. He shouted again, jumped, waved his arms. Damn it, she wasn't hearing him.

Broahm screamed and screamed and screamed and screamed.

SULTON ARRIVED AT the small cottage. It belonged to a journeyman wizard named Bortz. If all went well, he'd sell him on the usual package, and the usual scheme would unfold from there.

It had been two months since he'd sent Lorran to rob Broahm's house and Lorran had vanished. Sulton wasn't exactly sure what had happened. Either something had gone wrong, and Broahm had gotten the better of Lorran, or Lorran had stumbled upon something truly valuable in the wizard's home and, not wanting to share it, had hoofed it into the night.

Either way, Sulton had lost a first-rate sneak thief, and it had taken weeks for him to find a suitable replacement.

Sulton was slowly but steadily getting rich. First, he robbed wizards' households, the ones he suspected had poor security. As an accomplished wizard himself, he was able to circumvent most of the usual wards. Then he'd sell security systems to the victimized wizards. After that, when the time was ripe, he'd rob them again. More accurately, the thief he had on payroll would rob them again.

Sulton knocked on Bortz's door.

A few seconds later a plump wizard in green robes opened the door and squinted at Sulton. He was short and innocuous.

"You must be Master Bortz. I'm Sulton from Wizard Home Security."

"What?" The fat wizard blinked at him. "Oh, yes. I'd forgotten you were coming. I was in the middle of a star chart . . . well, never mind. Come in. Come in."

Sulton followed the wizard through a narrow entryway and into a small sitting room. He made mental notes of the dwelling's interior. They'd come in handy later when he briefed his new sneak thief.

"You've contacted us at a good time," Sulton said. "The Wizard's Quarter has been ravaged by a rash of burglaries this past year. You can't be too careful when it comes to protecting your valuables. We can set you up with a system that will allow you to feel secure, knowing that your possessions—especially any rare magical items you might have—are safe and sound."

Bortz snorted. "Guarding my knickknacks is the least of my worries. I want to make sure my throat isn't cut in my sleep. Especially after the disappearance."

Sulton raised an eyebrow. *The disappearance?* "Yes, well, your concern is . . . understandable."

"I mean, wizards just vanishing? It's enough to make you wonder. That fellow just recently, the mage who lived a few doors down. Broahm, I think his name was." Bortz snapped his fingers. "Gone just like that. Not a note, not a word to anyone. Foul play wouldn't surprise me one bit."

Come to think of it, Sulton had heard something about Broahm being gone. Sulton had been curious but didn't ask anyone about the details for fear of raising suspicion.

In the meantime, Sulton intended to use the situation to his advantage. If Bortz truly feared for his life, then Sulton might be able to sell him an elaborate spell package for an inflated price.

"These are dangerous times," Sulton said somberly. "What's money compared to your life? We can spell your household in a way that guarantees your safety. The simple fact of the matter is that you *can* buy peace of mind. It's not cheap, but you'll sleep at night."

Bortz was nodding. "Yes. That's what I want. Okay, let's talk." Bortz gestured through a low, arched doorway. "I've just made a pot of tea in the kitchen. Come on. I'll pour you a cup."

Sulton stepped into the kitchen and—

Blue light flashed, blinded him, the world spinning.

Disoriented.

Sulton sat up, looked around, and saw that he was in a world entirely of blue.

BROAHM CAME DOWN the back stairs into Bortz's small kitchen. "He's in there?"

Bortz pointed to the blue quartz on the wooden table next to his teapot. "It worked just as you described. Has he really been ripping off wizards all over the Quarter?"

Broahm bent and squinted at the quartz, wondering if he could see a tiny Sulton in there. It had taken Broahm a little over two weeks to duplicate the capture gem spell and set it up in Bortz's kitchen. A nice little bit of wizarding if Broahm said so himself. The real trick had been raising the slain burglar. You can't interrogate a zombie. They just slobber and try to bite you. So Broahm had been a bit clever, combining the zombie-raising spell and a mind-reading charm and tying them together in a way that allowed the zombie burglar to be questioned. Bortz had helped.

"The burglar told us everything," Broahm reminded Bortz. "Sulton has been getting obscenely rich off his fellow wizards."

"I must admit," Bortz said, "when your house maiden woke me out of a sound sleep in the wee hours in the middle of a raging blizzard, well, it gave me quite a start."

"I'm just glad she finally heard me and was able to fetch you," Broahm said. The thought of being trapped forever in the blue quartz still gave him a little shiver.

"So now that you've caught him, what are you going to do with him?" Bortz asked.

"I don't know." Broahm grinned at the chunk of quartz in the middle of the table. "But I'm going to take my sweet time thinking about it."

Gray

PATRICIA BRIGGS

It was raining, a desultory, reluctant angry rain forced unwillingly from the gray clouds overhead. It dribbled with the fiendish rhythm of a Chinese water torture. Drip. Drip. Drip.

Elyna's windshield wipers squeaked until she turned them off. But the drops still came down to obscure her sight. From old habit, she pulled into the space that had been hers.

She'd first parked there a couple of times because the space had been open. When she'd moved in with Jack, a lifetime ago, it was seldom open again because her car was in it. After a while if it wasn't available for her little Ford, she'd curse the visitor who'd stolen it and find some other, less convenient parking place. When that happened, she'd go out to check before bedtime to see if it was open. If it was, she'd repark her car where it would be happy.

"Cars just are, darlin'," Jack would tell her with a grin as he escorted her out of the apartment to keep watch as she moved the Ford. "They aren't happy or sad."

Jack had been in love with her, though, and was patient with her little ways. He'd loved her and she'd loved him in that wholehearted eager fashion that only the young and innocent have—secure in the knowledge that there was nothing so terrible it could tear them apart. Having successfully overcome her Polish and his Irish parents' objections to their match had only given her more confidence.

She was less innocent now.

Much, much less innocent.

Parking in that old spot had been habit, but it sat in her belly like a meal too cold. This was a bad idea. She knew it, but she couldn't give it up without trying to mend what she had . . . *lost* was the wrong word. *Destroyed* might have been a more apt one.

She rubbed her cold arms with colder hands, then turned off the motor. Without its warm hum, it was very quiet in the car.

She got out at last, locked the doors with the key fob, and left her car in the parking place that probably belonged to someone else now. Blinking back the aimless raindrops, she tromped through the slush from what must have been last week's snow on the sidewalk.

Only then did she look at the gray stone apartment building ahead. *Did they still call it an apartment building when all of the apartments were being sold as condominiums?*

It wasn't a particularly large building, three floors, six apartments, surrounded by a small front parklike area that had always managed to insert a little color in the summer without requiring maintenance or inviting anyone to linger. This evening, with winter still reigning despite the rain that fell instead of snow, there was no color to be had.

The cut granite edges of the steps were familiar and alien at the same time, worn in a way they hadn't been when this had been *their* home—and that strangeness hurt.

Next to the door, blown into the corner of the building, lay a little Valentine's Day card with a heart on it. The ink had run, fading out the *BE MINE* to a grayish semidecipherable mush. Only the name *Jack* scribed in black crayon was still clear. It was both irony and a sign, she thought, but she didn't know if a child's wet card was a good portent or not.

She looked up to the topmost windows with longing eyes and murmured, "Be mine, Jack?"

She rang the bell on the side of the door, a new plastic button surrounded by stainless steel, and a buzz released the door lock. The real estate agent must have beaten her here.

She wiped her tennis shoes off on the mat in front of the door and stepped into a small foyer. At first glance, she thought the room hadn't changed at all. Then she realized that the names written in Sharpie below the numbers on the box were different from the names she had known, and the wooden handrail next to the stairs had been replaced with the same polished steel as the doorbell.

"Our place, Elyna, just think of it!" Jack's voice rang in sudden memory, full of eagerness and life.

The wooden handrail had had a notch in it from when they'd hit it, she and Jack, with the sharp edge of her metal typist desk, carrying it up to their new home. She hadn't realized she had been looking forward to seeing that stupid notch until it wasn't there.

She looked down and saw that the new handrail was dented a little, too. She knew better than to do something like that; she had better control. But that notch had been a memory of laughter and . . . poor Jack had hated that desk, its industrial ugliness an affront to his artistic eye. Still, he'd helped her carry it all the way up the stairs to their third-floor apartment.

She'd paid him back, on top of the desk wearing (at least at first) a cream-colored lace teddy her mother had given her in a small, tastefully wrapped package with instructions to open it in private. Jack hadn't minded the desk so much after that.

And those kinds of thoughts weren't going to help Elyna tonight.

She continued up the stairs, trailing her hand over the new metal handrail, hard-won control keeping her hands open and light as they skimmed over the cold surface. On the third floor the real estate agent awaited her in a peacoat with damp shoulders. He had a closed rain-dampened umbrella in one hand.

"Ms. Gray," he said, taking a step forward and reaching out with his free hand. "I'm Aubrey Tailor."

"Yes," she said, shaking his hand gravely. "Thank you for making time to meet me here. When I saw the ad, I just knew that this was the place."

"You're cold," he said, sounding concerned. Delicately built and pretty, she tended to arouse protective instincts in some men. "There's no heat in the condo right now."

"It is February in Chicago," Elyna told him. "Don't worry, my hands are always a little cold."

"Cold hands, warm heart," he said, then flushed, because it was a little too personal when addressed to a single woman who was his client. He shook his head and gave her a sheepish smile. "At least that's what my mother always said."

"Mine, too," she agreed. She liked him better for losing the slick salesman front—which might have been his intention all along. He let her go into the apartment first, closing the door between them. He'd wait outside, he'd told her, while she looked her fill.

Here was change that made that handrail pale in comparison.

The old oak floors Elyna had polished and cursed, because keeping them looking good was an ongoing war, were scarred and bedecked with stains that she hadn't put on them. Her lips twisted in a snarl that made her grateful that the real estate agent had stayed outside.

Vampires are territorial and this was *her* home, the home of her heart.

One of the pretty leaded-glass windows that looked out on the street had been replaced with plain glass framed in white vinyl, giving the living room a lopsided look. Someone had started to tear down the plastered walls—messy work that had stopped about halfway. A piece of wallpaper showed where someone had broken through layers and layers of paper, plaster, and paint to a familiar scrap.

She pulled the chunk of plaster displaying that paper off the wall and sat down on the floor with the plaster in her lap. Was it her imagination or was there a rusty stain on the paper?

"Jack?" she said plaintively. "Jack?"

But, other than the normal sounds of a building with six apartments . . . condos . . . in it, five of them occupied, she heard nothing. She looked at the rest of the apartment—most of which she could see from where she sat—the gutted kitchen without the white cabinets, just odd-colored spots on the walls to show where they used to be. Bare pipes stuck out of the floor where the sink should have been, and wires dripped from the ceilings where once lights had illuminated her life.

Unable to look anymore, she put her forehead on her knees.

After a while she said, "Oh, Jack." Then she took a deep breath and worked at getting herself put back into some kind of public-ready shape. She'd fed before she drove over, but emotional distress makes the Hunger worse, and her teeth ached and her nose insisted on remembering how good Mr. Aubrey Tailor had smelled when he'd blushed.

Something made a sighing noise in the empty apartment and she jerked her head up, all thoughts of hunger put aside. But nothing moved and there were no more sounds.

What had she expected? Time hadn't stopped for her, why would it have stopped for this apartment? Since seeing that first newspaper article about it, she'd done her research. She'd walked in here knowing that the stripping of the old had already been begun, awaiting replacement by the new. The in-progress remodel hadn't even bothered her until she saw it with her own eyes.

What was she doing here? The past was the past. She should strip it away just as the old plaster had been stripped from the living room wall. She should wash herself clean.

Outside, the rain slid down the windowpanes.

WHEN SHE HAD the vampire within tamped down until it would take another vampire to see what she was, she opened the apartment door.

"As you can see," the real estate agent said heartily—without looking at her—"it won't take much to get it ready to become whatever you'd like. It's good solid construction, built in 1911. You can put new flooring in, or strip the oak. It's three-quarter-inch oak; you don't see that in new construction. My client's price is very good."

"You had it sold twice this year," Elyna said, keeping the anxiety and need out of her voice. She had money. Enough. But not so much that bargaining wouldn't be a help.

"Ah." He looked disconcerted. No one expected someone who looked as young and frivolous as she did to have half a brain. He cleared his throat. "Yes. Twice."

"They both backed out before the papers were signed."

He frowned at her. "I thought you didn't have your own agent?"

"I took the downstairs neighbor, Josh, out to dinner yesterday." He was a nice man about ten years older than she looked. She'd treated him, despite his argument. It had been only fair that she pay for his dinner since she'd intended he should serve as hers afterward. He'd not remember the dinner clearly or what they'd discussed. Nor would he see that it was a problem that he didn't.

Elyna's Mistress had had a talent for beguilement. She could have given him a whole set of memories clearer than what had actually happened. Elyna, whose talents lay in other places, made use of the more common vampire ability to cloud minds and calm potential meals.

"I see." Elyna could tell from Aubrey's tone that he knew the story that Josh had related to her.

Even so, she laid it out for him. "He told me that the man who bought the building to turn it into condos stayed in this apartment and fixed the others, one at a time. He finished the one over there"—she tipped her head toward the door to the other third-floor apartment—"moved in and started on this one. Only odd things started happening. First it was tools and small stuff disappearing. Then"—as the destruction increased—"it was perfectly stable ladders falling over with people on them. Sent an electrical contractor to the hospital with that one. Saws that turned themselves on at the worst possible time—they managed to reattach that man's finger, Josh said. Chicago is a big city, but contractors do talk to each other. He couldn't get a crew in here to work the place." Elyna gave him a big friendly smile. "Some of that I already knew. I read the article in the neighborhood paper before I called you." That article was why she had called him.

She could see him reevaluate her. Was she a kook who wanted a haunted house? Or was she just looking for a real bargain?

"I'm older than I look," she told him, to help him make up his mind. "And I'm not a fool. Haunted or not, anyone looking at this apartment is going to start by getting appraisals from contractors. You haven't had an offer on this place in six months."

"A lot of bad luck doesn't a haunted place make," he said heartily, taking the bait. "All it takes is a few careless people. The man who lived here before my client, lived here for twenty years and never saw any ghost. I have his phone number and you can talk to him."

"It doesn't matter if I'm convinced it's not haunted," she told him. "It matters what the contractors think."

He looked grim.

"I'm willing to make an offer," she said. "But I'm going to have to pay premium prices to get anyone in to do the work, and that affects my bottom line."

And they got down to business. Aubrey had the paperwork for the offer with him. They took care of signatures, she fed from him, and then both of them went their separate ways in the night. Aubrey, with a new affection for Elyna, would be determined to make a good bargain for her regardless of the effect it might have on his commission. She felt guilty— a little—but not as much as she would have if he hadn't tried to take advantage of her supposed ignorance.

ELYNA'S PHONE RANG while she was in the hotel shower. She answered it with her hair dripping onto the thick green carpeting. Only after she answered did she remember that she wouldn't be punished for not answering the phone right away anymore.

"Elyna," said Sean, one of the vampires who'd belonged to Corona with her. Without waiting for her greeting, he continued, "You are being foolish. There are plenty of places without seethes where you could settle. Colbert doesn't play nicely with others and you won't be able to hide from him forever."

Pierre Colbert was the Master of Chicago, and a nasty piece of business he was. He'd driven the Mistress and what he'd left of her seethe out of Chicago about thirty years ago. Elyna had met him only once, and that was enough. He wouldn't bother driving her out. He'd just destroy her— if he noticed she was in his territory.

"Elyna," coaxed Sean's voice in her ear. "Come back to Madison. Take your rightful place here."

Never. That much Elyna was certain of. Sean had been her lover sometimes—two frightened people finding what solace they could. Usually they'd been friends, too, and more often allies. But Elyna wasn't strong enough to hold the seethe—and Sean knew it. If she went back, he'd kill her to establish his power. Or maybe he was working for someone else, someone more powerful: There were several that came to mind.

"What of Sybil?" Elyna asked him. Sybil wouldn't need to kill Elyna to take power, but she'd enjoy doing it.

"Sybil's been dealt with," Sean said with considerable satisfaction.

"Good," Elyna said, meaning it. If Corona had been brutal, Sybil, her lieutenant, was fiendish.

Sybil had enjoyed hurting others: vampires or regular people, she didn't care. She had a special hatred of men, and Sean had suffered under her hand as much as any in the seethe except maybe Fitz. Fitz was ash and gone, but he'd provided Sybil with months of entertainment. "That's good. With her gone, Brad or Chris can take over as Master."

"Where are you staying?" said Sean.

Elyna sighed, making sure he heard it. He was being too obvious. Ah, the joys of vampire politics. No one even made an attempt to hide the bodies.

"I'm not really as dumb as I look," she told him gently. "I would have thought that you, of all the seethe, would know that."

"Colbert will find you," he told her. "That's his talent, you know, finding vampires when he wants them. You'll be dead anyway and we'll be in the middle of a fucking civil war—"

She ended the call while he was speaking—answering rudeness with rudeness. She didn't approve of swearing. Or prolonging conversations with stupid people. She hadn't thought Sean was one of the stupid people, and it hurt.

She walked over to the mirror on the bathroom door and stared. Did she really look so gullible and helpless? She blinked at herself a few times. She could admit she looked harmless, but surely not stupid.

Colbert could find vampires, any vampire. She'd known that when she'd come here.

Still staring at herself, Elyna flexed her hands, then fisted them. All vampires had talents of one sort or another. There were some magics that almost all of them who'd survived past the first few months had to one degree or another, such as the ability to cloud minds. Vampires who had to kill everyone they fed from were eliminated as a threat to the rest of them. Too many dead bodies brought too much attention.

There were rarer talents, like Colbert's ability to track other vampires. Her former Mistress Corona's ability with minds was rare only in how powerful she had been.

Elyna had a rare talent, too. She could hide in plain sight. As long as she didn't move, she was invisible in a room full of vampires. She'd kept that quiet, once she'd understood the implications. Finding the will to use it had taken a long, long time. A lifetime and more—because a vampire must obey her maker.

That was the first thing she had learned. If her Mistress had taken control of her a day earlier, or if her Mistress had made more certain of the rope she'd tied Elyna's dead body with, things would have been different. To Corona's credit, most vampires take years of mutual feeding to change from human to vampire. She'd had Elyna only a couple of weeks when someone slipped up and drained her dry. As Corona told Elyna when she'd finally tracked her down, they had assumed that Elyna was as dead as she looked; the rope had been merely a precaution. Sometimes, the Mistress had told her, there were people who turned much easier than others. Who knew why?

Stubborn Pole, Jack had called her when at his most exasperated. Fair enough; she'd called him a hot-headed Mick in return, and there had been more than a cup of truth in both epithets.

So, stubborn Pole that she was, despite expectations, Elyna had awoken tied up in a shed in Corona's backyard. The ropes had taken her a little while to break. Confused and dazed by the transformation from human to dead to vampire, she had run home, where Jack had been waiting.

If she survived to be a thousand, she would never forget the joy on his face when she'd opened the door.

But she hadn't been Elyna O'Malley, Jack O'Malley's wife, anymore, not then. She had been vampire, and she'd been hungry.

She'd fed and then fallen comatose into their bed until Corona found her the following evening. By chance the bedroom's thick curtains had been drawn and kept the sun at bay, or else Elyna would never have awoken again. It was a long time before she quit being bitter about those heavy curtains.

Corona wouldn't let her kill herself on purpose, so Elyna settled for second best. She couldn't kill Jack's murderer, so she decided instead to kill Corona, who'd made her and not made sure that Jack was safe from her. So she'd learned to control the vampire, learned to be the best vampire she could, learned to be Elyna Gray instead of Jack O'Malley's wife.

Four weeks ago, the time had been right. The ties that kept her loyal to her Mistress broke at last. Elyna's stubbornness had been rewarded and she was free.

Elyna moved from the bathroom. Her hotel room was eleven stories to the ground and had a fine view of the Loop and the big lake beyond that.

In contrast to the thirst for vengeance that had driven her since her death, hope seemed such a fragile thing.

• • •

IN THE END, she paid a little too much for the apartment turned condo, but a lot less than she'd been willing to pay.

She moved into a furnished efficiency apartment whose greatest assets were its location a few blocks from her home, its basement entrance where no one would see her comings and goings, and a storage room with no windows.

She went shopping at a few thrift stores and then took her newly acquired laundry to the nearest Laundromat. Three middle-aged women eyed her as she sorted her laundry. When she put the first load in, a grandmotherly woman came up to her and explained the ins and outs of the neighborhood laundry.

By the time she'd folded the last of her towels, Elyna had learned a nifty trick to get lipstick out of washable silk; that there was a scary-looking man who washed his clothes on Tuesdays who was a retired Marine, horribly shy, and a dear, sweet man, so she wasn't to let him frighten her; and that there was a local man, someone's cousin's sister-in-law's nephew, who was a contractor.

PETER VANDERSTAAT WAS a neighborhood man, a police officer who ran remodel jobs with his partner and a half-dozen other people on the side. He'd agreed to meet Elyna at her condo and look at it, even though what she wanted wasn't the kind of project they looked for. He usually bought a place, fixed it up, and sold it at a profit, but he was between projects.

He looked to be in his midforties with tired, suspicious eyes. Short and squat, Jack would have said—built like a wrestler. Peter didn't talk a lot, just grunted, until they came back to the living room.

"Where is the money coming from?" he asked. "I don't want to have my men put hours in and then not get paid."

Elyna had money. She'd started by stealing a little bit from her victims and continued with investments. Investments she'd successfully hidden from Corona.

"My family has money," she told him. "I can pay you."

She had been painfully honest when she had been human. Lying was one of those skills she'd had to learn to be a successful vampire.

Vanderstaat bought her story, turning his attention back to the apartment. He frowned at the mismatched windows. "You want me to match the vinyl?"

"*Please*, no," she said, involuntary horror in her voice.

He looked at her and lifted a shaggy eyebrow.

"Vinyl is good. I'm sure that would look terrific in a modern place, but . . ." She let her voice trail off.

"But," he agreed. "What do you intend to do with the floors? Some of those boards can't be saved, expensive to find replacement boards of the same quality. There are some very good laminates on the market; I can get you fair prices."

"Can't you fix the floors?" she asked in a small voice.

That time she got a grin. "A girl after my own heart," he said. "Not the most profitable way to go—but we're in it for fun, too. No fun slapping together crap no matter how much more money you make at it."

Peter and his men worked evenings, he told her, five days a week but not on Saturday or Sunday. They'd stop at ten every night for the neighbors' sake, which made for a long remodel—the reason they usually didn't take on a contract like this. They shook hands on it and agreed that he would start in two days to give him time to put together his crew.

GHOSTS AND CATS don't like vampires. Dogs, on the other hand, didn't mind Elyna—which was good because more often than not, Peter brought his yellow Lab as one of the crew. Peter was initially dubious of Elyna's need to help, but when she proved useful, he started ordering her around like he did the rest of his crew.

The first job was finishing the demolition, clearing out the old for the new. They started with the bedrooms and moved forward. Some nights it was just Peter and Elyna; other nights they had as many as eight or ten men.

"Hey, you guys," said Simon, a twentysomething rookie cop and drywall man who had pulled down a chunk of plaster from the living room wall and held it up for everyone to see. "Look how this is stained. Do you think this is blood? My mom says that back in the late twenties a man was killed up here in this apartment. Or at least he left a lot of blood behind and disappeared."

No one was looking at Elyna, which was a good thing.

"I remember that story," agreed one of the other men. "Something to do with the gangsters, wasn't it? And the Saint Valentine's Day Massacre."

"The massacre was 1929," commented Peter.

"Yeah," agreed Simon. "The guy who lived here was an architect just hired by John Scalise—one of Capone's men. Story was that the architect's wife went missing a few weeks before Valentine's Day. Right after the massacre, the neighbor across the hall and several police officers broke down the door—"

Everyone, even Elyna, looked at the front door, which showed all sorts of damage. If it wasn't the door that had been there when she'd lived here, someone had found an exact match. And then aged it for eighty-plus years.

"But"—Simon dropped his voice and whispered—"all they found was blood. Lots and lots of blood."

There was a crash in the kitchen.

Peter whacked Simon upside the head. "Kid, Elyna's going to be living here. You think she needs that in her head?" And then Peter tromped off to see what the noise in the kitchen had been.

"Sorry, Elyna," Simon told her sheepishly. "Boss is right. I wasn't thinking."

"No worries," Elyna said, straining her ears to listen for any more noises. "I've heard the story before. I did my research before I bought this place."

She must not have been convincing, because he followed her around like Peter's dog for the rest of the evening, mistaking grief and guilt for fear. Peter couldn't figure out what had made the noise, but they decided it was one of the tools falling off some precarious perch. Even so, Peter's crew was jumpy for the rest of the night.

Weeks passed without further incidents. They moved from tearing down to rebuilding the plumbing and electric. And Peter started to schedule times when he, his right-hand man Frankie, and Elyna would sit down with catalogs to choose what the apartment would look like when it was finished.

As soon as the bathroom and most of the electric was finished, Elyna put up blackout curtains in the master bedroom and moved in. She didn't have much more than would fit into a pair of suitcases.

The first thing she bought after moving in was a twin bed. The second thing was a small bookcase, followed by a double handful of books. She kept the efficiency apartment for the coming summer days when the sun's setting time meant Peter's crew would be arriving in daylight. She encouraged Peter to assume that was where the rest of her things were, waiting for the floors to be finished so she wouldn't have to move the stuff around. Peter, Frankie, and the rest of the guys had gotten quite protective of her.

Other than something falling in the kitchen while Simon was telling his ghost story, there had been no sign that the apartment was haunted, let alone haunted by Elyna's dead husband. Sometimes, sitting on her bed and reading a book, Elyna would pretend that Jack was just in another room.

Reading was something they'd shared. It had started when he caught her reading E. M. Hull's *The Sheik*. The scandalous book had left her blushing like a ninny and him rolling his eyes.

"Bastard needed to be put down like a mad dog," he'd told her. "Instead he gets to keep the girl he kidnapped and raped. Doesn't sound right to me. Is that the kind of hero you really want?"

So he'd read *Tarzan of the Apes* to her, and she'd agreed that the ape man would be a much better choice than the sheik—and that had led to a merry few minutes with Jack jumping around on the furniture and her laughing her fool head off until the neighbors knocked on the walls.

They read every odd thing: Charles Darwin, Zane Grey, F. Scott Fitzgerald. Sometimes they read them separately, and sometimes they read them to each other.

She hadn't read in the seethe. She hadn't wanted to give Corona even so much as a glimpse into her real thoughts—and Jack always had said you knew a person by the books they read . . . or didn't read.

When Elyna went shopping for books now, she was bewildered by the offerings. She found a copy of *Tarzan*, but the rest were all new to her.

She'd been reading *The Sackett Brand* for about fifteen minutes before she realized it was something Jack would have liked. She turned back to the beginning and started over out loud, reading for hours. She read *Tarzan* next, commenting on some of the things that science had proven since it was written. But she also went out and got twelve more books by Louis L'Amour for Jack.

As she read to him, she pictured her husband sitting in his favorite chair, eyes closed with that intent expression on his face that meant he was enjoying the book.

Reading wasn't the only pleasure she regained. It had been a long time since she'd had a friend. Inside Corona's seethe, Elyna hadn't been able to trust anyone. She could only show them the broken, fragile thing they all thought her to be. Someone to be discounted. She couldn't afford to care too deeply. The lover who gave her solace one day would torture her the next, because no one disobeyed the Mistress. Even the few who could have done so successfully (because they were older, stronger, or not of the Mistress's making) didn't disobey her. At least not after the Mistress gave Fitz, who had been her favorite, to Sybil.

To Elyna's lonely heart, Peter and his moonlighting friends were like a warm blanket on a cold night. She knew she couldn't afford friends, not if she was a stray living surreptitiously under the radar in Colbert's territory. More accurately, her friends could not afford her. But she couldn't help the affection she felt for them.

Between the books and work on the apartment, Elyna's time fell into a pleasant order that was so much better than anything that had happened to her in a very long time. One evening she woke up and realized she was happy. It was a very disconcerting feeling.

ELYNA LISTENED TO the irregular rhythm of the jazz guitar and breathed in the scent of sixty or so humans crowded together in the dark drinking mixed drinks and listening to the music.

A smart vampire doesn't feed in her own backyard if she can help it. Elyna had been hunting in a small club district several miles away from her home. Unfortunately, even a big city is composed of dozens of smaller places. When the bartender of the Irish pub that she'd been going to nodded at her and set a screwdriver on the bar in front of Elyna without asking, she knew she had to move on.

That was why she was sitting in a popular jazz club in the Loop. The Loop attracted tourists, and it was easier to blend in. At least that was her working theory. She'd come to this club four times in the last week; not feeding, just getting the lay of the land.

Anywhere she thought to be good hunting ground was going to appeal to Colbert, too, but she'd seen no sign of any other vampires. So tonight she'd come dressed to kill. She'd picked up the white sheath dress at a thrift store, but it was real silk and suited her flat stomach. When she'd been human she'd always carried an extra few pounds, but keeping the weight off was not a problem anymore.

She closed her eyes and let a soft smile stretch her lips as she nodded her head to the music. *Come here,* she announced without saying anything at all, *come here and I might be yours.* She didn't use any magic yet, just human mating rituals.

Corona had been bitterly envious of Elyna's ability to attract men this way—Corona had been in her seventies when she died. Though she had once been beautiful—stunning, Elyna suspected—she continued her life-after-death as an old woman. Corona lured her prey by vampire magic, which meant she had to feed more often and more deeply than Elyna, who could usually find someone willing to follow her to a dark corner without use of coercion or power. She wasn't beautiful the way Corona once had been, but she was attractive enough.

"Hey, doll," said a rough tenor voice next to her. "You look like you're having a good time."

She hated this. Making connection, making small talk, getting a glimpse inside someone she'd never see again. She understood the vampires who kept menageries of sheep: humans no one would miss. Menageries reduced the risk of being found out, of having to go hunting, of feeding from strangers, and they served as a sort of crèche from which new vampires were born. After a while, the sheep could be made to forget who they had been, and most of them learned to love their vampire, who slowly killed them. Maybe that had been the problem. Elyna hadn't been a sheep for long enough to learn to love the monsters. Sure as God made little fishies, she couldn't be made to keep humans as sheep just to save herself from a little risk and distaste.

"I am now," she said to the man sitting next to her.

He told her his name was Hal, and she had no trouble coaxing him out into the dark outside the club despite the gold ring on his finger. He had no qualms about following her around the back to a small, dark space of privacy that had made her finally determine that this was the club where she would hunt. Hal would have hesitated to follow a man, but she was half his weight and a foot shorter: he didn't find her threatening.

He laughed when she nuzzled his neck.

When she finished feeding and blurring his memory, she eased him down on the ground. Crouched beside him, one knee on the ground to brace herself against his weight, she felt them.

Vampires.

Elyna moved as fast as she could into the little bit of half-alley trap, no bigger than ten feet by twenty, then froze against the outside wall as flat as she could, thinking, *No one here, no one here.* Power flickered over her and she felt the drain touch her faintly. An hour was the longest she'd ever held this magic to her, and it had left her weak and violently hungry.

She heard their footsteps stop when they spotted her victim. It was dark here, but vampires can see in the dark.

"Not from our seethe," said the woman, her vowels a little rich with the same accent that had colored Elyna's Polish mother's voice.

"None of ours would feed from anyone in Colbert's favorite club," agreed the man. "He's not been here more than a few minutes."

They did a meticulous search of her hiding place. Elyna stood with the stillness of the dead, all of her attention focused on her high-heeled raspberry sandals—not the easiest thing to do when deadly enemies are less than a handspan away. Vampires can feel people who look at them too hard or pay too close attention to them. It means survival in a world that would destroy them if possible.

After far too long the female vampire turned to her comrade. "Not here anymore. Damn. I could have sworn I saw something move in here, just before we found this guy."

"I've heard some of the old ones can fly," said the second vampire.

"Don't be stupider than you have to be," the woman said. "If a vampire that old and powerful had come to town, Colbert would know it. He'll find this one, too. Time to go inside and let him know."

Chicago was huge, but that wouldn't save Elyna, not once he knew she was there.

"Life is what you do next," she whispered to herself as soon as the other vampires had left. It was one of Jack's favorite sayings. She walked quickly toward the L. She'd left her car at her condo because it was hard to make a quick getaway in a parking garage when monsters were after you.

Safely on the train, she shivered and tried not to look at the other passengers—in short, acting just like everyone else. She got off one stop early and walked through alleys and side streets until she made it home.

Home.

She locked the door behind her and sat down on the floor with her back to it. Vampires could not cross the threshold of a home—unless it was their home, which was why she had been able to get in to kill Jack all those years ago. Thresholds were made of life and love—all those things that turn a dwelling place into a home. She hoped that her threshold would hold them out.

But even if it did, it would not be enough. Once Colbert knew where she lived, he had only to wait until she left to feed. She was under no illusions. If he knew she was here, it was only a matter of time until he caught her: her death warrant was signed. Her only escape was to leave.

She could do that. Find some place that had no seethes. They were out there; vampires were not so common as fae or the weres. But it would mean leaving Jack again.

Jack was probably not here anyway.

She looked through the living room entranceway and stared out the window, where the sun was just beginning to lighten the sky. She had a third choice. Perhaps it would be enough penance for her crime if she died here, too. Popular knowledge was that vampires had no souls. Popular knowledge also said that ghosts were not souls of the dead, just leftover bits and pieces that remembered what they had been once. Maybe if she died here, her leftover bits could find Jack's leftover bits as well.

Gold touched the edges of the rooftops across the road from her and washed over the now-matching windows in her front room. She smiled and took one last deep breath as the pain from the sunlight reached her at last.

She had to close her eyes against the light.

"I'm sorry, Jack," she said. "I love you."

Because her eyes were closed, she didn't see the living room blackout curtains snap shut—just heard them the instant before her body died for the day.

SHE AWOKE IN a crumpled heap in front of the door. The skin on her face was tight from the sunburn, but the bathroom mirror assured her that the curtains had shut before the sun had done much damage.

Staring at her wide-eyed reflection in the mirror, she said, "Jack?"

He didn't answer, not then.

But when she and Peter were deciding which of several designs were closest to her original cabinets, a stray breeze fingered through the pages of a catalog they'd set aside and left it opened to a sleek modern style in hickory. She liked those, she thought, pulling the catalog in front of her. But she was trying to recreate her old home, not build a new one.

Maybe she could do both.

"What do you think of this one?" she asked Peter.

"Not very vintage," he told her. "But they would look fine with the countertops you picked out. Good wood goes with almost anything."

A FEW NIGHTS later she finished the book she'd been reading to Jack and replaced it in the bookshelf. The next night there was a book sitting on her chair, ready for her to begin: an Ellery Queen mystery.

The next evening, Jack rearranged the cardboard cutouts that Peter had made to let Elyna see how her kitchen would come together. She put them back as she'd had them, but he was relentless. He never moved them while she was in the kitchen, but if she left for more than a few minutes they were back the way he wanted them.

"And you called me stubborn," she sputtered at him finally, standing in the empty room. "I'm a vampire, Jack. I don't care where the stove is. Why should you?"

Something fluttered lightly on her lips, like a butterfly's kiss. She froze. "Jack?"

But there was no further sign that she wasn't alone in the room. She touched her lips with light fingers.

PETER ROLLED HIS eyes when she told him that she'd changed her mind on the kitchen layout. Frankie just laughed, a great big booming laugh that filled the air.

"Hah," he said. "Told Peter it wasn't natural the way you just let him dictate your kitchen. Never was a woman yet who let a man arrange her kitchen."

"Hmm," said Elyna.

The kitchen progressed rapidly after that. Stainless steel sinks, marble countertop, and all. Elyna bought a teddy bear for Simon's new son and told Frankie what to buy his wife for their anniversary.

When the men came in to lay the kitchen flooring, they were grim-faced and unhappy. Elyna, as she had done before, coaxed the story out of them. Being police officers in Chicago was not for the faint of heart. Vampires are territorial, and somehow this group of hardworking men had become hers just as the home they'd helped her put together was hers. Her mother had taught her to take care of what was hers. She had to use a touch of persuasion to get a name and address.

"Sorry to invite this in here," Peter murmured to her as they were getting ready to leave for the night. "Evil belongs out in the street, not in your home."

Elyna looked down at her hands. "Evil exists everywhere," she told him.

That night she broke the neck of a murderer who had gotten free on a technicality, just as she had killed the drug dealer who'd handed a ten-year-old the heroin to overdose on and the lawyer who liked to kill pros-titutes.

THEN CAME THE evening that Peter didn't come.

"You get a call, Elyna?" Frankie asked her. "He told me he was going to be coming here after his shift."

She shook her head. Everyone became increasingly worried as an hour crept by without word. Peter didn't answer his cell phone, and as he was ten years divorced, no one was home to answer the phone. They called the station and were told that Peter had left at his usual time.

Finally Frankie stood up and stretched, cracking his spine. "We're getting nothing done here, sweetie," he told Elyna. "We need to go out and look for him. He has a few mates and some places he goes to for a bite or glass."

"Call me when you find him."

"As long as it's not too late," Frankie promised, and he and the rest left Elyna alone in her home.

There were all sorts of reasons why Peter might not have made it over tonight. But the one she believed was that she had made him hers—and Colbert had noticed.

She remembered quite clearly how easily Colbert had ousted Corona and her seethe from this city. Half her seethe, anyway; the other half was gone to ashes and sunlight, never to rise again.

She pulled out her cell phone and dialed. "Sean," she said, "get me Colbert's phone number, would you?"

She felt his hesitation through the phone lines. He was angry with her—and would happily have sacrificed her on his road into power. But she had killed his Mistress, and for a while more the urge to obey would stay strong, even with the physical distance between them. She snapped her phone closed, confident that Sean could get the information and would call her back.

She walked into the living room, where Jack had died at her hands, and touched the floor where the wood was just a little darker than the boards around it, despite sanding and staining.

"My fault, Jack. I was mad because you were late again. Jealous, maybe. You were the newest rising star among the architects of Chicago, and I was a housewife. There was a new singer at that speakeasy we used to go to, and you'd promised to take me there. When you couldn't, I decided to go by myself."

The air in the apartment was still and hot despite the new HVAC system. Waiting.

"My fault. I knew it was stupid when I did it." Her eyes burned, but no tears fell. "The new singer was an old woman with a voice like a lark. She came to my table and said, 'You're all alone here, aren't you? I think I'll take you home with me tonight.' If I'd waited until you could go with me, she'd have left us both alone."

Elyna bowed her head. "She and her fellow vampires fed on me for a couple of weeks. I don't remember a lot about that time. Someone got careless and I died. It's unusual for someone to turn after such a short time; mostly they just die."

Stubborn Pole.

Elyna turned slowly, unsure whether her mind had supplied that voice or she'd really heard it.

"When vampires rise the first time, we are nearly mindless, and hungry. *Scared.*" She remembered that most of all. She'd been so scared. "I ran home and you were waiting for me." She swallowed. "Thing is, Jack, I don't think I'll be coming back here after tonight. The local vampires have taken Peter." Peter might already be dead, though certainly they'd have toyed with him while they were waiting for her to figure out what had happened. "I just . . . wanted you to know that my death wasn't your fault. I wish . . . I wish you'd had a chance to marry again, to grow old and watch over your grandchildren, never knowing what had become of me."

In the silence, her phone's ring was very harsh.

"Elyna," she answered.

"Elyna," said a man's voice, "I heard that you wanted to call me."

When she was through talking to Colbert, she slipped the phone back into her pocket. It was traditional for vampires to dress up when they treated with each other, a convention that traced back to older times. Elyna didn't bother changing out of her work clothes.

She opened the door to leave, paused, and said, "I love you, Jack."

THE JAZZ CLUB wasn't the same one where she'd run into Colbert's vampires. This one had a CLOSED FOR REMODELING sign on the door and wasn't in nearly as nice a neighborhood. Elyna got out of the cab and paid the driver.

"You sure you want off here?" he asked, a fatherly man who'd entertained her all the way here with stories of his daughter's almost-disastrous dance recital. "It's late and there's no one here."

She smiled at him. "I'll be fine."

The cab waited, though, until she opened the club door before driving off.

She took a step into the dark room, and with a click someone turned a spotlight on her. With the light in her face, she couldn't see them, but the vampires could see her just fine.

"Such a lot of trouble for such a little girl," purred a man's voice. Over the years, he'd lost most of the French accent she remembered. Colbert sounded a lot more like a TV newscaster than the eighteenth-century vintner he had once been.

"You have someone who belongs to me," she said, tired of playing games. Corona had liked games, too. "Show me that he is alive or this ends now."

Something heavy was tossed onto the floor in front of her, a body.

She went down to one knee and felt the body in front of her. She still couldn't see, but one hand touched something wet. She brought her fingers up to her mouth and licked the moisture away. It was Peter's blood. The body it had come from still breathed. She petted him gently and stood up.

"What do you want?" she asked. "And would you turn off the stupid light? You can't possibly be that afraid of me."

He laughed. The spotlight was turned off, and others were turned on.

Elyna found herself in a large room full of tarps, sawhorses, and tools. The walls had been newly painted a burnt orange. She didn't allow herself to look down and see how much damage they'd done to Peter, just stared at the vampires.

Colbert didn't look imposing. He was only a little taller than she was, wiry rather than bulky. His face looked as if he'd been turned as a teenager, though his dark hair was thinning on top. Only the expense of his attire hinted at his power.

Two vampires stood with him—a woman who was taller than he by four or five inches and a black man with the eyes of a poet and the body of a Chippendale dancer. Both of them were pretty enough to be models.

Arm candy, she thought. There were others here, on the other side of the wall to her right. Sheetrock was not much of a barrier to vampires, but it hid them from sight and made them easy to forget about. Not that it mattered. Doubtless either of his arm candy guards could wipe the floor with her, if Colbert didn't choose to do it himself.

"I am Pierre Colbert," he said.

The way he said it, it rhymed.

"You find something funny?" Colbert asked coolly.

She waved her hands around the building, leaving her right hand pointing at the wall behind which he had more of his people waiting, so he'd know that she understood they were there.

"All of this," she said, "for me."

"Elyna Gray," he said. "Who killed Corona and refused to take her seethe."

"I struck her from behind," Elyna said. "If I'd faced her in a proper fight I'd be ash. If I'd tried to take over the seethe, I'd have been dead in two days."

"Still," said Pierre, "you killed your Mistress and then came into my territory."

"I killed the monster who made me, and then I ran home," Elyna told him. "I admit it is a subtle difference, but significant to this conversation."

"Ah, yes," he purred. "Now that wasn't smart, Elyna Gray who was Elyna O'Malley. If you'd found somewhere else to live, it might have taken me longer to find you—you've been very discreet in your hunting habits other than coming into my favorite club a few weeks ago. I thought perhaps you had a menagerie, but that sheep"—he indicated Peter—"was a virgin pure."

His words accomplished what she'd tried avoiding by not looking at Peter. Rage rushed in and she felt her skin tighten and her eyes burn with fire. Someone looking at her would know that they were in the presence of Vampire.

"Mine," she said, barely recognizing her own voice. "He was one of mine and you harmed him."

"He tasted *mmm* so good," said the woman. "Bitch."

Behind Elyna something fell to the ground with a sharp crack. She took a quick look behind her to where a sawhorse lay on the floor, two legs on one side broken off.

"Now," said Colbert in an interested voice, "how did you manage that?"

Elyna had thought it was someone on his side. She shrugged.

The pretty man turned in a slow circle. "Master," he said, biting out the word as if he found it distasteful. "Master, there is a ghost in this room, can you feel it?"

"Elyna." Colbert looked at her. "You are just full of surprises. But the ability to control ghosts is not uncommon; why do you think they hide from us? And, as it happens, I am very good at it." He looked around the room. "Come out, come out, wherever you are."

Familiar big hands landed on Elyna's shoulders.

"Jack," she said horrified. "Jack, you have to get out of here."

"Too late," said Colbert, smiling. "Jack is it? Break her neck."

No.

The pretty black man looked from Elyna to the ghost behind her and started to smile.

"Jack, come here." The Master of Chicago's voice cracked with power. His pretty pet woman took a step forward and so did Elyna.

Jack patted her shoulder and then moved around her. His hands had been so solid, she thought that the rest of him would look that way, too. Instead, he looked more like a mist of light, a shimmering presence mostly human-sized but not human-shaped.

She'd done this to Jack, brought him to be enslaved by this vampire. She had to do something about it. Everyone in the room was paying attention to Jack and to Colbert. No one was looking at her.

You aren't interested in me, she thought, calling on all the power she had to fade out of notice in this fully lit room full of vampires.

Colbert extended his hand until it touched the cloud of light that was Jack. "Mine," he said in a voice of power.

But vampires can move fast, and Elyna had already crossed the room and found a weapon.

"*You*"—Elyna hit the Master vampire across the back with a piece of the broken sawhorse and knocked him away from her husband—"leave him alone."

Colbert turned on her—and there was nothing human left of him. "You *dare*—" He would have said more, but another piece of the wooden sawhorse emerged from his chest. He looked down, opened his mouth, then collapsed.

It took Elyna a moment to realize that Jack had used the other leg.

Beside Elyna, the black man threw back his head and laughed in utter delight. When he stopped laughing, it cut off abruptly, leaving echoing silence behind. His face free of emotion, he turned his attention to Elyna. He gave her such an empty look that she took two steps away from him until she hit the solid, feeling bulk that had been Jack O'Malley.

"He forgot," said the man who had been Colbert's. "Evil has no power over love." He smiled, his fangs big and white against his ebony skin. "And we are evil, aren't we, Elyna Gray?"

She didn't say anything.

"What now?" he asked her. "Do you want this seethe, Elyna? Do you want to be Mistress of Chicago?"

"No." Her response was so fast and heartfelt that it caused him to laugh again. His laugh was horrible, so much joy and beauty coming out of a man with such empty eyes.

"Then what?"

Elyna looked at the woman, Colbert's other minion, who had fallen to the ground in that utter obeisance sometimes demanded of them by their Mistress or Master.

"Who is the strongest vampire in your seethe?" she asked.

"Steven Harper," he told her. "That would be me."

Jack's reassuring presence behind her, she smiled carefully. "Steven Harper, I would seek your permission to live in your city, keeping the laws and rules of the old ones and bearing neither you nor yours any ill will. Separate and apart with harm to none. Yours to you and mine to me—and this human"—she tilted her head to indicate Peter, who was lying very still just where he had been dropped—"is mine."

The new Master of the Chicago seethe looked at Peter, then over Elyna's shoulder at Jack, and finally to the floor, where a splintered piece of wood stuck out of Colbert's limp body. "You have done me a great favor," he said. "I swore never to call anyone Master again, and now I no longer have to. Come and be welcome in my city—with harm to none."

Elyna bowed, keeping her eyes on him. "Thank you, sir." She took a step back, paused, and said, "The really old ones turn to dust when they are dead and gone."

He looked down at Colbert's body. "I guess he lied about how old he was."

"Or he is not, quite, gone." Elyna had made a point of finding out things like that. Corona had been ash before she touched the floor.

"Ah," Steven said, pushing the corpse with his toe. "My thanks."

A pair of Steven Harper's vampires drove her to her apartment building and helped her negotiate the way into her apartment while she carried Peter, unwilling to trust him to anyone else. She could no longer see Jack, but she knew he was with her by the occasional light touches of his hands.

Harper's vampires didn't try to come in, nor did they speak to her. She set Peter down on her bed, since she didn't have anywhere else to put him. Then she went back out and locked the door. When she returned to the bedroom Peter was sitting up. She'd been pretty sure that he was more awake than it had appeared, because a smart man knows when to lie low.

Without a word, she cut the ropes and helped peel off the duct tape that covered his mouth. Then she got a wet hand towel and brought it to him.

"There's blood on your face and neck," she told him.

He took it from her, stared at it a moment, and then wiped himself clean. The wounds had closed, she noticed, as vampire bites do. They hadn't actually hurt him very badly—not physically, anyway.

They stared at each other a while.

"Vampire," he said.

She nodded. "If you tell anyone, they'll think you're crazy."

"Could you stop me? Make me not remember? Isn't that what vampires are supposed to be able to do?"

She shrugged, but chose, for his sake, not to give him the whole truth. He'd sleep better at night without it. "Hollywood vampires can do lots of things we can't," she told him, instead. "You don't have to worry about Harper coming after you, though. He agreed that you are one of mine, and he won't hurt you. We vampires take vows like that very seriously."

"You don't look like a vampire," he said.

"I know," she agreed. A stray breeze brushed a strand of hair off her cheek. "We're like serial killers; we look just like everyone else."

Peter grunted, looked down at his hands, and then made another sound—something she couldn't interpret.

Then he said, "That man who killed his girlfriend's baby, the one where the evidence got bungled and the charges were dismissed a few weeks ago. The one who turned up dead in a place full of people who never were sure who killed him. That was you?"

Elyna nodded. He eyed her thoughtfully, then nodded.

He cleared his throat. "There were others after that, just a couple. The ones we talked about while we worked. Like the well-connected lawyer who liked to pick up hookers and beat them to death. Fell down his stairs and died a month or so back. That was you, too?"

She ducked her head. "Vampires don't have to kill people," she told him. "Especially once we are older, more in control of ourselves. I try not to. But . . . it doesn't bother me very much, not when they are"—she looked him in the eye and gave him an ironic smile—"evil."

"In my business," Peter said slowly, "you come into the job seeing the world in black and white. Most of us who survive, the good cops, learn to work in shades of gray." He smiled slowly at her. "So, Ms. Gray. What have you decided about the lighting fixtures in the kitchen?"

The brass lights are nice, but I think the bronze will look better, Jack whispered, his lips brushing the edge of her ear.

"I think I like the bronze," she told Peter.

Squatters' Rights

ROCHELLE KRICH

In the beginning she heard them inside the bedroom wall.

The sounds originated above Eve's head and had kept her awake for countless hours every night since she and Joe had moved into the house three weeks ago.

Scratch, scratch, scratch . . .

Mice, Eve had thought the first night, but she hadn't found droppings in the bedroom or anywhere else in the house, where speckled beige tarps had formed hills over their furniture and the stacks upon stacks of boxes filled with their belongings.

Joe hadn't heard a thing.

"It's all in your head, babe," he told her, his sympathy thinned the third time she woke him—at two in the morning, so she couldn't blame him. "The house was just fumigated, right? Even if something *was* in the walls, it isn't there now."

Unless it was a ghost.

The thought was ridiculous, and Eve was pretty sure believing in ghosts didn't fit with Judaism, although hadn't King Saul asked a witch to summon the spirit of the prophet Samuel?

Eve wouldn't have thought about ghosts at all if the broker hadn't told them the previous owner had killed her husband and herself, in the house.

"By law I have to inform you," the broker had said, his shrug and rolling of eyes inviting Eve and Joe to share his opinion of said law. He was a tall, wiry man with silver hair and a restless habit of bouncing from foot to foot that made Eve think of a Slinky. "It's morbid, I'll give you that, but a lucky break for you guys. This place is selling way below what it's worth. I'm sure you've seen the comps, so you know."

Bad *mazel*, both sets of parents had said. Eve and Joe had dismissed their forebodings, swayed by the potential in the three-bedroom, two-bath fixer-upper on Bellaire Avenue in Valley Village, and by the price. They had the down payment, most of it money Eve had inherited from her grandmother, but even with two incomes—Joe was a nursing home administrator, and Eve taught kindergarten at a private Jewish school—it was unlikely that they could afford another house in the foreseeable future, if ever, unless they were willing to leave Los Angeles, which they weren't. Their jobs were here, their friends, family. Eve's parents lived in Beverlywood, a thirty-minute drive from Valley Village. Joe's parents lived in San Francisco, where housing was even more out of reach.

To save rent, Eve and Joe planned to renovate the house after they took occupancy. It had made sense to have the hardwood floors refinished while the house was empty, and they painted the master bedroom themselves the Sunday before they moved in.

That first evening, while Joe and his cousin Marty were returning the U-Haul in the city, Eve stood inside the bedroom. It looked just as she had imagined—beautiful, serene, a haven where she and Joe could retreat during the many months the house would be undergoing work. She would have placed the full-size beds on the wider east wall, but two closet doors made that impossible. So the beds were on the south wall. Eve had chosen the bed near the windows that looked out on the yard even though it was farther from the closets and connecting bathroom.

The bathroom was their first project. The chipped porcelain finish on the tub and sink was ringed with rusty Rorschachs, and a leaking shower pan had caused dry rot in the floor joists and mud sill. Earlier that day Eve had yanked off half a panel of blistered, peeling wallpaper but stopped when she saw ominous Technicolor patches of mold and an accompanying cloud of dust.

Eve made numerous trips hauling armfuls of clothing to the bedroom closets, dresser, and armoire, the furniture's matte espresso stain rich against the Benjamin Moore Kennebunkport Green, which looked gray in the fading light. She considered moving some of the dry and canned goods into the kitchen, but she didn't have the energy to line the pantry and cabinet shelves. She took a box of Raisin Bran for Joe and instant oatmeal packets for herself. She gave up looking for the coffeemaker. She'd ask Joe to do it.

Even with the windows open, the house was warm. Eve felt sticky and grimy. Project number two, she decided: air-conditioning. After a quick shower in the guest bathroom (she made a mental note to tell the plumber about the weak water pressure), she put on coral capri pants and a white tank top and unearthed a tablecloth and two place settings, including goblets for the wine chilling in the fridge next to a bottle of Fresca and lunch leftovers from a nearby kosher pizza shop. Humming Crosby, Stills, Nash & Young's "Our House," she arranged everything on the small drop-leaf faux butcher block table in the dark ocher breakfast nook, which would look cheery and cozy when it was painted, maybe a buttery yellow.

Joe surprised her with sunflowers.

"You are so, so sweet," Eve said, standing on tiptoe to kiss his lips and nuzzle his cheeks, a little rough and darkened by two days' growth of beard and smudges of dirt, but she didn't care.

"You smell great," he said, his strong hands on her hips. "You look great, too." His smile was intimate, inviting. "You showered, huh? Guess I'll do the same."

Before Joe, Eve had felt self-conscious about her body, which fluctuated between a size ten and twelve, huge by L.A. standards. Joe made her feel beautiful, sexy. He loved her curves, he told her, and wide hips were great for having babies.

"How was the shower, by the way?" he asked.

She told him about the water pressure. "It's fine for now."

While Joe showered, she found a vase, a wedding gift from her best friend Gina, who had posted Eve's profile on J-Date. Eve had sworn off J-Date and other Jewish online dating sites after thirty-plus dates ranging from painfully boring to disastrous. She had initially declined to answer Joe's post, but she didn't want him to think she was rude, and (she hadn't admitted this to Gina) she was taken by his humor and his photo, even though photos usually lied. She and Joe, as it turned out, had much in common. They were twenty-nine years old, both only children committed to modern Orthodoxy, family, and sushi. They enjoyed hiking, word games, and *Curb Your Enthusiasm*. From their phone calls she discerned that he was smart and funny and self-deprecating. He had been married briefly at twenty-two—"We were both too young," he'd told Eve—and was ready for a serious relationship. Two weeks after their first post they met in the Coffee Bean and Tea Leaf on Larchmont. She caught her breath when she saw him coming toward her, six foot three and good-looking with wavy thick dark brown hair and okay, a small paunch, but his smile! His smile made her palms sweat and her stomach muscles curl. Pilates for the heart, she thought.

The sunflowers brightened the ocher walls. Over dinner, salmon fillets and tomato-and-basil angel hair pasta that Joe had picked up from the Fish Grill on Ventura, Joe uncorked the Asti. They toasted Gina and their good fortune in having found each other and the house. They drank a second glass of wine. They joked about the house's many defects and, after a third glass that made them giddy, about its macabre history. Joe said, "Promise you won't kill me, babe?" and Eve said, "Not tonight, I have a headache," and they groaned with laughter until tears streamed from their eyes. When the meal was over and the bottle empty, they were suddenly mellow. They held hands across the table. Joe fingered her wedding band and said, "I can't imagine life without you," and Eve was so happy she almost cried.

Later, when Joe was asleep, she stood in front of the window, the newly varnished dark walnut floors cool and smooth under her feet. The moon was kinder than daylight to the yard, a field of shaggy yellowed grass and weeds and bald patches of parched earth. She envisioned a dark velvety green lawn, tall trees hiding the cinder block wall, perennial shrubs and annuals—petunias, lobelia, pansies in the fall. Maybe a hammock where she could stretch her legs and brush her fingers against the blades of sweet-smelling grass while she read a book and, God willing, one day soon, would stroke the downy hair of a baby in the jasmine-perfumed air.

The noises started as soon as she slipped back into bed.

JOE HAD TO prepare for a health department inspection at work, so he was long gone when the contractor, Ken Brasso, arrived at seven thirty in the

morning with two Latino workers, Fernando and William. Eve would
have offered coffee and had a cup herself—God knew she needed caffeine
after having had almost no sleep—but Joe had forgotten to dig up the
coffeemaker and the fresh-ground dark roast she'd bought last Friday at
Whole Foods, was that too much to ask? She apologized about the coffee,
finishing with a little laugh that left her feeling awkward. She did have
the Fresca, which all three men politely declined.

Eve had been anxious about the floors and was gratified to see Fernando and William working with care as they laid tarps in the hall and
master bedroom. After covering the beds, dresser, and armoire, they taped
thick plastic over the frame of the door connecting the bedroom and bath,
leaving one flap open.

"There's gonna be dust when you're smashing tile," Ken had told Eve.
"But my guys will clean everything up."

Ken, short and compact and in his late forties, had come highly rec-
ommended by her parents' friends, the Bergers, for whom he had recently
done a kitchen remodel. The Bergers had left Ken and his crew alone in
their house for months and trusted them without reservation. Eve could,
too. She would have liked to watch the demolition, but the drive to the
school on West Pico would take at least twenty-five minutes. She did hear
the first thunks as she was leaving and felt a rush of excitement as she
pictured hammers attacking the godawful wallpaper and cracked tiles.

At work she made Memorial Day projects with the fourteen children
in her class. She loved her kids, each one adorable and inquisitive. She loved
sharing stories about them with Joe, who was a great listener and would
be a great father. Once or twice her mind slipped to the house on Bellaire,
and she wondered how the work was progressing. Throughout the day she
found herself yawning. During nap time she was tempted to lie down on
one of the tiny cots, just for a few minutes. Of course, she couldn't.

When Eve returned home, she was pleased to see the Dumpster in the
driveway filled with debris. Stepping into the house, she was greeted by a
lively Hispanic tune that she traced to the boom box on the floor of the
master bath, now an empty shell. Fernando and William were removing
the tarps from the beds and furniture. The music was loud, and they didn't
notice her arrival. When they did, they smiled at her. A coating of dust
had whitened both men's hair and eyebrows, and William's moustache.

Eve smiled back and patted her head. *"Mucho polvo."* A lot of dust.

Fernando nodded and stooped his shoulders. *"Sí, sí. Somos bien viejos."* We are very old.

Both men laughed, and Eve joined in, brimming with goodwill and happiness.

Ken took pride in giving Eve an update. They had replaced the warped plywood and joists. They had installed the drain assembly in the shower and poured mortar onto the wire mesh layered over the tar paper.

"See that?" Ken pointed to the grayish-brown mud on the shower bottom. "No dips, no humps. The slope is perfect. Water will flow right down to the drain. That's what you want."

"Wonderful," Eve said, thinking Joe would be more interested in the details than she was. The moist, earthy smell of the mortar was making her a little nauseated.

"Tomorrow we frame the window and put in cement backer board for the wall tiles. Moisture won't affect it, so it's great for bathrooms. Then the floor tiles. Cabinets, countertop, and faucets are last. And you've got yourself a beautiful new bathroom."

Eve smiled. "I can't wait."

She and Joe had enjoyed selecting the materials: white marble for the walls and floors with accents of one-inch green glass tiles above the sink; polished chrome trim for the sink, Jacuzzi tub, and shower faucets; dark brown cabinets; white marble for the countertop. A spa in their own home.

"One thing." A note of warning had entered Ken's voice. "That mortar's solid, but don't step on it, not even tomorrow. It'll be hardened, but still soft enough to be easily chipped or gouged with just about anything hard enough to do damage."

"The shower is off-limits," Eve promised.

"Thursday, we put in the shower pan liner and the second layer of mud. When that's dry, we install the marble. You ordered extra, right? Like I said, you have to allow for breakage."

TUESDAY NIGHT THE scratching was more persistent. Eve hated waking Joe. He was still tired from lugging furniture and boxes and a long day at work, where a patient had been missing for hours, right in the middle of inspection. After fifteen minutes she couldn't stand one more second of the noise. "Poor baby," Joe murmured, "try to get some sleep." Which pissed her off, because it wasn't as though she weren't *trying*, for God's sake. Minutes later he was snoring, his arm still around her, his breath a little rank as it tickled her cheek. She loosened his arm and nudged him until he was lying on his back. Turning onto her stomach, she pressed her pillow against her ears. No relief. In the living room, she rummaged through several boxes before she found cotton balls that she fashioned into earplugs. Months earlier, planning a trip to Israel, she'd filled a prescription for Ambien. In the end she hadn't taken the pills. She took half a tablet now, and with the cotton crammed into her ears, she lay down and shut her eyes. Silence. She exhaled slowly and felt her body relax.

The noises came back.

The scratching had been replaced by a whooshed exhalation that formed a word, *heave*, whispery at first, then gaining in volume. *Heave, heave, heave, heave.* And something was hovering over her face, pressing against her body, solid and warm and—

Eve. That was what she heard, *Eve.* Joe calling her name, *Eve*, dear Joe, he felt bad for her, or maybe he wanted her, which was fine, she couldn't sleep anyway. Smiling, she raised her arms and embraced air. She opened her eyes. He was lying on his back, fast asleep. *Thanks for the concern, Joe.*

The voices were louder now, sharper. Not *Eve*, she realized with a start, not *heave*.

Leave.

That was it. *Leave. Leave. Leave.*

Oh God, Eve thought, lying rigid with fear on the bed, what was happening? Ohgodohgodohgod.

At some point, when the first hint of daylight began tinting the gray walls green, the noises stopped. Eve slept. At five forty-five her alarm rang. She slammed the snooze button. Fifteen minutes later the alarm rang again. She slammed the button again. Joe, running his electric shaver over his chin, said, "Ken'll be here by seven, babe, so you may want to get up." She wanted to smack him. She crawled out of bed.

When she entered the breakfast nook a half hour later, Joe was sitting at the table reading the *Times*, a large mug in his hand. He put down the mug and pulled out a chair for her.

"Hey." He smiled. "I picked up doughnuts for Ken and his guys, like you asked, babe. They're on the counter. I found the coffeemaker *and* the coffee. Plus two mugs, hot cups, plastic spoons, and paper plates. I think you're set."

"Congratulations. I'll submit your name to the Nobel committee."

He ignored her sarcasm and patted the chair. "Sit. I'll pour you a cup of coffee. You'll feel better, I promise. The coffee's pretty good, I have to say." He rose and took a step toward the kitchen.

"I'm glad you're all sunshine and joy. I slept an hour. *One hour.* Coffee isn't going to fix that."

"I'm so sorry, babe."

"I could pack all our stuff in the bags under my eyes. I look like crap, Joe. I *feel* like crap. There was almost no water coming out of the damn showerhead, and what did tinkle out was lukewarm."

He took her hand. "Eve, honey—"

She yanked her hand away. "Don't 'Eve honey' me. The shower in the guest bathroom sucks, Joe. I'm sure it was hot when you showered, so of course you don't have a problem with it. The shower sucks. This house sucks." She started to cry.

In a flash he was at her side, his muscled arms hugging her to his chest. "I feel terrible, Eve. I wish I could help."

"Something's in the wall, Joe. Something alive."

Joe sighed. "Eve—"

She pulled away and glared at him, her blue eyes intense. She clenched her hands. "I heard it, Joe. Over and over and over, so many times I stopped counting. So don't you *dare* tell me I'm imagining things. Because I. Will. Scream."

Joe placed a hand on her shoulder. "I hear you, Eve. I'll call an exterminator."

"I don't know if an exterminator can help."

Joe frowned. "You want to ask Ken to open the wall, see what's in there? Whatever it takes."

She took his hand. "Promise you won't think I'm crazy."

"Okay," he said, drawing out the word, his tone wary.

"The voices I've been hearing?" She tightened her grip on his hand. "Last night they whispered what sounded like 'Leave.' And I felt something breathing on my face, Joe."

Joe covered his mouth with his free hand and forced a cough. Eve knew he was struggling not to laugh. She felt a twinge of anger but couldn't blame him.

He dropped his hand to his side. "What are you saying, Eve? That there are ghosts in the house?"

"The people who owned it before us . . . The woman killed her husband, Joe. She killed herself. What if their troubled spirits are here? I know we're not supposed to practice witchcraft, but that doesn't mean spirits don't exist. It's possible, isn't it?"

Joe drew her close. "You know what I think, honey? I think you and I had way too much wine the other night, and we were talking about the people who owned the house, being disrespectful. So that's on your mind. Plus our parents scared us with all that talk about bad *mazel*."

"I heard the voices, Joe. I felt them breathing on me."

"Maybe you did, Eve," he said, his voice soft as cotton. "And maybe you had a nightmare that seemed incredibly real. Isn't that possible? Hasn't that ever happened to you? It has to me."

She'd had those kinds of dreams, more than once. "You're right. I'm being silly."

"You're not silly. I'd be frightened, too." He released her and cupped her face in his hands. "Look, if it happens tonight, wake me right away. I'll stay up with you."

The bands around her chest loosened. "I love you, Joe."

"I love you, too, babe."

"I'm sorry I was such a bitch."

"You? Never." He smiled. "Gotta go, babe."

Fernando and William arrived on time. They thanked Eve for the coffee and doughnuts, which they hurried to finish when Ken showed up minutes later. Eve ate a glazed doughnut with her coffee and slipped a cruller into a plastic bag to take to work. She was walking to her Corolla when Ken called her name. She turned around.

"Show you something?" He looked stern.

"Is there a problem?"

"You tell me."

She followed him down the hall into the bathroom. He pointed to the shower floor.

"I thought I made myself clear," Ken said.

She stepped closer. The gray-brown mortar with its perfect slope showed markings and cracks in several areas.

"I have no idea how that happened," Eve said. "We didn't go *near* the shower, Ken."

Ken harrumphed.

She peered closely at the markings. "Doesn't that look like a bird's feet? We left the windows open all night, because it was so warm. Maybe a bird flew in."

"Through the screens?"

She sighed. "I don't know what to tell you, Ken."

"We lay tile on that surface, you'll have cracks, that's a guarantee. We'll have to redo the mud. That's half a day's work, and it's not coming out of *my* pocket." Ken was scowling.

"Of course not." Eve wondered how much a half day's work would cost. Not that they had a choice. "So when will you be able to install the marble?"

"You're looking at Tuesday at the earliest—unless you have more birds visiting."

EVE SHOWED JOE the marks on the mortar.

"That *is* strange," he said. "You're right. The marks *do* look like they were made by a bird. Or maybe a chicken. *Bock, bock, bock.*" Joe flapped his arms. "Is that the noise you've been hearing?"

She stared at him, wounded. "I can't believe you're making fun of me. I haven't slept in two days, Joe."

His handsome face turned red. "I'm really sorry, Eve. I was trying to get you to see the humor in this."

"The shower's going to cost us hundreds more, Joe. Where's the humor in that?"

Wednesday night Eve took a whole Ambien instead of a half and fell into a deep sleep. She dreamed she was at a grave site where she saw somber-faced people, most of whom she knew. Gina, the staff and teachers from her school. Her mother and father, Joe, Joe's parents. Everyone was crying. She didn't see herself, and it took a few seconds before she realized that it was *her* funeral. Her chest ballooned with sadness. She wanted to cry, too, but the voices were back, *leave, leave, leave, leave,*

leave, and she couldn't wake Joe, couldn't move because something was pressing against her chest, breathing on her face, its odor foul and musty.

In the morning Joe said, "I watched you, babe. You were sound asleep. Feeling better?"

"A little," she lied. She'd had another nightmare. That was the only rational explanation, so why worry Joe? There was nothing he could do.

She was sluggish at work, but the kids didn't notice. An hour after she returned home her mother, Ruth, arrived with bags of fruits and vegetables. She had brought dinner—a large pan of eggplant parmesan—and home-baked chocolate cake, Joe's favorite.

"You're the best," Eve said, and kissed her mother's cheek.

Ruth smiled. "I try." She noted the dark circles under Eve's eyes. "You didn't sound like yourself on the phone, honey. You're not sleeping well, right?" She nodded. "It takes time to get used to a new house."

"It's not that." Eve told her mother about the dream, but not about the voices. She braced for a comment about the house's bad *mazel*, but Ruth said, "Your own funeral? *Chas v'sholom*"—God forbid—and shuddered. Eve's grandmother, Rivka, would have spit on the floor.

"It's just a bad dream, honey," her mother said. "Try chamomile tea before you go to sleep. Or a glass of red wine."

Eve's eyes teared. "You warned us, Mom. You all said the house has bad *mazel*. I should have listened."

"Evie." Ruth hugged her daughter tight. "Don't let a nightmare ruin your happiness." She moved back and lifted Eve's chin. "You loved the house, right? You bought it. You'll make your own *mazel*. Okay?"

Eve tried a smile. "Okay." Her mother always made her feel better.

"So, show me what they've done. This is *very* exciting."

"They finished demolishing the bathroom." Eve led the way and was surprised to find her spirits and enthusiasm reviving with each step. "They're working on the shower, and they installed a moistureproof backing on the walls for the marble. It's going to be so beautiful, Mom."

"I'm sure it will."

In the bedroom doorway Ruth came to an abrupt stop. She *tsked*.

Eve turned to face her. "What?"

Ruth was frowning. "That's your bed?" She pointed to the bed close to the windows that looked out on the yard.

"Yes. Why?"

"That explains the dream, Eve. Your bed is directly across from the doorway. Your feet are pointing to the door."

Eve crinkled her forehead. "So?"

"It's bad *mazel*, honey. When a person dies, he or she is carried out feet first. You probably heard it before and forgot, and your dream is reminding you."

Jewish feng shui. That explained the sounds Eve had been hearing. *Leave.* It was her subconscious nudging her into protecting herself. The feeling that something had been breathing on her, pressing against her— that had been a nightmare, like Joe said.

That night after Eve and Joe enjoyed the eggplant and two servings each of the cake, she helped him move the beds closer to the closets. The beds were off center now. That bothered Eve, but off center was better than bad *mazel*. Eve debated and took an Ambien. She lay in her off-center bed with a light heart and fell asleep within minutes.

She was at her funeral again. Her heart ached for her parents and Joe's, all of them weeping as her casket was being lowered into the grave. She was most concerned for Joe. He had stepped back from the grave and was standing with his head bowed, his shoulders heaving. How she wished she could comfort him. He turned around and looked up, as though he sensed she was watching him. She saw him lock eyes with a tall, brown-haired young woman prettier and slimmer than Eve would ever be. Then Joe, her Joe, I-love-you-more-than-life-babe-I-can't-live-without-you Joe, gave the woman the lazy smile that had won Eve's heart. He winked at the woman, and Eve had no choice but to watch that lying bastard flirt *at her own funeral.* The voices started again: *Leave, leave, leave, leave, leave . . .*

Not the house—no, the house was fine, the house was not the danger. *Leave Joe.*

FRIDAY MORNING SHE woke up with a migraine and nausea. Joe notified the school that she wouldn't be coming in and offered to cancel Ken. Eve reminded him that Ken and his crew wouldn't return until Tuesday.

"That's good, then." Joe arranged a cool damp washcloth on Eve's forehead and kissed her cheek softly. "I don't want to wake you if you're sleeping, so call me when you can, okay, babe? If you need me, I'll come home."

She nodded, her eyes shut to block out the soft filtered light that, with her migraine, felt like an assault. Joe was so tender, so solicitous. She could tell he wasn't faking. She felt guilty having harbored hateful thoughts because of a nightmare that seemed ludicrous when she was awake.

"Don't worry about cooking for Shabbos," Joe said. "Your mom is taking care of everything." He kissed her again before he left.

She lay in bed until the migraine's accompanying zigzagging aura stopped and the ferocious pain receded to a dull ache. She made her way gingerly to the kitchen and saw that Joe had filled the hot-water urn and set out tea bags and dry crackers. And a note:

If you're up, that means you're feeling a little better. Call me. I love you, babe.

The tea and crackers settled her stomach. She showered in the guest bathroom and washed her hair, careful to avoid sudden movements that made her feel as though loose parts were rattling around in her skull.

She craved fresh air. Wearing jeans and a T-shirt, and sunglasses to protect her still-sensitive eyes, Eve walked out the front door. A thirty-something woman with curly red hair was in front of Eve's walkway, pushing a stroller back and forth while she kept her eyes on a redheaded boy furiously pedaling a tricycle up the street.

The woman smiled at Eve. "You're the new neighbor. I'm Sandy Komin."

"Eve Stollman."

"Nice to meet you, Eve. I planned to introduce myself before, but with three kids under eight, my intentions rarely pan out. If I can take a shower, I consider it a good day." Sandy smiled again.

Eve smiled back. "How old is your baby?"

"Lily is eight months." Sandy beamed at the infant asleep in the stroller. She pointed to the toddler on the bike. "Michael's two and a half. Our oldest, Geneva, is seven. She's in school, thank God. Do you have kids?"

Eve shook her head. "We want to start a family. That's one of the reasons we bought the house."

"Well, if you want to practice, you can borrow mine whenever you want." Sandy laughed. "Seriously, let me know if I can help with anything. Dry cleaners, markets, carpet cleaners, plumbers, gardener—I have tons of numbers."

Eve thought, *What about ghost busters?* "Thanks, I'll take you up on that. I hope the noise from the remodeling isn't bothering you too much."

"Not at all. We're up early. And I'd rather hear hammering and drilling than Barney. Barney the purple dinosaur?" she said when Eve looked puzzled.

"I've never watched it."

"Lucky you." Sandy adjusted Lily's blanket. "The couple who owned the house before you, Nancy and Brian Goodrich? They did some minor remodeling. They were planning to put in a new kitchen, but then . . ." Sandy's voice trailed off, and her expression had turned somber. "You know what happened, right?"

Eve nodded. "The broker told us."

"God, what a tragedy." Sandy sighed. "We were all shocked. Nancy and Brian seemed happy, and I never heard them arguing." Her eyes narrowed. "Michael, turn around and come back!" she called. "You're too far!"

Eve waited until the boy obeyed. "What happened, exactly?"

"The police think Nancy woke up when she heard someone entering the bedroom and thought Brian was an intruder. She must have been disoriented, maybe because she was on antianxiety medication." The baby whimpered. Sandy resumed the back-and-forth motion of the stroller. "Nancy shot him. When she realized she'd killed Brian, she killed herself." Tears welled in Sandy's eyes. She wiped them with her hand. "It's heartbreaking. It's . . ." She shook her head.

"Why was Nancy on medication?"

"I heard she had a nervous breakdown. She seemed stressed the month or so before she died. I didn't see her in the final weeks." For a moment Sandy was quiet, lost in thought. Then she looked at Eve and her face brightened. "Hey, I hope you don't let the house's history bother you. What happened to Nancy and Brian has nothing to do with you and your husband. What's his name?"

"Joe."

"I saw him. He's a hottie, Eve, a keeper." Sandy winked. "How'd you meet?"

Eve told her.

"That is *so* romantic. Tom and I dated in high school. We always knew we'd get married. Boring, huh?" She smiled. "I'm glad we finally met, Eve. Welcome to the neighborhood. I'm sure you're going to be very happy here. Michael, what did I tell you? Not so far!"

• • •

JOE AND EVE ate Shabbat dinner in the dining room, uncluttered now that he had moved the boxes into the living room, and she hadn't even asked. The light switch for the chandelier had stopped working. Eve didn't mind. The fixture was ugly, and some of the globes were cracked. She much preferred the honeyed glow from the candles in the two silver candelabras, an engagement gift from Joe's parents. The lighting, lovely and soft, hid the spiderweb of cracks on the walls and ceiling.

Over Ruth's potato leek soup, Eve told Joe about Nancy and Brian Goodrich.

"Two lives gone because of a tragic mistake, just like that." Joe snapped his fingers. "I don't know about you, Eve, but this makes what happened less creepy. You and I—we're nothing like the Goodriches. I feel better about the house."

"Me, too." She really did. "Speaking of the house, I saw cracks on the bedroom wall, above the headboards."

Joe nodded. "The house is settling. It happens."

"But we painted less than a week ago, Joe."

"I guess the house has its own schedule." He smiled. "We have touch-up paint, babe, so there's no problem."

Joe insisted on clearing the table and doing the dishes. Eve, still suffering from the hangover-like aftereffects of the migraine, took two Advil tablets and had read a chapter of *The Girl with the Dragon Tattoo* when Joe joined her.

Joe fell asleep first. Eve took an Ambien and twisted the outer shell of the Shabbat lamp on her nightstand until the room was dark. Drifting off to sleep, she realized she'd forgotten about the Advil she'd taken earlier and wondered if mixing the two pills was dangerous. She could check the package warnings, but unless she was prepared to make herself gag and cough up the Ambien, which she wasn't, what was the point? She wasn't really worried.

This time she dreamed she was at her parents' house. Her mother and father were seated on low folding chairs in their living room. Sitting *shiva* for Eve. The third low chair, Joe's, was unoccupied. Eve found Joe leaning against a wall. She saw the slim, brown-haired woman sidle next to him, saw them link their hands, just for a second, when no one was watching.

No one except Eve.

Saturday morning Eve stayed in bed while Joe attended Shabbat services at the synagogue on Chandler, a five-minute walk from their house—another selling point.

"Sure you don't want to come with me, babe?" Joe said before he left. "You might feel better if you get out, and you'll meet people in the community."

Eve was sure.

She *wasn't* sure, for the first time since they had started chatting on J-Date, about Joe. She accepted that the nightmare was a product of her unsettled imagination, compounded by the tragedy that had befallen the house's previous owners. But dreams had a purpose, didn't they? Wasn't she supposed to learn something from them?

And what did she really know about the man she'd met on an Internet site less than two years ago? She had never caught Joe in a lie, but then, she'd never questioned anything he'd told her. She'd checked him out before they met—that was only prudent, and she would have done so even without her parents' urging. She had spoken to his rabbi ("A great guy, Joe!"), had heard positive comments from friends of friends. The Stollmans, her mother had learned, were solid people, well liked by the San Francisco Jewish community.

Eve knew that Joe had spent a year in an Israeli yeshiva after high school and had worked as a day trader in Brooklyn before returning to San Francisco, where he obtained his administrator's license in a nursing home. Eve knew little about his six-month marriage. Joe didn't like to talk about his ex-wife. All Eve knew was her name. Karen.

None of which was damning, Eve had to admit.

Eve knew what Joe would say if she told him about the woman in the dream. *A figment of your imagination, babe. You're insecure. You've always been insecure about your looks.*

That was true. But . . .

Eve got out of bed and searched through Joe's things, first in the armoire, then in the dresser. She found nothing suspicious, no references to another woman, no photos. In Joe's nightstand she did find every note she'd written to him since they'd met, every card she'd given him.

Joe loved her. How could she have doubted him?

The door to the bathroom was open. She stepped inside. The room would be beautiful when it was finished, airy and spacious, so elegant with the white marble.

She frowned. Nails were protruding from the cement backer boards. Stepping closer, she noticed gouges in the boards. She examined the bottom of the shower. The marks and cracks on the mortar were back.

"KEN IS GOING to quit," Eve told Joe when he returned from *shul*. "I wouldn't blame him. This is crazy, Joe."

Joe examined the nails, studied the mortar.

"Let's eat," he said.

He was quiet over lunch. When they finished dessert, he said, "I have to tell you something, Eve. You're going to be upset, but I'm hoping you can keep an open mind. Okay?"

Eve gripped the edge of the table. He wanted a divorce. He wanted to be with the brown-haired woman in Eve's dreams. "Okay," she said. As if she had a choice.

"I've been thinking about the bathroom," he said. "The marks, the nails."

The bathroom. In her relief Eve almost laughed.

"Is it possible—don't answer before you hear me out, okay?—is it possible that you've been walking in your sleep and doing stuff you don't remember?"

"You bastard." Her lips were white.

"You're taking Ambien every night, right? Ambien makes some people hallucinate, Eve. It can make people walk in their sleep and binge without knowing what they're doing. It was in the news, remember? We talked about it. There are cases of people who didn't know they were driving, for God's sake."

Eve shook her head.

"Think about it, babe," Joe said. "That's all I ask."

Eve went back to her bed. When Joe came into the room she turned on her side. A moment later he was lying next to her.

"Eve, you know I love you. The Ambien is the only thing that makes sense."

"The floors are ruined."

"What?"

"The hardwood floors we just paid two thousand dollars to refinish? There are tons of scratches. You probably made them when you were moving the boxes."

Joe rolled onto his back. "You didn't say anything."

"Well, now I am."

He sighed. "What is this, tit for tat?"

"There are scratches on our bedroom floor, too."

"You helped me move the beds, Eve. We were both careful about the floors. Maybe Ken's guys did it."

"Why don't you tell him that, Joe? He'll charge us double for redoing the shower pan, again."

Eve gazed out the window.

THAT NIGHT SHE didn't take an Ambien. She dreamed she was at her parents' house. Joe and the brown-haired woman—Eve hated her!—were alone in a hall. She heard Joe whispering, "You can't imagine the hell I've been through, Eve was so crazy." She heard the woman saying, "No one blames you, Joey, everyone knows she was suicidal."

And then the voices: *Leave, leave, leave, leave, leave.*

Sunday morning she told Joe she hadn't taken an Ambien.

"And?" he said.

"You were right. No nightmare, no voices."

He grinned. "Well, now we know. I'm sorry about the floors, Eve. I should have been more careful. We'll get them redone after everything's finished. And don't worry about Ken. I'll smooth things out, guy to guy. It'll cost us, but the main thing is you're okay. This is great, babe, isn't it?"

"It really is," Eve said, trembling with hate so strong, it frightened her.

Joe would tell Ken. They would laugh about it, guy to guy, *Hahahahah, women*, when it was Joe who had damaged the shower and walls, deliberately.

The noises she'd heard the first night had been animal sounds. Cats or squirrels, maybe birds. But her anxiety had given Joe the idea to frighten her. He was very clever, her Joe. He'd probably made a tape that he played when Eve was sleeping. *Leave, leave, leave, leave, leave.* The weight on her body, the breath on her face? That was Joe. He'd moved quickly and pretended to be asleep when she'd opened her eyes.

It had taken Eve a while to puzzle out why Joe would do something so cruel and hateful. When she did, she was angry at herself for being so stupid.

Joe wanted the house. He didn't want her. He would make her so terrified that she would beg him to sell the house. He would refuse. They would divorce. He would remain in the house and everyone would say, "No one can blame him. Eve was crazy."

Eve tried to define the moment Joe had stopped loving her. Then she wondered if he had loved her at all. Maybe it had always been about the inheritance, which she had foolishly mentioned when they were dating.

Well, Eve had news for Joe. She wanted a divorce, too. And guess what, *babe? You'll get far less than half of what the house is worth, almost nothing.* Eve had inherited the money *before* she met Joe, so it wasn't community property.

Eve decided to bide her time before confronting Joe. She needed proof. She considered moving out, but she had to stay in the house, to protect her claim.

Squatters' rights, *babe.*

Of course, Joe wouldn't leave. Oh, no. Joe would continue his campaign of fear to drive her out.

She was stronger than he knew.

A MIGRAINE KEPT Eve in bed the entire day, and the next and the next. The nightmares and voices disturbed her nights. The headaches, along with increasing fatigue and listlessness, made getting up in the morning impossible.

On Thursday the school principal called again. Eve told him she wasn't coming back.

Joe looked genuinely worried. "Maybe a therapist can help you get a handle on this, honey. Do you want me to make some calls?"

You'd like that, wouldn't you, Joe?

A day earlier Eve, listening in on the phone extension on her nightstand, had overheard Joe telling Ken they had to put the project on hold. "My wife isn't well. I'm sure you understand."

Her mother came every day. "Tell me what's wrong, Evie," Ruth implored, stroking Eve's cheek.

Eve couldn't tell her about Joe. Her mother wouldn't believe her. No one would. She had found no proof, not in any of his papers or on his BlackBerry, which she'd accessed on Sunday while he was out buying groceries.

One morning, the nightmare fresh in her mind, Eve realized she'd underestimated Joe.

"You can't imagine the hell I've been through, Eve was so crazy."

"No one blames you, Joey, everyone knows she was suicidal."

Joe wanted her dead.

He would inherit the house they'd fallen in love with and bought with Eve's money. Oh, he would pretend to be heartbroken, and after a decent period of mourning he would remarry—"He was so lonely, poor Joe, he deserves happiness after what he's gone through."

Joe's wife—the brown-haired woman or someone else, who knew how many women he had in his life?—would live in Eve's house and sleep in Eve's bed. She would luxuriate under water streaming from the rainforest showerhead in Eve's marble-tiled shower and relax in the tub, letting the Jacuzzi jets massage her body. She would see the backyard bloom with flowers Eve would never have picked. She would lie in a hammock and rock a baby that wasn't Eve's.

Eve cried.

JOE AND HER mother drove Eve to her internist in the Third Street Towers in the city.

"Her vitals are fine, except for her blood pressure, which is a little high," Dr. Geller said, addressing only her mother and Joe, as if Eve weren't in the room or couldn't hear. "She's lost over ten pounds and she's withdrawn, almost nonverbal. I suggest you consult with a psychiatrist."

Eve had lost weight because she couldn't be sure if Joe had tampered with the food he coaxed down her throat. Eve thought, wasn't it ironic that she was thinner than she'd ever been in her life, her hips slimmer than slim?

Her mother said, "Evie, why don't you stay with us for a few days? I can take care of you until you feel better."

Eve wanted to say, *Yes, please, yes, God, yes.* She longed to lie in the safety of her bed in her old room, where she could sleep without fear of the nightmare or noises, or Joe.

But Eve couldn't leave the house, and she couldn't see a psychiatrist. A psychiatrist would listen while Eve talked about the voices she heard and the thing she felt pressing against her. A psychiatrist would nod while Eve told him that Joe was behind the voices, behind everything: strange marks on the mortar, popping nails, scratches on the floors, light switches that were no longer working, cracks that were spreading like vines on the Kennebunkport Green walls.

Eve would be committed.

Joe would have the house.

EVE KNEW HER parents were desperate when they brought a rabbi to the house late one Sunday morning. His name, Ruth told Eve, was Rabbi Ben-Amichai. The rabbi was a *mekubal*—a holy man, a master of Jewish mysticism—who lived in Jerusalem and was visiting Los Angeles. Eve's father, Frank, had met the rabbi that morning at *shul* and had asked for his help.

"First the rabbi wants to check the *mezuzahs*," Ruth said.

"But they're all new."

A week before they'd moved into the house, Eve and Joe, following Orthodox tradition, had bought eight rolled parchments, inscribed by hand with verses from the Torah in Hebrew. One *mezuzah* for every doorway in the house.

"Rabbi Ben-Amichai says even if they're new, a letter may be missing, or part of a letter, or there may be some other imperfection. If something's wrong with a *mezuzah*, Eve, it won't protect you."

Eve stayed in bed. She pictured the rabbi hunched over the small table in the breakfast nook where the lighting was best, inspecting the *mezuzahs* Joe and her father were removing, one by one, from the doorposts.

An hour later her mother returned. The rabbi had pronounced the *mezuzahs* fine.

Eve had known they were fine. The problem wasn't *mezuzahs*. The problem was Joe.

"The rabbi wants to talk to you," Ruth said.

"Why?"

"He's a wise man, Evie. Maybe he can help."

"Can he stop my dreams, Mom? Can he stop the voices?" *Can he stop Joe?*

"Eve, get up. *Now*. Get up, put on a robe."

Ruth's tone, knife sharp, sliced through Eve's lethargy. Eve struggled out of bed. Her mother helped her into her robe and slippers. She found a scarf and tied it around Eve's matted hair, unwashed for days.

"Perfect," Ruth said with hollow cheer.

With her hand under Eve's elbow, she escorted a wobbly Eve into the breakfast nook. Her father was there, and Joe.

The rabbi was old and stooped, with a long silky white beard and white hair covered by a black velvet yarmulke. His face had a thousand wrinkles.

"Sit, sit." In a deep, unwavering voice the rabbi ordered everyone else from the room.

Eve sat opposite him and tried to place his accent. Yemenite? Definitely Sephardic. His eyes were the eyes of a young man, the dark brown of molten chocolate.

"Your husband tells me you have been hearing voices," the rabbi said. "When did they start?"

Eve had expected skepticism or pity, but the rabbi sounded genuinely interested. "The first night we moved into the house, I heard scratching sounds. I think an animal made them. Then I started hearing the voices."

"What do the voices sound like?"

Eve described the whooshing sound. "They tell me to leave. I'm not crazy," she said with some defiance. "Did my husband tell you I'm crazy?"

The rabbi shook his head. "Your husband loves you very much. He is worried about you."

Eve's smile was thin. "He told you that, too?"

The rabbi studied her. "You don't believe your husband loves you?"

Eve lowered her eyes under the intensity of his piercing gaze. "I don't know what to believe."

The rabbi nodded. "These voices that you hear in your bedroom, Mrs. Stollman. Do you hear them anywhere else?"

She shook her head.

"You also have bad dreams, yes?"

"Every night."

"Tell me about the dreams."

Eve started talking. The rabbi closed his eyes, and she thought, *Great, the old man fell asleep*, but the moment she stopped, he said, "Please, continue."

When she had finished, the rabbi was silent for a while. Then he said, "I can see why you are so troubled. But something else is bothering you."

"My husband didn't tell you?" The sarcasm had slipped out. Eve flushed with embarrassment, but she wasn't really sorry.

The rabbi's smile was a gentle reproof. "I would very much like to hear this from you."

So Eve told him about the cracks in the walls, the broken light switches, the scratches on the floors, the recurring strange markings in the shower.

"Who do you think is doing this?" the rabbi asked.

Did she dare? "My husband," Eve whispered. "He wants to make me think I'm crazy. He wants—he wants the house. He doesn't love me." She hadn't meant to cry, but tears streamed down her face.

"And you know this from your dreams?"

Eve felt silly.

The rabbi said, "Your husband loves you deeply. This I know to be true."

"How? How can you know?"

"I know."

"You *do* think I'm crazy," Eve said. Maybe she was.

The rabbi pushed himself up from the chair with a sudden movement that startled her. "Come."

Eve followed him to her bedroom. How odd, she thought, that the rabbi seemed to know the way, as though he'd been here before. He stopped in the doorway of the master bedroom, as her mother had.

"They are very angry," he said quietly. "I feel them."

Eve shivered. "Who?"

Squaring his shoulders, the rabbi stepped into the room and stood motionless for several long minutes. He took his time examining the wall behind the beds, then the other walls and the floors. In the bathroom he looked first at the protruding nails. Stooping down, he peered at the markings on the bottom of the shower. He returned to the bedroom, Eve following.

"Show me where you hear the voices," the rabbi said.

Eve walked to her bed and pointed to an area above the headboard. "There."

"Do you hear them now?"

Was he testing her? She shook her head. "Can you—do you hear anything?"

"Mrs. Stollman, they have no quarrel with me."

The rabbi sprinted out of the room and down the hallway as though he were fleeing. Eve, out of shape and out of breath, had difficulty keeping up. Her parents and Joe were seated at the dining room table. They stood as the rabbi and Eve passed through the room and looked at the rabbi expectantly. He motioned to them to remain where they were and continued to the breakfast room, Eve at his heels.

The rabbi sat at the table. Eve did the same.

"Mrs. Stollman, did you close up any windows in your bedroom? Any doors?"

"No. Rabbi Ben-Amichai—"

"The people who lived in this house before you—your husband told me about the tragedy. Two deaths, *Hashem yerachem*." God have mercy. "Did they seal a door? A window?"

"I don't know," Eve said, stifling her impatience. "Rabbi Ben-Amichai, when we were in my bedroom, you said you felt them. Who is 'they'?"

"*Shedim,*" the rabbi said, his voice low. "Some feel that even to say the word is not advisable."

Demons. Eve flinched.

"They are made of air, fire, and water. The sages tell us that in three ways *shedim* are like angels. They have wings. They fly from one end of the earth to the other. They hear what will happen in the future." The rabbi paused. "In three ways they are like humans. They eat and drink like humans, they reproduce like humans, they die like humans. They are here right now."

Eve felt a prickling up and down her spine. She looked around.

"Trust me, they are here, Mrs. Stollman," the rabbi said quietly. "The Talmudic scholar Rav Huna stated that every one of us has one thousand *shedim* on his left hand and ten thousand on his right."

Eve squirmed.

"Sometimes we can sense them. Have you ever felt crowded even though no one is sitting next to you?" The rabbi leaned toward Eve. "These *shedim* are what you feel pressing on you every night, breathing on you." He eyed her with sympathy and a touch of sadness. "You do not believe me."

"It's . . ." Eve shook her head.

"Sprinkle ashes on the floor around your bed, Mrs. Stollman. In the morning you will see their footprints, resembling those of a chicken."

Eve flashed to the markings on the mortar. Not possible, she thought. Still, she felt a frisson of fear and revulsion.

"If you are determined to see them, take finely ground ashes of the afterbirth of a black cat and put them in your eye. You will see them." The rabbi raised a finger. "I must warn you, this is dangerous. Rav Huna saw *shedim* and came to harm. Luckily the scholars prayed for him and he recovered." The rabbi fixed her with his deep brown eyes. "Now it is you who are thinking, 'This old man is crazy,' yes?" A smile tugged at his lips.

Eve blushed and looked away. "The markings in the shower could be from a bird." Or Joe.

The rabbi didn't respond.

"Suppose you're right," Eve said, facing the rabbi. "Why would these *shedim* be tormenting me?"

"You or someone else has interfered with them. I believe that there was a window or door on the wall where you hear the voices. You say you did not seal off a window—"

"I didn't."

The rabbi nodded. "You do not know if the people who lived here before you sealed off a window or door."

"They did make changes," Eve said, remembering what the neighbor had told her. "I don't know what kind. Why does that matter?"

"*Shedim* have established pathways, Mrs. Stollman. When you interrupt those pathways, they are resentful. They take vengeance. These *shedim* resided in your house long before you moved in. To them, you are intruders, trespassers."

Eve wanted to say, *That's ridiculous*. But how could she insult this bearded holy man sitting in her home? "Rabbi, why doesn't my husband hear the voices? Why isn't he having similar nightmares?"

The rabbi shook his head. "That I cannot answer. Your dreams trouble you more than the voices, am I right?"

"Yes."

"They have robbed you not only of sleep, but of peace of mind, of trust in your husband. They have convinced you he means you harm."

Eve felt as though her heart would crack. "Yes."

"Why do you assume these dreams are true?"

"I have the same dream, over and over. Why would that be unless my unconscious is telling me something, warning me? You said *shedim* can tell the future, Rabbi. Do they share that knowledge with humans through dreams?"

The rabbi nodded. "They do."

Well then, Eve thought.

"But *shedim* love to confound humans, to mix truth with lies," the rabbi said. "Remember, they are not here to protect you. Quite the opposite. At the very least, find the location of the window or door that was sealed off. Make a small hole through the wall so that the *shedim* can resume their movement unobstructed."

"And that will stop the voices? The nightmares?"

The rabbi sighed. "This is a house of misery and bad fortune, Mrs. Stollman. Two people have died unnatural deaths. I'm afraid the *shedim* will never leave you in peace."

"*SHEDIM?* ASHES OF black cats?" Joe said after the rabbi had blessed Eve and Joe and left with her parents. "Sounds like *Macbeth*, or Halloween. I don't really believe in this stuff, babe. Do you?"

"Not really," Eve said, wishing she did.

Her parents had been less skeptical. Her father had looked somber and her mother had said, "Oh my God," several times and shuddered.

Watching Joe tap his fingers on the wall above her headboard in expanding circles, Eve thought, wouldn't it be something if the rabbi were right—frightening, yes, but at the same time wonderful?

"Sounds solid to me, Eve," Joe said.

"Oh."

"I can call the broker tomorrow and ask him to find out if the Goodriches sealed off a window. Or I can have Ken open the wall."

"You can ask our neighbor, Sandy," Eve said. "She might know."

"She may not be home," Joe said. He saw the look on Eve's face. "Okay. I'll go check."

Standing in front of the breakfast nook window, Eve juggled hope and despair for what seemed like an eternity until she saw Joe coming back up the walkway.

"What did Sandy say?" Eve asked, knowing the answer from Joe's shaken expression.

Shedim.

"They sealed off a bedroom window," Joe said, his voice subdued and so quiet she had to lean in to hear him. "Sandy wanted to know why I was asking. I said we were wondering, because the wall sounded hollow."

"Good thinking," Eve said. They were around her, around Joe, everywhere. Thousands, the rabbi had said.

Joe pulled Eve into his arms. "I am so, so sorry I doubted you, babe. I feel terrible that I accused you of sleepwalking and doing all that stuff."

"You couldn't know."

He pulled away and stared at her. "This is surreal, isn't it? Scary as hell."

"It is." Eve's heart soared.

RABBI BEN-AMICHAI HAD advised selling the house, but Eve and Joe saw no harm in trying a less drastic measure. They would ask Ken to bore a hole through the bedroom wall. If that didn't appease the *shedim*, they would sell, probably at a loss, but they would have no choice.

Joe said, only half joking, "We'd have to ask the rabbi if we're obligated to tell the broker about the *shedim*."

In the morning Joe would drive Eve to her parents' home, where she would stay until Ken made the hole and the rabbi determined that the house was safe for Eve.

"I can take you now," Joe said. "I don't want you to suffer through one more night of voices and nightmares."

Eve said, "Tomorrow is fine, Joe. Now that I know what's going on, I'm not scared."

Joe bought dinner from Cambridge Farms: sushi, Eve's favorite saffron rice with cranberries, grilled steak. Eve, feeling better than she had in weeks, was ravenous. Later Joe murmured, "You and me forever, babe," and she fell asleep in his arms.

Eve dreamed. She was in a long narrow room filled with Hebrew texts and men wrapped in prayer shawls. A *shul*. She saw a white-haired man with a long white beard sitting on a bench at a table piled with open texts. He was so familiar, who—

Rabbi Ben-Amichai.

A man approached the rabbi, his back to Eve. He shook the rabbi's hand and sat across from him. The two talked. Eve heard the man say, ". . . at my wits' end, Rabbi . . . need your help." The rabbi raised his hands, palms up. The man leaned forward and continued. Eve couldn't hear what he was saying, but she sensed the urgency in the hunch of his shoulders, saw the rabbi's responding sigh. The rabbi said, "I cannot promise, but I will try." The men shook hands again across the table. Then the man turned and Eve knew before she saw his face that it was Joe. She watched as Joe, crossing the room, greeted her father and brought him to the rabbi's table.

The image shifted to the cemetery. Eve saw her parents and Joe's, crying at her gravesite. She saw Joe and the brown-haired woman stealing glances, their hands touching. *". . . everyone knows she was crazy, Joe, don't blame yourself."* Rabbi Ben-Amichai was standing to the side, his white head raised toward the sky, his faced etched with grief, tears streaming from his dark brown eyes as he beat his chest with a clenched fist.

Then the voices, the rabbi's among them: *Leave, leave, leave.* Not a whisper, no, a cry.

Joe had fooled the rabbi. He had almost fooled Eve. *"I don't believe in this* shedim *stuff, do you, babe? We'll make the hole through the wall, and if that doesn't work, we'll sell."*

All to get her out of the house.

Eve woke with a start and blinked her eyes open. Her heart was beating so rapidly she was sure Joe heard. She gazed at Joe, lying on his back, asleep.

Lover or traitor?

And *how* would she die? Would she take her own life, driven mad by the voices and dreams and despair? Or would Joe lose patience? Would he poison her? Drug her? Smother her with a pillow as he leaned in for a final kiss?

Shedim lied.

Shedim lied, Eve reminded herself. The rabbi had said so. *Shedim* lied. *Shedim* lied.

Were they urging her to leave, showing her a future they hoped she would avoid? Or were they laughing at her with malicious glee, trying to shatter her newfound faith in Joe?

How could Eve know what was truth and what was fabrication?

Lover or traitor?

Careful not to wake Joe, Eve slid off the bed. She tiptoed down the hall to the kitchen. She eased open a drawer.

She would never leave, never, unless she was taken out feet first, and then she wouldn't go alone, oh no.

She loved Joe so much. She really did.

Eve lay on her back, the knife tucked under her thigh, sharp against her skin.

Blood on the Wall

HEATHER GRAHAM

There it was—that stench of stale blood again.

DeFeo Montville stood and stared at the desecration of his family's handsome temple tomb, set almost dead center in the peace and beauty of the cemetery—this "city of the dead" where some of the finest names to ever grace Louisiana found their rest. Even in a cemetery where the dead rested in style, the Montville vault was a thing of sheer grandeur. The façade was pillared and porticoed, a gloriously winged and weeping angel sat atop the vaulted roof, and a cast-iron gate opened to the small altar area that separated the rows of the family's individual tombs.

Naturally, the gate was kept locked.

But that didn't stop hooligans from their graffiti and vandalism.

He inhaled. Pig's blood, he thought. And he knew how it had come to be there, or he was almost certain that he knew. Austin Cramer.

Cramer was the self-proclaimed god of a so-called voodoo-vampire cult, though what the man didn't seem to know about the contemporary American practice of voodoo would surely fill enough volumes to cross the ocean. He was a dropout, but a dropout who had a way with women, motorcycles, and oration. He rode a Harley and wore black at all times;

maintained a head full of sleek, pitch-black hair; and had *the look*. He wanted the world to think of him as a New Age Aleister Crowley—in his mansion in the Garden District, he had collected a harem of Cramer-worshipping girls and, of course, a following of young men who wanted to be just like Cramer, or to have young women worshipping them—as they did Cramer. As far as DeFeo knew, the jerk and his friends were just into girls, unlike the real Crowley, who would sleep with just about anyone—or anything.

He called himself the Father of the Brotherhood, and he preached a lifestyle that wasn't exactly Satanism, but something like it. Cramer had borrowed from Crowley and, DeFeo was fairly certain, from the religious view of demonology during the days of the witch burnings.

And, of course, because DeFeo's ancestor, Antoine Montville, had been suspected of Satanism during his day (a complete lie!), Cramer—a man he could *just tell* had been a nerdy-brat-turned-cult-master—liked to bring his acolytes to the cemetery, perform a sacrifice ritual, and cast blood over the tomb. They snuck in and carried out their ridiculous rites when he was working, which meant he was going to have to be working a case in the area if there was any hope of catching the little bastard and his crew. He had long ago gotten his license and hung up his shingle as a private investigator; it kept him friendly with the police. He liked the fellows in this district, but he knew, too, that they were busy with gangs, robberies, and other cases of violent crime. They'd do their best, but they couldn't just hang around the cemetery watching for a vandal.

DeFeo shook his head, turned to the bucket of water and soap he'd brought, and started cleaning. Eventually, workers would have come in to do the chore; he wouldn't wait for "eventually." He finished cleaning the tomb and decided to head down to Frenchmen Street, hope a real jazz band was playing somewhere, and try to drink some of his aggravation down. There were some interesting things going on in the city, but for now, he'd take a night off, look forward to some enjoyment, and calm his simmering inner rage against a petty—idiot.

He parked on Esplanade and walked down Decatur until he reached his favorite little pub, a place called Your Favorite Pub on Frenchmen. Before he had even taken his seat on a stool at the bar, Joe, the owner, had a drink in front of him. "It's a DeFeo special," Joe told him, but he wasn't jocular, he was grim.

"Thanks, Joe. Anyone singing tonight?"

Joe seemed surprised and perplexed by his question, but he answered.

"A lady named Regina Hansen; she's got one of the best blues voices I've heard in my day."

Joe could croon out a tune himself, like no other. He was a slim African American with a voice like silk. Joe always welcomed DeFeo with his "special" drink, and it was always on the house. Once, DeFeo had managed to take care of a serious problem for Joe—an off-the-books job, so to speak—and though DeFeo assured Joe that it had been nothing, the old man was still grateful.

"I'll stick around a bit then," DeFeo said. He was still pondering a way to pin *something* on Cramer and his band of whacked-out believers.

"You got time to stick around?" Joe asked. He sounded edgy. "I thought you just dropped in on your way to work."

DeFeo frowned. "Sure. I'm here for the drinks and the music. Same as last week."

"Yeah, but last week, we didn't have *this* happening in the city." Joe said, pulling out his phone and hitting the touch screen to bring up a recent news report.

Before he even read the report, DeFeo leaned back, stunned that such a picture had gotten to the media *and* that the media was showing it.

He was seeing the body of a woman, so mutilated that he couldn't be sure what parts the remnants of her clothing were covering. He didn't need to ask Joe where she had been found; he recognized the Masonic tomb in a nearby cemetery.

It made the blood on the Montville tomb seem like child's play.

He stood, gulping down the drink Joe had given him, and said hoarsely, "I guess I'm not staying."

As he spoke, his phone began to vibrate in his shirt pocket. He glanced down. Yes, he was being called in. His usual connection, a lieutenant from homicide, was the caller.

"I'm on my way," he said, before Lieutenant Anderson could speak.

"Quickly," Anderson ordered, knowing from DeFeo's tone that he had heard the news.

DeFeo hung up, nodded at Joe, and hurried out.

• • •

"DRINK THE BLOOD, and you will be whole, and the strength of the true essence of life will fill your body and your being, and you will be one with the Brotherhood," Austin said, lifting the fake-jewel-encrusted chalice high above Adriana Morgan's head.

It was such rot. And, of course, he knew it.

But Austin had spent his junior high and high school years in pure misery. He was the skinny kid who had acne. He had spent his afternoons playing computer games while the jocks were out on the football field—cornering all the girls. The jocks were cruel. Several times, they'd tossed his tray of food on him at the cafeteria. They'd thrown him in the Dumpster at school, along with all the refuse from the bathrooms.

Then, Austin had found the way. Well, *his* way. And it had all happened by accident. They'd been about to throw him into Mr. Johnston's water sprinklers one day when he had actually found the nerve to fight back—verbally, at least. He'd cursed them, telling them that all the demon dogs from hell would come after them. By happenstance, Mr. Johnston's giant Rottweiler, Juju, had come running out of the house at that moment. Austin had played with Juju since he'd been a puppy, and Juju took offense at Austin's mistreatment. Billy Trent, quarterback, missed the next three games because Juju took a nice piece of flesh right off Billy Trent's big muscled butt. And the story spread—and suddenly, Austin knew how to bring up all the powers of Satan himself.

It worked. He liked it. So he used his computer game time to study cults, world religions, and superstitions. He came up with the Brotherhood. Cool. That, too, worked. Who would have ever figured that he, geeky Austin Cramer, would have women throwing themselves at him? It helped that he grew another five inches and put on a little bit of muscle. At heart, however, he was still geeky Austin Cramer.

Adriana Morgan was his newest recruit, and she was beyond beautiful.

He had seen her once before, right here, in this cemetery, mourning a loved one; he was sure of that, since she'd had flowers with her.

It had been instant love for him. Or lust. No, he was in lust and in love.

She had mile-long hair, and it tumbled down her back in sleek blond tresses that shone in the sunlight, and in the moonlight. She had huge, dark blue eyes and a figure that should have graced a Victoria's Secret catalog.

She looked up at him adoringly, took the chalice, and drank. Pig's blood. It was always his choice. His Uncle Stu managed a slaughterhouse, and the blood was easy to come by. Adriana sipped the blood, and he drew her to her feet. "Now, my dear, you cast the remains in the cup on the side of the tomb, and you ask the power within to be your strength so that you may live your life seeking pleasure where you will, as is your human, carnal, and animalistic right. Tonight you will fast and cleanse, and tomorrow begin your life in the Brotherhood, living as you will!"

He'd taken a chance coming here again tonight at midnight—he'd just indoctrinated a girl last night, Angie Sewell, and he might have returned to find that the blood from the previous night was still on the tomb. But he had gambled well. A Montville was a PI who worked in and around the Vieux Carré. He seemed to like working a graveyard shift, so he wasn't around to catch anyone in the action, and frankly, the cops thought his obsession with the old family tomb was a bit much. They had tried now and then to catch Austin in the act, but they'd never thought to just stake out the cemetery. Of course, they thought he had to crawl over the ten-foot wall to get into the place—dumb bastards never realized that he'd come in the daylight and found time to make a putty impression of the lock on the gate, and therefore had a key.

Adriana was worth the risk. It felt as if he had coveted her forever. And now . . . now he had to force himself to remember that everything had an agenda, and he couldn't freak out and beg her just to let him kiss her lush lips, entangle himself in the scent of hair, lie with her naked.

Get a grip, he warned himself.

Adriana splashed the blood on the tomb and repeated the words as he had told her. Just as she did so, the clouds that had been covering the moon drifted past, and the full orb made the cemetery glow with an eerie light.

Austin looked up. Hell, somebody loved him, he thought, laughing inwardly. Not. The law of physics had simply sent a breeze, and the clouds had moved.

Adriana turned to him, and his knees almost turned to jelly. "I'm one with you! I'm one with the Brotherhood!"

He drew her against him and felt the fantastic warmth of her body and the richness of her full breasts. He drew away quickly, damning himself for the ritual cleansing he had given to this rite. Tomorrow night, she'd be his.

He heard a sound: a cell phone buzzing. She stepped back, looking at him apologetically. "I'd put it on silent. I'm so sorry. I haven't ruined anything, have I?" She fumbled with the black cape she was wearing, found her phone in the pocket of her form-fitting jeans, glanced at it, and quickly shoved it back.

"No. Though I thought I told you not to have it on you?" He was irritated. She had arrived late to her night of confirmation into his flock, and now—she had the damned cell phone on her!

"I'm sorry—I'm on call. At the hospital." She was an RN. "I have to go to work."

"Of course." He never encouraged any of his "followers" to quit their day jobs; keeping up the mansion was a costly task, and he'd also acquired some expensive tastes since he turned his experience with Juju into his life's work. He loved hundred-year-old tequila and aged Cognac, and a Havana cigar now and then, as well.

Austin set his hands on her shoulders. "Don't forget; this is your one night of abstinence. No men, no food. The blood you drank will cleanse your body of the past; it will cleanse your soul of what you believed to have been the sins of your past, and it will allow you to enter your new world where life is what you crave it to be, filled with earthly, sensual, and erotic pleasures."

"There will be no other men for me!" she said, staring up at him. Her voice was breathy, so sensual. He cursed himself again. Oh, well, they needed money, and she was going to work. He couldn't have taken advantage of this moment no matter what. That was the bad part of being the Father. He had made the rules—he had to remember that his whole religion could come crashing down if he changed them because he couldn't control his own libido.

"Go, my child. Tomorrow night, you and I will seek to understand the truth to be found on Earth; and we will give one another strength, and share all that is our essence!" He kissed her on the forehead. *What rot!* But, damn, it worked so well. He stepped back quickly; she made him tremble, and he couldn't have her knowing that he was just another average guy so hot for her body he could just about melt on the spot.

"Go now. We'll have tomorrow."

"Yes!" she whispered. "Tomorrow."

He nodded; he let her turn and leave the cemetery first, watching her and swallowing down the urge to run after her. She'd given him the worst boner in history. Had to get that down a bit, too.

He followed a minute later, locking the gate, and headed for the mansion, still in discomfort. Ah, well, he had just indoctrinated Angie Sewell last night, meaning she was now available. She wasn't as drop-dead gorgeous as Adriana, but she'd do.

When he got there, he was surprised to see members of his flock on the floor in front of the television, so enrapt in what they were watching that they hadn't even heard him enter.

"What's going on?" he asked. He looked around. He saw Lena, Sue, Sara, Jeanine, and Lila, his first girls—who were actually beginning to bore him—and Tom, Brian, and Joe. Joe, ironically, had once shoved him into his locker at school. Joe was now his most ardent follower.

He didn't see Angie. "Where is Angie?" he asked.

They didn't hear him.

"Hey!" He had learned how to just about roar the word with total authority.

They all turned to him, en masse, all those eyes, dazed and staring up at him. There was real fear in the looks they all gave him.

"She's—she's—" Sue stuttered out, pointing at the television.

"Dead!" Lila croaked.

Austin frowned and stared at the screen. A young anchorwoman was standing in front of the gates to one of the old town cemeteries. He could see the rise of an I-10 ramp behind her. "Police have arrived on the scene of this brutal and gruesome murder, discovered by high school students who had broken into the cemetery on a dare. They found the mutilated, decapitated, and dismembered body parts of a young woman in the center of one of the paths through the famous 'city of the dead' just thirty minutes ago, and it appears that the most seasoned of our detectives has been stunned and dismayed by the ferocity and violence of the crime. I can't get a statement from anyone close to the crime; no one has left the cemetery yet. Oh! I see the private investigator—DeFeo Montville! Montville specializes in occult cases. They've called him in on this, obviously. DeFeo Montville seems to have an ear to the ground and hears the beat of this city in the night. He is just now exiting the gates. I'm going to try to have a word with him."

She turned, and the display on the television seemed to jostle as her cameraman tried to follow her.

"Mr. Montville! Can you give us any information?"

Montville was probably just what a private dick should be—and not the used-up-over-the-hill-pudgy-old-bastard image set in the minds of many. Montville was tall and well muscled. There didn't seem to be an ounce of fat on his body. He had yellow-gold eyes that seemed to home in on the woman, and his expression was one of irritation and disbelief.

He spoke curtly. "A young woman was murdered. And it's appalling that someone in the media took a picture and let it out to the newspapers so that it can be viewed by anyone with Internet access. The victim surely has family, and to let that picture be shown is an outrage."

"But, Detective Montville, we need information for our viewers—"

"Here's the information. Stay home, or stay in a crowd. There's a murderer on the loose."

"Do you suspect that this might be the work of a cult—such as the Brotherhood?"

Austin couldn't stop himself in time. He gasped out loud. It didn't matter. Everyone in the room gasped. Any remaining spasm of desire that might have lingered in him disappeared as his penis went as limp as over-cooked pasta.

"We'll be looking into all possibilities; the killer will be found. Now excuse me." He pushed past the woman and headed out down to the street, presumably to his car.

The anchorwoman started talking again, but Austin didn't hear her. The others—his flock, his adoring flock—turned to stare at him with horror in their eyes.

Sue and Lena inched closer together. Brian and Joe took a step back from him. They all stared at him with wide eyes and blank expressions. It was one thing to drink pig's blood and have orgies, it was quite another to be accused of murder.

Austin desperately tried to pull his wits about him. They were all ready to bolt.

"I'll prove that we were not responsible for this." He lifted his hand. "We are all about pleasure, not pain. There is no need to worry." He turned to exit with a grand determination, but he could hear them whispering behind his back.

"Oh, my God! He is Satan!" Sue said, her words barely audible.

"Then—then we need to run, get the hell out!" Joe said.

"He'll kill us if we run," Brian gulped out.

"He'll kill us if we stay!" Lila whimpered.

Shaking his head in disgust, Austin walked on out. DeFeo Montville would be coming for him. Montville might tell the police to check up on anyone else themselves, but Montville would be coming for him personally. Austin knew that he'd be questioned for the murder. DeFeo might not know that the dead girl had been with him, but the man was quick to put two and two together, and he'd suspect Austin no matter what.

Officers would be going to the house; they would probably round up his group. He didn't want to be taken by just any officers. He had to talk to Montville first, convince him that he was innocent.

A lethal injection was not part of his life plan.

Montville would not look for him at the mansion because he'd know that Austin was too smart to just sit there and wait to be picked up.

No, there was one place Montville would wait for him. At the tomb.

DEFEO, IN ALL his days, had never seen anything as savagely carried out as the murder of the poor girl discovered in the cemetery. Of course, the medical pathologist from the coroner's office had barely had time to give them a preliminary report, but it appeared—because of the amount of blood—that she had been chopped up while alive, and maybe . . . half consumed. Perhaps—it did seem that large chunks of blood, flesh, and bone might be missing in the jigsaw of the body parts. She hadn't been dead more than an hour or so before the students had stumbled upon her.

Maybe they had a sick modern-day Jack the Ripper on their hands, this time a killer who kept fleshy body parts and bone and later mailed them to the head of a vigilance committee.

He had a feeling kids wouldn't be playing around in cemeteries after dark anymore.

The girl's trunk, head, and body parts had been laid out on one of the main central paths between the tombs, almost as if they were part of a guide map to different gravel trails and interments.

Her head had lain in the center of a path. Eyes still open. She had been decapitated, and then her arms and legs had been severed from the body.

The whole of the body had been loosely brought back together so that the pieces were there—minus chunks, DeFeo was certain!—gathered back together again so that just a foot or so lay between her torso, her head, and each limb. The crime scene unit was still busy, but he and others had searched, and there had been no sign of a murder implement—or the tools that would have been necessary for hacking up a human body. The killer had taken them with him. Along with pieces of the body.

"What caused the jagged look on the flesh, Petey?" DeFeo asked the medical pathologist from the coroner's office.

"I don't know. Looks like she was ripped apart—blood slurped up and flesh eaten. This is bad, really bad," Dr. Pete Long said.

"DeFeo!"

He stopped and looked back. Lieutenant Anderson, who had left his desk to come out for the gruesome murder sure to bring the city to the point of screeching hysteria, was coming after him. Anderson called his officers and coworkers by their surnames; he had never seemed to realize that DeFeo was his given name, and Montville was his last.

"They've already tried that Satanist's mansion in the Garden District. They pulled in some of his followers, though they believe some had already hiked it out. Cramer wasn't there."

"I'll find him," DeFeo said.

Lieutenant Anderson, a good guy who was gruff at times, shook his head.

"You need help on this one, DeFeo," he said. "This killer is an animal—you shouldn't be out there alone."

"I work best alone. That's why I'm a PI. You know that, Lieutenant."

Before Anderson could argue, DeFeo shut his car door, turned on the ignition, and put the pedal to the metal after he eased out into the traffic.

DeFeo knew where he was going.

He left his car two blocks from the cemetery. He didn't use the gate, but bounded the wall and walked straight to the Montville tomb.

He found Austin Cramer there just as he had expected—studiously scrubbing blood off the wall of the tomb. DeFeo shook his head; he'd scrubbed the damned tomb already. Austin Cramer had apparently been busy that night with another initiation. And now he was trying to clean it all up. Interesting. Didn't look like the work of a rabid murderer.

Austin Cramer didn't hear him at first. He was too busy inspecting the tomb and scrubbing.

Standing just a few feet behind him, DeFeo said, "Well, this is a new twist."

Austin nearly leaped atop the tomb, he was so startled by the sound of DeFeo's voice. He backed against it. He didn't look like a great cult leader, but a young man of about twenty-two, terrified.

Austin shook his head, unable to find speech at first.

"I already did that tonight," DeFeo said, his voice harsh. "Thanks to you, I spend half my life trying to take care of that tomb."

Austin worked his mouth for a few minutes. "I'm sorry, hey, it's not like it's your home or anything—it's your old family tomb."

"It's way more than just a home; it deserves more reverence than a home," DeFeo said, his tone just as harsh. "And you spend your life making sure that it constantly needs domestic repair!"

"I'm sorry; I swear to God I'm sorry."

"You need to be sorry to that poor girl you ripped to shreds," DeFeo said. "I'm taking you to the station where you'll be arrested—not for vandalism. For murder."

"No, no—that's why I'm here, and you have to know it! I didn't do it. I swear to God, I didn't do it! Look—you can see. I was here tonight! I was here, with a girl. I couldn't have done it. Please, I swear to you. You have to help me."

"Why would I want to help you?" DeFeo demanded.

"Because you're a decent guy—and you know I didn't do it!"

DeFeo looked at Austin Cramer and, for the first time, realized that the little prick was actually intelligent. He was staring at him with a strange certainty and pride, as if he knew the facts of the situation and believed that DeFeo saw them clearly as well. He was also terrified, cleaning off the blood because he knew that his vandalism was like a bone stuck in DeFeo's throat. It had been a game of cat and mouse with the two of them, DeFeo always furious and longing to pounce, and Austin Cramer always happy he could get away with it. He was careful not to leave prints or evidence, and he almost always picked nights when DeFeo was working. They both knew the cops didn't have the time to sit on the cemetery nightly, and they hadn't a whit of proof or evidence against him.

Austin had to be absolutely scared silly about what DeFeo just might do to him—after all, the two of them were alone in a dark cemetery. DeFeo could beat him to hell—and claim that he'd swung first. He could probably get away with shooting him, and the law and the people of the city would look at the situation with blind eyes—good riddance to the devil incarnate.

But he was here, and he was facing DeFeo, shaking, but desperate and determined.

"You didn't do it?" DeFeo asked quietly.

"I swear to you! As God is my witness—"

"God?" DeFeo interrupted.

"Oh, please, you know that my thing is an act! Hell, I finally got the bullies to quit picking on me! The Harley dealer *gave* me a big bike! Girls flock to sleep with me. I couldn't get a girl to let me buy her a beer on Bourbon Street before all this. It's an act, man, please—look at me! You've got to believe me—and help me! If the cops pick me up, I'll be convicted before they seat a jury!"

He is nothing but a scrawny, computer-geek nerd—who has found an act, DeFeo thought.

"You keep wrecking my house!" DeFeo told him.

"It's a tomb, man, it's a tomb. Okay, so it's a tomb that's nearly two hundred years old, but come on, it's a tomb! But, I swear, I'll never do it again. I swear, I'll paint it once a year. I'll keep flowers around it, I'll rip out the weeds, I swear I'll keep it in pristine condition. I'll do anything— please; you've got to help me."

"Really? And how do you propose that I help you? You're definitely at the top of the suspect list as far as the police are concerned. Maybe things will change; the autopsy is going to be done *now*, this is such a savage event; the killer has to be stopped before he strikes again."

"I didn't do it, and that's it—the killer is out there somewhere tonight. Maybe he doesn't intend to strike again tonight, but, dear God, Jesus, Lord! We have to find him."

"Do you know how many crimes go unsolved—forever? Do you know how much desk work, forensic work, and legwork usually go into apprehending a killer? But you think that *I* can solve this tonight. With you, of course."

"Where would you start looking in a normal investigation? Say she'd just been strangled and left in the cemetery?" Austin asked him.

"I'd look closest at her associates—oh, that would be you!" DeFeo told him.

"Me—and the rest of my group."

"They've brought in most of your group already," DeFeo said. "And guess what? I'll bet your loyal followers will be pointing the finger at you!"

The Father—who now looked so pathetically like a little kid—shook his head fervently. "I didn't do it!" he repeated. He stared at the ground blankly, and then he looked at DeFeo. "Who didn't they get? Who didn't they bring in?"

"I don't know. And we don't know exactly who might have been living in that mansion of yours."

"I do—I know exactly who I've been in contact with, and if you tell me who they have, I can tell you who they don't have. And then we can do some of that computer stuff. You know, look up their backgrounds, find out if they smothered kittens and liked to set fire to dogs' tails and stuff like that!"

DeFeo had to admit it; the kid had a point.

"Well, if I take you to the station, they'll start interrogating you, and the way the cops are feeling tonight, you will finally confess to anything."

"I've got a computer!"

"There are unmarked patrol cars and plainclothes detectives watching the mansion."

"No, no—my home. My real home. It's a two-bit shotgun house, the other side of Esplanade. I've got a computer there. My folks left me the house."

"They died?"

"They moved to St. Pete."

DeFeo stared at him as seconds ticked by. If Austin hadn't killed the girl, it was likely that someone he knew, someone in his association—maybe some other idiot involved in one of the other area vampire/demon/Satan cults—had. Or someone in his realm, at the least. Unless a new whacko had suddenly come to New Orleans, drawn by the legends, voodoo, and the city's reputation.

But, used the right way—and not set down beneath a brilliantly burning bulb, deprived of water, dying to use the john—Austin Cramer just might have the key to the murder.

"Let's go," DeFeo said.

"Oh, my God. You're not going to regret this. I swear, I will be your willing slave in the future. I will take such good care of that tomb—you'll never need to do the least bit of maintenance again. I swear, oh, thank you—"

"Stop slobbering on me!" DeFeo said. "Let's do this!"

Austin Cramer slunk down in the back seat of DeFeo's car as they wove through the city to a small, ramshackle house in a poorer area of the city. The place still smelled of mold—almost as if someone had decided after the summer of storms to simply abandon it. Maybe that was what his parents had done.

The house had a living room, a kitchen, a dining room, and two bed-rooms.

The computer was in what had once been Austin Cramer's bedroom. There were rock band posters and *Sports Illustrated* swimsuit model pic-tures taped to the wall. There were books in rickety wooden shelves, and a plethora of old gaming boxes. It was the typical room any nerd might have—any poor, unpopular kid who spent his life in his room.

But the computer, set on a simple desk, was brand-new, and when Austin touched the keyboard, the screen snapped to life, showing a zillion applications.

He pulled up two chairs and DeFeo watched as Austin keyed in one of his word-processing programs, and then slid it over to open a Web page.

"There—there's the list of the people in my group. Should I pull up their Facebook pages, or something like that? I know how to find out if they have criminal records!" he said proudly.

DeFeo grated his teeth, brought his finger to his lip, and called in to the station. He read off the names and asked the sergeant on desk duty how many of those he had listed had come in. "We've got them all, now. Except for Brian—Brian Langley," the sergeant told him. "They're all claiming that it was Austin Cramer—he took them to the cemeteries and made them drink human blood and then throw it on the wall."

Austin could hear the sergeant, despite the fact that DeFeo was pacing with his phone. "It was never human blood!" he said in horror.

"Where the hell are you?" the sergeant's voice cracked over the phone again. "Montville, the lieutenant brought you in on this, but when you've got something, you're not a cop. You've got to keep us in the loop. You're a PI, man. Not a cop!"

"When I've got something, the lieutenant will know. Right now? I'm on a search in the city," DeFeo said. It was more or less true. He glanced at his watch as he spoke, and he frowned. It was already one A.M. He looked at Austin, feeling his jaw tighten. "Trust me; you'll be informed. I'm going to find Brian Langley," he said, and hung up.

"Wait!" the desk sergeant said. "What's that one girl's name—Sue. Sorry, I wasn't looking right. We have Sara, but we don't have Susan Naughton."

"So, Brian Langley and Susan Naughton are still missing?" DeFeo asked.

"Of the names you gave me, yeah. Hey, where did you get that list?"

"Just something I'm working on." DeFeo was growing irritated. "I'll let you know when I've got something and you can tell the lieutenant," he said, and hung up quickly.

"So—Susan, and Brian Langley. Where would Langley go?" he asked Austin.

DeFeo stared back at him. "Brian? Oh, my God, Brian! Yes, he's the biggest chump of them all. He used to be a bully, a big football hero—only he flunked out on his college scholarship. He's always been an asshole who wanted to beat the hell out of everyone."

Austin was elated, thinking that Brian was the killer.

"Doesn't sound right," DeFeo said.

"What do you mean? I told you—he was a bully!"

"Guys who get physical with their fists don't usually turn into this kind of a murderer."

"You have to be strong to hack up a girl, right?"

DeFeo shook his head. "You just need to know something about human anatomy—and own a good saw—like a bone saw. I know a few medical pathologists down at the coroner's office who aren't all that big or strong, and they can take a body apart pretty damned easily." He hesitated, thinking about the way the body appeared to have been *chewed*. "Hell, let's go find Brian. Where would he be?"

Austin was reflective. "I—I don't know. I made a big deal about our constitutional rights, and the fact that we didn't need to hide from the pigs—sorry, cops." Austin offered up a weak, ironic smile. "Sorry, hide from the cops—use *pig's* blood."

DeFeo rolled his eyes. "Come on, think. He's from this area. Where would he hide out? What about his folks?"

"They're gone, too."

"So did they move out and leave him their house?"

"No—they actually died. And the state took over the house for back taxes," Austin said.

"Great," DeFeo muttered.

"Oh, oh! There's an old abandoned church down near Magazine Street. He used to go there. He might be hiding out there. Derelicts and prostitutes use it sometimes, too. I don't think the cops have ever caught on. It's like a safe house for the street people of the city."

"Let's go," DeFeo said, rising.

They returned to his car. Austin hid in the back.

But they never reached the abandoned church on Magazine.

DeFeo's phone rang.

It was the desk sergeant.

"You're not going to believe this—but it's gotten worse. Found both of those kids you were talking about."

"What?"

"Susan Naughton and Brian Langley. Can't be that they're guilty; they're chopped up like doll parts. Lieutenant is on his way. They found them in an abandoned-church-turned-nightclub up in Metairie. I'd get there quick if I were you."

FIFTEEN MINUTES LATER, Austin Cramer sat huddled in the worst misery and despair of his life.

Hell, he'd never expected this. He was *in* the Montville tomb at the cemetery. He'd wanted DeFeo to leave him at his old house, but DeFeo had told him that the cops weren't stupid, and they owned computers, too. It wouldn't take long for them to discover that he owned the place, and they'd be looking for him there.

His face was known; there was no safe place in the city for him to hide.

Except for the Montville tomb.

It was very dark and heavily shadowed. Pale light from the full moon made it through the high grate at the rear of the tomb, but it didn't do much to alleviate the darkness inside.

The thing that was weird about the place was that it wasn't dusty; the marble that covered the shelves of caskets was entirely free from cobwebs, and the floor had been well swept, if not polished as well. DeFeo really had a thing for his old family tomb. It was spotless. It was really beautiful, in an odd sort of way. The heat in New Orleans was so intense that a body was naturally cremated in about a year; in fact, for a tomb to be "reused" or for a recently deceased family member to be interred with others, the rule was "a year and a day." That way the fragments of the body that remained could be swept to a holding area just beyond the length of the individual tomb, and another dead family member could join those who had gone before in this final resting place.

Austin sat in silent torment for a while and then nearly jumped sky high, feeling movement near him.

Then he heard a soft buzzing sound. It was his phone. He answered it with a quavering voice.

"Who else?" DeFeo's voice barked to him. "Both Susan Naughton and Brian Langley are dead. Who else should we be looking for?"

"Who else? No one! I gave you every name—you saw my file!" Austin said. He felt small, beaten, and almost numb. He'd given the man everything.

No, he hadn't. And it seemed that members of his cult were being killed right and left.

"Oh! Wait. There's Adriana Morgan. That's why I couldn't have killed anyone and you know it. I was in this cemetery tonight, initiating her. You saw me—you saw me washing the blood off!"

"The first victim was murdered about an hour before you would have been there," DeFeo told him dryly over the phone. "Plenty of time to play with *human* blood as well. Where is this Adriana Morgan now?"

"She's a nurse; she works at the hospital. She had to leave fast because she's on duty tonight. You've got to get to her. DeFeo, you've got to get to her quick. This bastard is killing people around me—he's killing my entire cult."

"Stay where you are—don't even think about looking for your girl. I'll get someone to pick her up," DeFeo said.

"I won't move!" Austin swore.

He hung up. He did move. He had to shift his weight. No matter how nicely the tomb had been kept, it was a tomb, dark and stifling, and the floor was hard.

He sat there, shivering in the dark shadows, staring at the grating, and watching as the moon, glowing full, seemed to fill the night sky.

Time crept by. Then he nearly jumped again. He heard something, something that seemed to be rustling in the tomb.

"THE KILLINGS ARE being done by someone from the city, someone who knows the city like the back of his hand," DeFeo told Lieutenant Anderson. They both stood on the sidewalk, just outside the building that had begun its existence as a church and then been turned into Bats! Bats! had apparently been an alternative bar before going down. The décor had made use of the arrangement of the old church, with dusty bats in various sizes adorning the walls and hanging from the pulpit. And, of course, there were bats in the belfry as well.

"Yeah, that freak cult asshole—that Austin Cramer. We've got to find him, DeFeo. This isn't the beginning of a serial killer's vision—this is a spree murderer out in a vengeance." Anderson looked back at the church-turned-nightclub. "Gotta love New Orleans," he muttered.

"The youth of America," DeFeo said. "They have places like this in New York, L.A., San Francisco, you name it. Kids like the occult."

"The occult has gotten damned ugly—we have to find this nut," Anderson said. "Quickly. Tonight. Who knows how many will die next?"

The bodies of Susan Naughton and Brian Langley had been posed one after the other in what had been the church aisle. They'd been placed in the same pattern. Heads and limbs detached, arranged so that they were a foot or so away from the torso, where each limb and head should have been. And the edges of the torso and limbs were ragged.

Chewed? DeFeo wondered again.

They had been killed less than an hour before.

That left Austin Cramer in the clear.

"Did you get someone to go find the nurse at the hospital—that Adriana Morgan?" he asked Anderson.

"Sent them as soon as you gave me the name," Anderson told him. "Where the hell did you get those names, DeFeo?"

"I'm a computer whiz," DeFeo lied. "I'm going to start moving."

"I hope you have a plan. I was having all the cemeteries staked out—but now, now we've found these two new bodies. . . ."

Another one of the detectives, Brad Raintree, walked out to the sidewalk. He headed straight to the edge, leaned over, and vomited. He glanced up. "Sorry, guys. I was doing all right, and then . . ." He looked at DeFeo, who looked back at him with sympathy.

"Hey, you wouldn't be human, right?" DeFeo asked.

"You're doing all right," Brad commented. "Jeez, I was doing all right until the pathologist told me that . . . he wasn't so sure the limbs had been sawed off. He said that they'd been *chewed* off."

"I thought that's what it looked like; you didn't?" DeFeo asked.

Brad looked like he was going to be sick again.

"Sorry," DeFeo said quickly.

"I've never seen anything like this at all," Brad told him. "Bullet holes, decayed flesh, knifings. Nothing like this."

An uneasy feeling settled into DeFeo's gut.

"It's hard for all of us," he said. He turned to the lieutenant. "I know the city. Leave it to me," DeFeo said. He started to walk away. He vaguely heard Anderson's phone and wasn't paying attention—*hell, limbs chewed off?*—until the lieutenant called him back.

"Hey! DeFeo!" he called.

DeFeo stopped, turning back.

"You got one wrong. There is no nurse at the hospital by the name of Adriana Morgan. She doesn't exist, according to their records."

THE NOISE WASN'T coming from inside the tomb—it was coming from outside.

As he listened, Austin could hear footsteps—light footsteps—on the gravel that surrounded the tomb. He listened hard. Cops. Cops had probably come to stake out the place.

He just had to remain really quiet.

Whoever it was crunched on the gravel again. The person was trying to be stealthy, as if certain someone else was in the cemetery.

And they were looking for that someone. *Stalking them.*

Austin caught his breath. Yes, another *crunch.* And *another.*

He tried to shrivel into himself. He couldn't be seen; he was in the Montville tomb. DeFeo hadn't locked him in, but it surely appeared that the gate was locked. Whoever it was would go away.

But they didn't.

Crunch, crunch, crunch, soft, and yet there, and all around the tomb.

"Come out, come out, come out—wherever you are!" came a voice.

It was a quiet voice, a teasing voice.

A feminine and sensual voice.

Austin's blood ran cold throughout his veins. He wanted to jump up and run, run as far as he could possibly run. Staying still was almost impossible.

His heart!

His heart was thumping so loudly that it seemed like a marching band was playing in his chest! Surely, the sound would be heard. And his breathing . . . oh, Lord! Every inhalation and exhalation seemed like the winds of the worst hurricane on record.

"Come out, come out, I know you want to play. . . ."

He didn't want to play. He wanted to be Austin Cramer, computer geek, commanding animated figures on the screen.

"Austin!" The voice whispered his name.

She knew him. And, oh, God—he knew her. He knew the voice. It was Adriana Morgan who was out there, and it was as if she were sniffing him out, as if she had . . . radar! She knew where he was.

Crunch, crunch, crunch . . .

And then nothing.

But he could feel her. She was right outside the iron gate.

He rolled, as silently as he could. He had to get away. Where? He was in a tomb. He began flailing in the shadows, mindless; not even knowing what he was looking for. And then, as he kept inching back, he leaned a hand against the marble near the floor. . . .

And it gave.

He pushed it, and rolled.

He came to rest on a patch of dirt. Good old dirt. There was no coffin in the tomb. If someone had been laid to rest where he lay, their remains had long since given way to the furnace-heat of summer, and they had been swept back to the holding area. No, where he lay, it was completely clear and clean, a bed of fresh, natural-smelling *earth*.

"Austin, come on, come out!"

He heard the rusty gates swing open. She was coming for him.

"Austin, come on baby, I know what you said about a night of abstinence, but I'm ready. I'm ready to do what I want to do in all the carnal ways! Carnal. Well, carnivorous, maybe, too. Come on, Austin, I'm ready to show you the time of your life!"

He lay still, stunned and in shock.

Adriana?

No! It was impossible. Impossible. Impossible . . .

Adriana killing people . . . killing people like Brian! A big old strong football-hero guy. How could little Adriana have gotten to a guy like Brian?

Couldn't be, couldn't be, couldn't be . . .

"Austin, don't make me angry! All right, I do like to play with my food, but . . . hmm. I'd thought about leaving you for another night, but the full moon doesn't come around that often. I mean, really, it's great with the police thinking that it has to be you! Oh, they would string you up faster than a man can swat a fly!" She laughed, the sound of her voice still so teasing and petulant—and sensual. "Wait! They don't string men up anymore, do they? Well, they'll give you the needle. Actually, hmm, think of all the fear while you wait for them to make all the fussy arrangements, strapping you in and all that. I really would love to wait around and see, but . . . I'm still hungry, Austin. I had a few snacks tonight, but I had to be careful—had to make it look like you. But that doesn't matter anymore, 'cause the playing just didn't do it for me. I'm so, so hungry! So hungry for you!"

He didn't even dare breathe. He lay there, frozen.

"Austin! Silly boy—I will find you. I can smell you, you know that. I'll hear your little rabbit heart pretty soon . . . come on out. I can make it fun, and then . . . I can even make it easy. Catch that carotid while you're still shaking with bliss. Don't make me angry, Austin! I'm not fun when I'm angry. And I'm the most erotic thing you've ever experienced when I'm not."

Fear streaked through him with an icy vengeance. He could hear her sniffing—just as if she were a dog. Sniffing and sniffing the air. He heard her move, and he could almost see her, imagine her bending down, and figuring out that the marble slab that covered the bottom tomb wasn't really a marble slab at all; it was a swinging door. . . .

It opened. The moonlight in the main tomb seemed brilliant after he had lain in the slab-covered dirt area for many minutes. He saw her. Saw her perfect face, saw her smile. Saw the blond hair, sweeping down around her shoulders.

"There you are, Austin!" she said.

Then she cast her head back, and she let out an ungodly sound. It was a howl, it was worse than a howl; it was like a dozen wolves crying out beneath the moonlight in pure victory. . . .

Wolves!

She contorted. Her head snapped back; her arms bent forward at a bizarre angle. Hair—luscious golden hair—suddenly seemed to burst out all over her body, and she fell down to all fours. Her eyes narrowed and her nose grew, and she opened her mouth and it was filled with sharp white teeth that seemed to glitter and gleam in the moonlight.

She growled and lunged.

He felt her breath, hot and fetid, and he felt the dripping of saliva and he closed his eyes, screaming as he nearly felt the reach of those teeth, snapping for him with fanged vengeance. . . .

"Get the hell off him!" he heard.

And, miraculously, she was wrenched away from the tomb. The marble slab waved wildly, and Austin rolled out and as far across the tomb as he could, ready to lunge to his feet at any opportunity.

DeFeo Montville was there; he was back. And he had wrenched the Adriana-thing away from him just a split second before she could sink her fangs into his flesh.

She was massive; a massive golden wolf. But DeFeo had her by the scruff of the neck, shaking her. She yelped and growled, desperately trying to wrangle free and sink her teeth into him. But his grip was incredible. So strong.

Then DeFeo cast his head back and opened his mouth.

Austin let off a silent gasp of astonishment as huge fangs sprouted in DeFeo's mouth. He sank them into Adriana's neck.

She wriggled; she let out one last weak growl. . . .

And she went silent, wolf's head cast to the side.

He dropped her, shaking his head.

Then he stared at Austin. "Look, you've already got your occasional stray werewolf wandering into the city, the kooks who think they're aliens . . . don't ever, *ever* get involved in any ridiculous demonology business again, and I don't give a damn if you ever get laid again in your life!"

AUSTIN STOOD BACK.

The beautiful temple-style tomb with its pillars and portico and weeping angel looked magnificent, if he did say so himself. A little fresh plaster, and a nice new paint job, and flowers surrounding the gate. He had done a great job—really!

It had taken all day, and now dusk was falling, but he was done. He whistled while he finished his work, picking up the paint cans and the brushes from the last of his ministrations to the tomb. He crawled out of his work overalls, set them with his supplies in his wheelbarrow, and then hurried out. The gate would lock soon and he no longer kept a key.

He deposited the wheelbarrow and its contents in the back of his ordinary white van.

Letters advertised his new life's plan on the van. CRAMER HOME REPAIR.

He drove on to his new favorite hangout on Frenchmen Street. Walking in, he took a seat at the bar. Joe looked up at him, nodded, and poured him a beer.

"Is he on his way?" Joe asked.

"I haven't seen him yet," Austin said. "I imagine he'll be here soon."

"I'll get his special drink ready," Joe said. Joe kept DeFeo's "special" drinks in a refrigerator in the back. His daughter really was a nurse at the hospital, and she managed to keep him supplied with just what he needed.

"Anyone singing tonight, Joe?" Austin asked.

"A great girl. She can really sing the blues. And you'll love the guys playing with her. A jazz trio. It should be a fine night, filled with real local talent."

As he finished speaking, DeFeo walked in. "Hey, Joe!" he called, taking a seat. Then he turned to Austin. His eyes were sparkling. "You need a reference for that new business of yours, I'm your man. My home has never looked better!" he said. He lifted his glass and clinked it to Austin's.

"And there's great music tonight," Austin said, grinning. "Local talent."

In a few minutes, the music started up. DeFeo stood to watch. Joe stood by the bar near Austin. "Yeah, a great night! I love New Orleans!

What a great place to call home. Especially when the damned werewolf population has been taken care of again. The vampires, they're just fine, once they settle in. But you just never know when a wolf will turn on you, huh, son?"

Austin nodded.

"Hey, I may need some home repair next week, got a leak in the old roof," Joe said.

"I'm your man—unless, of course, DeFeo needs me for something at his place."

They both looked at DeFeo, but he was just swaying with the music.

He loved jazz and the blues, and he loved New Orleans.

And he sure loved his home. And from now on out, Austin would take the best damned care he could of that home.

The Mansion of Imperatives

JAMES GRADY

That three-story Gothic mansion rose like a hulking mirage from the desolate snowy prairie east of Montana's blue misted Rocky Mountains.

Five people came there that winter Friday.

Louise hoped rehabbing the old house with their friends Bob and Ali would spark a paternal instinct in her husband, Steve.

Steve hoped fixing up the deserted relic would get his wife off his case and let him hang out, *that's all*, just hang out with Ali, Bob's willowy wife.

Ali was there because doing what Bob wanted kept her comfortable.

Bob told himself that it was okay to keep secret how he was going to work their group investment because he was the guy who always turned a profit—and had the bankroll, the blond wife, and the do-gooder plaques to prove it.

Parker stood in the front yard outside the mansion that cold gray morning as Bob said, "What do you mean you've never set foot in here?"

"Wouldn't go in fifty years ago," said Parker. "Won't go in now. Stood here then watching Mom yell at my old man 'bout how he come to architect for Mister Rich—who had some heart attack, left this hulk and his fortune to my old man. Dad wouldn't quit here for us. Saw him push Mom off that front porch. Watched her disappear day by day, die waiting for him to come to his senses. After the UPS guy found him froze like a statue here last month, if I didn't need your money, I'd let this damn place rot to dust."

"We won't work in your pickup or our rental car," said Bob. "If a storm is coming down from Canada, the longer you argue about that, the harder it will be for you to drive the thirty-seven miles back to town."

"You folks really plan on staying here all night?"

"For four nights," said Bob. "Power's on—drafty, but the furnace works. Got a portable heater, fuel. Sleeping bags, food. Four nights now in December gives us ten percent of our ownership as occupants during our first calendar year—the minimum requirement for the homesteading tax credit."

Bob didn't say, *And with the hardware store receipts plus date-stamped pictures of us working, we prove renovation, increasing our equity.*

He told Parker, "Either you come in or we're all out."

Parker clumped up the porch steps as if he were climbing a gallows. Louise handed him coffee from a thermos they'd filled at a Starbucks 110 miles away in Great Falls. The four friends had flown into Great Falls the day before, from Denver. She followed Parker and Bob into the dining room with its legacy of scarred furniture that included a document-covered table.

Steve laughed while Ali strapped a tool belt around his waist.

Louise caught the glow in her husband's eyes.

Bob gets off on seeing that fire in other men.

Louise shook her head: *Why did I just think that?*

Montana recognizes legal verification other than notarization. A digital movie camera recorded the four friends processing sales documents with the mansion's heir. Parker wanted to *sign, sign, sign* and skedaddle, but Bob insisted on explaining each document to forestall future lawyers.

Fifty-four minutes later, Parker yelled, "Done!"

The front door swung open. They all hurried to its gaping view.

Outside snowflakes parachuted down like an invading army.

"But there's no wind yet," said Steve. "What opened the door?"

"Old houses," said Bob. "They're always settling."

Parker said, "I'm so outta here!"

Louise grabbed his arm. "You can't drive in a whiteout!"

Her husband, Steve, pushed the door closed.

Damn my logic, thought Louise. She didn't know why.

And again the door swung open.

"Whoa," said Ali. "That's weird."

As with a great *whoosh,* wind rose in the storm.

Bob closed the door. "Parker, if you die out there, the sale gets stalled in your probate. That blizzard will swallow you. What could be worse?"

"I don't wanna know." From his shirt pocket Parker fetched a steel lighter and a hand-rolled cigarette. The herbal smoke he exhaled revealed marijuana.

Bob said, "You're getting stoned? Now? Celebrate at home!"

"Ain't celebration." Parker took another hit. "Medication."

The door rattled.

"Didn't think the wind was blowing that hard," said Steve.

"*Not thinking*'s the way to be here," said Parker. "My old man didn't hole up here because he was a drunk. He drank because he holed up here. Staying outside or being stoned makes it harder for the thinking to get you."

"Look," said Bob. "*Thoughts, voices,* whatever you hear—"

Ali asked, "Why did you say that?"

"—doesn't matter," continued Bob. "We gotta fix this place up fast. Seal ourselves in or this storm will turn us into icicles. The leaky windows in the upstairs bedrooms: no time to replace them, but we can cover them up."

Louise heard her husband, Steve, say, "Ali and I'll do it!"

"Good," said Bob. "Louise, help me Sheetrock that basement insulating wall Parker's dad didn't finish."

Breaking glass!

They ran into the dining room and found the popped-off-the-wall shelf that Ali and Steve had laughingly named "Look-out Ledge" when they stacked it with bottles of red wine, the smoky Scotch Lauren ached to give up for motherhood, and the vodka Bob favored because it never breathed the secret of its sip. Plus Diet Coke and tonic water and two six-packs of beer.

The plastic bottles of Diet Coke and tonic water had survived—one Diet Coke bottle rolled across the floor to greet the five of them running in.

The liquor bottles were a jumble of broken glass cupping tiny pools of red wine.

Parker said, "Looks like you guys just lost your medical protection." He stubbed out the joint on the lighter and put them in his shirt pocket.

"Leave this mess," said Bob. "We gotta work. It's getting colder."

Bob led them to the living room and their stack of delivered hardware supplies, their luggage and sack lunches and read-on-the-plane newspapers.

He handed Parker a hammer. "We're all trapped in a house that needs fixing. Rip out the molding, reframe that window to keep out the cold."

Parker shrugged: "If you gotta, you gotta."

Steve grabbed a roll of plastic weathersheeting, duct tape. He would have dashed up the two flights of stairs to the bedroom level except Ali floated up the steps with that long-legged languor Steve didn't want to miss.

Louise blinked: *No, that wall didn't just pulse.*

Bob led her to the basement while their spouses climbed to the third floor with its wide-open stairwell bordered by a railing-protected corridor. Steve looked down the huge open shaft. Felt the vertigo of its inviting depth.

He and Ali worked on the smallest bedroom first.

"Like a cage in here," said Ali.

Steve spun the rolled weathersheeting so an end flopped down.

Ali lifted a utility knife from the tool belt she'd strapped onto this muscled man who seemed less boring than her husband. She cut a translucent sheet, held it over the only window. Cold air blowing in from outside flapped the plastic and goose-bumped her flesh. She heard Steve ripping free strips of duct tape from where he loomed behind her hips.

Why did I think of it like that? she wondered.

Felt him brush against her as he bent to tape and seal all the edges.

"We're done here." Steve stared at her. "This is a kid's room."

She felt her goose bumps receding as the now-sealed room warmed, wondered if he noticed her nipples had yet to go down under her sweatshirt. Then she heard herself share a secret out loud: "Kids cut into your chances."

"And all you can do is screw them up." *Never even told Louise that,* thought her husband, Steve, as he led Ali to the second bedroom.

Where, in the dust and cobwebs stirring with the drafts from two windows, the bed was big enough for a surging teenage boy.

Ali said, "Feel the furnace? Like it started blasting more heat."

Steve swallowed as she slid the zipper on her hooded sweatshirt down, down, spread her arms wide as she took it off.

For no reason she knew, Ali shook her blond hair free from a ponytail so it fell across her blue denim shirt with its pearl-white cowboy snaps.

Steve shook his head. *I want "driving down the highway, white hash lines coming at the windshield," and it's the going, not the getting anywhere.*

White pearl snaps.

They plastic-sealed the two windows against the howling wind.

Work together, Ali thought. *It's harder for the world to win if it's more than just you.* She felt like she was back in the trailer park, a girl hearing Gramma turn up the radio for some "Sealed with a Kiss" song. Ali knew how to do that, had done it and it wasn't bad, but it wasn't *that* kiss.

Ali said, "We should . . . keep going."

"Yes," answered Steve. *Yes. White hash lines. White pearl snaps.*

They walked the corridor along the third-floor railing. Rising from the living room came the *whump-ruh* sounds of Parker ripping out molding.

As Ali led Steve into the third, the last, the master bedroom.

Whump-ruh. Whump-ruh.

That bedroom door slammed. Closed. With them inside.

"Old houses—always settling," repeated Steve.

"Sure," said Ali. "Sure."

Covering the first window, Steve held the plastic in place while Ali taped it to the wall.

The heat swelled in that closed room. Steve shed his outer shirt. Its flannel smell sweetened the air for Ali as Steve savored the whiff of coconut shampoo from that morning at the motel when she'd showered naked.

Ali went between Steve and smudged glass to seal the last window.

Feels like I'm stoned, she thought as she finished. Her hips brushed Steve's loins. She turned. Her breasts brushed his arm. *Don't think* yes.

Like a tear, a bead of sweat trickled down from her temple.

Steve saw his fingertips catch that drop on her cheek.

She sucked in his finger.

Then he was kissing her, she was kissing him. White pearl snaps popped like machine-gun fire as he ripped open her shirt *No!* she said pressed his hands to her swollen breasts. *Oh* she pulled open his jeans *Don't want* he whispered as she leaped onto his neck like a vampire while he pulled off her jeans and panties, her legs thrashing them down to her still-on boots. They crashed onto the bed. Dust billowed. His mouth devoured her she knew she'd never come like this over and over again *Stop* she pulled him deep into her and it was like he'd never been this good, had this so good *Want High-ways* and *Not Him* and they cried out came collapsed on the bed.

Knew that in this house, they'd do that again and again and again, like running their hands along the bars of a cage until their fingers bled.

Whump-ruh. Whump-ruh.

"Listen," Bob in the basement told Louise. "Guess Parker can work."

"He'll do what it takes to get out of here." She positioned a sheet of drywall against the wooden studs of an insulating wall.

"Yeah." Bob reached for a hammer. "Took fifty years, but his dad ran out of the money he inherited with this place a few weeks before he died."

"We could fix the house up to live here," came out of her mouth.

"Who?" Bob drove a nail through the drywall to the stud. "*All of us?* Forget that. Me and Ali? Sticking us in Nowhereland isn't our deal. You and Steve? The only thing he'd want about this place is the hundred miles of highway between here and any job he could get, and one day driving that much road, he'd just keep on keeping on."

"Somebody's gotta live here!"

"Damn, Louise, what's your problem?" Bob hammered in a nail.

"I . . . don't know. I felt like . . . Somebody's gotta keep this place going."

"That's not our flip." Bob hammered in counterbeat to the noise upstairs in the dining room, the only noise that was close enough to hear.

Louise knew that look on Bob's face as they positioned new drywall. That was his ain't-I-cool look that paid off only if he confessed.

"What's going on, Bob?"

Whump-ruh. Whump-ruh.

Bob worked his hammer, too. "I was going to tell you guys when we got back to Denver. If I'd told you before, you might've settled for less than the big payoff.

"Didn't you wonder," he said, "who'd want to buy this nowhere place from us for enough cash to make us fixing it up worth our while?"

He hammered Sheetrock into place.

Said, "You know the Nature Preservation League?"

"You're on its national board of directors."

"If the economy's going green, green is how you gotta go."

"What did you do?"

"Our names aren't on the deed, just the limited partnership for a place that's being rehabbed as a 'luxury getaway home.' Figure the stats of a mansion, pictures of rehab happening, and the 'paper worth' becomes *what it could be* if this was *what it'll never be*, which is paradise.

"In five weeks, NPL will announce they've bought the land all around here for a new edge-of-the-mountains preserve. Of course, a house smack in the middle of that fucks up the NPL plan, so the board—"

"Which you're on."

"—so the board will offer the owners of this being-fixed-up mansion a buyout of what the place would be worth—"

"If this place were that paradise," said Louise. "Board member *you* will make sure it happens. And the rest of them will never know."

"Everybody gets what they want! We're doing well by doing good. This house gets rehabbed back to nature for people to love forever."

"I want something to love forever," whispered Louise from her bones.

"No forever here," said Bob. "This house is headed to the bulldozers."

She said, "Why is it so quiet?"

"That asshole upstairs quit working," said Bob.

Louise left him in the basement.

Walked upstairs.

Alone.

Bob swung his hammer, *Bam!*

His plan was beautiful. *Bam!* Perfect. *Bam!* Nothing could stop—

Screaming!

Upstairs!

Bob ran from the basement to where Louise stood in the living room.

To where Parker sprawled on his spine in an oozing pool of blood, the back of his head impaled by nails jutting from a chunk of discarded molding.

"Holy shit!" Bob checked: no heartbeat, no breathing. Stared at the chunk of wood jutting from under Parker's head, knew nails on the other end of the wood stuck deep into that skull.

Bob nodded to other chunks of wood scattered around the room.

"If he hadn't been stoned, if he'd worked neat, not left trip-and-fall-on-me danger lying around . . . Easy explanation."

Clumping feet ran down two flights of stairs.

Ali charged into the room, stopped.

Louise wondered, *Why is she looking at Bob and not the body?*

Ali cried, "Tell me what happened!"

Her husband said, "An accident. Must have been."

In ran Steve, wearing his Bruce Springsteen concert T-shirt that had been under his flannel shirt. Louise thought, *Why is Bruce on backward?*

Bob pulled his cell phone from its belt pouch. "No signal."

The blood pool oozed toward them.

Louise suddenly knew Steve would never give her morning sickness.

Ali stared outside at the raging blizzard. "What are we going to do? We can't get to help and help can't . . ."

"We figured to be here four days," said Bob. "Now we got no choice. No phone. Heat, enough food, but . . . We can't live in here with a corpse."

Bob and Steve zipped into their ski parkas. Put on gloves.

Dragged the body through the door held open to the storm by Louise.

The chunk of wood stayed nailed to Parker's skull.

Louise wiped clean the fogged glass of the newly framed window to watch Bob and her *just a husband* drag the corpse through shin-deep snow to Parker's pickup.

Steve and Bob plopped the corpse in the pickup's passenger seat. The wood chunk nailed to a skull bumped the rear window. They slammed the pickup door, then struggled through bitter cold swirling snow to the house.

"It's over," Bob told everyone as he and Steve shed their coats in the front hall. "Done. Tragedy, but it ain't the being dead, it's the dying, and we'll get through the storm—Hell, fix the place up. The probate will work as long as we've got a straight story."

Ali whispered, "What do I know?"

"Honey," said her husband, "we all know . . ." Bob stared at his wife. "Why are your snaps done up crooked?"

Louise heard Steve say, "All this, what's happening, it's like . . ."

Steve shook his head. Like he couldn't free the right words.

Ali reached out her hand to Bob. Whispered, "Please!"

He lurched toward her like a robot.

"Please get me out of here!" she told her husband.

Bob dropped to his knees before his wife. His strong hands cupped her perfect moon hips as he buried his face in the front of her jeans.

A bellow tore from Bob: "That's not our smell!"

Bob rocketed to his feet, lifted Ali off hers. Threw her away.

Ali flew through the dining room crashed onto the table/bounced off it to the floor. Bob charged Steve, yelling, "That's not the deal!"

Steve backpedaled as dizziness swirled Louise. She saw Bob slam into her husband, knock Steve onto the table, choke him.

Louise leaped onto Bob. He reared away from Steve to shake the wildcat off his back. Louise felt herself flung from him, flying—

Slamming into the dining room wall.

That absorbed her collision softer than wood should: *Why*—

Bob's fist hooked toward her face.

As Steve swung the hammer and cracked Bob's skull.

Bob crumpled to the floor.

Steve swung the hammer down on him again. Again. Again.

Stopped. Turned to look at his wife.

Louise saw her legal mate splattered with blood and bits of brain.

He dropped the hammer beside dead Bob, said, "You okay?"

"What's happening?" she whispered.

"We had to do it!" yelled her husband. "Bob, he . . . he went crazy!"

Ali moaned on the floor across the room.

Louise helped her sit up and lean against the wall. Saw the bend in Ali's arm that meant *broken*.

Steve loomed beside them. Said, "Is she . . . What happened upstairs . . . We . . . It's like it's all gone crazy in here! If you think about it—"

Louise whispered, "Parker said *not thinking* was the way to be here."

"Parker's dead," said Steve.

"So is Bob." She looked at her husband.

Steve pressed both hands to his temples.

"Story," muttered Steve. "We just need . . . a story. Bob went crazy, killed . . . killed them, and we, we're okay, we—*Don't want hate this place!*"

Louise grabbed her husband's blood-flecked arms. "If we know it's here, we can hear what it knows."

"What are you talking about? Ghosts? No such thing as ghosts. When you're dead you're dead, don't want to die don't . . . *Wait*."

"Yes, *wait*: not ghosts. Not . . . people. *The house!* The house itself!"

Ali moaned.

The wind howled.

Steve staggered from the dining room where he'd killed a man to the living room where another man had been killed.

Louise ran after him.

Found him standing staring down at the floor.

"Blood," he whispered to her. "We could clean it up. Make this place look great, be great, fix it solid again and . . . and . . ."

Sorrow twisted Steve's face: "I didn't want to fuck her!"

"Yes you did!" Louise grabbed his forearm. Dug her nails into his flesh. Felt the exertion push away wind in her skull. "Of course you wanted to fuck her! Everybody wants to fuck Ali! But you wouldn't have because you want other things more even if—"

Doesn't matter what I'm thinking if it was true before!

Louise blurted, "Even if you don't want our baby to love forever! You care about other stuff enough to not fuck her except we came here!"

Match what makes sense with who you are, thought Louise. *Use it like . . . like in that aikido demonstration on YouTube.*

She yelled, "Parker realized it when he had a child's mind! He stood outside and felt or thought something and knew enough to stay away and . . .

"His dad: maybe he pushed Parker's mom away to save her!"

Words blurted from her: *"Only needed him."*

"And then he ran out of money to keep you fixed up!" Louise yelled.

Steve blinked: "You . . . *who?*"

Louise grabbed him: *"Us! The house hijacks our thoughts!"*

Steve shivered.

Then she felt it, too, *cold air*, like . . .

She ran back to the hall between the living room and the dining room.

The front door gaped open to the whiteout swirl of the blizzard.

"Where's Ali?" she whispered and ran to the dining room.

Found only Bob's bludgeoned body.

Ran back to the hall where Steve stared out the open door.

Footprints in the snow led off the porch, past the white-mantled pickup truck, past their drift-buried rental car. Vanished in the blizzard.

"She chose," said Louise. "Ali was *that* strong. Never realized—"

The door slammed shut in their faces.

Blessed heat circled them.

Steve said, "She broke the first imperative: self-preservation."

Louise shook him. "Focus on what you knew before! Self-preservation isn't the first imperative! Remember? Sophomore biology and the first imperative, *the first imperative* is preservation of the species!"

"You're just saying that because you want to have a baby."

Steve stepped toward her.

Louise took a step back.

Like we're dancing.

"We don't need a baby," said Steve.

He took a step toward her. She took a step away.

His voice came out flat. Hammered. Fixed.

As he said: "We need a story for outsiders. To make them let us stay."

"You want to leave me!" Louise backed into the living room and he danced with her. "Please remember you want to fuck Ali and leave me!"

Blood on the floor tried to stick her shoes to the wood.

"Just need our story," he whispered. "Could say . . . Bob, Bob went crazy when we found out his plan."

Louise stepped farther into the blood. "How do you know his plan?"

"And then he . . . he killed Parker and . . . and hurt Ali, that's the truth! Tried to kill me and that's the truth! But we fought him off and they're all gone now and it's just us and we have to, we'll say we won't let Bob steal our dream to fix this place up—we'll say it's in honor of Ali. And Parker!"

"No!" Louise stepped backward out of the blood pool.

Steve cocked his head. "Fixing all this could be a one-person job."

He smiled. Held out his hand to her as he had for their wedding dance. Stood in sticky the color of raspberry swirls in their chocolate wedding cake.

Louise slapped his hand away. His boots slipped and his legs flipped out from under him. His crash shook the house.

The hammer Parker'd used. Lying on the floor by the newly framed window—*No*: not lying, *moving*, as like a wave, floorboards rippled to surf the hammer toward the blood pool and Steve's waiting hand.

Louise ran up the stairs.

"Wait!" she heard Steve yell. "We can fix this!"

His footsteps charged up the stairs behind her.

She made it to the second floor. Raced up to the third, past bedrooms where visions of her husband fucking Ali fueled her fear with rage. She ran beside the hallway railing around the open space drop to the first floor.

Looked across that gap and saw Steve running after her, his face twisted and his fist full of hammer.

Stopped, as if on command, both of them crouching near the rail to glare across the stairwell chasm centering the heart of this crumbling house.

Across the chasm, Steve smiled: "Easy, hon. We're home."

Blasts of dust blew from the corners flanking Steve. Floorboards snapped up to slap back down again with a machine-gun racket as two energy waves rippled toward him. They met with a *crack!* and the wood he stood on exploded in splinters. The railing in front of him blew apart and the hole suddenly made in the mansion dropped him into the chasm of its heart.

He fell three stories without a scream.

Louise shut her eyes. Heard him land. Opened her eyes to a mushroom cloud of dust. She peered over the railing.

Steve lay sprawled on his back on the first floor, homicide's hammer by his limp right hand, a railing chunk driven into his chest as another crimson pool formed around his outline.

You owe me filled her mind.

She ran down the stairs.

Okay, it's all okay now, you're okay.

"No!" yelled Louise as she ran down from the second floor.

You were always the one.

"Oh God oh God oh—"

Whatever created us must want us here. This must be right.

"Stop it!" yelled Louise as she reached the first floor of the house with two dead bodies. "I've got to stop thinking so I can see what to do!"

Flashes. Bob's calculations of probate problems after Parker's death *just need a good story* and protracted conveyance keeps bulldozers away and *might use who comes to clean up*—No, Louise can do it. *Say:* Steve went stir-crazy, murdered Parker, raped Ali, killed Bob, crumbling house saved her *I saved you* keep the place, live in it, *fix me up* tell rescuers it's like getting back on the horse. *Could work.*

Louise ran for the door before the house *got* what she realized.

She had the door halfway open when it snapped rigid in its frame.

But halfway was wide enough for her to fling herself out into the blizzard. Cold bit her as the door slammed shut behind her. Snow swallowed her legs up to her shins as she stumbled down the porch stairs. *Cold so cold Oh my God yes wonderful because it's real!* Snowflakes wet her skin and tried to refreeze. Thick white afternoon light let her see Parker's snow-buried pickup. Its steel handles burned her bare hands, but the driver's-side door swung open to her pull and slammed shut after she was in, behind the wheel. Parker's corpse sat rigid on the seat beside her.

The dead man stared at the windshield as her shaking hands fished in his shirt pocket . . . *Yes!* Found his lighter, a half-smoked joint and a small plastic bag. Her trembling hands clicked open the metal Zippo lighter, thumbed a blue flame, lit and hoovered a deep hit.

"Staying stoned makes it harder for the thinking to get you," the dead man beside her had said. *Hope he was right about that.*

She took another quick hit before she stubbed it out: *So little left!*

I am freezing in a blizzard-trapped pickup with a dead man.

She saw a bulge in the left front pocket of the dead man's blue jeans.

Keys! She leaned the stiff corpse against the passenger window, wriggled her hand into those jeans. The chunk of wood jutted from Parker's skull but she knew, *she really knew*, that out here, such wood had no power.

The pickup ground to life, blew heat into the cab.

A quarter tank of gas.

Even with the chains on the pickup, even with four-wheel drive, she'd need to rock the pickup back and forth to create tire tracks to follow. Even if she found roads in the whiteout, that vehicular effort needed a full tank.

Like an electric cloud softened other voices in her brain.

Can't drive away. Can't stay here. Enough gas to idle for a couple hours. Don't look at the dead man, his open eyes. Don't look at the board nailed to his skull. She searched his pockets, found a few bucks, coins, and in that shirt pocket, *a plastic bag . . . with another joint! Could stay stoned for . . .* maybe until dawn. She checked her watch: three fourteen P.M. *Make that until midnight. If I come in and out of the house, run the engine . . . every three hours . . . My mind and I will make it to dawn, maybe to the end of the storm.*

Told herself: *It's not what the house can do, it's what I choose to do.*

Only junk in the glove compartment. Nothing on the floor but the thirty-foot orange extension cord Parker used to connect an old-fashioned headbolt heater in the pickup's engine to any building's electricity.

Three hours. Stoned enough, staying strong enough, I can survive three hours in there. I can keep me. Louise turned off the pickup, left the keys in the ignition: one less trick for the house to play.

She ran from the pickup, stumbling through the eye-stinging snow and the knee-deep white powder that slowed her stumble up the steps and—

The house door refused to open.

Arctic air shook Louise so hard she fell into the snow on the porch. She ran back to the pickup, turned the engine on to blast heat over her, melting the snow and dampening her clothes *cold, that's cold, too*, but—

Louise closed her eyes. Like Parker'd said: *If you gotta, you gotta.*

She ran back into the storm carrying the orange extension cord, her mind playing the movie of how she'd tie one end to the porch or the door, tie the other end to the pickup's front bumper, and it wouldn't matter that the pickup could only charge a few feet, its horsepower against old wood—

The house door opened.

"Fuck you," whispered Louise. "You get one chance."

She backed off the porch, dropped the extension cord end far enough from the last step that it didn't touch wood, tied the other end to the pickup's bumper to show she meant business, ran back into the house.

The door slammed shut behind her.

Louise ran to the living room with its dried pool of Parker's blood, with its stacks of four friends' suitcases that had flown full of dreams from Denver, and sacks with their packed lunches and old newspapers, sleeping bags and the portable heater with a generator and a red plastic jug full of fuel oil that wouldn't work in a pickup. She closed her fist around the plastic bag with its one-plus joint and metal cigarette lighter as she switched her wet clothes for dry garments, unrolled a sleeping bag.

MIDNIGHT.

Louise sat rocking back and forth on the decrepit mansion's living room floor. She'd smoked all but an inch of the last joint. Felt her still chemical-addled mind mostly free from capture. To help, she'd crawled on her hands and knees, lapped up drops of the mixed brew spilled in the jumble of broken glass on the dining room floor near Bob's body.

What more are you than the home you build for your life?

Can't have a baby without Steve and who would want you now even if some rescuer comes. No rescuer's coming. Not in time. And when someone does come, someone with a weaker mind than Ali oh poor Ali.

Lucky Ali. She knew how to use what she had to get what she could.

There's what's real and there's what you believe.

What's real is that outside in the cold she'd die in an hour.

What's real is she could feel who she was slipping away.

Here could be home.

The something to love forever that's been her lifelong dream.

If she keeps this place fixed up, the place will fix what she believes.

She can come up with a story for all this.

After all, it's what works, not what's real.

She clicked open the metal lighter. Knew that was real.

Clicked it shut. Knew she was still here. For now.

Forever is a moment.

Like now. Louise clicked open the lighter.

And now. Clicked it shut.

The imperative to survive is all the house cares about.

The metal lighter clicks shut.

This is the moment you click open the lighter.

This is the moment you click it shut.

This is a moment when you're still Louise.

Not some species of zombie slave.

She clicked the lighter open.

"We're all trapped in a house that needs fixing."

Bob said that. When he was alive.

He said, *"It ain't the being dead, it's the dying."*

Louise thumbed the blue flame to life and fired up the last inch of the joint. Felt the house sigh.

Like, *odds are*, there'll be more months of sunshine on its wood.

You could be not dead here for a long time.

All you need to do is let go of every imperative except existing.

Louise sucked in a caustic cloud of smoke.

Held it as the house trembled its floor to shake her balance.

Like a movie queen, Louise flicked her lit joint onto the pile of yesterday's newspapers and birthed a flickering blue flame.

Dust and debris fell from the ceiling like smothering rain.

She grabbed the red plastic jug for the portable heater and splashed fuel oil through the room.

A ball of fire *whumped* up in front of her.

Fire consumed all the house's thoughts as flames licked its walls.

Louise grabbed her coat, gloves. Fought open the front door that, unlike her, had no feet to flee.

And as she stood outside in the snowy night next to the inferno where a house once lived, unzipping her coat to *heat* from the blaze whose coals might glow long past dawn when rescue would or would not come, Louise hoped she was right about the worth of the imperative that to survive as who you are sometimes requires fixing your house with flames.

The Strength Inside

MELISSA MARR

When Chastity bought the only house on the cul-de-sac with several acres between her and the nearest neighbor, it wasn't an *accident*. Privacy was a priority. At the time, her plan seemed sound. At the time, she hadn't yet met the Homeowners' Association or their subcommittee, the Architectural Review Board.

"Well?" Alison prompted when Chastity walked into the kitchen with the mail. Unlike Chastity, her sister was in comfortable jeans and a long-sleeved shirt. The dirt on her cheek—and the muddy footprints on the floor—told Chastity that her sister had been gardening again.

"Another form." Chastity clutched the latest ARB letter in her hand. By now she could recite the first paragraph:

> The River Glades Community prides itself on high community standards. As such any and all exterior architectural alterations must receive approval of the Architectural Review Board. Please submit the attached form to JUSTINE sixty days prior to the date upon which you would like to begin any alteration, addition, removal, or other visible change.

Chastity forced herself to release her grip. She laid the paper on the kitchen counter and smoothed it out. "Every damn form includes the same paragraph. It's like it's their letterhead."

"What do they want this time?" Alison unbraided her hair, finger-combed it, and twisted it up into a loose ponytail while Chastity read—and then reread.

Chastity made a growling noise before saying, "Sufficient neighbor signatures from . . . any house with direct line of sight with or without foliage."

"Umm." Alison walked to the door, opened it, and pointedly glanced to the left and right. "They do know we are the last house, right?"

"I'm sure they do." Chastity kicked off the ridiculous low heels that she wore to work. Her skills were more about focus, so office work made sense. If it didn't include such uncomfortable clothes, she'd be far happier. Alison floated from job to job when Chastity said they needed more money, but she couldn't hold a job that involved too much time indoors. Chastity, for better or worse, was content in closer spaces.

Which is why we need both a house and a big yard.

For a moment, the sisters stood face-to-face in their kitchen. It was a lovely space. Beautiful granite countertops, sleek stainless steel appliances, and black tile with black grout. Greenery hung from the ceiling, lined windowsills, and clustered along all of the walls. Like much of the house, the kitchen was as close to an exterior space as possible—but without too many wild creatures or insects. Through the open door, Chastity could see the yard that was Alison's passion. It was well on its way to resembling a formal garden that had been allowed to grow wild. Alison had the admirable ability to persuade most every plant, shrub, or tree to thrive even when they weren't native. The result was a fabulous space filled with wildlife and ample places to hide.

"It's worth fighting for," Alison reminded her. "I could persuade the woman if you say the word."

Chastity pushed away the mental image of the conversation her sister would have—or she herself would *like* to have—with the ARB chair; the process was made easier by the fact that she'd not yet *met* Justine. She shook her head. "I can do this." She paused for a moment, scanned the form again, and looked at her sister. "How many signatures are 'sufficient'? How do I know that?"

"You could always go to the committee meeting and ask." Alison widened her eyes in faux innocence. "Take a covered dish, perhaps?"

Chastity flipped her little sister off. "We're trying to get along here, Ali, not encourage the neighbors to show up with pitchforks and torches."

Alison shrugged and stepped away from the still-open door. Given her way, she wouldn't ever close the doors. "So, go fill out your paperwork. I'm going to read."

"Don't let the littles con you into treats because of fake hunger pains while I'm out," Chastity reminded Alison. "They need to learn to *schedule* their meals."

After a derisive snort, Alison wandered farther into the house. Somewhere in the plant-filled rooms, their siblings hid in dark shadows, but she pretended—for their amusement and hers—that she was unaware that they stalked her. In human years, and to the casual observer, the children appeared to be young teens, but as *Bori* they were the equivalent of toddlers—precocious toddlers, lethal toddlers, but toddlers all the same.

Like some mammals, a *Bori*'s physical growth meant they had strength far beyond their emotional growth. If the littles were left in the wild, they'd be mistaken for feral children—such nestless young were the source of the human stories about children raised by wild animals—but Chastity and Alison weren't going to let such a fate befall their siblings. A very long time ago, the sisters had struggled as parentless *Bori*; they'd lived in the old ways.

Which is exactly why we won't fail the littles now.

Despite their considerable longevity, few *Bori* were left in the world. Too often over the centuries humans declared them demons and murdered them, caged them as freaks in carnival sideshows, or destroyed their habitats. Protecting young *Bori* from such horrible fates was daunting. Chastity whispered a silent *Thank you* to whichever deity had granted her Alison as a sister. She could've handled the littles without extra help, but having Alison there made it far more manageable. Alison was maternal in a way that made her playmate as much as authority. Chastity, on the other hand, wasn't fun. It simply wasn't part of her skill set. There were plenty of things that Chastity considered as *skills* she possessed: she was a hard worker, kept her promises, killed easily, and generally could get along with just about anyone. She might not genuinely like seven out of ten of the people she smiled at, but now that blending was important for survival, faking friendly was essential.

Faux smile in place, Chastity took the papers in hand and went out to start knocking on doors.

"CAN I HELP you?" The older woman stood in the open doorway, not inviting Chastity in but not refusing to answer the door like the people at the first house.

"I'm Chastity. My sister and I bought the house at the end of Eden Street." Alison held up the paper. "I'm trying to get approval for a fence for my younger siblings."

"And Miss High and Mighty said no, did she?" The old woman lifted the glasses from her chest, where they dangled like a necklace. "You know, she tried to tell me I couldn't have azaleas up front. Azaleas! Who ever heard of azaleas being an issue?"

"I think they're lovely."

"Well, of course they are." The woman took the pen and paper from Chastity's outstretched hand. "I had to hire a gardener in order to get *approval*. That woman needs a job, or a hobby, or something."

Chastity smothered a laugh while the woman signed *Mrs. Corrine A. Kostler* on the form and held it out.

"You might as well skip the Hinkeys." Mrs. Kostler pointed toward a red brick colonial that sat kitty-corner from her house. "They do whatever *Justine* says. Edward files complaints on me right regularly. You just wait until he wants me to sign a form. Ha!"

Wisely, Chastity made a mental note to never anger Mrs. Kostler—and to invite her to tea. *Maybe even a human meal.* The food humans ate was peculiar, but there were things that Chastity could stomach. *The littles would have to eat early, but we could work it out.*

"Did you want something else?" Mrs. Kostler prompted.

"No, ma'am."

The old woman took her glasses off, smiled, and announced, "You're not half as weird as Justine said you were, girl. I should've known. Go talk to the others. Not the Hinkeys, mind, but the Valdezes and the Johanssons are decent enough."

"Yes, ma'am." Chastity nodded. She paused. "Thank you."

"Don't step in the grass this time. I have a sidewalk for a reason." Mrs. Kostler scowled. "Bring those children for cookies some afternoon."

Then she closed the door before Chastity could reply.

Like Mrs. Kostler, the rest of the neighbors seemed friendly. They looked at the signatures on the form, made a few comments—mostly polite small talk, but more than a couple bitter remarks about Justine—and signed. After the fourth house, Chastity figured she might as well keep knocking. More signatures couldn't hurt her case.

WHEN ALISON ARRIVED at the builder's office the next day, she was reassured. She had been discreet in her inquiries. *Chastity isn't the only one with a plan.* Once she'd narrowed in on the builders in the area with the sort of specialization skills they required, the choice was immediately clear. Damek Vaduva had achieved an odd, almost cultish following for his designs, but he also provided the more traditional building skill she needed. Unfortunately, his reputation for design made it near impossible to get a meeting, so Alison had to persuade the receptionist that she had, in fact, made an appointment but the poor dear had forgotten to enter it into the book.

What Chastity doesn't know won't hurt me.

Alison shook her head. "I can reschedule."

"No, no. It's my mistake, and Mr. Vaduva had a cancellation earlier, so he's in. Maybe I told him, but didn't add it in *my* book. I'll go in and tell him," the young woman murmured. Then she nodded to herself, apparently pleased that she'd resolved the dilemma satisfactorily.

"It's not a problem if he's busy, I can reschedule—"

"No, of course not!" The woman stood. "We were having such a lovely chat when you called that I must have forgotten."

Alison didn't know how much she could reorder the woman's mind and Damek's, so she glanced at the nameplate: DARLENE. Names helped.

"Since you've already told Mr. Vaduva I'm here, I will just wait out here for our appointment." Alison motioned to the overstuffed burgundy leather chair in the corner. "You go on to your lunch, Darlene."

The receptionist frowned briefly as her mind tried to assimilate the revision of reality that Alison was forcing on her. Then, she nodded, picked up her purse, and came around the front of the desk. "That does make sense, doesn't it?"

"It's always lovely to talk to you, Darlene . . . Goodness, it feels funny to call you that whole name after the things we've discussed." Alison leaned close enough that Darlene's little human heart pitter-pattered like a bunny on speed. "You will tell me if you decide to be more than, well, *curious*. Won't you, Dar?"

For a moment, Alison wondered if she'd overtaxed the poor human girl. Judging how much reality alteration they could take was always tricky, and some biases were a bit more deeply seated than others.

Then Darlene tore a piece of paper, scribbled a number on it, and pressed it into Alison's hand. "Oh, yes! It feels so liberating to even admit it."

Alison almost laughed in joy. Humans could be so unexpected. *A relationship might be a fun way to mainstream.* Being a *Bori* meant that one had a regular need to be needed; most of that need was satisfied by adopting and raising a pair of young *Bori* the way the sisters had, but there was something very satisfying about being needed in other ways.

She reached out one hand as if to touch Darlene's cheek. She held it there until the bunny heartbeat went from bunny-on-speed to bunny-on-speed-with-a-crack-chaser. Once Darlene seemed ready to burst with tension, Alison brushed her knuckles over the girl's face. "Sweetie, you haven't even *started* feeling liberated."

Darlene blinked, but said nothing.

"Go on with you, Dar. I have work to do." Alison shooed her out the door, admiring the way the girl added an extra sway of her hips.

Definitely worth pondering a relationship.

Once the door was closed, Alison walked over, flicked the lock, and took a moment to herself. Keeping the appearance of a human while exerting influence could be a tricky thing. Utilizing *influence* made a *Bori*'s eyes revert to their natural oblong shape which, sadly, tended to attract attention. It also had the strange result of making far too many humans unsettled even when they couldn't see the *Bori*'s shifted appearance. For a young *Bori*, exerting *influence* precipitated a form shift. Typically, for most older *Bori*, only the eyes changed, but there was always the chance of a more complete shift—and explaining why there was a wolf or an enormous bird where a human had just stood could be awkward. Alison hadn't slipped in years, but she did try to adhere to Chastity's insistence on mainstreaming, enough so that these little sessions were all the more exhilarating for their rarity.

Unnecessary if we just moved home where we belong.

However, the unfortunate truth was that Chastity was right: the littles were growing up in a world where global awareness had changed everything. So few places were truly sequestered, and by the time the littles were on their own, Alison couldn't imagine how the world would've changed.

A century from now, they'll need *to be able to assimilate far more than they would be able to if we stayed away from the humans.*

When the sisters were hatched centuries ago, it wasn't so unpleasantly difficult to nestle away in a village or mountain. By the time they were ready to take mates and have young of their own, the telephone had changed things, but it was the Internet that really was ruining things. Her youngest nestmates would need all the tools she could provide if they were to survive in the future that loomed.

Alison rolled her shoulders, cracked her neck, and concentrated on making her features both human and attractive. Her eyes hadn't recolored, but they tingled as they tended to when their shape started reverting to her natural oblong pupils. It would be easier if she could force her eyes to hold a human shape, but unlike Chastity, Alison could master that trick for only a short time. Alison resorted to contacts, which felt unpleasantly tight as her pupils reshaped.

She slipped her cell from her side pocket as it buzzed. A text from the littles read: "Need kibbles." It was immediately followed by a second text message: "Rave lies. Caught yellow birds at Chassys feeder. No kibble."

Alison smiled as she texted back: "Bury evidence. Do NOT eat all Chastity's finches."

Not all technology is bad.

The littles had responded well to the terseness of texting. They didn't yet like to use words if they didn't need them, but they did so when they needed to communicate with either of their elder sisters—or in cases where they wanted to talk to only one sister, typically when they needed to talk to Alison without Chastity knowing.

The next text read: "Three bird? Chassy sleeps now."

Alison grimaced at the thought of the littles eating too many of Chastity's finches and replied, "Only what you caught so far."

And that's why we live in this area. If they lived in the city where the littles had to steal house pets or try to find disease-free rodents, their diets would be a mess.

Resolved, Alison opened the door between the waiting area and the builder's office. The man at the desk didn't look up. He was darling for a male human: muscular, sun-darkened skin, a few pleasant scars on his exposed forearms, and old enough to be skilled at sex. Perhaps a relationship for Chastity would be wise, too.

Alison tapped her long, lacquered nails on his desk as she assessed him. He still didn't lift his gaze, so she murmured, "Mr. Vaduva? Mr. Damek Vaduva?"

"I am Damek." The man looked around with the gaze of one who was not expecting anyone to be in the room. When his gaze settled on her, he frowned. "Well, your sort don't usually come to the office." He pushed his chair back from the desk and folded his hands together. "Darlene is safe?"

"She is." Alison sank into the cozy chair in front of Damek's heavily carved desk.

She opened her handbag and pulled out a cloth. She didn't hesitate, despite the difficulty of coming to terms with what was wrapped inside it. She laid it on the desk. "I have a job for you."

To his credit, Damek did not unwrap the bundle in front of him. "Tell me."

Alison weighed her words with the same care she used in selecting the right stones from the earth. "I need my home made stronger. I can provide the materials."

"Everything I need will be there?"

"Yes," Alison agreed. "Everything."

Damek leaned back. "Then I will come next week."

SEVERAL DAYS PASSED calmly, and then another form arrived. That night, Chastity tore open the mail with a scream that might've caused concern if not for the sound-dampening spell they'd had the foresight to get for the house.

"Good day at work?" Alison called from the kitchen.

"I hate Justine with an unhealthy degree of enthusiasm." Chastity didn't bother trying to hide her irritation. Outside, she had to be sweet, normal, all of those pesky mainstreamer things, but in the house, she dropped the façade. "If she had any idea what happened to the last woman who—" Chastity stopped herself as Alison came to the doorway and gave her a bemused smile.

"We could move somewhere remote," Alison suggested.

"No. Times are changing. The littles must become socialized." Chastity took three calming breaths and walked into the kitchen.

Alison shrugged. "Now what?"

"Samples. We need to get samples." Chastity stared at the paper, reread it for the third time, and then tossed it on the table.

"Of?"

"Any and all building material visible to those in the community." Chastity closed her eyes and began counting very slowly in her mind. *One . . . two . . . three . . . I can do this . . . four . . . five . . . mainstreaming is good for the littles . . . six . . .*

Alison snorted. "Damek is to be here in two days. The builder I said was coming? I think you'll like him."

"We don't have the money, and *I* don't have time to like anyone, Ali." Chastity pulled open the fridge and got out several cardboard boxes. There were fresh bloodworms, a partially eaten chickadee, and at least half a squirrel left over.

"So you keep saying. The littles and I are not enough for you. You do not want a *Bori* mate, so you should select a human for a while. He is striking if you like males."

Pointedly ignoring her sister, Chastity returned to the fridge. "Did you want to go out for dinner or have leftovers?" She rummaged around and found an opened jar of red sauce. "I could do a casserole."

"Please, gods, no." Alison sniffed the air. "I smell you. If you expect to sneak up on both of us, you need to bathe more often, Remus."

A low growl came from the living room.

"And not react to every barb, sweetie," Chastity added. "Ali has a much better nose, so I wouldn't have known she was right if not for the growl."

The growling boy in question made a noise that sounded like a *chuff*.

The sisters exchanged a look, and while Alison's head was turned a black blur came at her from the other doorway. Chastity started, "Al—" but before the second syllable, the blur in question had toppled Alison and the chair she was in.

Perched on Alison's chest was a feral girl with almost solid black eyes and dark snarled hair. The girl tilted her head at an inhuman angle and stared at Chastity. She snapped her mouth in a self-satisfied way.

"Human words, Rave." Alison reached up to ruffle the girl's hair—and got a sharp snap on the wrist for it. "Clever thing, aren't you?"

Raven preened a little.

Chastity shook her head. "He agreed to being the decoy?"

For a moment, Raven pulled her stare from Alison to Chastity. Then she opened and closed her mouth. In a scratchy voice, the child said, "Bigger share of dinner."

"Clever," Alison repeated.

WITH A HAPPY yip, Remus charged into the kitchen. Chastity's edict against shapeshifting was helping the children learn to appear human, but their behavior was still more animal than human. Alison was grateful that she was the younger sister, though; she wasn't entirely sure she had the confidence to make some of the family decisions. Chastity's choices were akin to laws, so it made for a family without conflict. Luckily, their eldest sister was also realistic.

Remus leaned his body against Chastity and butted her hand with his head. His skin was smudged with dirt, but his hair was damp and leaf-free. She suspected Raven had groomed his hair again. Gently, Chastity murmured, "You will bathe in *water* later."

"Hate water." Remus looked at her beseechingly. "Used *words*. No water?"

"Maybe," she said. For all of her attempts at mainstreaming, Chastity still remembered that they weren't human. She lectured, and she reminded, but she didn't expect them to change entirely. If Alison were more curious, she might ask her sister if there was a master chart or spreadsheet where the number of admonishments and praise was measured out.

Alison watched her sister and the littles with a sort of peace that they hadn't always known—the sort of peace they were going to ensure for the family. *Not all nests are created equal.* This particular nest was one she would fight to protect.

"So, about Damek," Alison started.

The littles were unconcerned. Raven remained perched atop Alison, and Remus sat beside Chastity with his eyes closed contentedly. Chastity herself was suspicious. She leveled her gaze at Alison. "I'll talk to him, but the fence is the first priority."

"Sure, but the unfinished rooms downstairs—"

"Ali, we've talked about this. The money has to go to the fence first. I *will* get it approved. Getting the fence in, then spelled, and"—Chastity had stopped petting Remus, and he whined plaintively—"the inside is not the priority this year. Maybe next year if money is available."

"Chas?"

"It's not like I don't *want* them to have a better—"

"Chastity!"

"What?" Her sister resumed petting Remus, who had become unsettled by the tension in the sisters.

"I have the money." Alison held up a hand to forestall any questions. "Damek will be here to assess the site in two days. All you need to concentrate on is the fence. I have this."

For a strange moment, Alison felt the weight of all three of her nestmates' stares. Raven and Remus were experts in nonverbal communication, and Alison's studied lack of expression was obviously fascinating to the littles in a way that words or gestures rarely were. Remus prowled closer and sniffed her; Raven tilted her head from one side to the other. The littles exchanged a look, then studied Chastity. Remus chuffed at his sister, and she released a screech that only Remus could understand. Then, the littles gave both sisters their renditions of assuring affection. Remus licked their hands, and Raven rubbed her forehead against their shoulders. With no signal that Alison and Chastity would recognize, the littles vanished into whatever dens they had elsewhere in the house.

Once they were gone, Chastity sighed. "They're still sleeping in the rafters in the attic."

"They'll be fine." Alison reached up and laced her fingers with her sister's. "We weren't that verbal so young."

"I know." Chastity looked at her. "Do you miss the not-words?"

"Sometimes, but what I really miss are the tufts of fur you'd drag home from whatever you'd killed. We had a fabulous nest." Alison thought longingly of the way they'd lived before Chastity decided they had to mainstream. The nest was a true nest then. They'd had a cave with shiny bits of stones that she'd found, and the warm-soft pelts that Chastity brought.

It was so much easier.

Quietly, Alison said, "But we made the right choice."

"We?"

Alison laughed. "Yes, *we*. If you think I didn't choose it, too, you're spending too much time around humans. I'm here. That means I chose it."

"Thank you." Chastity squeezed her hand. "Do I need to ask where the money came from for the repairs?"

Alison shrugged. "I brought a few of those shiny rocks from the old nest. Humans make them into body ornaments. I gave them to Mr. Vaduva."

"You used some of your *gems* for payment?" Chastity's mouth hung open oddly on the last word. When she realized it, she closed her mouth with an audible smack.

"Go find your samples. The ARB meeting is in two days." Alison paused and rubbed her forehead on her sister's shoulder as she had when they hadn't learned words yet.

ON THE DAY of the meeting—the same day that Damek Vaduva would arrive at their nest—Chastity stood examining a white brick, a small bucket of some sort of masonry compound, and a three-inch sample of the metal rods that would reinforce the brick. She thought they had pretty good odds—and then the doorbell rang.

She looked through the peephole in the door to the thin, perfectly made-up woman, and she knew without a doubt that this had to be the ARB chair. The artifice that was conveyed in every detail of the woman's outfit was proof enough that no matter what form they filled out, no matter how innocuous—or logical—the request, it wouldn't matter. This was a woman who cared for appearance. Her clothes were the sort of poorly chosen frocks that admitted that the wearer didn't dress for her personal style, but for the society-approved idea of fashion. If Chastity knew anything about designers, she would be able to be falsely impressed, but the idea of being concerned with brand over style made no sense to Chastity.

"You have got to be joking." She sighed, affixed a smile, and opened the door.

"Miss Faolchu?"

"Yes. I'm Chastity Faolchu." She stepped aside. "Please come in."

Behind her, Chastity heard the littles. She glanced over her shoulder as Raven and Remus crept down the stairs. They perched on the edge of the landing midway down the staircase. Neither spoke. They stared at Justine.

Justine had stepped into the house. The expression on her face was polite, but the tone of her voice was chilly. "I didn't know you had children. Do they go to a private school?"

"No."

At that, Justine's polite demeanor slipped a little. "Oh, I haven't noticed the bus stopping here."

"It doesn't."

The ARB chairperson pursed her lips and blinked, as if forcing clarity to come to her. "Do you drive them? They don't look old enough to drive themselves yet."

"No." Chastity moved to the side so she could see the littles.

"So . . ." Justine prompted.

"We homeschool." Chastity gave her a tight smile.

The temptation to ask for more information vied with the natural discomfort most people experienced when they were confronted by the littles. Justine's gaze darted to them, and then back to Chastity. "Why did you say you moved here again?"

Chastity's dislike for Justine boiled inside her, but she wasn't ready to completely give in to it. She kept that anger out of her voice and said, "Children need yards. *Fenced* yards. In the city, we didn't have enough space for their growth."

"They seem a bit old for you to worry about fences," Justine said.

Charity briefly imagined telling Justine exactly how much trouble a pair of young *Bori* would inflict on their area. *Her tiny sweater-clad dog is lucky to be alive still. Bird feeders all look like buffets.* She forced her tone to remain level. "Nonetheless, we need a fence."

"I see."

The littles exchanged a look that conveyed how truly they believed that Justine did *not* see.

"Would you like to have a seat?" Chastity belatedly remembered that keeping a guest standing in the foyer was not friendly.

No matter how much I study humans, I still slip up.

She gestured for Justine to precede her into the small living room to the left of the foyer. It was more conservatory than living room, but such a thing wasn't terribly peculiar; a lot of people had greenery-filled homes, maybe not to the degree that they did, but humans brought nature into their homes, too.

Chastity tensed as Justine took a seat on the settee, but aside from pursed lips, the ARB chairperson made no note of the thick plastic that covered the furniture. It crinkled noisily as she shifted on it.

"I was getting ready to water the plants," Chastity lied. *And the littles have released several squirrels in the house again,* she added silently.

"Oh."

"I didn't want the furniture to get damaged," Chastity continued. *By the children disemboweling squirrels.* There was something oddly disconcerting about trying to make small talk, but the habit of adding silent truths typically made it more palatable. Today, it wasn't helping.

After as friendly a smile as she could muster, Chastity broached the subject of the fence. "I have the materials to bring to the meeting. I'm hopeful that we can resolve this and—"

"I doubt it, Miss Faolchu. I simply don't see that a privacy fence is conducive to fostering a healthy community." Justine folded her hands in her lap. "I don't think we need to start walling ourselves into little territories."

"Really?" Chastity's temper slipped a bit. She felt the pressure in her eyes, but she held on to the human shape of them. It wasn't that she had a short fuse, but the nitwittery of the ARB had frayed her nerves.

Justine waved a hand. "We don't control who buys the houses here, but I *do* have a measure of control over this community. It is my privilege to protect it from threats."

The rustle of leaves behind Justine revealed the hiding place where the littles waited. Their presence went far to remind Chastity why she was doing this—both controlling her temper and mainstreaming.

They deserve a home.

"There you are, Chas." Alison walked into the room. "I wanted to tell you that Damek arrived while you were out and discuss the schedule for the next step, but here you are . . . and with a *guest.*"

Alison smiled in such a disturbingly friendly way that Chastity realized that they were not going to resolve this politely.

At all.

Before Alison turned her attention to Justine, she walked over to stand beside Chastity, put one hand on her hip and the other on Chastity's shoulder, and said, "Rave? Remy? I see you."

The littles came out from behind a cluster of leafy potted plants; their movements were in perfect synchronicity. Raven tilted her head, and Remus stared fixedly at Alison. They didn't move away, though.

"Why don't you go find us something interesting to eat?" Alison said softly.

The littles zipped toward the door too quickly to be mistaken for anything remotely human. Chastity pursed her lips, but said nothing.

Justine's eyes widened. "They're . . . quick."

WITH HER TEMPER barely hidden, Alison turned to face the human who had caused such turmoil in the nest. "Oh, you have no idea."

She was a perfectly serviceable human. Her hair was a soft brown, and her eyes were a glimmery blue. *Like the rocks I can't ever find.* Alison tilted her head and assessed the woman further. She trembled some; fear was such a primal thing.

"I probably should go." Justine's voice quivered so slightly that it was almost unnoticeable, but Alison had spent centuries reading the nearly imperceptible cues of humans. Justine continued, "I simply wanted to stop in and let you know that there is no need for you to attend the meeting."

She stood and then paused.

"Stay. I'd like to discuss the fence." Alison stepped toward Justine. "My sister is surprisingly . . . *normal*. She dates males, works in some sort of . . . What is it you do, Chas?"

"Technical writing." Chastity obviously heard the dangerous edge in Alison's voice; she came to stand shoulder-to-shoulder with Alison.

"Right. Tedious normal things. I, however, am not quite as civilized."

"Alison." Chastity reached out for Alison's hand and pulled her away from Justine. She smiled reassuringly at the now visibly nervous human and said, "Please forgive my sister. She's a bit overprotective."

Justine looked from one to the other. "I don't think I like your attitude, Miss Faolchu." She visibly composed herself. Her shoulders straightened, and she smoothed her sleeves down. "I will be going now."

"No. I don't think you should, Justine." Alison glanced at Chastity and said quietly, "Leash me or step back."

Chastity shot her another quelling look, but she did not order her to stop.

Alison looped an arm around Justine's waist. The ARB chairperson stiffened and attempted to pull away, but Alison kept her arm where it was. "Did Chastity tell you about the work Mr. Vaduva is doing? Today is his first day here, but we're very excited about the project."

At that, Justine paused. "*Damek* Vaduva? Here?"

"The same."

"I've seen his work in *Architectural Digest* and *Metropolitan Home* and . . . He's a genius."

"Would you like to meet him?" With her free arm, Alison gestured toward the stairway leading to the lower level.

"Justine has a meeting to attend," Chastity said.

Alison glanced at her sister. "Of course . . . the *meeting*. Chastity is going to that meeting, too. Maybe you could ride over together. She's hoping to petition the board for approval for the fence, so maybe you could discuss it on the way."

Justine looked toward the stairwell. "I suppose I could miss one meeting."

"I don't think that's fair," Chastity said. "If you aren't even there to hear my petition—"

"You can talk to me while I'm here," Justine amended. "I was the only one objecting, but I can see now that you have good taste . . . perhaps, I could reconsider my stance. I mean, if Vaduva is here. He *is* really here?"

"Come meet him. Then call your committee. Maybe afterward you can talk to Damek. He's been nattering on about some architectural trip that he's leading . . ."

"Damek. You call him Damek?" Justine whispered.

"We come from the same place." Alison shrugged. "Not family, mind you, but we have an old connection."

Alison saw Chastity stiffen at the mention of Damek coming from the same place, but she did not ask the question she so obviously wanted to. She wouldn't in front of outsiders.

"Come downstairs, Chas." Alison held out her free hand. "You should meet Damek."

Silently, Chastity accepted Alison's hand. She squeezed it briefly, and then she opened the door to the basement. "I'm glad we're able to work this out, Justine."

"Of course." The ARB chair sounded positively friendly now. She smiled as she started down the stairs.

AT THE FOOT of the stairs, Chastity stood silent as Alison introduced Justine to Damek Vaduva. She wasn't prepared for the way he looked at her; the familiarity of his assessment made her blush like a far younger *Bori*. He didn't speak to her, not yet. Instead he listened as Justine gushed at him, senseless words about his artistry, about how she had tried to get an appointment but was callously rebuffed.

"It's almost unfortunate," Chastity said quietly. She caught her sister's gaze. "You didn't tell me he was from *home*. I didn't know there were any traditional builders here."

"You can tell me to cease," Alison reminded her. "You make the final decisions."

Chastity folded her arms and looked from the builder to her sister. "Mr. Vaduva?"

"Damek," he corrected. "To you, I am only Damek." He caught and held Chastity's gaze then as he added, "It is an honor to work in your nest."

"Their nest?" Justine echoed. "Oh, the house. In English, it is *house*. A *nest* is what animals have."

Damek motioned for Justine to come closer to him, but his gaze remained fixed on Chastity. "Do you wish me to do this work?"

"Yes."

There was a moment when neither *Bori* nor builder moved, and then Damek turned to Justine. "Come here." He pointed into the section of the wall that had been torn open. The drywall was gone, and a peculiar stone-and-wood structure was now alongside the original studs. The stone wall was already built almost knee-high.

"You see the beams. They are good beams. A structure must have the right support."

Justine leaned forward and looked into the partially built wall. "I see."

"No. You must come closer." Damek stepped over the stone and stood in the opening. He laid one hand on the beam. "Inside is the support. This is where the strength comes from. In here."

Then he stepped out and motioned for Justine to step into the opening. Obediently, she did.

"Look there . . . to the side." Damek stepped closer, invading Justine's space, and bodily blocking her exit from the partially built wall. He pointed. "Do you see the weakness of the beams? They need more support."

Once Justine was looking away, Damek made a gesture at his side with one hand. Alison tugged on a rope, pulling a board from above Justine and releasing the sludgy mix Damek required. It poured over Justine, who shrieked as she lost her balance.

"You idiot!"

"Hold still." Damek reached out with both hands, but instead of steadying her, he wrapped his hands around her throat and squeezed.

Eyes widened in fear, she stared at him as she clawed at his arms.

Once she crumpled, Damek looked toward Chastity. "You must hold her up."

With one hand, Chastity pushed Justine backward until her shoulder was flush against the exposed beam behind her. Damek took Chastity's other hand and put it on Justine's throat. "Squeeze if she wakes."

Damek knelt at Chastity's feet and continued building the wall. He hummed softly as he worked, and he paused only to look admiringly at Chastity—who pretended not to notice.

Justine was walled in up to her hips when Chastity finally allowed her to stir. "What are you doing?" She pushed against Chastity's grip. "Stop."

"Support matters," Damek told her with a frown. "My buildings . . . they never fall. You say you want to understand. You are learning a secret now."

"No." Justine slapped at them with hands caked in the clay mixture and scratched Chastity's arms. Her fingernails gouged Chastity's forearms, leaving behind tiny red cuts atop the thin scars already there.

"I share this secret." Damek frowned. "Many years ago people understood. Now? Things have changed."

Chastity nodded and shoved Justine more firmly against the wall. The ARB chair struck Damek and clawed at him, scraping her now-broken fingernails on his face. She grabbed Chastity's wrists, bruising them. Damek and Chastity ignored her.

"They have. It's not that I can't appreciate the benefits, but I worry. The littles are so young, and this world . . . It was different before. I worry—" Chastity stopped herself.

Damek paused. "I understand."

As they stared at one another, Justine shrieked and struggled against the stone, brick, and spell-laden mortar that now encased her legs. "You people are sick. You can't *do* this. People will notice. It's—"

"People never notice. Sacrifice helps buildings," Damek said.

"I won't tell. I will sign your fence form and—"

"No," Alison interrupted. "We needed someone with strong emotions. You are the right person for this job, Justine."

There was a flash of sorrow in Chastity, but not so much that she would fail to do what must be done to keep her nest safe.

While Damek worked, he said, "People see that my buildings are good. They write the articles. Now, I build for people with money, and when it is important, I build some special things in the old ways."

"No!" Justine tried futilely to dislodge the stones and bricks. "This isn't happening."

As Damek worked, the only sounds other than the grate of brick against brick or tool against stone were those of Justine's mix of screams, objections, and pleas. Then, even those faded, and only the rhythmic scrape of tools remained.

Chastity watched the bricks as Damek built them up around the exhausted, yet still weeping ARB chairperson. Quietly, she spoke to Justine. "It is for the good of the community. You understand that, don't you?"

Justine lifted her head and stared at Chastity. "You're a monster."

"Yes." Chastity nodded. "Not so different from you. You wanted to *protect* your community from fences and divisiveness . . ." Her words drifted away for a moment as she realized that she felt strangely sad. "I understand now. We both are trying to protect what we believe in. I have to protect my nestmates. The littles need safety, stability, a home . . . and you are helping provide that for them. Our home will be safe from any damage now. It cannot be broken into. Even our windows will not break."

"You're insane," Justine said wearily.

Only her head was still exposed.

"No." Damek lifted a trowel of mortar and carefully spread it on her face. "My buildings are safer. You make this building strong. Your rage. Your sorrow. Your death. It is good. Strong feeling from you and for you."

He lifted several more trowels of mortar, and Chastity scooped it from the trowel with her fingers and packed it around Justine's face and smoothed it into her hair.

The littles had come into the room at some point and now sat nestled against Alison's body in the middle of the floor. Raven was tucked under one arm, and Remus was curled on the other side.

"You wanted to make a difference, to be noticed, to be important. You have been. You will always be important to us now, Justine." Gently, Chastity covered Justine's eyes.

The last couple of tears had left tracks in the mortar on the ARB chairperson's cheeks. Chastity left them there.

She stepped back, looked at her sister and at the littles. Then she nodded to Damek.

Silently, he finished strengthening the building. Each brick and every stone he placed solidified its security and strength.

When he was done, the sisters and their young siblings went up the stairs, and Damek began humming again.

SEVERAL DAYS PASSED as Damek continued his work in the house. On the third day, Chastity found another letter in the mail. Nervously, she clutched it in her hand as she read the first paragraph:

> The River Glades Community prides itself on high community standards. As such any and all exterior architectural alterations must receive approval of the Architectural Review Board. Please file the attached approval FOR FENCE CONSTRUCTION for your records.

She smiled.

"What does it say?" Alison came to stand shoulder-to-shoulder with her sister.

Chastity held up the paper so they could both read it. "They've approved our fence!"

Alison let out a whoop of triumph, and the littles came careening into the room.

"I told you it would all be okay." Alison bumped her shoulder against Chastity's. "The littles will have their safe home and safe play yard."

"We owe thanks to Justine." Chastity nudged her sister back. "And to you."

Remus bumped his head gently against her hand. "Go catch yellow birds now?"

At that, Raven and Alison exchanged a worried look, but Chastity smiled at him and then said, "If you keep eating them, we won't have any left."

"Is a feeder though," Remus complained. "Feeder is for food."

Chastity laughed. "True. We need to mark the fence line anyhow. Come on."

And the sisters led their younger nestmates into their soon-to-be-fenced yard.

Woolsley's Kitchen Nightmare

E. E. KNIGHT

There's a joke over in Europe that if you find yourself in America's Upper Midwest, it's time to switch your GPS. Any reputable routing service provider should program its devices to keep you well clear of these bleak woods and cornfields, connected by old two-lane highways linking bits of crossroad nothing.

They can't imagine why anyone would want to be here. Bland as processed cheese, either too hot or too cold and dreary in the spring and fall. Whatever the charts say, the region's not on anyone's cultural map—devoid of interesting incident since the last Sioux uprising was put down during the American Civil War and populated by flannel-wearing bumpkins; they might say antipathy is the best policy . . .

Feck the snobs, I say. I've been there a couple of times. Few of the snobs will say that. What's more, I look forward to returning, which none of the snobs would say, even if it were true. You may laugh, but it's a land of quiet surprises and secret treasures. One moment you're on a winding country road counting cows, the next you're in a Swiss village or Cornish mining country, with Norwegian troll statues grinning at you from the roadside.

That's just Wisconsin, perhaps my favorite of the Midwest states. It's a rich land in its own way, sharing the stolid wisdom displayed by the locals in my own home county in Ireland, and with life in the country moving to the rhythm of the livestock and harvest. The grass is the same emerald green as well, at least until the July sun hammers the countryside into straw and clay. Maybe that's why it always seems half-familiar to me.

Ah, Ireland. You can leave it, but it never leaves you, even if you escape. I grew up wild and woolly with nothing but ravens and barn rats for friends, sneaking from one paddock to the next and scrounging from bins and feed sheds. I left the Auld Sod with a caravan of translife first chance I got. Quite an eye-opener, that, learning there were others not unlike me, full of anxiety and appetite. Because I was the new guy they dumped the worst duty on me: food prep and disposal. Of course the weres and the troupe's leader, a one-eyed vamp named Jack who taught me the Discreet Art of Wandering Translife, had all the fun of procuring the food. Once the blood was drained and the excitement of sticky red died down, I took over and turned the meats and vitals into road cuisine that would see everyone through to the next carefully chosen kill.

Then on my night rides I'd get rid of the bits of evidence that weren't reduced to sauces and stock.

That was how I found out I had a knack for cooking—a gift, even, as the others styled it. Dear old One-Eyed Jack plunked down the cash for my first translife eatery in Paris and handed over the deed. It was a dying bistro beneath an old nunnery when he bought it.

Two holes and a corner, it was, connected to the vast Paris sewers and a smuggler's tunnel on the Seine that dated back to Napoleon's Continental System. I put in twenty-two-hour days for a year and made a go of it. Word got out and I opened a second in Prague—my first and only instant success. I did a true restaurant in New Orleans, following with Shanghai, Lisbon, Buenos Aires, and finally my crown jewel, Nippers, in London, not far from Jack the Ripper's old kills. I did well in that very competitive market. The Secret Eyes, who pretty much run things in the translife world, put my London staff on retainer, doing the catering for their seasonals. That took me and my team all over the world, since the Secret Eyes never meet in the same city twice in the traditional human life span of threescore-and-ten. "Everyone served anywhere" went on my business cards.

But arse-over, such public recognition made me some enemies. Rivals in the translife foodie world got my place in Prague shut down. You'd think even white-hot jealousy wouldn't make any of us night folk do a deal with the Templars, but that was just what happened. Someone sent a note or an e-mail and three promising caterers on my team there saw their last night. The Templars dispatched and exorcised them in the prime of translife. What could happen in Prague could happen in Paris and Shanghai and so on, so I sold off my catering empire.

Tragedy, right? Worst year of my life? Not a bit of it. I'm a born wanderer, I'm happy to say, always kicking on for a new horizon. I needed to earn money so I went into consulting—you go through a lot of cash as a translife, between covering your tracks and bribing the local constabulary. So now I advise other would-be or troubled restaurateurs in the translife catering trade. I like going somewhere with fresh faces, fresh preferences, fresh customs, and fresh victims. Fresh horses, too, for a good, sweaty night ride, since most translife eateries keep out of the cities for safety's sake.

So, the call came to go to Wisconsin in the early summer, in the southwest corner on the bluffs overlooking that big, winding river through the heart of North America. Beer and dairy farm country, smelling of hot asphalt, manure, and crabapple trees. Sounded like a challenge; that bit of the world's almost off the translife grid, culturally and logistically. I had to wonder who'd be mad enough to try to cater to translife in the middle of a teat-pulling human nowhere.

A madman or a visionary, I guessed. I drew up a mental sketch of a discerning vampire retiring from hectic urban life, or an old banshee reconnecting with her childhood roots. As usual in matters unrelated to food, I was wrong.

THE SECLUDED SKYLINE Restaurant had a promising enough setting for catering to translife appetites. From the outside, not even visible from any highway, it didn't look like anything much—just another distressed barn in a part of the country full of them.

I had to follow the verbal directions given by the owner, as the little farm access road leading to the Skyline didn't appear on any database. The road had cheap, mass-produced red-and-white NO TRESPASSING and NO HUNTING signs, with a BEWARE OF DOG as you came to the flat ground surrounding the barn. I pulled up in my rental van—in this business you never know what you might have to run out and acquire at the last minute, and a van is perfect for discreet haulage—and decided I liked the look of the place. The barn was green rather than the more usual reds or whites, with a pinkish-white roof. Lonely, windy, remote. Cold as Jadis's tit in January, certainly, but on a deliciously firelit Beltane . . .

A walkaround reaffirmed my positive first impression. The building was shabby-looking and plain from a distance, but up close I could see that it had been largely rebuilt in the past ten years or so. One might wonder why a barn had a superb view from high on the bluffs overlooking the Mississippi Valley, perhaps halfway between La Crosse and Dubuque, or well-kept gravel paths leading into an abandoned quarry, or a small planted trellis over the stairs leading down into the former pigpens. Someone really curious might venture around to the valley-facing side and wonder at all the windows and the little patio around brick fire pits.

But I'd have to enter to find out if this place passed my most important criteria.

First, security. If I don't think a location is safe, or run with the well-being of its translife clientele in mind, I won't touch it, no matter what the fee. Location, location, location, as the real estate fleshies say. I'm a hungry Irish night-rider, not a wizard; I can't do anything about location.

Second, staff. Staff can sometimes make me walk right out the door within an hour of entering, if I think there's absolutely nothing that can be done with them. I looked forward to meeting them, starting with the owner.

The Skyline's owner, Mason Mastiff, came out to greet me, looking flushed and out of breath. He walked with short steps and crackled with a touch of other worlds about him, but he was as human as any of the dairy drivers whose rigs I'd been caught behind on the drive over from Madison. A wig cut to resemble the youthful, carefully crafted parted-on-the-left hair of a politician rested on his head, as out of place as a napping dove. I've always found wigs on men a little unsettling. Or maybe it's the kind of men who wear wigs that I find strange. I should have trusted my instincts that Mason Mastiff would be arse-over trouble. Staring, suspicious eyes, vaguely mad and dangerous like Rasputin or an Old West gunfighter thirsty for blood and whiskey, blazed out of a fleshy, pale face.

"Chef Woolsley, I apprehend," he said. His high-pitched voice rang out across the hills. He peeked over my shoulder into the van, perhaps wondering if a more impressive figure was waiting to be introduced.

I don't look like much in the day, I'll grant. My arms are out of proportion to my body and I'm a bit bowlegged. Haggard and limp when I'm not riding. I usually tell humans I'm between chemotherapies. Once the moon is up I'm not much better, but my hair comes alive and I'm hungry for fun.

Mastiff wore a brilliant azure smoking jacket and neat twill trousers that made him look as though he should be leading a marching band in a salute to John Philip Sousa. A cravat with a little golden skull stickpin at his throat screamed trouble.

I mean it literally. The feckin' thing was enchanted.

"Welcome, monsieur, set yourself down," it sang out.

Strike the enchanted, probably possessed.

"Quiet, Hellzapoppin," Mastiff said. "Business, not a customer. Have trouble finding the place, Woolsley?"

We exchanged politenesses. As we toured his grounds, Mastiff told me a little about his background. He'd started out as a restaurant writer and critic, or at least that was his dream. Strictly for human consumption back then. There was too much competition for the big names and the Michelin-guide stuff, so he started to specialize in dive eateries, bohemian cafés, and theaters where you could get a bit of performance art with your canapés and coffee.

"I was killing an hour with a custom appliance installer in a little Seattle bistro, asking him about odd little places he'd seen. The dear man had had a few tales to tell and told me about a place he'd done when he lived in San Francisco. Not in the city, mind you, out in the wine country. There were some cages behind the kitchen and a special table that looked like something out of an episode of *CSI*. He figured it was some kinky sex establishment.

"I smelled a unique story there, and dredged up every piece of information I could about it. I tracked it down and tried to get in. No luck, private club, membership card only, that sort of story. No record of it with the health department, no advertising. So I started watching the clientele going in and out, always in late at night, always out again well before dawn or leaving in a well-tinted limo the next day from a lightless garage. I managed to meet the owner and talked him into letting me work there."

He nudged some cold embers back into one of the fire pits with a polished dress shoe. The skull pin broke into the dwarf "Whistle While You Work," but quietly.

"I met my first translife there. From then on, I was hooked. So many legends, so much human history, quietly filling forgotten corners, unrecognized."

"We like it that way," I said.

"At first, I thought I had a food exposé that would win me a Pulitzer, but I found the customers were more interesting than the story—and the money! The money, my dear Woolsley. I learned everything I could about the business and found this place. Sunk my life savings into it, but the game hasn't gone my way. Hoped you'd tell me where I've gone wrong, dear fellow."

"Let's take a look inside," I suggested.

Third, décor. An easyish fix most of the time. We walked in through the front door. If Mastiff's own eyes couldn't tell him where he'd gone wrong, nothing short of a burning bush on a Sinai mountaintop could.

As soon as I saw his interior I decided this would be an easy job. All I needed was to find a couple of crowbars and a flamethrower.

The barn's interior was architecturally interesting, inspiring even, with the high, thick-timbered ceiling and small loft at one end, currently occupied by the bar. Big, airy, yet intimate in the way all those beams ate up the sound. Most translife don't care for noise and clamor. The tall windows facing the Mississippi gave a beautiful show of a green-and-blue river valley, vaster than the Grand Canyon and very nearly as deep, with the Minnesota bluffs a blue smear on the horizon.

There were definite possibilities in the way you looked down into the kitchen. He'd opened up the barn floor so you could see into a bit of the cooking line setup in the old pigpens. He'd set up sort of an open-air dumbwaiter. Above the big kitchen hatch hung what I first thought was an art piece. Some chains and a big platform featuring a surgeon's table not unlike the one used to animate Dr. Frankenstein's go at creation gave me all kinds of ideas for culinary showmanship.

However, as we toured the inside, I felt like putting on welding goggles to keep out the ugly. All that sturdy beauty to work with, and Mastiff decided to cover it up with garish flourishes.

Mastiff had ruined with décor what should have been won with space and view. Ghastly brass and fern fixtures that managed to combine the worst excesses of the late seventies and early eighties clustered here and there on the barn floor like scattered dog turds. Pointless plaster mini-Greek columns stood next to vintage washtubs and gas-station Coca-Cola machines, and a Tesla coil buzzing here and there. Imagine Castle of Dr. Frankenstein meets bricky urban loft meets postindustrial rave.

Curtains and linens in purple and black and pink with flecks of red with billowing gauzy cotton hung in festoons from the ceiling, trying to look ethereal but succeeding only in adding to the tatty feel and hiding the interesting details in the ceiling. Pointing out his acquisitions with one arm while the other remained anchored across the small of his back in a ducal pose, Mastiff prattled on, gassing about where he'd obtained the fabric and how much time it had taken to get the draping just right.

Small spotlights on conduit riggings suspended ten meters below that lovely wooden ceiling lit fabric, floor, and tables haphazardly, ruining the rustic effect.

He led me up the stairs to the loft-bar. There, old polymer countertops in dreadful puddle shapes, everything rounded and looking like tongues, lapped around too-thin high-backed chairs with pointed, stamped metal moons crowning the backrest. The chairs seemed eager to do someone an injury.

He led me to the railing overlooking the dining floor.

"We put musical guests on the rising platform," Mastiff said, pointing to the central Dr. Frankenstein rig on its chains. He gripped the rail like an admiral surveying his battleship from the bridge in a storm. "Or go-go dancers on singles' night. I know an absolutely brilliant troupe from the Twin Cities, two succubi and a harpy—"

"In short there's simply not, a more congenial spot . . ." sang the golden stickpin. Clearly the spirit inside was blind, deaf, and mad.

I only half-listened as it sang on. Singles' night! Arse-over, I was trapped in an eighties grease-and-grind meat market. All that was missing was a backlit sign featuring two Regency silhouettes and a name like *Snugglers*.

The crowning insult to the eye was the centerpieces on every table in the bar: lolling skulls with bloodred wax candles atop, dribbling down on both skull and tabletop. I leaned over to get a better look.

Arse-over. "Is someone filming a metal video tonight?" I asked.

"Tee-hee, dearie," Mastiff said, losing a little of his lordship's air.

This sort of excess had been popular for about ten minutes in some London and New York and L.A. clubs two decades back, a mixture of an old Universal horror set and furniture shaped like various pieces of the human digestive system. It lingered now only in Tokyo, where the Japanese translife put their own twist on it by adding enough neon to represent the Human Genome Project and pumping up the technopop.

It stuck out in the rolling hills of the Mississippi River Valley like high heels on a cow.

He'd sent me his numbers. Unless his accountant was as cluelessly skeevy as his decorator, a few customers were still braving the fugly to eat here every week. Perhaps the service staff and food would be the Skyline's salvation.

"I'll want to watch a service tonight," I said. "And we'll still need to see the kitchens."

Last, food. It can be an easy fix, or it can be like tunneling in wet sand. All depends on the staff and owner. Mastiff took me downstairs into the old pigpens. His kitchen crew was already at work.

A golem ran the kitchen with the help of two zombies.

My heart sank.

If there's anywhere you don't want a golem, it's managing a kitchen. As for zombies, they have their uses, but not where food's being prepared. You don't want earlobes sloughing off into the mustard.

Mason Mastiff was inordinately proud of his golem and the great expense a Jewish Kabbalist in Marseilles had charged to create it. To his mind, with a golem all the cost was up front. It worked for free from then on, often for decades, without needing much more wizardry, barring accidents. I suppose it looked impressive enough, this mountain of copper and tin, ladles, skewers, pans, and tongs. A pair of blue butane lights serving as eyes regarded me across a slab of stainless steel.

Look on the bright side, Woolsley, I told myself. At least there wasn't the usual suspicion when I was introduced to the chef of a troubled kitchen.

"Let's see it make me an omelet," I said.

Mastiff stuck his tongue in his cheek in thought. "You're serious?"

"It's supposed to cook. I didn't ask it to fart out the 'Stars and Stripes Forever.'"

"Chef Cuivre, an omelet if you please."

The golem clanked into motion. A nine-inch pan clicked out of its forearm and the mountain of cookware and utensils turned to the stove.

"Butter. Eggs," it said. It took me a moment to realize it was talking to the zombies.

They stood there in their hairnets, stupidly, faces even more green when contrasted with the kitchen whites. They wore baseball caps advertising what were local radio stations, I assumed.

"Buck! Tooth! You heard the chef," Mastiff said. "Sorry, everyone is used to orders being printed out on a ticket."

"Is that the problem?" I said.

Thanks to dropped eggs and butterfingers, my two-egg omelet took five from the fridge. Why do Americans insist on refrigerated eggs?

The golem extruded a silicone spatula and went to work on the beaten eggs. It worked well enough, but moved with such deliberate, noisy concentration I wondered what would have happened if I'd asked for bacon, fried tomatoes, and toast to go with it.

It did cook the omelet perfectly, going by my eye and nose. Taste would tell . . .

Then one of the zombies picked it up with a black-nailed finger and set it on a plate.

"Bollocks," I said, and Mastiff fled back upstairs.

The sight of that put me off eating. I watched the kitchen activity for as long as I could stand it. After seeing his kitchen staff doing their prep work, I was afraid to use the toilets for fear of what I might find floating in the bog. I returned upstairs.

"What did you think of the kitchen, then?" Mastiff asked, resetting a dripping candle atop a skull.

Maybe meeting some of the front staff would lift the growing sense of doom. "I'm trying not to. Do you have a hostess?"

"I take care of that, dear Woolsley," he said, his hand disappearing behind his back again. An operatic gesture toward the little stand by the door next to a case of cuisine trophies (I later examined them and found out they were all antiques from other restaurants) showed a little lectern on a podium so he could greet his guests from an intimidating height. "I like to attend each customer and tell them about the specials. One should treat each customer as an individual, no? Noblesse oblige."

Maybe that was the source of his mania for this place. He ran on fear. By serving translife, he was empowering himself over them.

The rest of the staff arrived. A bent, aged vampire named Ravelston served as the headwaiter. And the only waiter, considering how slow business was at the moment. He worked with the aid of two polished, animated skeletons. That I approved of. They looked clean and worked quickly, sounding like rolling dice as they worked.

I took a liking to Ravelston. He had grandfatherly wrinkles all about the eyes and smelled of lime talcum powder and extra-strength breath mints. "How ARE you, sir?" he said in a deep Southern accent upon being introduced. He had an interesting habit of both emphasizing and drawing out his verbs. "I HAVE heard about you. We ARE so PLEASED you made the trip. IS that an Irish accent I detect?"

We chatted a bit about my home county. He knew Dublin and Cork but didn't lecture. He did make one feel special, as though you made his day by simply walking through the door.

Still, he seemed willing to talk until the restaurant opened, leaving the skeletons idling like waiting cabs. I broke away from him and found Mastiff in his office, checking an Internet news site.

"Why in God's country are you using zombies, Mastiff?" I asked, though I knew the answer.

"Well, they're reliable, my dear. They never leave the premises, as a matter of fact. So they work as a security system as well, if you think about it."

"And they're cheap," I said.

"Well, yes. I am running a business."

"Into the ground. Look, I see the strategy, but sometimes, with zombies and animated skeletons and all that, it hurts you in day-to-day tactics. You lose all ability to have staff that thinks on its feet. Reacts to new situations."

"You haven't met my bartender yet. She's sharp as a spinning slicer, my dear. She doesn't come in until just before opening. Besides, now you're here. You'll get things put right, won't you? I'm entirely at your disposal, my dear."

"I'll hold you to that," I said.

"Consider yourself at home!" sang the golden skull as we shook.

I gave myself an unreality check. I'd taken a dislike to Mason Mastiff and his restaurant. Could I give fair value in consulting to a man I despised?

Perhaps it was his human nature. I like humans—especially served seared and roasted with butter and an herb crust of rosemary, sage, garlic, and parsley—and usually have little difficulty dealing with them. Mastiff rubbed me the wrong way. Perhaps it was his eagerness to court the trans-life world. I'd take a Templar, even a Black Templar, over a human who was so eager to profit on the preparation and consumption of his fellows. Since the soulrift, it's been them and us, or them versus us I should say, alternating roles as hunter and prey for millennia. This recent mixing of life and translife—put me down as Not a Fan. It won't end well. *The farmer and the cowman won't be friends,* as that demented little stickpin might put it. I can guarantee that each little story and encounter is being transcribed for the Templar archives. They're paying attention. Organized. We in the translife world spend too much time in a navel-gazing funk, or jealous of the fleshies and their daisy-chain lives.

Everyone served anywhere. Wisconsin was an anywhere and Mason Mastiff an everyone. Luckily for the world, everyone didn't wear a gold-braided smoking jacket and strut around a barn like Mussolini with three feet of PVC up his arse, thinking the world's ugliest dining room was some kind of tribute to Christo and H. R. Giger.

THE SERVICE THAT night, such as it was, depressed me. Few customers ordering fewer entrées. I tried a bit of the cuisine. A medical school lab equipped with a microwave and a salt shaker could have come up with a tastier dinner. The specials were an Unattended Death paella—an old lady and her cat, by the look of the kitchen bin—and Quad Cities suicide scramble.

Ravelston, the vampire waiter, spent more time talking to his friends among the clientele than shuttling food and drink. While I admired the gentlemanly charm and the smattering of knowledge and interesting anecdotes he could summon up on almost any subject, each involved him planting his feet at the edge of the table for ten minutes. The original third-wheel waiter.

Mastiff was serving emergency room food at private clinic prices. Twat.

Most of the clientele sat in the bar, chatting with each other or the barmaid. A pair of werewolves in purple Vikings jerseys hooted at the television.

Traffic died early in the bar. Strange for a place catering to translife, but then, it was a long drive back to any of the cities.

The barmaid was the one bright spot in the whole front of the house.

She was clearly out of the Eastern heritage of translife. Young, beautiful, pale green skin, and wide red lips. She had six arms and a graceful walk, gliding behind the bar from bottle to tap while wiping, placing coasters, and picking up money. I guessed she was a Devi.

"How did you manage to make it to the West?" I asked her.

"Mastiff petitioned the Secret Eyes," she said.

"That must have taken some doing."

"He never fails to remind me of that," she said, a red-green smile traveling across her face as if it were in a hurry to get elsewhere.

"What's your name?"

"Call me Megha."

"Devi?"

She gave me that brilliant smile. "I didn't sew these arms on."

"How do you like Wisconsin?" I asked.

She gave a matched set of shrugs. "It's pretty. The air and water are wonderful. No pollution. You can't imagine how bad India is with the exhaust these days."

"Like bartending?"

"I've always been a listener, and I'm proud to say the bar never gets behind." She checked the screen on her electronic assistant, opened a fresh jar of olives, and replaced the ice scoop. "Our patron, he's something of an old letch. Those wigs should come with goat ears. I think he brought me over because he liked the idea of a girl who could rub his prostate, give him a reach-around, and fill out his taxes all at the same time. But I get tired of the bar. He wants a glamour girl here."

She reached up with two of her arms and adjusted her fleshy breasts in their dressy bustier. "Regardless of what you've heard about minor Devi girls, we don't all go for the stage makeup and jewels. Doing six sets of fingernails three times a week is tiresome. What's a human life span again?"

"I give Mastiff three more decades, at best."

"Vishnu's discus," she said. "These last two years have felt like ten. I don't suppose you have American citizenship through the Secret Eyes."

"Not even a green card," I said.

• • •

THE PLACE HAD possibilities, no question. But at the moment, Mason Mastiff was playing checkers with some very expensive chess pieces, moving his queen like a pawn while his bishops sat back tossing off.

"This weekend will be better," Mastiff insisted, as we talked over the dismal dinner service. "I've something special to celebrate the rebirth of the Skyline." Mastiff let out a titter.

I HAD TO ride and think this through.

In all my travels I've yet to find a perfume sweeter than horse lather, and, given my nature, I doubt I ever will.

I found a small farmette surrounded by promising, moonlit fields. Their stable, under a buzzing incandescent floodlight coated in spiderwebs, didn't even have a lock. Inside a chestnut mare dozed.

Her ears pricked up as I touched her nose. In Wales and Ireland the legends say that the horses fear us; that's why they run so hard while we're astride. The truth is our scent excites them as much as their sweat pleases us.

I led her out, grasped two handfuls of thick mane, and swung up onto the beast's back. Muscles quivered between my thighs as I removed the tight restraining tie from my hair. I kicked her on. The mare galloped off into the night, accepted the challenge of the three-rail fence, and we were in the dark, free and away at last.

The pounding hooves soothed me and the fresh night air cleared my head, even if it came at the price of a swallowed bug or two. I'd return the mare, sweaty and trembling, by morning. A steamy mystery for whoever came first into the barn. For now, I'd give her the ride of her life.

THE NEXT MORNING I forced Mastiff to show me his surprise for the weekend.

I found him in his office. Megha had arrived early, or perhaps had never left, and was sorting bills into three piles: Delay, Delay Some More, and Final Notice.

"You've been hinting at some special cuisine for this weekend. I was hoping for some input on preparation," I said.

He winked and took me down to the kitchen. The zombies were taking turns working the mop back and forth—Buck would hand it to Tooth, who'd wring it out and hand it back to Buck, who'd wring it again and pass it back, without mop head coming into contact with the floor—as the golem slumbered in a corner, gently ticking and shifting like a refuse pile with a rat exploring within.

We passed through what served as an office and into the old dairy storage tank room. He'd converted the two tanks into cells, after a fashion, by installing reinforcing-rod grills over the cleaning hatches.

A white-painted dungeon. It smelled faintly of bleach and mice.

"Only one's occupied. Take a look."

"HELP ME! OH GOD, HELP MEEE!" a voice pleaded from within.

I hazarded a look. An attractive, tan, college-age human with bruises up and down her forearms and fists shot toward the hatch like an electrified cat.

"Help . . . out . . . please," she burbled.

It came to me. I'd seen the face on the airport news. The Stensgaard disappearance. The girl had vanished from the U.S. Virgin Islands while on spring break from her college in Syracuse.

She fit the profile for a missing woman the cable media would obsess over: upper middle class, attractive, a white girl-next-door with just enough body to warrant a second look—perhaps a third if she was in her swimsuit.

"Oh, this one was expensive," Mastiff said. "Very expensive indeed."

Idiot. He'd probably paid two or three hundred dollars a pound, plus finder's fees. He could have snatched a local Iowa high-school dropout for a tenth of that price.

Beyond cost, there was the danger that always came with a big media case. If word got out, it wouldn't be just a quiet little Templar raid—they'd call in Shaolin monks and Aborigine animist spirit men. One of the rules of the long war since the rift was to keep humanity only vaguely aware of the translife world. Rouse the superstitious, ignorant masses and you get inquisitions and jihads and pogroms that hurt both sides.

"This guy's crazy, you've got to listen!" she cried, white fingers gripping the bars.

"I'm inclined to agree with you," I told her, storming out of the storage room.

We returned to the office and I asked Megha to give us a moment.

"Are you mad? A big media kidnapping victim?" I asked.

"I thought it would create a buzz. I was in Europe last fall for the yearly declarations of the Secret Eyes, and no one had even heard of the Skyline."

"You're not just playing with your own safety, it's everyone who works for you. Me, too, while I'm here."

"Oh, come come, my dear. What's she going to do, chew through wrought iron or riveted tanks built to hold a thousand gallons of milk? Once she's on the table and surrounded by parsnips, your worries will be over—and at the plate cost I'm charging, I'll have a chance to put this month in the black."

"You're straining at a camel and can't even swallow a fly, Mastiff. You've got a six-armed demon on payroll who isn't being used to near her capacity, pouring with one hand, working her cell with another, and picking her bum with the other four."

"I will admit Megha's been a disappointment. Cold fish, my dear."

"Arse-over, more like. Quit looking at the two really great tits and think about those six arms and the creativity in the brain behind, right? You should put her in the kitchen, instead of that slow-motion junkyard."

"Then I'd have to find another bartender. I'd rather spend what cash I have left for a dazzling display of fresh food. That'll get them over from Europe."

Last person to try to blow this much smoke up my ass was a loquacious demon in San Juan.

"Fresh food! You're taking the piss, aren't you? Serving up one truly high-end dish surrounded by lashings of garbage that would choke a hellhound. Customers know a dodge when they see one. You're from here, Mason, yet your mindset's with those knobs in Marseilles and Prague who won't see beyond the tip of their cardamom-dusted noses. Your locals deserve better. Let's start with giving them your respect, right?"

"The locals! Depressed St. Louis vampires and Minneapolis ghouls. That's not why I went into this business."

Well, so Wisconsin grows a few snobs, too. Interesting. Still, I had to talk sense into him, or at least try.

"Forget about the fancy, high-concept menu items. You have great local sourcing, if you just think about it. In the summer, there's enough prospects on the waterways to keep three translife restaurants going. Drunken ski-boaters, sclerotic fishermen, college girls looking for a secluded stretch of beach where they can take their tops off without getting leered at, backpackers. In the fall, you have hunting season. Talk about a buffet! There are hundreds of different ways a couple of beered-up rednecks hunting out of their camouflage-painted truck might disappear. In the winter, just snatch someone off their snowmobile and then sink it in one of the lakes, or wait for a storm and go knocking on isolated ice-shack doors. In the spring, you have teens jaunting off into the woods for the first outdoor shag of the season. And all the bird-watchers. Bird-watchers are hardly ever missed by anyone."

"Have you ever eaten one of these good-ol'-boy deer hunters? They wouldn't be caught serving one of them in Paris."

"Listen, Mastiff, in Paris I could get twenty servings out of a fat old Normandy fisherman, skin salt-tanned right into a boot heel. Twenty servings at three hundred a diner, maybe thirty euros to find and haul him."

"I can't believe it."

"It's in the cooking, mate, it's not the quality of the cut. Your infatuation with college girls—Pilates classes and whole-wheat biscuits don't give you much flesh or any marbling. Your average Wisconsin plumber makes better grilling. Give me a braising pan and I'll make the most leathery old stream fisherman taste like sea turtle. Besides, local sourcing saves you a bunch of money and the potential for subcontractor mistakes. You can afford to cut prices, add variety, and these days even translife are on a budget."

"No! Tonight I'm putting on a show that'll impress even you, Sean Woolsley. You can help me by thinking up some side dishes to go with the Stensgaard girl."

Ahh, that's his bollocked-up plan. He thought he'd have me in, update the menu, then put on a show with his expensive little menu item every twenty-four-hour news channel had the hots for. Get a buzz about the old barn. Takes more than one pretty little dinner to turn around a restaurant, fleshie, believe you me.

I THOUGHT ABOUT climbing into my rented van and raising gravel. I could eat Oreos all the way back to London.

In the end, I stayed. For Megha and Ravelston, even for those two idiot zombies in the kitchen. Even those two deserved better than Cecil

B. DeRanged putting their translives at risk. Mason Mastiff had bitten off a good deal more than he could chew, and someone had to be there if he choked.

I took out some of my frustrations on a horse stolen from a riding club. I left it tied out back, knowing that I'd need another ride after seeing Mastiff's little show with the Stensgaard menu.

He'd been right about one thing. He'd generated a buzz. The old barn was very nearly packed. I even recognized a few diners from the translife foodie circuit from as far away as Memphis. Then I saw another familiar half-face.

Leave it to Mastiff to toss a turd into his own punch bowl. He'd invited yellow-skinned Charles Lasseur, a writer for the Nightcraft Roundtable, a one-stop Internet shop for all things translife. Some mix of ghoul and vampire and lich, he had an occasional column on restaurants, cafés, and nightspots, draining the life energy from would-be restaurateurs more thoroughly than a starving vampire. The old bastard had a scarred-up face minus the nose that might have been the inspiration for Lon Chaney's Phantom.

He had a peculiar sideways gait and sidled up to me as though we were old friends.

"I heard you were orchestrating another culinary triumph," Lasseur said, looking down his nonexistent nose.

"I'm still evaluating matters here," I said. "After tonight, I'm sure I'll know what sort of changes need to be made."

"Beyond the décor, I hope," Lasseur said. "Please tell me you'll do something about the décor."

I wouldn't give Lasseur the satisfaction of agreeing with him, so I just grunted.

For the featured dinner tonight, Mastiff wore a metallic suit and top hat, sort of a cross between Willy Wonka and Liberace, with a tiny brown wig the size of a sleeping bat atop his head.

The Frankenstein platform rose. The poor Stensgaard girl stood on it, attached to the rigging arms like Fay Wray awaiting her rendezvous with King Kong.

She had a stout leather ball gag in her mouth but otherwise looked wide awake and thrashing.

I've heard of a few translife clubs in Amsterdam, Southeast Asia, and the Mideast making such a production out of food preparation, but I don't agree with such spectacles. I'd warned and rewarned Mastiff not to attempt his plan, and here he was going ahead anyway. Tonight would be my last night at the Skyline. He could spend his way into bankruptcy without attaching my name to the fiasco.

"The world has gone mad today. And good's bad today. And black's white today. And day's night today," sang his stickpin.

"Ladies and gentlemen, mesdames and monsieurs, *meine Damen und Herren*," Mastiff began to an audience of English-speaking, Upper Midwestern translife, "let me introduce you to our fabulous main course, on special tonight for only nine ninety-nine a plate. That's nine hundred ninety-nine dollars, for the privilege of tasting the most talked-about woman in America today, Lisa Stensgaard. That price includes, of course, fresh blood to accompany your meal.

"She's exclusive to the discriminating clientele of the Skyline. Only you will be able to answer the question on everyone's lips: What happened to Lisa Stensgaard?"

Don't play with your food. First lesson old One-Eyed Jack ever taught me. Leave it to a human to go for sexy presentation. Sparkle might fill movie theaters, but it doesn't do much for cuisine. Hollywood gives the humans such lame ideas about translife.

Both zombies were pulling hard on her arms, forcing her down into the guttered autopsy table. Fresh jugs waited under the drain to collect every precious drop of blood, and Ravelston stood ready with wineglasses.

As the golem bent over her, chef's knife at the ready, she suddenly threw herself toward Buck. Or perhaps it was Tooth. One zombie plus one desperate woman plus the tipping platform managed to yank Tooth (if that was who it was) off his feet and impale him on the golem's outstretched knife and sent Buck backward off the platform.

Both zombies grunted in outrage as they bounced bloodily into the kitchen pit.

Stensgaard scooted backward as the golem mechanically wiped the knife and struck again.

"Chef! Stop her!" Mastiff shouted.

Breathing hot and hard, Stensgaard jumped off the platform and among the diners. She sprinted between the widely spaced tables, upending a busboy cart that one of the guests had pushed into her way. Otherwise the rest were satisfied with just watching the escape attempt.

Perhaps they thought it was dinner theater.

"Stop her," shouted Mastiff, waving his shiny top hat in frustration from the balcony.

The skeletons went about their business of mechanically filling knocked-over water glasses and picking up dropped forks. *You get what you pay for, Mastiff.*

Stensgaard didn't bother with the door. Instead she grabbed the busboy cart and followed it through one of the great river-facing windows and down onto the patio.

All I could do was shake my head. If she got away, the Templars would be investigating all of southwest Wisconsin and the surrounding states inside twenty-four hours.

"Looks like the special's off . . . and running," Lasseur said. "I can't wait to see what's planned for dessert. A heroin addict launched from a cannon, perhaps?"

Someone had to set this mess to rights, and for the sake of the staff of the Skyline, I'd undertake it. I grabbed Ravelston by the arm and pulled him toward the hole in the glass.

"Ladies and gentlemen, it seems . . ." Mastiff said. "It seems . . ."

"Starting here, starting now, honey, everything's coming up roses!" sang the stickpin.

"THIS NEVER WAS my kind of show," Ravelston said, his arms tight across my back as the horse trotted through the cloudy Wisconsin night. The tall quarterhorse was deeply unhappy about carrying a vampire. "Running down food in the dead of night."

I'd had to bring him. I could ride quickly, but I couldn't track a bus driven through a glass blower's.

"How do you keep yourself fed? Just the restaurant?"

I couldn't see his face much out of the corner of my eye, but it looked like a cheek muscle twitched.

"Tweed suit," he said.

Wasn't sure I heard him right so I yelled over the hoofbeats. "Come again, please?"

"She WENT downhill here, sir. TURN to the right, if you please. A tweed suit. Just put on a tweed suit. Especially if it's a few decades out of date. No one suspects you of anything. I tell you, if you ever need to lie low somewhere, find yourself a secondhand tweed suit. When I must eat, I visit the hospitals and nursing homes. Someone like me, smelling like mothballs, wool hat in hand wandering around a nursing home peeking into doors—no one gives me a second look. I look for those on their last legs. Dementia, pain . . . not much vitality in their blood, of course, but I feel as if I'm doing them a service."

"Was it always like that, or did you change over time?" I'd known a vampire or two who'd quietly starved themselves to death because the routine got to them. Talky old bloke would probably go that way.

"It was my daughter, poor creature. She'd had it all, smarts, looks. WANTED, NEEDED to keep it. Best turn left here, I think she's down this gully."

"Your own daughter."

"We lost my wife early on, so it was just the two of us. I think the possibility she wouldn't have to outlive me got in her head. She'd been away years, just a postcard here and there from various spots in Mexico or Rio. Then she came back. I SHOULD have known something was odd about her, years traipsing around Puerto Vallarta and the Caribbean, but pale as moonlight. Still, who wouldn't hug their daughter even if there was rather too much white about the pupils."

"How did she get into it?"

"Some young hotshot. Hardly KNEW the art himself, and here he was building a posse. That's what he called my daughter. Part of his *posse*. Nothing so dignified as *bride*, or *mate*, or with the implied responsibility of *sister*. She was in his posse. The world and its young hotshots. Those are just the kind of customers Mason wishes to cultivate. As if they are going to be touring the Mississippi Valley, antiquing for old farm implements and rare beer bottles."

"What ever happened to her?"

"The Templars, I think. She called me, once, said some men were after her and I MUST move and change my name. She loved the game, *the game* she called it, and played it risky. Just here—I can hear panting from those trees."

I thought about asking if she'd ever tried his tweed suit, but even the horses I exhaust don't deserve that much cruelty. In any case, we were almost on top of Lisa Stensgaard.

"Shall you take care of her, or shall I?" I asked.

"Must we?" Ravelston asked. He stared at the copse of hillside poplars. I couldn't hear anything but the wind and the horse stomping, but his instincts were intact with the night at its zenith.

"It's that, or the Templars will be burning you all out by noon the day after tomorrow."

"Perhaps—Oh, I suppose you're right. She's just about the age of my daughter. Funny how the bits of human existence linger on. Like a nursery rhyme from childhood."

"Along came a spider," I muttered.

Wait a tick—

"Come out, my dear," Ravelston said. "I'll make it quick, and I GUARANTEE it's pain free and rather pleasant. I went through it myself not so many years ago, you see."

"No. Let me go, please. Please!" she said, stepping from the copse. Her legs were scratched by thorns, and they shook.

"Lisa," I called. "Lisa, I know you didn't ask for this. You didn't ask for anything but a holiday in the sun. The only thing you did was talk to the wrong guy in a bar, I suppose. Bad break for you. But I think I can give you a choice. You can just accept that you're a casualty of an ancient battle, or you can help us out. Maybe even get revenge against the man who imprisoned you in that tank."

"Is this a trick?" she asked.

"More of a treat," I said. "For us, at least."

A WEEK LATER the Skyline had been cleaned of the dreadful décor and refurnished with some simple Arts and Crafts chairs and tables Ravelston had found at an Amish furniture roadside shop. A new bar was on order.

Megha, working the kitchen, had the zombies in thick rubber gloves and surgical suits washing dishes and polishing glassware. The golem was chopping vegetables, working methodically from the bins.

I'd loaned her a substantial sum to pay off the Skyline's debts. She'd proven herself an eager pupil and looked forward to her new role as chef.

The relaunch was a stunning success. Not a soul recognized pale, newly dyed-and-shorn Lisa Stensgaard as the new waitress. A delicate black choker hid the healing bite marks in her neck, and her nice eyes and cheekbones drew attention upward in any case.

Ravelston was behind the bar, pouring out aquavit—a local favorite— and anecdotes.

The menu, designed by me and executed by Megha, was a success. The special tonight was a juicehead fricassee in a New Ulm winery sauce. Some drunken college jocks had overturned their canoe on the Wisconsin River—with a bit of a nudge from Buck—and the police had managed to dredge up only one of the victims.

Even Charles Lasseur was impressed. I issued an invitation for a revisit personally, and he'd called Megha to his table to compliment her on the second-string Badger linebacker. "You've brought expertise back to fine dining here in the Midwest. I expect you'll find a grateful and loyal clientele," he said.

"Thank you," we said in unison.

"I look forward to trying you again tomorrow. Can I assume the new management has a fresh surprise to delight the tooth?"

"You can count on it. As our guest, of course," Megha said.

Megha knew how to stay on the old ghoul's good side. Counting her tongue, she was making at least four obscene gestures. Five if the lascivious wink was included.

Lasseur's lips had long since shriveled and pulled away from his gumline, but he licked where they'd once been. "Give me a hint?"

"Yes," I said. "As a matter of fact, tomorrow night we're serving the old management."

Through This House

SEANAN MCGUIRE

Now until the break of day,
Through this house each fairy stray.

—WILLIAM SHAKESPEARE,
A MIDSUMMER NIGHT'S DREAM

"So this is Goldengreen." May stared around herself with undisguised curiosity, taking in the high weeds choking the footpaths and the brambles that did their best to conceal the drop-off to the Pacific Ocean waiting a hundred yards or so below the cliff. Not one of California's finer views, although at least it wasn't raining. "It's a fixer-upper, that's for sure."

"Shut up," I snapped. I kept circling the rusted-out old shed that used to link the field behind the San Francisco Art Museum to the knowe of Goldengreen, Seat of the County it was named for. The door connecting the mortal world and the knowe had been created and maintained by the former Countess, Evening Winterrose.

Trouble was, Evening had been dead for nearly two years, and few enchantments are strong enough to last that long in the mortal world without maintenance. Goldengreen was sealed when she died. No one maintained the connections, figuring, I guess, that someday there would be a new regent, and it would be their problem.

Guess who the new Countess of Goldengreen was?

Good guess.

I gave the shed an experimental kick. It shook slightly, but that was all. No magical sparks leaped out to char my shoe, no lingering wards activated—whatever magic Evening had used here, it was long gone. I sighed, stepping back. "Come on, May. We're going to need to try one of the other doors."

"Awesome." May walked over to me, beaming. "It's an adventure."

"Yeah," I said dryly, and started walking toward the edge of the cliff. "That."

A LITTLE BACKGROUND, before this gets too confusing: My name is October Daye. I'm a changeling, which means my father was human and my mother was fae. I'm less human than I used to be, also thanks to my mother, who used blood magic to push me more toward fae in order to save my life. I'm still not sure whether to be pissed off about that.

About two years ago, Countess Evening Winterrose was murdered by my former mentor. I was the one who proved he'd done it. In the process the Queen of the Mists—current regent of Northern California—wound up in my debt. It was a position neither of us found particularly comfortable, since she thinks I'm changeling scum and I think she's dangerously insane. As soon as she had the opportunity to discharge that debt, she did . . . by giving me the title to Goldengreen. Yippee.

I never wanted to be a Countess, and I definitely didn't want the responsibility of reclaiming an entire fallow knowe. Faerie hills get weird when they're untended for too long, and Goldengreen had been empty since Evening died. Unfortunately, I also had a few dozen new subjects to worry about—the former denizens of the Japanese Tea Gardens, who were left homeless when their regent, my friend Lily, was murdered. They'd been camping in the entry hall, a huge, empty space that offered neither warmth nor comfort. It was the only place in the knowe close enough to the mortal world for us to access without actually prying a door open.

Reclaiming Goldengreen wasn't something I could afford to put off. We just had to find a way to get *inside*.

May stopped at the edge of the cliff, teetering on her tiptoes as she looked down to the rocks far below. "Whoa. That first step's a doozy, huh?"

"Something like that. Can you take a step to the left?"

"Huh? Oh, sure." May took an exaggerated step sideways, offering me a bright smile at the same time. "How's that?"

"Good. Good." To the mortal world, May's my sister. Faerie knows her for what she really is: my Fetch, a death omen summoned into existence by my impending demise.

That was several impending demises ago. May's been living with me since the first time I failed to die, and she makes a pretty good roommate. Best of all, being a Fetch, she possesses one trait that was about to come in extremely handy.

Fetches are indestructible.

While she was peering down at the waves beating themselves against the base of the cliff, I positioned myself behind her, checked my footing, stepped forward, and shoved. May screamed as she fell—more with surprise than actual fear—but the sound was cut off after only a few feet, when she vanished into thin air.

"I *thought* this was the back entrance," I said, and jumped after her.

MY FALL ONLY lasted a few seconds. Reality did a dizzying dip-and-whirl of transition as I passed from the mortal world into the Summerlands, and my feet hit the solid stone floor of Goldengreen's main hall. May's palm hit my cheek about five seconds later.

"A little *warning* next time?" she demanded.

I'm not fond of being slapped, but I had to allow that she'd been justified. "Would you have let me push you if I'd warned you?"

"What? No!"

"Well, that's why you didn't get a warning." I waved a hand to indicate the hall around us. It was twilight-dim, saved from absolute darkness only by fae vision and the traces of a distant glow from somewhere up ahead. "We're here. That was the goal. And what's the worst that could have happened?"

"I could have been eaten by a giant shark swept out of its natural habitat by freak ocean currents caused by global warming."

I let my hand drop back to my side, eyeing her. "That's it. No more late-night horror movies for you. Come on. Let's see if we can't find the light switch."

May fell into step beside me, sticking a little closer than was strictly necessary as we walked along the darkened hall. I couldn't exactly blame her. The air had a sepulchral quality to it, like we were walking into a tomb that had been sealed since time began. Even our footsteps failed to echo, dampened and deadened by the shadows pressing in around us. In Faerie, the regent is the land. By leaving Goldengreen untended, the Queen had left the land without a regent . . . and that's never good.

"It's like we're in a big zombie movie," said May.

I glared. "I was trying really hard not to have that thought."

Her smile was visible even through the gloom. "That's what I'm here for."

I started walking a little faster, making May hurry to keep up. She snickered as she quickened her pace.

"Oh, c'mon, Toby. If you just watched a few more horror movies—"

The hall shifted around us.

It wasn't a big shift—just enough to knock me off balance, sending me stumbling into May, who caught me easily. She looks like a changeling, but she's a pureblooded Fetch, and her balance is much better than mine.

"What was that?" she demanded.

"Oh, *now* you're not making jokes?" I straightened, tilting my head toward the join of wall and ceiling as I snapped, "Cut that out! I am the new Countess of Goldengreen, and I'm here by right of Crown and Claiming."

Maybe that wasn't such a good idea.

The hall shuddered, for all the world like a dog trying to shake something off its back. This time, May and I both staggered backward, stopping only when we hit the wall. Doors were slamming deeper in the knowe, and dust and cobwebs were beginning to rain down from the rafters. Unlike the first shift, this one showed no sign of stopping—although it *did* show signs of getting worse. If we didn't move, the knowe was going to bring itself down around our ears.

Being buried alive didn't sound like a great idea, and with Lily's subjects camped in the entry hall, I couldn't take the risk that the entire knowe would fall in. The Queen might approve—it would take out a lot of troublesome riffraff in one "regrettable accident"—but I certainly wouldn't. I didn't know why the knowe was objecting to us and not to them. That was something to worry about later.

I grabbed May's arm. "I've learned something from horror movies, too."

"What's that?" she asked, raising her voice to be heard above the shaking.

"When the house tells you to get out, you *get out*!" I took off running, hauling her in my wake and banking on the exits being easier to find than the entrances were. The knowe continued to shake around us, more and more detritus showering down from the ceiling, the few remaining furnishings and ornaments toppling to the floor. Then a door was in front of us, and I hit it shoulder first, sending us both into the cool night air of the mortal world. We went sprawling, May in a patch of ornamental ground cover, me into a sign that identified our location as the San Francisco Art Museum garden.

The door swung shut behind us, but not before I saw the knowe stop shaking.

May sat up, beaming as she brushed her hair away from her face. "That was awesome! What now?"

I groaned, sagging backward against the sign. "I have no idea."

MY ALLIES ARE a motley bunch, defined more by their stubborn refusal to stand back and let the professionals deal with things than any other characteristic. Danny showed up half an hour after I called, his cab roaring into the parking lot at a speed that would have been suicidal for most people. With Danny behind the wheel, it was just stupid.

He parked sideways across three parking spots before climbing out of the car, a process that took longer than would have been necessary for almost anybody else. Danny is a Bridge Troll—basically eight feet of mountain that walks like a man, with skin like concrete and hands large enough to wrap around a grown man's head. He wasn't bothering with a human disguise, probably because it was almost two o'clock in the morning, and stood revealed in all his craggy, gray-skinned glory. He would have looked right at home guarding the gate at a Renaissance faire, if not for the blue jeans and size 5X San Francisco Giants sweatshirt.

"Tobes!" he declared jubilantly, spreading his arms in greeting. "An' May! How's it going, girl?"

"Pretty good," said May, walking over to hug him. "Jazz sends her love. She's off with the flock this weekend. Something about the annual migration."

"That's, uh . . . that's special."

May grinned. "You get used to it once you've been dating a bird for a little while."

The two of them continued exchanging pleasantries as I walked around Danny's car and peered in the passenger-side window. The bronze-haired teenage Daoine Sidhe sitting in the front seat with a Barghest sprawled halfway across his lap offered me a timid smile. I knocked on the window.

Quentin obligingly rolled it down. "Hi, Toby."

"Don't you 'Hi, Toby' me. What are you doing here?"

"Danny said he was coming over, and I asked if he'd bring me along."

There were so many issues with that sentence that I barely knew where to start. I settled for asking, "Why were you with Danny to know that he was coming over?"

"He picked me up from the Luidaeg's."

I pinched the bridge of my nose. "Do I want to know why you were at the Luidaeg's?"

"Just visiting."

It's a sign of how much time Quentin has spent with me that the idea of "just visiting" the Luidaeg didn't seem to strike him as odd. Most people refer to the Luidaeg by her title: the Sea Witch. She's Firstborn, almost as old as Faerie itself, and tends to be viewed as one of the bogeymen under our collective bed. No one "just visits" her. No one but me, and now, apparently, Quentin.

Quentin and the Luidaeg met when his human girlfriend was kidnapped by Blind Michael and transformed into a horse to serve his unending Ride. We got the girlfriend back, Blind Michael's Ride was stopped for good, and Quentin wound up forming a personal relationship with one of Faerie's greatest monsters. Nobody can say our friendship hasn't been educational for him. I just hope his parents—whoever they are—will agree. Quentin is a blind foster at Shadowed Hills, which means I don't know where he's from, beyond "somewhere in Canada."

If he doesn't come from a really liberal family, I am eventually going to have to do some serious explaining.

"Get out of the car," I said, dropping my hand. "You're here. You may as well make yourself useful."

Quentin grinned, scrambling to open the door. Danny's Barghests poured out before Quentin had his seat belt undone, swarming around my feet making the weird yodeling noises that passed as their happy-to-see-you bark. I took a step backward, trying to maintain my balance. "Danny!"

"Aw, heck, sorry about that," said Danny, and planted two enormous fingers in his mouth, giving an earsplitting whistle. I winced, waiting for the museum security guards to put in an appearance.

Luck was with us for a change; no guards appeared as the Barghests stopped circling my ankles and went racing over to dance around Danny, scorpion tails wagging in wild delight. There were only three of them, if *only* is the appropriate word when talking about corgi-sized semicanine monsters with venomous stings and retractable claws. Danny runs a Barghest rescue service, and they tend to go everywhere with him when he's not driving mortal clientele. I don't think he's ever managed to adopt one out. I also don't think he cares.

I shook my head. "Which ones are these?"

"Iggy, Lou, an' Daisy," Danny said proudly, bending down to pet his venomous charges, who yodeled more in their delight. "Daisy's the smart one. She figured out how to open the door on the mail truck. You shoulda seen the mailman's face."

That was another line of thought I didn't really feel like pursuing. I shook my head. "Okay, great. Come on. We need to find a way to get into Goldengreen without the knowe deciding to kill us all."

"Sounds like fun to me," said Danny, and grinned, showing a mouthful of teeth like broken concrete.

"Wish I shared the sentiment," I said, and started down the path toward the cliffside entrance.

"**LOOK AT IT** this way, May," said Danny encouragingly. "At least you were the first one off the cliff. Tobes or the kid woulda drowned, and I'd be walking along the bottom to get back to shore."

May glared at him, continuing to wring the water out of her hair. "I can swim, but I still *fell*."

"Yeah," Danny agreed. "It was funny."

"We don't really have time for you to kill each other," I said, stepping between them before my sodden Fetch could lunge. "So the cliff entrance has sealed itself, the garden entrance is one-way, and the entrance in the old shed is gone. The only other entrance I know of is in the museum itself, and that's not going to work without breaking and entering."

Quentin looked up. "Wait—you mean there was an entrance in that old shed we passed?"

"Yeah." I nodded. "That's how I used to get in."

"I think I have an idea."

I raised an eyebrow. "Did you miss the part where the entrance was gone?"

"Yeah, but . . . 'What's been leaves marks on what is.'" He was clearly quoting something. All three of us looked at him uncomprehendingly. Quentin smiled, a little sheepishly. "I've actually been paying attention to my magical theory lessons."

I didn't have a better idea. "Okay, if you think you can get us in through the shed, let's give it a try. It's got to be more effective than chucking May off cliffs."

"Not as funny, though," said Danny.

"Hey!" protested May.

Danny kept chuckling all the way back to the shed.

It hadn't visibly changed; it was still rickety, ancient, and choked over with rust. Quentin waved for the rest of us to stop a few feet away while he circled it slowly, the steel and heather scent of his magic gathering around him as he walked. I watched carefully, less because I wanted to see what he was doing—I'm learning to admit that the Daoine Sidhe can do things that I can't—and more because I wanted to see *how* he was doing it. Quentin hasn't used much magic beyond simple illusions in the time that I've known him. If he was going to start branching out, I wanted to see where he was going.

After his third trip around the shed, Quentin leaned forward to touch the open padlock, murmuring something that I couldn't quite hear. An answering whisper echoed through the grass around us, sounding like the dying protests of the wind. Quentin said something else, dropping his hand to the shed's rusted latch. The whisper this time was louder, and lasted longer. The smell of heather and steel was getting heavier by the second, chasing everything else away. It was just Quentin's magic, the whispering grass, and the night.

And then the door swung open, revealing a square of blackness too profound to be anything but magical. Quentin looked back over his shoulder, sweat beading on his forehead, and offered a wan smile. "I got the door," he said. "But we should probably hurry. I don't know how long I can hold it."

"You did good," I said, motioning the others to follow as I walked quickly forward. "What did you do?"

"Countess Winterrose was Daoine Sidhe. You, um, aren't." He shrugged a little, looking uncomfortable. His hand never left the doorframe. "I told the knowe that I'm her. It believes me, for right now. But that's going to change real soon."

"That's fine. We're going." I offered a quick smile and stepped past him, into the dark.

THE DOOR LED to the main courtyard, a vast, circular room with crystal panels in the domed ceiling. They let in at least a little light from the starry Summerlands sky overhead, where four lilac moons hung high. The knowe was tied to the mortal world but wasn't a part of it. That was the issue. I don't know about most people, but I've never walked into a dead woman's house and had it order me to get out again. That sort of real estate problem is reserved for Faerie.

Danny and the Barghests were the next ones through. Iggy, Lou, and Daisy promptly scattered, tails wagging as they ran around the room trying to sniff everything at once, while Danny stopped beside me, planting his hands on his hips as he considered the room.

"You really planning to keep people in here?" he asked. "What, are you gonna sling hammocks or somethin'?"

"It'll be a home improvement project. If it lets us start." I turned in time to see Quentin follow May through, and stepped over to offer him my arm. "How're you feeling?"

"Winded. Like I just ran a marathon. But awesome." Quentin offered me a bright smile. "Did you see what I did?"

"I did. That was cool. I'll be sure to let Sylvester know that you're progressing in your illusions. And right after that, I'll tell him you were visiting the Luidaeg on your own."

"Hey!"

"Take the good with the bad, kiddo." Inwardly, I was miffed. The Luidaeg hadn't spoken to me in weeks. The fact that Quentin was able to casually visit stung. And besides, Sylvester Torquill is the Duke of Shadowed Hills, which makes Quentin his responsibility. If he didn't know that Quentin was sneaking into San Francisco to visit the Luidaeg, he needed to be informed.

Quentin wrinkled his nose at me, but didn't protest again as I turned to study the courtyard. Danny's Barghests were still sniffing their way around the room. Danny seemed to be keeping a close eye on them, which was a relief; I wasn't sure how many halls were connected to the courtyard, and I didn't want to add Barghest hunting to my list of things to do today. May, meanwhile, had wandered into the center of the room and was looking up, studying the Summerlands stars through the crystal panels in the roof. The knowe wasn't yelling at us yet. That was a nice change. Of course, once Quentin's spell wore off . . .

"It's too bad I don't know where the other exits are from here," I muttered.

"What?"

"Nothing. Let's see if we can't figure out where the lights are."

I started slowly forward, watching the shadows that collected at the base of the walls for signs that something was going to lunge out at us. Nothing seemed to be moving, but that could just be because we had yet to move far enough away from the door. If Goldengreen was truly tired of our intrusions, it might want to make sure we wouldn't be able to escape. What a charming thought.

Sylvester always said he could "feel" Shadowed Hills, like a second heartbeat echoing the first. Every other landholder I've spoken to said something similar, even Countess April O'Leary of Tamed Lightning, whose ideas of "normal" are heavily skewed by the fact that she's the world's only Dryad living in a computer server. They can feel their territory—their knowes, and their lands, are a part of them. All I felt was the creeping fear that Goldengreen might decide to rise up and smash us at any moment. I don't normally feel that way about parts of my own body, and on the rare occasions when I do, I tend to reach for the ibuprofen.

The floor was uneven, the cobblestones cracked and shifting in their settings. We were going to have some serious repair work to do once we managed to get the lights back on. Evening must have been neglecting her upkeep for years before she was killed—that, or the place had been sustained so entirely by her magic that when the magic was removed, the foundations began to crumble. I hoped that wasn't the case. My magic can't hold a candle to Evening's, not even now that I'm starting to understand what my magic really *is*, and if I was supposed to power this place, we were going to have a very short residency.

Thinking back, I couldn't remember the last time I'd been in this room. Evening had a small Court, almost unattended; I hadn't heard anything about what happened to the denizens of her fiefdom after she died. They must have managed to blend into the Counties and Baronies around Goldengreen without so much as a ripple. I'd asked Sylvester if he could help me find any of them when the Queen first gave me the title to Goldengreen, and he hadn't been able to name a single one, much less tell me where to look. If anyone out there knew the knowe's secrets, they weren't talking to me.

"Toby?"

May's voice was soft but still pitched to carry. I turned toward it, starting in her direction. "What is it?"

She was standing next to one of the decorative crystal fixtures on the wall. They were shaped like ice cream cones, held to the wall by thin copper loops. I remembered them lit, burning with a calm white light that never flickered or dimmed. She didn't say anything. She just pointed a quivering finger at the fixture, face gone pale. I blinked at her, confused, before reaching out and unhooking the offending fixture from the wall.

There was a glass dome tucked inside, where it would be normally hidden from view. I unscrewed it carefully, tipping the cone so I could see what was inside.

The dried-out husk of a pixie fell out.

It hit the floor before I had a chance to try catching it, shattering on impact and sending tiny, broken limbs and bits of wing in all directions. I jumped in surprise, cone and dome slipping from my hands and shattering next to the pixie's remains. Given what they'd contained, I couldn't find it in myself to be sorry that they were broken.

Raising my head, I gaped at May in horror. "How do you think it managed to get trapped in there? The poor thing must have starved to death. And why didn't the night-haunts come?"

"They couldn't get through the glass," said May. Her voice was just as soft as it had been before, and her eyes were distant, not quite focusing on me. "I don't think it got trapped in there by accident, Toby. I'm still a Fetch, even if I'm not exactly yours anymore, and I can feel their deaths all through this room. Dozens of them . . ."

Her words sank in slowly. I swept my horrified gaze along the wall, taking note of the crystal fixtures set at regular intervals. She was right; there were dozens of them, once you made a full circuit of the courtyard, and if they'd all contained live pixies at one point . . .

"But the knowe's been sealed since Evening died," I said. My words seemed distressingly loud. "She would never have allowed something like that."

"You always saw the pretty side of the nobles, Tobes," said Danny, looking back to us. He paused, then added, "No offense, kid."

"None taken," said Quentin faintly. He had walked over to stand next to me, staring down at the broken pixie on the floor with horror that mirrored my own. "I've . . . I've heard of people doing this. Before. It . . . they . . ."

"Pixies aren't covered under Oberon's Law," I finished for him. He nodded, very slightly.

Oberon's Law forbids the fae to kill each other. It's the only absolute rule he ever made, and it's enforced in every Kingdom. Of course, there are loopholes. Killing is allowed during an officially declared war. Changelings aren't protected by the Law. Cait Sidhe are allowed to kill each other, since that's a major part of their succession process, and the Law is enforced on the killer of a Cait Sidhe only if the local King or Queen of Cats requests it. Monsters, like Danny's Barghests, and small folk, like the pixies, are completely exempt from the Law. Kill them all you want. No one will stop you. No one will punish you.

Most of the fae won't even care.

Kneeling, I scooped the remains of the pixie into my hand. There was no way to avoid all the broken glass. A chunk sliced my forefinger. I stood quickly, hissing through my teeth. I wasn't fast enough to keep from bleeding on the floor—just a few drops, but every one of them seemed to glow like a tiny star. The Daoine Sidhe work with blood. The Dóchas Sidhe *are* blood, in some way that I still don't quite understand.

"Hold this," I said distantly, pouring the pixie's dusty remains into May's hand. It didn't occur to me to question how she knew to be ready.

She was my Fetch for a long time before the bond between us was broken, and she knew how I was likely to react to almost anything. Even things that had never happened to me before.

Kneeling, I lightly pressed my fingertips against the blood that had spilled onto the floor. I was still bleeding, gleaming, sluggish drops that fell to widen the stain. I still didn't feel the knowe, not really, but when I reached through the blood, I felt *something*. It was as if Goldengreen were stirring, becoming aware of our presence on a conscious level for the first time.

Of course, I had no way of knowing whether that was a good thing. I pressed my fingers down with a little more force, speeding the flow of blood. The knowe was definitely waking up, some deep, slow process that was too strange and too old for me to really understand.

"Uh, Toby?"

"Hang on, Quentin. I think I've got this."

"No, I don't think you do," said May, voice carefully lowered.

I turned toward her, raising my head just in time to see the flock of pixies that had been massing in the hallway door swoop down on us, their wings buzzing in the confined chamber like a million pissed-off mosquitoes on the warpath. I had time for a startled, wordless shout, and then they were on us, blocking out even the faint ambient light with the pressure of their bodies.

NO ONE REALLY knows where the pixies came from. Unlike Faerie's larger races, all of whom trace their ancestry back to Oberon, Maeve, or Titania, the pixies simply *are*. Some people say they're the natural by-product of magic, and I can believe it. Not much else explains the existence of an entire species of tiny, semisentient humanoids with a fondness for roast moth and clothes made out of candy wrappers.

Most pixies are wild and occasionally vicious, but it takes a lot to goad them into actually attacking something the size of a Daoine Sidhe, much less someone as big as Danny, who practically qualifies for his own ZIP code. These pixies were something else. Their clothes were made from scraps of silk and pieces of old tapestries, not garbage scavenged from the mortal world. Their weapons looked handmade, carved from pieces of ash and rowan wood. We had no way of knowing if they were dipped in equally handmade poisons, and I didn't want to find out.

The pixies chattered rapidly in high-pitched voices as they swept down on us, incomprehensible words almost drowned out by the buzzing of their wings. Danny's Barghests barked at them for a few seconds, distracting the flock. Then the Barghests turned, running full-tilt for a door in the far wall.

"Get back here!" Danny bellowed, swatting at the pixies that were dive-bombing his head.

"I have a better idea!" I shouted, straightening up and grabbing hold of Quentin's hand. "Follow those Barghests!" I ran after them, towing Quentin in my wake. May and Danny followed close behind, the pixies diving and weaving around all four of us as they lashed out with their tiny but potentially deadly weapons. The fact that we were running away didn't seem to be lessening the fury of their attack; if anything, it increased their enthusiasm, since now they were winning.

The Barghests ran through the door and down the hall, making a sharp left after about twenty yards. The four of us followed, speeding up as best we could in our effort to escape the flock of pixies, which seemed devoted to stabbing us. May yelped in pain but kept running. Good girl. When we reached the place where the Barghests turned, we did the same, and found ourselves in a small, rounded room with tapestry-cushioned walls. There was another skylight set into the ceiling, filling the room with cool moonlight.

It was pretty, but I was more concerned with getting the massive oak door shut against the pixie influx. I shoved against it; it didn't budge. "Danny, a little help here?" I asked.

"On it." He reached over and gave the wood a small, almost dismissive shove. It swung away from me so fast I nearly fell, and slammed shut with a concussive *boom* that echoed through the entire room. "Better?"

"Much," I said, and turned to study the others.

Quentin and May were both bleeding from a variety of small cuts, and one of May's barrettes was missing, making the hair on that side of her head stick out at an odd angle. Only Danny looked relatively unscathed. He leaned against the door, folding his arms.

"You didn't warn me about the attack pixies," he said. "I woulda brought a flyswatter. Maybe a can of Raid or somethin', too."

"You can't use Raid on pixies!" said May, looking horrified. "It's . . . it's . . ."

"Probably messy." I shook my head. "I didn't tell you about the attack pixies because I didn't know they were *here*. I thought the place was empty."

"The cliff exit," said Quentin. We all turned to look at him. He shrugged, looking embarrassed. "There was that time right after Evening died, when you fell? Remember?"

"How could I forget? But how do *you* remember? You weren't there."

"I told him," said May. I raised an eyebrow. "What? It was funny."

"No, listen—the cliff exit didn't have a door on it. The pixies probably got in that way and decided this was a good place to stay. No one was killing them. That's sort of an improvement over the way things worked before." Quentin paused before adding, reluctantly, "Maybe they even saw it as a sort of victory over the Countess Winterrose. She's gone, and they're still here."

"Which also explains why they reacted so badly to us. They think we're going to start killing them again." I glanced at the door. "Anybody feel equipped to explain the lightbulb to a swarm of feral, pissed-off pixies?"

"Not it," said May.

Danny's Barghests paced the edges of the room as we spoke, their semicanine muzzles pressed low to the ground and their scorpion-like tails wagging. They abruptly stopped, muzzles swinging toward the same patch of wall as they began growling.

When a Barghest growls, smart people pay attention. I straightened, to face them. "Danny . . . ?"

"Iggy! Lou! Daisy! You stop that right this second!" Danny pushed away from the door, striding toward the Barghests. "Behave, or Toby's not gonna want to take you guys for guard dogs!"

"What—" I began.

I didn't have time to finish. A spider easily the size of a goat lunged out of the shadows between the hanging tapestries, where it must have been pressed practically two-dimensional in order to stay out of sight. The Barghests yelped, the smallest cutting and running to hide behind Danny while the others held their ground and began to bark cacophonously.

May shot me a look. "Remind me to *never* start another home improvement project with you."

I didn't dignify that with a response. I was too busy pulling the knife from my belt and charging forward, toward the massive spider.

The folks at Home Depot definitely didn't have any pamphlets for this sort of thing.

IF THERE'S AN art to fighting enormous spiders, I somehow managed to live to adulthood without learning it. The creature seemed to consist entirely of lashing limbs and fangs the size of my forearm, which was enough to give even the Barghests pause. Danny grabbed one of them by the tail, jerking it clear just before it would have been impaled on one massive, hooked forelimb. I darted forward, slashing at the spider's leg. It responded by hissing and scuttling backward, looking for a new angle of attack.

"We need an exit!" I said, taking up a defensive posture while Danny pulled the other Barghest to safety.

"The pixies are still out there," said Quentin. He sounded dismayingly calm, given that we were sharing the room with the sort of thing that inspires arachnophobia. Maybe it was the fact that he had a Bridge Troll between him and the giant spider.

"Have you ever heard the phrase *the lesser of two evils*?" I asked, jumping back as the spider took another swing at me. It seemed to realize that this approach wasn't working as well as it could have, because it turned and raced six feet up the wall, hissing at us. "Open the damn door!"

"It's your funeral," said May. She grabbed the door handle, pulling as hard as she could. It didn't budge. "Quentin? A little help here?"

"On it."

The spider hissed again, spitting a long stream of something sticky-looking in my direction. I dodged to the side. The sticky substance splattered against the floor instead of against my legs. "Danny! Help them with the door!"

"This day just gets better and better," said Danny, and leaned over to yank the door open. May and Quentin were swept along with it, the wood shielding them as the tide of pissed-off pixies came boiling into the room. They stopped when they saw the spider, chattering rapidly among themselves in high-pitched voices. They weren't attacking; that was something, anyway.

I was so distracted by the pixies that I didn't notice the second spider until it dropped from the ceiling and grabbed me. Then I was being jerked into the air, so rapidly that I lost my grip on both my knives. Something pierced the skin at the back of my neck, sending what felt like liquid fire pumping into my veins. May screamed.

After that, everything went black.

I'VE WOKEN UP in a lot of strange situations, including "in the Court of Cats" and "halfway to being transformed into a tree." That probably says something about how much time I spend unconscious. Waking up wrapped from feet to shoulders in a silk cocoon and dangling upside down from the rafters of Goldengreen's throne room was a new one on me, though.

I blinked, trying to get my eyes to adjust as I strained to see what was around me. More cocoons hung to either side, the heads of my companions poking out the ends. Danny was to my left, with the Barghests behind him, and Quentin was hanging to my right. That just left— "May?" I tried to whisper. My voice still echoed in the empty room. I would have winced, but the cocoon didn't leave me with that much freedom of motion.

"Worst knowe *ever*," whispered May angrily. It sounded like she was hanging to my right, somewhere on the other side of Quentin. "I realize that your memory isn't always totally reliable, but couldn't you have at least *tried* to remember the giant spiders? That seems like the sort of thing you'd want to mention *before* you came for a visit."

"They weren't here before!" The puncture wounds at the back of my neck were a dull, distant throb. I could really get used to this whole accelerated healing thing. "Neither were the pixies."

"Well, they're here now," replied May. "Quentin and Danny are still out."

"Swell." I heal fast; May's functionally indestructible. In this case, that just meant we got to be awake when the giant spiders came back and decided to liquefy our insides for breakfast. I wasn't sure either of us would survive *that*. "What did I miss?"

"The spider grabbed you, and then two more grabbed Danny, while the pixies herded Quentin and me into the first one. We never had a chance."

"Hold on—the pixies are working with the spiders?"

"Maybe it's a tribute thing? They feed us to the spiders, the spiders leave them alone."

"No, really, hold on." The spiders *couldn't* be eating the pixies. Their fangs were too big for that. Any spider trying to eat a pixie would just wind up with a skewered pixie, and no breakfast to speak of. "They're working together. They have to be."

"What, we managed to blunder into the middle of the great pixie-spider alliance? Oh, that's just fantastic. This place gets more entertaining by the minute."

I tried squirming again. I still couldn't get any real purchase against the silk, and I gave up after a few seconds, letting myself hang limp. The answer was obvious. It was all but staring me in the face the whole time. I'd just been distracted by its many, many teeth. "They're not spiders."

"Eight legs, fangs, wrapping us up in giant snack-pack cocoons—if they're not spiders, what are they? Pretty pink ponies?"

"They're bogies."

There was a moment of silence as May considered my words. Then she groaned. "Oh, crud."

"My thoughts exactly."

Bogies, like pixies, bridge the gap between the intelligent and bestial fae. They're shapeshifters. Shapeshifters are pretty common in Faerie, but most shapeshifting fae have a limit to the number of forms they can assume. Bogies don't. They can take the shapes of a thousand types of creeping, crawling things: spiders and centipedes, scurrying beetles, and even, occasionally, really big frogs. They're territorial, like their pixie cousins, and they tend to live in large family groups, defending each other to the death.

Danny made a grumbling sound, like rocks grinding together, and the cocoon to my left shifted. "Anybody get the number of that dump truck?" he asked, sounding woozy.

"We found a bogie nest," I said, without preamble. Best to rip the bandage off cleanly.

Danny was still swearing when Quentin woke up a few minutes later. "Hello?"

"Hey, Quentin," I said. "Don't bother to struggle. We're bogie-caught."

". . . Oh," he said. "That's new."

"Yeah, I know." A distant humming sound was filtering into the room, like the beating of a hundred tiny wings. "Danny, shush. I think the pixies are coming back."

"Oh, that's *exactly* what I wanted," muttered Danny, and went silent.

The pixies brought light with them when they came pouring into the room, their tiny bodies glowing like low-watt Christmas lights. There were at least fifty of them. They swarmed to surround us, jabbing tiny spears and daggers at our faces—but not, I noticed, actually making contact. In fact, except for the bites from the bogies, we hadn't taken nearly as much damage from the knowe's inhabitants as we could have.

Maybe the Goldengreen's new denizens were trying to play nicely. Sort of.

I cleared my throat. "Uh, hi," I said, to the pixie that was flying back and forth in front of my nose. Pixies don't hover well. It was a male, maybe four inches tall, glowing with a rich, royal blue tint that didn't quite go with the scrap of buttercup-yellow sheeting that he was using as a loincloth. "I'm Toby Daye."

"And now she's talking to pixies," said Danny, in a long-suffering tone. "We're all gonna die here."

"Danny, shush," hissed May.

I did my best to ignore them, focusing instead on the pixie. "I think we may have managed to get off on the wrong foot."

The pixie eyed me suspiciously, not saying anything. That made a certain amount of sense. The language barrier between the small folk and the human-sized fae meant that while he might have been able to understand me, I had no real way of understanding *him*.

"I'm starting to get an idea of what used to go on here, and I'm sorry. I had no idea. The things that Evening—"

That answered one question: the pixies definitely understood at least a little English. The flock went nuts when I said Evening's name, shrieking in high-pitched voices as they all started flying wildly around us. Almost all. The blue pixie continued flitting back and forth, eyes narrowing with suspicion.

"I'm sorry! I'm sorry!" I said, hurriedly. "It's okay, really! We're not here to do the things she did. Do you understand me? We're not here for that at all!"

The blue pixie swooped a little closer, wings buzzing into a blur behind him as he aimed his spear at the tip of my nose. It was difficult to resist the urge to go cross-eyed looking at it.

"My name is October Daye. I'm supposed to be the new Countess here. The Queen sent me." The pixie shook his spear. "Hey! It wasn't my idea, okay? She didn't ask me. But as far as she's concerned, this knowe is my problem now, and she's not going to take it well if we never come back out. Do you understand? If we disappear, more big ones will come looking for us." There was something charmingly perverse about the idea that I was counting on the Queen of the Mists to avenge my potential death; she hates me, after all, and would probably be thrilled if I conveniently disappeared. But form would still insist she send someone into Goldengreen to look for us, and once whoever that was found our bones— and the homicidal local ecosystem—a mass extermination would follow.

"Sweet Maeve, I don't believe I'm worried about the pixies getting in trouble for killing us," I muttered. More loudly, I said, "Do you *understand*? We aren't here to hurt you, but if you hurt us, the people who come after us won't be this nice."

"What is she doin'?" whispered Danny. Hearing a Bridge Troll whisper was something like hearing a gravel truck trying to be quiet. It would have been funny under most circumstances.

"She's trying to reason with the pixies," said Quentin.

"Can she even *do* that?" asked Danny, abandoning his attempts at whispering. "Pixies aren't that smart—hey! Ow!" Pixies swarmed around him, stabbing out with their tiny weapons. Bridge Trolls have thick skin, but even thick skin can be punctured if the attacker is dedicated enough.

May laughed. "Looks like they're smart enough."

"Guys, can we settle down? Please?" The blue pixie was still hanging in front of me, a wary, quizzical expression on his face. I sighed, focusing on him. "Sorry about my friends. All the blood's going to their heads, and it's probably messing with their brains."

"Hey!" said May.

"So please. Let us down. We can talk about this rationally, once we have our feet on solid ground." The pixie didn't look convinced. I took a deep breath. "All right, you want me to swear? I'll swear. I swear by oak and ash and rowan and thorn that we did not come here intending harm. I swear by root and branch and rose and tree that none will raise a hand against you, unless hands are raised against us."

The pixie hesitated before turning and jabbing his spear at the rest of the flock. The pixies abandoned their swarming to come and circle around him, their various glows blending into a single off-white glow. A flurry of high-pitched exchanges followed. It seemed like every pixie had an opinion on the matter—that, or they just really enjoyed yelling at each other.

"Toby? What's happening?" asked Quentin.

"The pixies are deciding whether to let us go," I said. "I think."

"Or maybe they're getting ready to eat us," said May dolefully.

"Oh, *swell*," said Danny.

The pixies seemed to come to an agreement. Most of the flock flew toward the far wall, getting clear of our cocoons. The blue pixie turned to point his spear at the doorway, barking something that sounded very much like a command.

"Okay, he's doing something . . ." I said.

The sound of feet running along the ceiling heralded the return of the bogies—conveniently still shaped like giant spiders. They were smaller now, only about the size of terriers, which wasn't all that much of an improvement. Two of them ran down the length of my body, waving their serrated forelimbs at my face. I took a sharp breath, willing myself not to scream. I think of myself as pretty tough. That doesn't mean I appreciate having giant spiders clinging to me while I'm tied up and helpless to get away from them.

"He's calling his spider buddies to come and eat us," said May. "Good job, Toby."

The pixie barked another long string of squeaky commands . . . and the bogies started chewing through the cocoons. I let out a slow breath, closing my eyes. "Oh, good," I said. "It worked."

Danny was still swearing when we began dropping toward the floor.

THE BARGHESTS PRESSED themselves against Danny's legs, growling deep in their throats. Danny wasn't actually growling, but he didn't look much happier than the Barghests did. That was understandable. We were completely surrounded by bogies—most still shaped like giant spiders, although a few had transformed into less mentionable things—while the pixies zipped around us in an ever-shifting circle. The blue pixie remained stationary, hovering in front of me with his arms folded across his chest.

I brushed some stray cobwebs out of my hair, offering the pixie a respectful nod. "It's good to be back on the ground." I didn't know for sure that the prohibition against giving thanks applied to pixies, but I was trying to be polite, and that meant I wasn't going to risk it.

"Now what?" muttered May.

"I'll let you know when I figure it out," I replied. The pixie glared at me. "Sorry! Sorry. We don't negotiate with pixies very often."

He unfolded his arms, chattering rapidly at me.

I sighed. "I'm sorry. I don't understand you."

The pixie repeated himself, more slowly. He was clearly making an effort to be understood.

"None of us speak . . . uh, pixie," I said. "How about this? I'll try to guess what you're asking for, and you'll let me know when I get it right. Is that okay?"

The pixie nodded.

"Good enough. I, uh . . . Do you want us to leave?" The pixie didn't react. "Do you want us to let you leave?" The pixie scowled.

"Ask him if he wants to know how you're going to keep your promise," said Quentin.

I turned to blink at him. "Good call." Looking back to the pixie, I asked, "Is that what you want?"

The pixie nodded again, more vigorously. The motion of the swarm slowed, all their eyes focusing in on me at once. This was clearly important to them . . . and really, I couldn't blame them. It's hard for people that small to find places where they can let their guard down—and the longer I spoke to the pixies, the easier it became to think of them as people. I didn't understand a word he said, but he understood me, and in Faerie, that's better than you sometimes get.

"I'm supposed to be in charge here," I said, slowly. "That means this knowe is mine. I have my own people to protect, and they need to be here if they're going to receive that protection. Another promise. If you'll let me claim this place, I will do my best to give you the same protection that I give to them. No one will hurt you here. No one who comes here will be allowed to hurt you. Not on my watch." The bogies chittered. "That means *all* of you, as long as you can extend the same courtesy to my subjects. You don't attack them, and they won't attack you."

The pixie dipped a little lower in the air, glow brightening. Then, abruptly, he turned and zipped out of the room, leaving me staring dumbly at the spot where he'd been.

"Either you just messed up bad, or . . . actually, I don't got an *or*," said Danny. "Should we be running?"

"I'm considering it," I said. "Give it a minute."

The four of us stepped closer together as the seconds ticked by, the majority of the pixies still circling. May was indestructible and Danny was tough as a rock; Quentin and I didn't share those advantages. If the pixies and the bogies decided to attack in earnest, we were going to have problems.

I was getting ready to suggest we start moving when the pixie returned, clutching a chunk of rose quartz the size of a duck's egg to his chest. He flew to a stop in front of me, holding out the rock. It glistened, gleaming from within and putting out a silent sound that somehow managed to serve the purpose of a spell's magical signature. It was the knowe. He was trying to hand me the knowe.

There was only one response to that offering. "Okay," I said, and took it.

Goldengreen shuddered around us again, the motion still feeling very much like a dog trying to shake off a flea. May yelped, staggering backward into Danny, who caught her casually and held her in place with one massive hand. I barely noticed. I was too busy trying to sort through the sensations that were crashing through me, flowing first through the stone, and then—in a moment of transition that was barely a transition at all—through the entire knowe.

Goldengreen was one of the first knowes opened in San Francisco. Evening didn't open it. A red-haired woman I didn't recognize did the opening . . . working in tandem with a blonde woman I *did* recognize. Amandine. My mother. No wonder the Queen was willing to give the knowe to me. She knew it would talk to me, even if it wouldn't take me. Fae law says that changelings can't inherit, but a knowe knows the bloodline that pried it open in the first place. The realization only had a moment to register. Then the shape of the knowe as a whole was slamming into me, sending me to my knees. The stone rolled free of my hand. The images flashing through my head didn't stop.

Amandine didn't stay with the knowe. She helped the red-haired woman open it, and then she left, leaving Goldengreen to grow under a single custodianship. The redhead left, replaced by an unfamiliar Daoine

Sidhe who was replaced, in turn, by Evening Winterrose. Her arrival signaled the descent of the knowe. It was thriving before she came, filled with people and with life. All that ended after Evening, and the knowe fell into a long twilight that ended only when she died and it was sealed away, forbidden to Faerie.

And then the pixies came, and the bogies, and made the knowe their home. It *liked* them. It liked that it was needed, that it was *wanted*. For the first time in over a hundred years, Goldengreen had something to protect. That was why it was fighting us. It wanted its inhabitants to be safe.

I bit my lip, hard enough to draw blood. It was a moment's work to raise my hand and wipe the blood away, touching it to the floor. The pressure of the memories decreased, even as I felt my connection to the knowe grow stronger. "I promise," I whispered. "I am not Evening. I *promise*."

There was a momentary pause, as if the knowe were holding its breath. Then two things happened at the same time: The images stopped coming.

And the lights came on.

"THAT WAS A nice trick," said May, sitting next to me on the edge of the broken fountain in the main courtyard. Danny leaned against the wall, while Quentin sat to my other side. It was a comfortable moment, even with all the cleaning that we knew was waiting just ahead.

The pixies swarmed around us, picking up bits of broken cobblestone and whisking away cobwebs with quick sweeps of their wings. The bogies were nowhere in evidence; probably lurking in the shadows, waiting for someone they could jump out at and terrify. They were going to be waiting for a long time. After the day I'd had, my threshold for terror was very, very high.

At least the lights that were burning now were powered by magic, and not captive pixies. The pixie-power lights must have been purely decorative. Which didn't make them any less horrible, but meant we weren't going to be forced to deal with installing a new lighting system while we were doing everything else.

"It worked, didn't it?" I asked. I could still feel Goldengreen at the back of my head, but it was fading quickly. The knowe was willing to talk to me, even willing to tolerate me—that didn't mean that it was mine. The

Queen had given me these lands. The lands themselves were still reserving judgment.

"Next time, risk somebody else's neck," suggested Danny amiably. "Like, I dunno, the Queen's. Bring her next time."

"Yeah, there's a real life-extender." I snorted, leaning over to ruffle Quentin's hair. "Besides, now we have a built-in workforce to get all the crap down from the ceilings."

"You're going to make us clean, aren't you?" asked Danny.

"And repair, and replace, and probably paint." I stood. "Now that we have the doors open, let's go beg the local nobles to lend us all their Hobs and Bannicks."

"I'll go for beer and pizza," said May.

"I'll drive her," said Danny.

Quentin sighed. "I'll get a mop."

"Good call," I said, and grinned before I started for the nearest exit. The bogies slipped out of the shadows, joining the pixies as they followed me all the way to the door, wings buzzing and legs tapping against the floor. Reclaiming Goldengreen was going to take a lot of work, and a lot of favors from the local hearth-fae community, but it was going to be worth it. Changelings and pixies have at least one thing in common: it's rare that we have places where we're safe. Goldengreen was an opportunity to change that.

With all the time I've spent feeling like I was on the outside, looking in, it was going to be nice to finally have a place I could say, with absolute conviction, was my home. The giant horror movie spiders, well . . .

Those were just a bonus.

The Path

S. J. ROZAN

"The Trent Museum," I sighed to my friend, the Spirit of the South Mountain, "refuses to return my head."

"You are wearing your head." If mountain spirits can be said to have a weakness, it is this penchant for stating the obvious. "Furthermore, you are a ghost. Even if you desire a second head for reasons you have not explained, the head you speak of, if it has gone off somewhere from which it must be returned, is clearly corporeal. Were it to be returned, you would have no ability to use it." They also tend to expound at length on any topic before them.

"It is not, literally, my head," I clarified. "I speak only out of a sense of attachment, a spiritual obstacle of which I daily struggle to rid myself, now no less than when I lived. The hermit monk Tuo Mo, my most recent incarnation, who died one hundred and three years ago as you might remember—"

South Mountain Spirit shrugged. Flocks of birds arose squawking from his trees, to settle once again when the tremor subsided. "Time has a different meaning to me," he said.

"Yes, of course." I watched a last edgy bird circle, finally fluttering onto a branch. "In any case, the body of Tuo Mo has returned to dust long since; and that dust (including, of course, the dust that had been the head) has reentered the cycle of existence. The head I mention is that of the Buddha statue in my cave."

"Ah, yes. One of the many carved from the sandstone cliff by monks such as yourself? I have always wondered, actually, why Cliff Spirit permitted that."

"From reverence for the Buddha, I would imagine."

"You have never asked him?"

"He's rather forbidding, not approachable like yourself."

"And you, even as a ghost, retain the timidity of the little monk you once were." Sunlight bathed his slopes and a light breeze rustled the trees thereon.

"I'm glad I provide you with amusement," I said, attempting a grand air of dignity. The trees danced even more merrily. "But yes." I deflated. "It is as you say: here in the spirit realm I retain all the flaws I had in my last life as a man. It is quite disheartening."

"Never mind about that," said my friend, who, craggy and precipitous though he may sometimes be, is often also gentle. "We were discussing your head."

"The statue's head," I said, only too happy to turn away from consideration of my own flaws. "Yes. Well, the cave in which I lived as a hermit monk contains a large carving of the Buddha, created by monks seven centuries ago. From it, shortly before I died, an expedition from the Trent Museum, in New York City, America, removed the head."

"Did they? For what reason?" Though once familiar with these events, South Mountain Spirit nevertheless required some prompting of his memory. Spirits of Place are universally better at being remembered than at remembering.

"Do you not recall their arrival?" I inquired.

"Vaguely, I do. A loud and unpleasant bunch, with growling vehicles, clanging pots, and boisterous voices, building smoky fires larger than they needed. They came to your caves from the north, however, and did not approach any closer than my foothills, so I did not consider them of consequence. Over the course of millions of years, you understand, one sees so many things."

"Yes, I imagine."

"In fact, a similar group has arrived at your caves now, I believe? Sometime in the last decade, if I am not mistaken . . ." Mists gathering, he drifted into reverie.

"Six months ago. You are correct."

The mists thinned, stretching apart. "They are different, however, I think. More respectful, surely?"

"Yes. They have come for another purpose. They are here to restore the caves."

"What does that mean?"

"To make things as they were."

"Why would one want things as they were? Or expect them to be so?" My friend gave me an uncomprehending look. Fog, thicker than the mists of a moment since, began to gather at his brow. He is the spirit of an ever-changing mountain, whose trees grow, leaf, and fall, whose waterfalls break rocks from boulders and, washing them into streams, alter their courses. I knew at once this was a concept he would never grasp.

"It is a notion of men," I said, an explanation I have often used in conversations since entering the spirit realm. At first I had been astonished to hear myself, not because the phrase is incorrect, but because conversation itself was an activity I, as a man, had hardly been capable of; and explanation or correction, never. Spirits, I have found to my surprise, are much less terrifying than men.

"Ah, I see," said South Mountain Spirit, the fog lifting. Humans, with their dissatisfactions, rushings-about, and simultaneous attempts to change some things and prevent others from changing, are inexplicable to most Spirits of Place. Thus South Mountain Spirit accepted this pronouncement, if not as the elucidation he sought, then as the explanation for why such elucidation was not forthcoming. "In any case," he said, "we were not discussing this new expedition of men. Our subject, as I have had to remind you once already, was the Buddha head." Spirits of Place, as they are tied to very specific objects of the physical world, can on occasion be doctrinaire.

"Indeed," I agreed. "Well, apparently the Emperor of China"—again, the fog began to gather, so I reminded him—"at the time, our secular ruler."

"Oh. Yes, of course. Is he no longer?"

"The Emperor died long ago. Long in human terms, I mean. We are now ruled by"—I knitted my brow, as I do not fully comprehend the meaning of this myself—"the government."

"Ah." Seeing my confusion, South Mountain Spirit said, "Another notion of men?"

"Precisely."

Essentially uninterested in men, he did not request further illumination, but waited for me to continue my tale.

"The Emperor," I said, "had, it seems, given permission for the expedition from the Trent Museum, in New York City, America, to remove from our caves whatever items they cared to carry off. This exalted art, the Emperor explained, would be better looked after—and would more strongly redound to the glory of China—in a museum in America than on the walls of a cave in the desert."

South Mountain Spirit considered that. "What is a museum?"

"As far as I understand, though my appreciation of these concepts is poor, it is a building in which people place beautiful things."

"For what reason?"

"To look at, I believe."

"As in the case of monks' caves and temples, as aids to meditation?"

"I do not believe so, though I can offer no other explanation."

"Personally," he said, as gusts of wind came up and tossed the branches on his slopes, "I have never understood the need for any of it." A family of deer, startled by the sudden breeze, bounded across a brook. "Are not my forests and rivers beauty enough? The layers of red rock on North Mountain, the pale sands of the desert?" The winds eased. "I apologize. You are here to tell a story. Pray go on. The Emperor, you were saying, permitted the removal of many objects, including this head with which you are now concerned."

I shrugged, which had little effect on the wildlife. "Possibly Explorer Trent and his expedition left behind some indication of their gratitude in the Emperor's coffers; who am I to know? In any case, our monastery, which seven hundred years ago had housed a thousand monks—"

"I remember those days! You do not, I believe?"

"No." It is unlikely I was there in that incarnation. In any case, as with all ghosts, the only incarnation I remember, of the hundreds (or, in the case of one as hapless as I, no doubt thousands) I have lived through, is the most recent.

"Such chanting," South Mountain Spirit said joyously, the sun glittering off his watercourses. "Drumming, and bells, and dancing, bright prayer flags snapping in the wind! Some monks made the journey as far as myself, to perform rites and hang prayer flags from tree to tree across my valleys. You used to do that, when Tuo Mo lived. By then you were the only one."

"Yes." I smiled, remembering the three days' walk from my hermit cave to South Mountain, sandals slapping the desert trail, prayer flags rolled in my monk's bundle. "It seemed the proper thing to do, though it was a difficult journey. It is easier to visit with you now that I am incorporeal."

South Mountain Spirit, who has always been incorporeal but who cannot, of course, leave South Mountain, was here faced with yet another concept he did not understand. He began to brood. I have learned not to approach him when thick clouds are gathering, so I waited. As usual, his mood changed rapidly. "Continue," he instructed after a few minutes, his brow clearing. "I am interested."

"I'm gratified to hear it," I told him. "As I say, the monastery had once been large and bustling; but by the time I came to live there, it was greatly reduced in size, and when the expedition arrived, we were eight small monks. We chanted and prayed while they chopped and pried. Attachment to the things of this world, our abbot daily reminded us, is one of the chief impediments on the spiritual path. We watched them remove our statues and altar cloths, and tried to think of it as a blessing, an opportunity to practice detachment."

"Were you successful?"

"Those who were spiritually mature did succeed, to varying degrees. In fact I hear our abbot went on to become a bodhisattva. But I, sadly, was not far enough along the path to be able to use this lesson. I was unable to rid myself of a strong attachment to these objects, and a powerful desire to see them remain. This attachment created in me a great sense of loss when the objects were taken away. None more so than the Buddha head."

"That is unfortunate."

"More than you know." I sighed again. "Now: at the time the expedition arrived, I was ill."

"Tuo Mo, your incarnation, was ill, you mean."

"Yes, exactly." I attempted to keep my patience with this literal-mindedness, which was, after all, merely his nature. "And a few days before the Trent expedition left, Tuo Mo died."

"Freeing you, as a spirit, to continue your journey along the path." He peered at me and dark clouds began to gather again on his brow.

"Yes," I said, "I think you begin to understand."

"You," he said portentously, thunder rumbling, "are still here."

Mournfully, I said, "I am."

He paused in reflection. "The spirits of humans," he spoke slowly, "remain in this spirit realm for forty days before assuming a new incarnation. As I mentioned, I am not very precise about the smaller divisions of time, but are we not well beyond your forty days?"

"We are one hundred and three years beyond my forty days. Time, as you say, has a different meaning to you. But even a Spirit of Place can no doubt see that, though I have departed the worldly realm, I cannot continue my journey through the cycle of existence, arriving eventually, as all sentient beings will, at Buddhahood, if I cannot leave this spirit realm to be reborn."

"Well," he demanded, "why have you not left, then?"

"I cannot." I shook my head with sorrow. "Three days before I died, the expedition removed the head of the Buddha statue from my cave. This saddened me; and, unknown to me at the time, caused great uproar. Not in the realm of the living, where we monks continued chanting and praying. But among the cave spirits, I later learned, there arose much consternation. The statue, you see, had from the beginning been the guardian of the spirits of all the other images painted and carved on the walls: not only the humans, but the horses, the foxes, the tigers and cranes and peacocks. With the head gone, the statue was incomplete, and therefore unable to perform its function. Demons began to gather. My cave, formerly a peaceful retreat, became fear-filled, the air sharp with anxiety. The image spirits joined together in an attempt to keep the demons at bay. They held them off for a time, but it was clear that they would not be able to continue until the coming of the Buddha of the Future."

"And if they failed?"

"Demons would flood the cave. The spirits would flee, leaving behind the images, which, uninhabited, would start immediately to deteriorate.

The demons, of course, would gleefully hasten that process, cracking statues and peeling paint from walls. The labor of centuries of monks to create and maintain a place whose purpose was to assist men along the spiritual path would come to an end."

"An unfortunate outcome," South Mountain Spirit rumbled, "as men do appear to need assistance."

"Oh, yes, most certainly. Now, I knew nothing of this, of course, at the time of my departure from the realm of men. I left the body of Tuo Mo and presented myself to the Lord of the Underworld. His scribes showed him the accounting of my virtues and imperfections. He pored over their scrolls, finally turning his terrifying visage to me. 'You have come at an opportune time!' he thundered. I must tell you, I have met the Lord of the Underworld a thousand times now, and he frightens me anew each time."

"I believe that is his function, is it not?"

"It is, and he performs his duties with enthusiasm. While I anxiously awaited instructions as to my next incarnation, he glowered silently, taking much longer than usual. Finally he roared, 'Ghost of Tuo Mo, you will be given a task to fulfill!'

"Hearing this, at first I was excited: Did it mean I had made enough spiritual progress in Tuo Mo's lifetime to move on to a higher realm? Was I now one small step closer to the enlightenment I so dearly sought? Alas, as it turned out, that was not the case.

" 'The spirits in your cave are in a state of great distress!' he howled. 'They have lost their guardian and will soon be at the mercy of a cloud of demons. Ghost of Tuo Mo, why did you not attempt to stop the removal of the Buddha head?'

" 'I? The expedition—the Emperor—our abbot—I was a small monk—' I'm afraid I squeaked, shivering before him. 'I could not have prevented it.'

" 'You did not try! Who are you to know what effect your efforts might have had? But throughout this life, you were cowardly, Ghost of Tuo Mo. You were terrified of these strangers, you who trembled to speak in the presence of your brother monks. So terrified that you fell ill when the expedition arrived. And now you have died!'

"I hung my head. 'I did not intend to die, my Lord.'

" 'What care I for your intention? The expedition has removed the

Buddha head, and you have died. And as though those events were not enough, before you left the worldly realm the removal of the head created in you, Ghost of Tuo Mo, vast stores of attachment and regret that you were unable to resolve.' He leaned forward, eyes burning. 'Can you deny these things?'

"I could not. The Lord of the Underworld settled himself on his throne once more and continued. 'You must expiate these imperfections and the cave spirits must be protected. You will not move on from this realm in the usual forty days. You will instead return to your cave and become the new guardian!' "

At this point in my story I was surprised to hear South Mountain Spirit interrupt, ringing with laughter that echoed down his gullies. "Yes, now I remember your telling me this! It was the first time you visited me, soon after you arrived in this realm. How funny it struck me. The little round monk, he who quivered if required to speak to his fellows, charged with defending lion spirits from underworld demons."

"Yes, well, it has been very hard work," I sniffed. "As both you and the Lord of the Underworld pointed out, I am not particularly well suited to it. However, through my anxiety and fear, I have done it to the best of my meager abilities, and the benevolent deities have aided me, for my cave has remained a refuge from the chaos, trouble, and disorder of the world outside it. Though human visitors have not been many, still some have come, and after spending time in meditation, they have left with some small addition to their store of wisdom."

"In that case," cheered South Mountain Spirit, "I say, well done!"

"Thank you," I said humbly. "But you can understand, now, my distress when I hear that the Buddha head will not be returning."

"No," said South Mountain Spirit, still sunny and unperturbed. "I cannot."

I attempted to control my exasperation, short temper being an unhelpful attribute along the path. "If the head does not return," I explained, "I cannot leave this realm. I am to be Cave Guardian until and unless the Buddha statue can resume its former role. If it cannot, I will be here until the coming of the Buddha of the Future!"

Slowly, the sunlight faded behind collecting clouds. After a long, misty pause, South Mountain Spirit spoke. "I cannot, of course, feel the source of your unhappiness. It involves the flow of time, meaningless to me.

However, you are my friend, and I am distressed to see you in this state." Rain began pelting from the black clouds piled along his brow. "How do you know the head will not be returning?"

"The chief of the restoration project is a man called Leonard Wu. He is from New York City, America, but has been sent here with the consent of the government in Beijing. Leonard Wu was surprised and delighted to see the state of the images in my cave. He had anticipated, he told his chief assistant, Qian Wei, that the destruction caused by years of neglect would be much worse. Neglect! If only he knew how hard I have been working!"

"Why don't you tell him?"

As a ghost, of course, I do not have a heart; nevertheless, something in my spectral chest began to pound. "I? Speak? To a man?"

"Oh, of course, how foolish of me! The timid little monk." Again he laughed.

"Leonard Wu, however," I managed to go on, "has been speaking with the director of the Trent Museum, in New York City, America, throughout his time here. In the human realm this type of conversation is called 'negotiating.'"

"I believe humans 'negotiate' my paths. Is it the same?"

"Yes. It involves understanding, careful attention, and compromise. Still, it is not always successful."

"That is true on my paths, also. I try to be of help, pointing out places where they should and should not step. Those places are clear and obvious, it seems to me. However, often the humans cannot understand me, and sometimes, they fall."

"Human understanding is, alas, limited. The director of the Trent Museum, for example, failed utterly to understand the importance of the return of the head. This," I said, "even though, as you do here on your paths, I tried to help."

"You? In what way?"

"I became quite excited when I realized what was being discussed. The return of the head! My next life, finally looming! When it first appeared that negotiations were not proceeding well, I screwed up my courage and began hovering close to Leonard Wu. After some time, though I was trembling, I did what I thought I would never do: I attempted to whisper in his ear."

"*You* were trembling? You are the ghost! Leonard Wu is supposed to be trembling!" Again, the laughter of wind in the trees.

"As you mentioned," I said miserably, "my faults are no fewer in this realm than in the human one. It is difficult to understand how to correct them."

"And it is difficult for me to understand humans," South Mountain Spirit said affably. "No less so your spirits than your fleshly incarnations. So, my friend. Apparently this head is important enough to you that you overcame your bashfulness."

"I have not overcome it. It continues to haunt me. Yes, yes, I know, I am meant to be the one who haunts!"

He did not reply, though a small rockslide tumbled down one of his shoulders.

"The head's return is, however, as you say, very important to me. So I forced myself to approach Leonard Wu. But I could not speak. Incoherent from nervousness, I managed a croaking whisper. He shook his head, looking around as though he suddenly recognized nothing. Then he continued in his work. I tried and tried, but I could not make words come to me. Finally he left my cave that day, complaining of headache."

"Then he has not come to understand the importance of the return of the head?"

"In fact he has, though not through me. Leonard Wu, as it happens, is very fond of cats. It has given him joy to take special care with a painting on the north wall, wherein the Buddha allows himself to be eaten by starving tigers. The Spirit of the Mother Tiger, who has been of great help to me in defending the cave—and who, with reason, is not impressed by my prowess—has become close to Leonard Wu. She, more brave than I, has whispered to him, has told him stories of the way the cave once was, how things were here when the statue was whole. He will stop in his work when she speaks, dust-brush in hand, and stare at the painting or carving he is cleaning. Soon after she began whispering to him, he redoubled his efforts for the return of the head."

"That sounds quite hopeful."

"Oh, yes! I could hardly restrain myself from howling through the camp. All the cave spirits felt the same. We were so eager, so optimistic!"

"But from what you say, your hopes have not been borne out."

"No. Leonard Wu has failed. This morning he told his chief assistant, Qian, that the head would not be sent back. Together they stood mournfully regarding the statue, on which they have been hard at work in preparation for the reunion with its head. The assistant asked if that was a final decision. Leonard Wu said it was. I was quite stricken to hear this news, and hurried here for the consolation of a visit with you, old friend."

"I am honored," South Mountain Spirit gravely said. We sat together in silence for some time as his streams tumbled and his trees waved. As always, I felt comforted by his presence. "But surely," he finally said, "once you have taken solace in my wooded hillsides and rocky tors, your unhappiness must spur you on to further action?"

I blinked up at him. "Action? I am the ghost of a simple monk. My entire earthly life was spent in contemplation, in a cave to which I took in order to avoid 'action.' Whispering in the ear of Leonard Wu was beyond my abilities. What action could there be for me to take? No." I shook my head. "All that remains for me is to return to my cave and continue my efforts to protect the multitudinous spirits there, until time itself stops."

I felt quite low. South Mountain Spirit, however, did not, even in sympathy, share my mood. A splendid sunset broke through the glowering clouds encircling his peak. "Clearly, my friend, you must go yourself to the Trent Museum, in New York City, America, and retrieve the head."

GLEAMING SUNLIGHT ILLUMINATED the vast vertical cliffs that were the buildings of New York City, America. I stared up at them. Though I had only the faintest understanding of their materials—steel and glass—and though they were certainly larger by far than any manmade structures I had ever encountered, I had lived the only life I could recall in a cave in the side of a towering cliff. As fearful as I had been when considering this journey, I found myself strangely reassured by the sight of these looming structures.

Similarly familiar were the vehicles racing through the valleys between the towers. Though countless in number and moving without horses or oxen, they seemed to me not unlike the vehicles used by both expeditions to my monastery. At the beginning of my journey I had even ridden in one, hovering beside Leonard Wu as he drove away from the caves. Thus neither the structures nor the vehicles of New York City, America, were sources of alarm.

I was, however, not entirely comfortable there. What took me aback were the people.

My incarnation as a hermit monk born in a tiny desert village had, of course, limited my opportunities to traffic among my fellow humans, and my inclination toward timidity had, if anything, embraced those limits. I understood from conversations around the cooking fire between Leonard Wu and the members of his expedition that Beijing, and likewise New York City, were inhabited by vast crowds of people. Therefore I had thought it prudent to attempt to stretch my small imagination to the utmost, in order to ready myself for what I might find. I considered the flocks of birds that migrated over South Mountain in fall and spring. I contemplated the roiling of the fish in the monastery fish pond as I fed them. I meditated on the countless industrious ants, hurrying to and fro between anthills on the desert pathways. Once my journey with Leonard Wu began, I found myself among progressively larger numbers of people, first in the nearby village where Leonard Wu stopped for a meal, next in the town, and then in the airport where we boarded a plane to Beijing. In the Beijing airport, much larger than the one we had flown out of, I was unsettled by the crowds and stayed close to Leonard Wu's side. Still, by the time we reached New York City, America, I felt confident I would take the situation in stride.

As it turned out, I was woefully unprepared.

In New York City, America, human beings swarmed this way and that, seemingly not in concert, but impressively able to avoid plowing each other over. The bright colors of their clothing, their various ages and sizes, and the hues of their skin were multitudinous almost beyond my comprehension. I gaped, and stared, and gawked. "Oh, my friend," I whispered, thinking of the Spirit of the South Mountain, "if only you could see this sight!"

But he, on the other side of what I now realized was, in many senses, a very large world, could not. My words were heard only by the spirits in the streets of New York City, who, flitting along the roadways, perched in trees or on building ledges high above, or resting against lampposts and on stone walls, greeted me, observed me, or ignored me as was their wont.

I, of course, had no need to be in the streets at all, headed at a human pace for the Trent Museum, drifting beside the purposefully striding Leonard Wu. Being a ghost, I could have left my monastery cave in western China and appeared instantaneously at any location I desired.

That, however, was not the plan.

I had been quite astonished, and not at all pleased, when the Spirit of the South Mountain had proposed that I travel to New York City, America.

"I am the ghost of a hermit monk, born ten kilometers from the monastery in which I spent my life! The journey here to South Mountain is the longest I've ever made, either in body or as a spirit! How can I go to America?"

"It is precisely that you are now a ghost that makes this journey possible."

"Possible . . . well, yes. But . . ."

"As I said earlier, my friend: you are as timid now as when you lived."

"Yes, all right, that's undeniable. But as you also said: the Buddha head is of the physical realm, and I am not. If I were to travel all the way to America, and find it, I could not bring it back."

"That is the reason you must not go alone."

"But go with whom? You cannot go! Mother Tiger Spirit, the fox or peacock spirits? They are as ethereal as I am!"

"You will go with Leonard Wu."

Surprised into speechlessness, I had sat silent as South Mountain Spirit's winds began to blow. This happens often when he is thinking.

"Leonard Wu also desires the return of the head, does he not? You will go back to the monastery caves and discuss the situation with Mother Tiger Spirit. She will persuade him to undertake a trip to New York City, America, to retrieve it."

"Even if she is successful and he decides to go," I said anxiously, "the director of the Trent Museum has already refused to return the head. How will Leonard Wu convince him otherwise?"

"What happens then will happen then. You will be in New York City, America, with Leonard Wu. Between you, you will find the answer."

Terrified at the prospect, I tried to persuade South Mountain Spirit that this idea was not a good one, that I would not be able to accomplish the mission, that it was bound to meet with failure.

"Everything you say may be true," my friend had said equably. "But answer this: what have you to lose?" I had no rejoinder. Moreover, I realized, even had I an answer, there is never any point in arguing with a mountain spirit. They will not be moved.

I bade a glum farewell to South Mountain Spirit, who was bathed now in a tranquil, fading sunset, and returned to the monastery. As had been true for some weeks, the cliffside caves were the scene of much hubbub. The restorers' hushed, delicate, painstaking work on the paintings and

carvings in the caves' interiors was balanced by the loud and messy sawing and hammering of the construction crews as they built temporary
walls for protection and walkways and scaffolding for access. Clouds of
dust kicked up by their vehicles engulfed men and tents before Desert
Wind Spirit cleared them away. (She is mercurial and arbitrary, but not
malicious, and she had told me she was quite enjoying all the bustling
about, so she was trying to be helpful.)

I made my way back to my cave, there to find Leonard Wu. He was,
as usual, working with great care, as he cleaned the painting of the bodhi
tree on the cave's rear wall. I stood beside him for a time, watching his
precise dabbing and brushing. Mother Tiger Spirit was curled at his feet.

"Mother Tiger Spirit"—I made an attempt to speak with an air of
authority—"Leonard Wu must go to the Trent Museum, in New York
City, America, and personally request the return of the Buddha head."

Mother Tiger Spirit half-opened an eye and looked at me. "What?"

I repeated my statement.

She licked a lazy paw and rubbed at her ears. "Why?"

"South Mountain Spirit has suggested it."

"The director of the Trent Museum, in New York City, America, has
already refused this request. How could Leonard Wu persuade him any
better if they were standing face to face?"

"South Mountain Spirit says"—I forced myself to continue—"I am
to go with him."

As with any feline, Mother Tiger Spirit's countenance does not reveal
her emotions. However, there was no mistaking her derision as she sat up
and roared, "You? The quaking monk, to travel to the ends of the earth?
With a man? What good will you be?"

"I may quake, but over the years I have managed to protect this cave
from demons—"

"With the help of a good many of us, may I remind you! And from
demons, not men! I saw you attempting to whisper to Leonard Wu. A very
amusing sight. If you go to New York City, America, with him, he will
not even know you are there."

Leonard Wu stopped his hand in mid-dab. He looked left, then right,
then shrugged and continued removing millimeter by millimeter the dry
remains of some long-ago desert plant that had been sent by a demon to take
root on the painting. I had prevented it, but what a struggle that had been.

"Nevertheless," I said, "Leonard Wu must go to America, and I must go with him. You and the other spirits must guard the cave assiduously while I am gone. And," I added, "you must persuade him to go."

"Because you dare not," she mocked.

"Yes," I admitted. "Mother Tiger Spirit, I am, if anything, even less convinced than yourself of the efficacy of this journey. Certainly I am not eager to undertake it. But the head will not be returning if we do nothing. Surely, the possibility of having your former guardian back must be an attractive one."

"Indubitably," she answered dryly.

"Then," I said, echoing my old friend, "what have we to lose?"

After fixing a long, unblinking stare on me, Mother Tiger Spirit, as cats will do, gave herself a thorough bath while taking time to think. I waited. After she was finished, she did not speak to me, but with a swish of her tail padded over to stand beside Leonard Wu.

"You must go to America," she told him. "To the Trent Museum, in New York City."

Leonard Wu put down his brush and, with a cloth, wiped his brow.

"You must speak to the director personally," Mother Tiger Spirit continued. "He does not understand the importance of the return of the head"—especially, I thought, to me—"but once you have explained it, he will."

Leonard Wu had picked up his brush, but now he paused in his work, again looking left and right.

"The statue," Mother Tiger Spirit said, "must be complete. You will tell the people at the Trent Museum, and they will understand, and you will return with the head and reinstall it on the statue. Think how grand it will look! Complete and majestic, towering in this cave as it did for six hundred years, before it was taken away! Before we were left with this fool of a monk for a guardian," she added.

Leonard Wu arose, putting down his brush and cloth. He walked around the headless statue in the center of the cave, to stand and look up at it from the front.

Mother Tiger Spirit bounded with him. "Majestic!" she roared. "Towering! Able once again to guard the myriad cave spirits from demons and fiends!" At that Leonard Wu frowned, looking, as South Mountain Spirit so often does, uncomprehending. "Towering." Mother Tiger Spirit hastened once again to tell him, now whispering in his ear. "Complete. Majestic beyond measure!"

Leonard Wu stood for a few moments longer, staring up at the headless Buddha statue. Then he spun around and left the cave, blinking in the sharp sunlight. I followed close beside him as he searched the camp for his chief assistant. "Qian!" he shouted, spotting the man. "I'm going to New York. This is ridiculous. I'm going to talk the Trent into giving us back that head."

I hastened to South Mountain to tell my friend of Leonard Wu's plans. He was delighted. "Now," he said to me, "you must go with him, and by that I mean you must accompany him on every step."

"Why?" I asked. "Even if I am to go, why can I not instantaneously appear at our destination, as I do when I come to visit you?"

"You must stay at his side as he travels among men." He was adamant, as mountain spirits often are. "It is my thought that perhaps you will become less alarmed in men's presence if you spend more time among them, so that when you arrive at your destination you will find yourself capable of speaking to Leonard Wu, and able therefore to assist him in his mission."

As always, I did what my friend instructed. Alas, what he hoped for did not occur. The journey, I will admit, was interesting. We traveled by vehicle, as I have said, and also by two airplanes. Having never, either as man or as spirit, been among any clouds beyond those on South Mountain, I was awed. I did not think South Mountain Spirit would look askance at my briefly leaving the side of Leonard Wu to converse with a Cloud Spirit or two. I greatly enjoyed these talks and learned many things, though the conversations were fleeting, as Cloud Spirits are constantly on the move. But hovering in the airplane's aisle as Leonard Wu ate, drank, read, and slept, I remained uncomfortable with the crush of people around, and the rest of our journey had not helped me in this regard.

Nevertheless, we were here. Now, with Leonard Wu navigating among numberless humans, and I among an equally countless host of wraiths, we arrived at the Trent Museum.

The building's exterior consisted of grand white stone blocks interrupted by large windows. Its interior was dark wood and white plaster, similar in some ways to the temple in the town where I was born, though

undeniably more grand. I gazed about, fascinated at the odd-shaped furniture, elaborate carpets, and unfamiliar paintings. Leonard Wu did not
spare them a glance. He spoke to a young man at a desk and was immediately escorted up the stairs to a bright antechamber. I hurried to catch
up. In the antechamber a young woman took over, knocking at a door
and admitting Leonard Wu, with me beside him, into a large, dim, car-
peted room.

The room contained many things: furniture, books, paintings. My
ghostly eyes ignored them all, fixing, the moment we entered, on that which
sat serenely on a plinth against the far wall: the Buddha head. I raced toward
it, Leonard Wu following almost as quickly. "Old friend!" I exclaimed.
Leonard Wu gazed at the head, leaning in to examine it, stepping back to
admire it. I said, "I am delighted to find you looking so well!"

Calmly, the Buddha head replied, "I have been well treated, Ghost of
Tuo Mo."

"You remember me?" I asked excitedly. "I am honored!"

"Of course I do. We sat together for endless hours in prayer and
meditation. Tell me, Ghost of Tuo Mo, how goes it with the cave spirits?
I have been concerned for them since I was removed."

"They are well." I proceeded to tell him all that had occurred since
he had come to America. He interrupted once—"*You?*"—and laughed
merrily, sounding not unlike South Mountain Spirit.

"Yes," I concluded. "I. I have done my best, and the cave has remained
a small island of peace in the chaos of the world. But the task has been
tiring and I am longing to move on to my next life. This gentleman is
Leonard Wu. He is responsible for the restoration of the caves. We have
come to take you back."

"Have you? That would be quite satisfying."

Now my attention was drawn from the head to the opening of the
door. The large round eyes and unruly brown hair of the pale man who
entered looked familiar to me and for a moment I thought I knew him.
Then I realized that was because he so resembled Explorer Trent, whom
I had seen at my monastery caves one hundred and three years ago.

"Dr. Wu!" the pale man said, coming forward to shake Leonard Wu's
hand with both of his own. "I'm Walter Trent. This is an honor! Your
reputation precedes you. Please sit down."

Leonard Wu did so, and the other man sat also, in a matching maroon leather chair. Leonard Wu said, "I'm pleased to meet you, Mr. Trent. Thank you for seeing me."

"Of course! How goes the restoration in China?"

"Very well, thanks. That's why I'm here, in fact. I'll get straight to the point: I've come to ask in person for the return of the Buddha head from Cave Thirty-seven."

"Ah." The young Trent appeared crestfallen. "I was afraid of that. It's right here—you've seen it?" He gestured to the rear of the room.

"Yes, just now."

"Impressive, isn't it? Everyone notices it. It's always seemed . . . alive, to me. You might think it would make me nervous, staring like that, but I actually like it. But I'm sorry you've taken so much trouble, coming all this way. I'm afraid I can't give it back to you."

"Because you like it?"

"No, no!"

From behind me, while the young man was searching for words with which to explain himself, came a growl: "Because he's an idiot!"

I turned. A large, rotund spirit wearing white whiskers, a stiff-collared shirt, and a vested suit hovered in the doorway. He drifted into the room, until he was beside me. "The boy's a lunkhead, that's the problem. Who're you?"

"Explorer Trent!" I stammered.

"No, I'm Trent." He peered at me through a glass attached to his jacket by a gold chain.

"Oh, yes, I know that. I'm sorry, I didn't mean—I'm just so surprised to see you!"

"Why? This's my house. And that's my idiot great-grandson. Wait, I know you. You're the monk from the cave where I got the Buddha head."

"I am the Ghost of Tuo Mo," I said. "Yes. Why are you still here?"

"Where? In the house? Can't I haunt my own house?"

"In the spirit realm. You must have died not long after I did. Why have you not moved on to your next life?"

"Have no idea what you're talking about. Next life. Didn't expect to be here this long, though, I'll grant you that. Thought I'd be getting some heavenly rest by now. Someone has to look after the place, though. Protect all this stuff from generations of nitwits."

I was fascinated. "Did the Lord of the Underworld not send you on to another incarnation?"

"Hmmm? I met some fat red-faced fool, I vaguely remember. Ranting and raving. Asked me if I had any idea where I was bound for. Told him, as long as my numbskull son was in charge of the collection, damned if I was going anyplace. He said fine, and he sent me back here." The spirit frowned. "Something like that, anyway."

"But as long as you are here, you cannot continue along the path."

"What path?"

"To enlightenment."

"Can't think what you're getting at. You're an odd one. Always were, if memory serves. What'd you say your name was? Moe? And what're you doing here, anyway?"

"I've come with Leonard Wu, to request the return of the Buddha head."

The spirit of Explorer Trent snorted. "Good luck."

"It is very important that the head return."

"It is? How come?"

"Until it does, I cannot continue on to my next life."

"Next life? Listen, you mean, whaddaya call it, reincarnation? That what we're talking about?"

"Precisely."

"Well, I'll be hornswoggled. You really get to come back as something else?"

"Every being does. Yourself included. I cannot hope for another life as any being better than a man, but I do hope to have the opportunity to be a better man than I was as Tuo Mo."

"You're making my head spin. And then what? Next man you are dies, you just go on like this forever?"

"For quite some time, hoping to gain wisdom with each life. Until finally, you have reached enlightenment and can meld into the not-made."

"The what?"

I was at a momentary loss, until I recalled something he had said. "Heavenly rest," I told him. "I think it would be like that."

"Oh? Sounds pretty good." He stroked his chin whiskers.

"You will be on the same path," I said. "Once you leave here."

"Hah. There's the rub. I can't leave until someone's in charge around here who's not a moron. When you look at these birdbrains, I think I have to plan on staying forever!"

"Please?"

He heaved a great sigh. "My son the idiot begat my grandson the jackass, who begat this simpleton here. Each one's worse than the one before him. I should've gotten out when I had the chance." He shook his head. "Can't leave now, though. Not one of them has a clue about anything in the collection. Best I can do is make sure everything's kept clean, gets repaired if it breaks, and stays together. That's why Walter here won't give you back the head. If I could've trusted any one of them even an inch I'd have let him make his own decisions about what stays and goes. But these imbeciles, they can't be allowed to think for themselves, because whatever they do, it'll be wrong! So I've drilled it into them: The collection stays together! Nothing leaves this house!"

"And you are remaining in this realm to make sure they behave correctly?" I tentatively inquired.

"You got it, Moe."

"But then . . . your next life . . . your path . . ."

"Does sound good, got to admit. Made some mistakes this time around, I don't mind telling you. That red-faced gent—what'd you call him, the Lord of the Underworld?—he pointed out a few. Might like a another chance, maybe see if I could correct 'em. But nothing to be done. Like I said before, can't leave now."

I regarded the ghost of Explorer Trent. Compassion stirred what would have been my heart, had I been corporeal. I remembered my attachment to the cloths and carvings in the monastery caves. Over the century of my guardianship of the spirits, those ties had loosened, until, I realized, I no longer gave a thought to any of these objects. In fact, as I contemplated them now, a hopeful warmth suffused me—an impossibility, of course, in my disembodied state, but nevertheless the sensation I felt I felt—at the thought that these works, having been spread willy-nilly around the world, might even now be aiding in their journeys beings who would never have reached the caves.

"You must let go of your attachment to these objects in your collection," I told Explorer Trent. "Or you cannot move on."

"Well, that's kind of the point, isn't it? That's why I'm here."

"But you cannot mean to remain."

"As long as dunderheads are in charge here, yes I do."

"As long as you remain here," I said, voicing a thought that was new but, I was suddenly sure, correct, " 'dunderheads' will be in charge."

"Eh? How's that?"

"Did you not say that each one is worse than the one before him? The Lord of the Underworld is clearly assigning, to be reborn in your family line, souls who, for whatever reason, must expiate the arrogance of pride— in their own intelligence and in their skills at decision making. Politicians, perhaps, or military commanders. They are reborn as directionless fools. As long as you remain attached to your collection, he will continue to send them here."

"That the way it is, huh? Well, as long as he sends 'em, I'll stay here and keep 'em from mucking things up!"

"You are not proposing to set yourself in opposition to the will of the Lord of the Underworld?"

"You think if I did, I couldn't take him down a peg or two?" The ghost of Explorer Trent swelled, then deflated. "Nah, really, that's not what I meant. But as long as all my stuff's here, and being watched over by morons, I don't think I can leave. No, I don't think so." He frowned, narrowing his eyes at me. "Wonder if I can help you out, though."

While we had been conversing, Leonard Wu and Walter Trent had been in discussions also. The ghost of Explorer Trent turned to look at them now, so I did the same.

"So do you see?" Walter Trent was inquiring anxiously of Leonard Wu. "It's not my decision. Everything of my great-grandfather's has to stay in the house."

"If I understand you correctly, though," responded Leonard Wu, "that's not written anywhere. It's not a legal or contractual obligation, I mean."

"Well, no." The young Trent shifted uncomfortably, provoking a snort from his great-grandfather's ghost. "But it's my mandate. Our mandate. Everyone's understood that, from the time my grandfather took over. It's the way it's always been."

"Wouldn't have been, if you hadn't all been muttonheads!" barked the ghost of the elder Trent. Walter Trent nervously rubbed the back of his neck.

"Well," said Leonard Wu, "the way it's been was suited to the times, maybe, but times change. Important artifacts are being sent back to their original sites all over the world these days. Restoration of patrimony is a big movement in the art and archaeology communities."

"Yes, I know. And I'd help if I could, I really would. The Fogg, in Boston, asked just the other day to borrow some bronzes for an exhibit they're doing. I'd love to send them, too." The younger Trent looked unhappy. "But I can't. I just don't feel I can make those decisions."

My heart, or whatever had been beating hopefully, sank. The head would not be returning? I would not be moving on to my next life?

The ghost of the senior Trent turned to me. "What do you say, Moe? This head really important to you?"

Miserably, I said, "It is."

"Make you happy if this half-wit here sent it back?"

"Yes." I allowed myself a tiny spark of hope. "Very happy."

"Well," said he. "Well." He stroked his whiskers, as before. Drifting across the room, he reached his great-grandson's side. He leaned down until his lips were at the young Trent's ear. I flinched involuntarily at the idea of approaching a man so closely. The ghost of Trent, who obviously did not suffer from such timidity, waited a moment before he spoke.

Or rather, he did not speak. He roared. *"GIVE THEM BACK THE HEAD!"*

Walter Trent nearly jumped out of his seat.

"Are you all right?" Leonard Wu inquired as the young man's face paled.

"Yes, yes, I'm fine." Walter Trent removed a cloth from his pocket and wiped his brow. "I'm subject to . . . attacks of some sort."

"Attacks!" growled the ghost of his great-grandfather. "Believe you me, I'd attack him if I could. You see what I'm saying? He hardly listens." He leaned to his great-grandson again, and this time he dropped his voice to an insinuating whisper. "Give them back the head, you boob, or I will personally put snakes in your trousers."

That was, of course, an empty threat. The ghost of Trent could no more handle actual snakes than I could the Buddha head. The only effect ghosts can have on humans is to frighten, inspire, or instruct them, and then only to the extent that the humans choose to allow.

Walter Trent, however, was obviously choosing to permit his great-grandfather's ghost a good deal of power. He swallowed, wiped his brow again, and stood. "Excuse me," he said to Leonard Wu. "I'm feeling faint."

"*Sit down!*" howled the ghost. "You're not leaving this room until you give that head back!"

Walter Trent dropped into his chair again. Leonard Wu was looking increasingly concerned.

"Now," said the ghost of Explorer Trent, "tell this nice archaeologist gent that you've changed your mind. Tell him he can have his head. Give the chief curator a call. Then you can go lie down."

Walter Trent's large eyes stared ahead of him. Slowly, he turned to Leonard Wu. "Do you know," he said, licking dry lips, "I may have been hasty. I believe it might be all right for me to return that head. If you're sure you want it?"

Leonard Wu's face lit up. "I certainly do!"

"All right." The young man blinked. "We'll draw up a formal agreement this afternoon, but for now, I'll just give the chief curator a call. That'll be enough to get him busy preparing the head for transport."

Leonard Wu began enthusiastically to thank Walter Trent; Walter Trent, weakly, insisted he had done nothing and was glad to help. I hovered, surprised and thrilled, beside the beaming ghost of the elder Trent. I was searching for words with which to express my gratitude when suddenly his head lifted.

"Uh-oh," he said. "Trouble at the loading dock. Another great-grandson in charge down there, as much of an idiot as this one. Got to go help out. You stay here, Moe, make sure this ninny gets it right." He spun and vanished.

"I . . ." But he was gone. So I did as instructed: I turned back to Leonard Wu and Walter Trent. Leonard Wu was smiling broadly, describing the beauty of the paintings and carvings in the monastery caves, inviting Walter Trent to come see them for himself. The young Trent, for his part, looked weak, but better than previously. Color was starting to return to his countenance, and he no longer sweated.

"I appreciate the invitation," he said, his voice still faint. "But a trip to China . . . I don't know . . . Here, let's get this process started." He pressed a button on a box on his desk. "Jerry? The big Buddha head up here in the drawing room—we're sending it back to China." A startled objection began to issue from the box, but Walter Trent cut it short. "Yes, I know, but that's what's happening. It's my responsibility and I can do this if I want to. Dr. Wu's coming down to give you the logistical details.

Thank you." He took his finger off the button and said to Leonard Wu, "Why don't you go ahead? I'll be right down. I just need a minute."

"Yes, of course." Leonard Wu rose. "I can't tell you how much we all appreciate this."

None more than myself, I thought, as he turned and left the room. I was on the verge of following. My task was completed; I had spoken convincingly to the ghost of the elder Trent, and thus the Buddha head would be returning to my cave. The cave spirits would be protected by a better guardian than I, and I would present myself once more to the Lord of the Underworld, to be sent on to another life. A most satisfactory ending.

As Leonard Wu walked through the door, though, I did not follow. An uncomfortable knowledge was beginning to take hold in my mind. I would soon be going on to another life, taking my next step along the path. But the ghost of Trent, who had helped me reach this longed-for day, would not. He was bound to remain in this realm, unable to advance spiritually, until the Lord of the Underworld ceased sending him fools to oversee the collection to which he was so tied. Which would not happen until his ties to his collection loosened.

I could see only one possible solution.

I hovered in my spot near the door, watching Leonard Wu trot happily down the stairs. I turned to my friend, the Buddha head. I said nothing, but he, as though he knew my mind, said, "You know it is right."

"It might fail. *I* might fail," I objected.

"Is that a reason not to try?"

No, I thought, terror is a reason not to try. But what must be done, must be done. My spectral heart pounding, I drifted across the room, nearing the young Trent. When I reached him, I found myself frozen, unable to move. And certainly, unable to speak.

"Continue," the head said calmly.

I leaned forward, as Trent's ghost had. I opened my mouth, but could produce nothing but a few croaking sounds. Walter Trent frowned and looked about.

"Continue," the Buddha head said once more.

I swallowed—how can a spirit's throat become so dry?—and, in a whisper so faint I was sure it would not be heard, said, "Walter Trent."

It was heard, however. The young man raised his head sharply, looking directly at me. I jumped. I glanced wildly at my friend the head, but he sat placidly silent.

I screwed up every ounce of courage I possessed. "Walter Trent," I whispered again, surprised to hear my words slightly stronger than before. "You must send the bronzes to the Fogg."

Walter Trent opened and closed his mouth.

"You must become a strong guardian of your great-grandfather's collection." I heard my own spectral voice but was incredulous at the idea that I was the one using it, even as I went on. "You must lend some items, and return others whence they came. You must allow scholars to come study pieces here in your rooms, and to remove them for further study."

The young Trent was shaking his head, over and over. Sweat had once again blossomed on his brow.

"I recognize your lack of confidence in your own judgment," I told him. "That is your lot in this life. You must do what I have instructed you nevertheless. Your action in the face of insecurity and fear will open new pathways for you. And also, for your great-grandfather, who needs to move on from this place." Walter Trent sat motionless, as pale as he had been previously. Then, haltingly, he began to stand. *Well*, I thought, *I've seen this done.* I gathered myself, and roared, *"Sit down!"*

Like a stone, he dropped into his chair.

I, meanwhile, hurried to flit back to his desk from across the room, where the force of my bellow had blown me. "You will shoulder your responsibilities!" I ordered him, in a voice only slightly shaking. "Do as I say!"

A still moment; then the young man minutely straightened. He ran a finger under his collar. With a deep breath, he pressed the button on his desk again. "Jerry? Dr. Wu down there? Good. And while you're getting things set with him, get this going, too: we're lending the Fogg those bronzes they asked for. Yes, Jerry," he answered the squawks from the box. "I'm coming right down."

Walter Trent stood, wiped the cloth along his brow, folded it carefully, and left the room.

Unable to move, I stared after him, until I heard my name calmly pronounced: "Ghost of Tuo Mo."

I darted to the back wall and spoke to the head. No; I hardly spoke, just stammered. "I . . . I . . ."

"Yes," the head replied serenely. "I think he will make an admirable guardian. As you have, my friend."

I found my voice and answered, "Thank you."

"I only speak the truth. What will you do now?"

I thought. "I will return to the caves. Leonard Wu does not need my company on his trip; he will have you. I believe I will be summoned by the Lord of the Underworld not long after you reach the caves and have been reinstalled. I would like an opportunity to bid farewell to the Spirit of the South Mountain."

"You will encounter him again on your journey," said the Buddha head. "More than once."

"I hope I do," I said. "As I hope I encounter you, also. But I will not remember. So in some sense, this is our leave-taking. Good-bye, my friend."

"Good-bye, Ghost of Tuo Mo. And," the head added, "thank you."

My spectral being infused with warmth from the Buddha head's parting words, I drifted down the staircase. I looked in on Leonard Wu and Walter Trent, deep in conference with three scholarly young people. The ghost of Explorer Trent was with them, also, looking astounded and pleased. I did not disturb them, but floated through the large wooden doors and out into the streets of New York City, America. I gazed on the towering glass cliffs, the multitudinous spirits, and the innumerable people, wondering if my path would lead me here again. Then I sped away, appearing instantaneously at the foot of South Mountain, to find my friend smiling and bathed in a glorious sunrise.

Rick the Brave

STACIA KANE

His wallet was empty, so Rick took the job.

It wasn't a job anybody else wanted—well, hell, if it had been, somebody else would have taken it already, specifically his sister's husband, who'd told him about it. Apprentice electricians didn't often get handed five grand off the books for what would amount to only a couple of days' worth of work. So much for Shelley telling him he'd never make any decent money. And calling him a wimp. And dumping him for that sleazy car salesman.

Would a wimp take a job in Downside? Ha, no. No way. Like anybody else in Triumph City with half a brain and without a particular death wish, Rick had never gotten closer to the area than the stretch of Highway 300 that ran past it—over it—and he'd never wanted to. It was the kind of place where even the police didn't go, the kind of place where you could find yourself a hooker or find yourself in mortal danger any hour of the day or night.

But here he was, with his tool bag slung over his shoulder in what he hoped was a nonchalant fashion, standing with two other guys in the dusty, empty main room of a ramshackle house, while outside the streets rang with laughter and screams and loud music.

A sort of grunting noise—it took him a second to realize it was some-one speaking on the next floor—and they trooped up the creaky stairs toward it, past shreds of old wallpaper that fluttered like ghostly fingers as they passed.

Now *that* was something he didn't even want to think about.

Looked like the other guys didn't feel the same.

"Any spooks up here, I throwing you at 'em," the guy in front—he called himself Delman, of all things—told the one behind him, who was apparently known as "Barreltop."

Barreltop laughed. Rick did, too, the sort of too-hearty laughter that always made him feel like an ass.

The others didn't seem to notice, though, or maybe they already thought he was an ass so they didn't care. It was quickly becoming obvi-ous that he didn't belong here. The others seemed to know each other and probably lived in the area, although why they'd live in Downside if they were making this kind of money often, he had no idea.

It couldn't be because they liked the ambience. The house stood only a few blocks away from the slaughterhouse, and while the breeze was luckily going in the other direction, the smell was still there when it stopped. It tingled his sinuses like a sneeze he couldn't get out.

A few oil lamps sat on the floor of the room at the left of the stairs, casting wide U-shaped shadows against the dingy walls with their broken plaster and loose wires. Before Haunted Week and the utter destruction caused by the rampaging ghosts, before the Church of Real Truth had taken power and banished them below the earth, this had been a grand home. Now it was a corpse waiting for cremation. Or renovation, which was why they were here: wiring it for power, reinforcing the floors with steel.

Thick sheets of that steel rested against the far wall, between two high empty windows. A few shreds of fabric danced in front of one of them, the remains of curtains still trying to do their job.

Which was what he should be doing. He looked away from them, back at the other two, and found them staring at him, arms crossed, eyebrows lifted.

That pose was mirrored by the hulking man leaning against one of the walls in black jeans and a black bowling shirt. Shit, he was big. Rick took an involuntary step back, then regretted it when the big guy smirked. Mean-looking, too; the expression wasn't pleasant on his scarred, broken face, shadowed by the black fifties-style greaser haircut. For the first time Rick began to seriously doubt he would make it out of the building alive, or at least with all his limbs intact. He could see that guy ripping out an arm and snacking on it, just for fun.

"You ready now?" the big guy said, and Rick realized they were still all looking at him, that he'd been openly staring.

He nodded. "Yeah. Um, sorry."

The guy's chin dipped. "You got the knowledge what needs doin', aye? Choose you a room, get them floorboards up. Half the floor, dig, then we get the steel in."

He pulled a cigarette out of his pocket, snapped open a black steel lighter. The room brightened for a second with the six-inch flame of the lighter, dimmed again when he snapped it shut and refolded his tattooed arms. Barreltop and Delman walked past the stairs, into the room opposite, leaving Rick alone with the big guy. Why were they both leaving? Weren't they going to take up the floorboards?

"Gotta problem?"

"I'm just wondering what you want me to do. Where you want me to start."

The big guy stared at him. "Over yon corner be good. Crowbar's there."

"But I'm an electrician, I don't—"

"You wanting payment, aye?"

"Well, yeah, but—"

"Crowbar's there."

Five thousand dollars, he reminded himself, crossing the floor and picking up the crowbar; he felt the big guy's eyes on him but didn't turn around to look. Instead he put the flat end of the bar under the edge of a floorboard and pushed down.

For five minutes or so the only sound in the house was the tearing and clattering of floorboards as they were wrenched from their places, and the chatter of the guys in the next room as they worked. Even this late—it was close to eleven—Rick's shirt was damp with sweat, his throat dry from rotten dust. Dead mice and insect skeletons littered the layer of wood beneath the floor.

He needed the money. He needed the money. His car payments were killing him—that fucking car *Shelley* wanted him to buy—and five grand would pay it off and give him a bit left over. Left over to buy presents for *another* girl, once he found one. A girl who would appreciate a more . . . cerebral man.

There were girls like that out there, right?

Of course. So a few nights of misery were worth it, because he could picture that the boards were Shelley's new boyfriend's face as he tore them to hell. And once the boards were up he'd get to do some wiring.

But good as the image of what's-his-name's terrified expression made him feel, he wasn't going to kill himself for imaginary revenge, either, so he headed for the cooler by the doorway and grabbed a bottle of water. Vicious brutes like himself got thirsty some—

A scream from the other room. A horrible scream, a terrified one, made even worse by the fact that it was a deep voice, a man's voice.

The big guy knocked Rick down as he ran past, sending him spinning to the floor. What the hell was going on?

Dust filled his nose and throat, stung his eyes and made it impossible to see. For one confused minute as he struggled to his feet he was only aware of thundering footsteps and the big guy cursing.

Then the others yelled, more yelling. Panic. Rick finally used his head and dumped water over his face, and saw them all backing into the hall, away from the ghost as it crossed the floor.

A ghost. A ghost. Holy shit.

He knew hauntings happened, of course. Ten years ago a family on his street had had one, and the resulting payout from the Church had moved them into a newer, bigger house somewhere else. Like any child growing up after Haunted Week he'd heard the half-serious laments of his parents, wishing they had a ghost themselves, just a small harmless one but one that would earn them a settlement, too, to pay for college for Rick and his sister.

But they'd never really wanted that—who in their right mind would?—and Rick had never seen one.

And now he had, and he was in an unfamiliar part of town where he doubted he'd survive ten minutes on the streets by himself, and he was about to get up close and personal with that ghost because he'd bought a too-expensive car to get into some gold digger's pants.

Life sucked.

But he still wanted to hold on to it.

Barreltop and Delman didn't seem to think this was the moment to get philosophical. They raced down the stairs so fast Rick wouldn't have thought their feet touched the wood if he hadn't heard the noise of it.

The big guy backed away from the ghost, his hands raised, and Rick jumped to his feet, realizing even as he did that it was too late. The ghost had almost reached the stairs. It would be blocking his way in another second, and he didn't particularly rate his chances on getting past it. It would attack him, kill him, try to steal his life for itself . . . Every hair on his body stood on end. It was like he could feel each individual air molecule hitting them.

"Ain't can hurt you less'n it gots a weapon," the big guy muttered as he kept backing up.

The ghost's hands were thankfully empty, but the chances of them staying that way were pretty impossible. Shards of wood littered the floor, and the ghost would probably spot them—and lunge for them—in about two seconds.

Funny how something so ephemeral, something that looked like nothing more than a person-shaped blob of light, could be so full of hate. So terrifying. Especially when it was so clearly female, tall and slender in a long gown, hair piled high upon its head. It had been a lovely woman once, he thought—he guessed, because the expression on her translucent face was so angry and contemptuous it made him shiver.

She stood there, looking back and forth between Rick and the big guy. Probably trying to decide which of them to kill first. And with Rick's luck, it would probably be him.

Sure enough, she lunged for him. Rick stumbled in his haste to jump back, fell to the floor with a teeth-rattling thud.

She advanced toward him; he crawled back, an awkward crablike movement over the slippery pile of rotted floorboards. He didn't want to die like this, didn't want this dilapidated husk of a house to be the last place he saw—

Something black swung through the ghost. She shrieked—she didn't *shriek*, no sound came out, but her mouth opened and her entire form wavered and expanded.

The big guy stood with a bar in his hands like a baseball bat. Not just a bar. It was the curtain rod from the window, and it must have been made of iron, because when he swung it again the ghost stepped back.

He glanced at Rick again. "Get up. Take this. Gotta make me a call."

A call? Like on the phone? Was he crazy? "Shouldn't we just get out of here, I mean—"

"Think it ain't gonna chase us? Take this. Now."

The sweat on his skin didn't help him grip the thing. Nor did the growing idea that if he slipped up the ghost wasn't the only one in the room who might kill him.

"Don't quit on the swingin', dig? You quit swingin', we both of us die."

"No pressure," Rick muttered, but he did as he was told, ignoring the frantic pounding of his heart.

Behind him the big guy started talking. "Hey. Naw, gots us a problem. Naw, naw, I'm right, but us got a ghost here. Guessing—aye. Aye, no worryin'. Got an iron bar, keeping it back. Aye."

Rick's shoulders had already started to ache by the time he heard the phone click shut. The ghost, infuriated now, grew bigger and *looser*, in some horrible way that he couldn't let himself think about, every time the bar sliced through it. The bar itself started to burn his hands, heating further with each pass through the ghost.

"Got somebody comin' help us out, dig. You need a rest-up?"

"What?" Swing. Swing. "No. I'm fine."

"You sure? Them arms lookin' shaky."

"I'm sure."

If he were honest, his shoulders were killing him, and the burning iron bar threatened to slip out of his grasp entirely. But nothing in the world could have induced him to admit it. Not yet, at least.

He didn't know how long he kept at it. Ten minutes, fifteen? Long enough for the loud, clattery music from the street outside to change a few times. He found a rhythm; swipe at the ghost, wait until it almost re-formed, swipe again. But he couldn't deny that his arms felt as if they were about to fall off, and finally when the big guy asked again if he wanted a break, he nodded.

Of course, the girl arrived about thirty seconds after that, just as Rick was letting cold water splash over his face and down the front of his shirt to rinse off the dust and sweat. Great. Who didn't want to look like a drool-covered baby in front of women?

She was slim—almost too slim, as if she didn't eat much—and pale, with thick black hair cut like a pinup model and thick black eyeliner to match. Despite the heat she wore skinny black jeans over a pair of battered Chucks, and the red of her T-shirt peeked through little holes in the gray cardigan covering her arms. A canvas bag, faded green like an antique army bag, hung off her shoulder. In her hand was a canister of some kind.

What was a girl doing here?

He stumbled to his feet. "Hey, um, miss, you shouldn't be—there's a ghost here, you should—"

She cocked an eyebrow. What was it with people looking at him like that? "I can see that."

"That's Chess," the big guy said. "She get rid of the ghost, aye?"

"How hot's that bar?" She walked toward the ghost, inspecting it; her thumb flipped open the top of the canister.

"Ain't cold."

She smiled. "No, I guess it wouldn't be."

"Is that normal, for the bar to get hot?" Yes, it was dorky. But so? He, Rick, had done most of the ghost-swatting, and now Mr. Greaser was getting all the credit. In front of a girl who, okay, maybe she wasn't the most gorgeous thing he'd ever seen, but she was pretty.

And despite the holes in the sweater and the ratty shoes and makeup, he didn't think she—no. She didn't talk like them, that weird patois, so she must not live in Downside. So who knew, right? Why not talk to her? "Because it wasn't when I started using it, but by the time I handed it over to him, it was."

"Yeah, that's normal. It's the energies mixing." Her bag sank to the floor with a sort of crunchy thud.

"Your name is Chess?"

She nodded.

"I'm Rick." He started to get up and extend his hand, but she was already moving away. She whispered something under her breath and upended the canister, dumping something white onto the floor. Salt, he realized, when she started creating a circle around the ghost.

"Little faster, Terrible," she murmured. "I don't want it to notice."

Oh, wait. The guy's name was Terrible? Really? Didn't anyone in Downside have a normal name? An adjective and a board game. Sure. Why not?

Terrible kept swinging at slightly shorter intervals, checking his back-swing while Chess walked around behind him. Her head was down, watching the line as it poured into place; when she was finished, Terrible and the ghost stood within a circle five feet or so around.

She whispered something else, then looked up. "Okay, get out whenever you're ready. Just don't—well, you know."

Terrible nodded, glanced down, and started backing up. Oh, right. The salt line would—wait. Normal people couldn't do that, right?

Sure, just about every house had a jar of Church-salt in the cabinets; like a copy of the *Book of Truth*, it was practically given to people at birth. Well, no practically about it, really. Copies of the *Book of Truth* and jars of Church-salt were standard gifts for baby Naming ceremonies. Rick had one of each himself. And supposedly if you ever saw a ghost coming for you, you could throw the stuff at it and it would give you a few seconds to make a getaway if you could.

But normal people could not create binding circles like the one Terrible was now stepping carefully out of.

Who the hell was that girl?

"Okay." She knelt and started marking the floor with what looked like a piece of black crayon or something, scrawling an intricate little symbol just outside the salt circle. The ghost re-formed inside it, its outlines clearing and defining again. When the girl leaned over and started drawing the same symbol inside the circle, the ghost swiped at her head with one long-nailed hand.

Rick gasped, then immediately regretted it when she just kept working. "Doesn't that hurt?"

"Not really. It doesn't have the energy to make itself solid, and nothing like a weapon or anything to solidify around, so it's just cold."

Okay, something was definitely weird here. How did she know so much? And this kind of magic, the kind of magic she was apparently doing, wasn't legal. Not for regular people.

"Hey," he said, aware that his voice sounded a little too loud, his joking tone a little too forced. "You don't work for the Church, do you?"

It was the wrong thing to say. Terrible looked at him. The iron rod still dangled from his fist. Shit.

But Chess replied, glaring at the ghost as it renewed its efforts to hit her. "Why? Does it matter?"

"No, no, I just . . . You seem to be really good at this, is all."

"Do I?" She finished the marking and started sorting through her bag. "What do you think, Terrible? Think I'm good at this?"

"Seen better. Knew a dame once controlled a whole flock of birds, just with she magic."

Chess grinned, a quick flash before she pulled a lump of fabric out of her bag. "That must have been seriously impressive."

"Weren't bad."

She laughed, for reasons Rick could not fathom, and nodded at the ghost. "Where did she come from, do you know?"

"Barreltop find her, lookin' like. Pulling up floorboards."

"I thought you were going to let me check over these places before you start tearing them up."

He shrugged. "You was workin'. Bump only choose the place couple hours past."

She looked like she wanted to say something, but stopped herself before starting again. "Okay, this should only take a couple of minutes, no big deal." She glanced at Rick. "You guys want to wait downstairs?"

"Actually, I'd—"

"Aye." Terrible's fist closed around Rick's arm, lifting him from the floor. Damn, could the guy be any more insulting?

But to say anything would only make things worse, so he followed Terrible across the room and down the stairs, taking one last glance back to see Chess unfolding a long black stick and setting it into some sort of base on the floor.

TEN MINUTES LATER she came stomping down the stairs. "It's not working."

"What?" They both spoke at once.

"I can't get a portal to open, and the only reason I wouldn't be able to do that is if there's already one here."

Terrible rubbed his chin. "Like where?"

"I don't know. Show me where she came from, we'll see if maybe it's there. The ghost is masking anything else I might feel, so I'd have to get closer to whatever it is to find it."

"What do you mean, feel?"

Chess started to answer him—at least he thought she would, she opened her mouth—but Terrible spoke first. His thick brows drew together. "Why you askin'?"

"Just curious."

"Aye? Don't be."

Chess's voice cut into the silence. "Show me where the ghost came from, okay? I'd like to get out of here."

"But—" Rick snapped his mouth shut. "Never mind."

"No, what is it?"

"I just—you have the ghost locked in that circle up there, right? So why can't we just leave? And maybe call the Church and have them come take care of it."

Terrible folded his arms over his massive chest and glared, but Chess shook her head. "The wind could blow the salt away any second. And if there's an open portal in here, that means more ghosts, and they'll find their way into the streets. We can't let that happen, right?"

That still didn't really explain why he had to stick around, but neither was he going to try to leave. His tool kit was still upstairs, and he had the distinct feeling that if he tried to grab it and run he'd end up facedown on the floor.

So the three of them headed back up the stairs and into the other section of the house.

No windows at all back there, at least not ones people could see through. Boards crisscrossed the empty eyes in the wall. For some reason Rick felt almost as if they'd suddenly stepped underwater, or into some kind of jail cell. Probably the jail cell was more accurate.

But as much as he hated this—and he did hate it—he had to admit he was kind of having fun, too, now that the situation seemed under control. It wasn't every night that he got to fend off a ghost with a curtain rod and hang out with a girl who might not be a Church witch but was definitely a witch of some kind. How many of his friends were having this kind of night? They were probably all sitting around Alex's living room watching bootlegged porn.

Barreltop hadn't gotten very far with his crowbar. One board was splintered at the end and split down the center, but that was all. Probably fortunate, really. The thought had no sooner entered his mind than Chess gave it voice.

"Good thing he was lazy. If the ghost came out of here with loose

boards and shit lying around, you guys could have had a serious problem.
A more serious problem, I mean."

Terrible didn't reply.

Chess sighed. "Can one of you pull this board up all the way so I can
look underneath?"

She said "one of you." But she looked at Rick, and he, sensing an
opportunity to actually not look like a total wimp in front of her, seized
it and headed back to the other room.

The ghost still stood in the circle, her fists clenched at her sides and her
long gown moving as if in a faint breeze. She bared her teeth. Her furious
gaze followed him as he grabbed the crowbar from where he'd dropped it.

He ignored her. Or at least tried to. It wasn't very easy, ignoring the
presence a few feet away of something that had—maybe not personally,
but still—killed three of his grandparents and several aunts and uncles.
Not to mention millions and millions of other people during Haunted
Week, leading to the rise of the Church and the fall of all other govern-
ments and religions. The urge to spit at the thing, to hurt her somehow,
rose in his chest, but he fought it down. He couldn't hurt her. She was a
ghost; they didn't feel pain. And she wouldn't care if he spit at her.

Better to pry up that board and let Chess destroy the portal or whatever, and send the ghost to the City of Eternity where it belonged.

Assuming Chess could. If she was Church, she could, but she couldn't
be Church, not if she was hanging around Downside in the middle of the
night. But if she wasn't Church—whatever. No point in wondering, he
guessed. They wouldn't tell him.

They were both kind of smiling when he walked back into the room,
watching him. Maybe she'd told Terrible to get off his back? That would
be nice.

Terrible reached for the crowbar, but Rick pretended he didn't see.
He'd just fitted the flat end under the edge of the board when Chess spoke.

"Hold on. If that came out when he'd only lifted the edge of the board,
I have no idea what lifting the rest of it might do. So . . . be careful, okay?"

He forced a grin. It felt more like a grimace, but he had to at least try.
Chess didn't look scared. Terrible certainly didn't look scared. Rick was
damned if he was going to be the only one who did. "I held off a ghost
with an iron bar for like fifteen minutes before you got here. I think I'll
be fine."

The board came up with a satisfying crack. He reached down and tossed it aside.

Chess produced a flashlight from somewhere—had she had that before?—and handed it to Terrible, who shined it into the space beneath the boards while she knelt beside it and peered in.

"See anything?"

"No."

"Feel anything?"

"Not really. I mean, yes, the whole house feels off, but it doesn't seem particularly strong here." She straightened up. "There's no portal or anything under—shit. Get back. Both of you."

"Huh?" Rick looked toward the doorway, where her gaze was pinned as she stood up. From her hand dangled one of those cloth bags Rick saw earlier.

Terrible grabbed him and shoved him against the wall. He thought he heard his bones creak; he certainly felt them. "Hey, what—"

Oh.

Another ghost wavered in the doorway. It held a crowbar in its spectral hand.

Pure terror shot up Rick's spine, the kind of terror he hadn't felt since he was seven and his older brother dangled him off a bridge for touching his stuff. That was his life, that crowbar, swinging like a metronome in front of the ghost's wicked smile.

Terrible picked up the iron bar, while Chess stepped forward, her right hand hidden by the cloth bag. An odd collection of syllables poured from her mouth and she flung something at the ghost, something that made dark speckles against its pale glow.

The ghost froze. Almost before Rick had time to register that, to wonder at it, she'd upended her salt canister and started pouring another line, stretching it across the length of the room.

Okay. That made sense, he guessed. But it also blocked their escape. What were they supposed to do, sit there all night? All day? Ghosts hated the sun, but not much sun would come in with the windows boarded up like they were.

As if in reply, Terrible turned and smashed his heavy foot into the boards. Rick joined him, feeling the boards give under his boot, until finally they split and fell into the yard below.

It was a cloudy night, a dark one, but Rick's eyes adjusted well enough to see a patch of overgrown weeds and some rusted lawn furniture. A rotted awning hung in tatters off a frame protruding from the side of the house.

So much for jumping. If the fall didn't break their legs they'd impale themselves, and he had a feeling it would be both rather than either/or.

Chess's gaze darted between them and the ghost. "Can you guys get down?"

"Naw. All broken metal down there."

"Shit! I—what the hell?"

Ghostly feet had appeared just below the ceiling. As they all watched, the feet sank to the floor, another ghost revealing itself inch by inch from the bottom up.

And another.

Holy shit. Rick's heart pounded so hard in his chest he thought it might literally explode. He almost wished it would, because at least that would be a quicker death. In that other room lay a pile of broken boards, some studded with nails. Probably enough debris filled the other rooms to turn himself, Terrible, and Chess into nothing more than bloodstains and piles of goo, even if the ghosts couldn't cross the salt line. Ghosts could throw things, after all.

Chess spun around, tugging that black crayon or whatever out of her pocket. "Boost me up. I need to mark the ceiling."

Rick started to bend down to cup his hands, but Terrible got there first. In one smooth movement he had Chess lifted high enough that she could scrawl another of those little symbols on the ceiling.

"That should hold," she said, as she slid back down. "But I need to get up there."

On what planet was that a good idea?

He must have said that out loud, or made some kind of sound, because she looked at him. "The portal is up there. They're not coming up out of the floorboards, they're coming down through the ceiling. I need to close it."

Terrible frowned. "Lemme come along, aye?"

"How are you going to get up there? Rick can't lift you."

"Ain't want you on your alones up there, Chess. Ain't just one or two, aye, an' we ain't got any knowledge what weapons might be up there."

A pause, while Rick's heart sank into his shoes. Then, as if in slow motion, they both turned to look at him.

"Sure." Was that a squeak in his voice? He cleared his throat and tried again. "Sure, I'll go with you. Just tell me what to do."

She smiled at him. Terrible made some kind of growling noise.

"I'm going to salt off a section up there," she said. "Just like this one, as soon as I get up. I don't know if there's any debris or anything in that attic, but I assume there is, so you're going to need to grab whatever you can—if you can—and put it in that area, where they can't get it. Okay?"

She slid past them and marked off another section of the floor behind her line, forming a square with the line already existing. "Try to get through here."

He didn't look happy about it, but Terrible nodded and stepped into the square, ramming the iron rod at the ceiling. Plaster fell around him. For a moment it looked bizarrely like snow, until the plaster stopped and chunks of wood began.

In less than a minute, or so he thought—time seemed to be going by awfully fast, and every passing second moved Rick that much closer to what he was certain was his date with death by ghost—the hole in the ceiling was big enough for them to get through.

"Okay." Chess looked at Terrible. "As soon as you get us up there, step back, okay? Don't stay under here, at least not until I get it marked off on the floor."

If Terrible nodded or said anything, Rick didn't hear it, not over the rasping of his own breath in his throat. He closed his eyes for a second or two; when he opened them, Chess's feet were disappearing into the ceiling.

His turn. *His turn.* Terror numbed him so effectively that he barely felt his feet hit the dusty floor.

But Terrible didn't bend down to cup his hands, not immediately. Instead he grabbed Rick's arm and squeezed, hard. Hard enough that Rick wondered if biceps could liquefy. Terrible's eyes were black holes in his brutish face, and he said, "Aught happens to her, I kill you, dig?"

It didn't seem like the kind of question that was really a question, and Rick was glad, because he didn't think he could have replied if he wanted to. So he just nodded mutely, and Terrible bent down for his foot.

Something hit the wall above them, and the noise reverberated through the room. Rick barely had time to register it before Terrible practically threw him through the hole in the ceiling.

He'd thought maybe he'd need a minute for his eyes to adjust to the darkness, but he didn't. Not just because the small, round windows in the attic room weren't boarded, but because it was so full of ghosts it glowed.

For a second he just knelt there, his mouth open. He'd never seen anything like it before. Yes, before this night he'd never seen a real ghost, so by definition any ghost was something he'd never seen before, but this . . . this was amazing, and frightening, and beautiful in a terrifying and awful way.

Through the mass of their bodies, the tigerish pattern of light and darkness, he saw other shapes, the thick outlines of furniture. Not too much, thankfully, but enough to make his heart sink further. Across the attic space were more porthole-like windows; through one of them a streetlight shined like a single star in a clouded sky.

Chess crouched not far from the hole. She'd already marked off a large square around it with salt, and apparently the ghosts realized it, because Rick had barely seen the line when glass shattered above his head, raining chips on him that stung his shoulder and arm.

"Chess! You right up there?" Terrible shouted from below.

"I'm fine," she called back, digging around in her bag.

She glanced at Rick. "It's definitely here, the portal. I have no idea how it got here or what the deal is or why, but it's here."

"Is that going to be hard to fix?" A chunk of wood came flying at them. They jumped back and it clattered against the wall.

"Don't know."

"What? What do you mean?"

Bluish light moved across her face like a reflection of water, making her features seem to shift and change shape a little as he looked at her. "I mean I don't know. Until I know how it happened, I won't know how to close it. Or even if I can close it."

Great. Just great. He'd come up to help "clear debris" or whatever, and now he was on the front line of some sort of portal that this girl who may or may not be a witch may or may not know how to fix. Oh, and don't forget the huge, very scary guy below them who looked like he ate babies and had just promised to kill Rick if anything happened to the aforesaid maybe-witch.

This night just kept getting better and better. And he had no—"Ow! Fuck!"

A shard of glass had embedded itself in his arm, thrown by an angry ghost.

Chess's eyes narrowed. "Did you just get cut?"

He lifted his arm to show her.

"Damn it! They're going to sense that, it's going to make them mad."

Witch or no witch, she was starting to piss him off. "Sorry. I didn't mean to let myself get injured after risking my life to come up here and help you. How careless of me."

To his surprise, she smiled. "You would have risked your life more if you hadn't come up to help, and I kind of think you know that. But yeah, I guess you're right. Sorry." She lifted her hand, the black crayon in it. "Come here. I want to mark you."

He wanted to ask what the hell that meant, but he was tired of saying "What?" over and over like some sort of idiotic parrot.

So he scooted over, closing the few feet between them. "Would Terrible actually have killed me if I hadn't agreed to come up?"

"It's entirely possible, yeah." She said it like it was no big deal. Like it was normal or something, rather than psychotic. Who the hell were these people?

Her fingers touched his jaw, cool and light. "Close your eyes."

She smelled faintly of shampoo and a sort of herbal scent, with a little cigarette smoke mixed in. The crayon wasn't a crayon at all, he realized, but some sort of woodless grease pencil, and it moved across his forehead in a tingly line. Circles, maybe, some kind of swirl with an angle? He wasn't sure. It made his head buzz, though, enough that he opened his eyes a crack to try to shake the dizziness.

The pencil moved down to his cheek; another little symbol there, and then she lifted his hand and drew on the back of it. It looked almost like a crab, but he couldn't seem to really trace the pattern.

Instead he looked up at her. He'd thought before that her eyes were dark, but they weren't. Inside the thick black eyeliner and mascara they were lighter than that: hazel, almost blue but not quite. Pretty.

He opened his mouth to tell her so, driven by some sort of imminent-death impulse, but she dropped his hand and pulled back before he could speak.

"Those should help keep you safe." She tucked the pencil back into her pocket. "They won't be able to drain power from you, and you won't feel the cold as much when they touch you. Okay?"

He would have nodded, but ducked instead when a large chair flew at them.

She grabbed his arm with her left hand, grabbed his eyes with her own. "But listen. They like fear. They can sense it, it excites them. You need to try to sublimate that. You cannot show them you're scared. You cannot let them see when they hurt you. Now take off your shirt."

"What?"

"Take off your shirt. Give it to me. We need to bind that wound of yours to try to mask"—a crash broke through her voice, as what looked like a table leg hit the wall—"the smell of your blood."

He tried to smile. "You know, if you wanted to see my bare chest, all you had to do was ask."

Terrible's voice cut into her reply. "Chess! What's on up there?"

Damn it! He'd finally managed to say something funny, too.

"We're fine," she called.

Rick peeled off his shirt and handed it to her. The attic was so damn hot it barely made a difference.

She wiped his cut with it, ducked as glass smashed behind her, and wound the fabric into a bandage, which she tied around his arm with the air of someone used to dealing with such things. "I need to get out there and look around. So you need to start grabbing stuff, okay?"

He glanced out again at the sea of ghosts, at the way the light they cast reflected off the naked ceiling boards and patchy walls and somehow thickened the air.

"They can't hurt you unless they have a weapon," she said, in a softer tone. "Without magic powering them they can't solidify themselves without an object to solidify around, remember? And those sigils will help protect you. So just keep your eyes open, and get everything you can behind that line. And for Truth's sake, do *not* break the line, okay?"

The sound of wood scraping wood drew his attention; a team of ghosts, four or five of them, were pushing what looked like an enormous wardrobe.

Chess saw it, too. "We'll worry about that when we have to. Just go, and go as fast as you can."

She stepped over the salt line and into the mass of ghosts, who whirled around her, grabbing for her with impossible white hands that failed to take hold.

Rick's breath rattled in his chest. Ghosts out there. Terrible downstairs, probably with all sorts of weapons and eager to kill someone. He could move, or he could die, and while neither of them really appealed, he figured moving seemed like a better idea.

They were so cold. So damn cold. He'd never really thought about it. He'd been brought up to think of death as something peaceful, something that meant you got to go live in the City below the earth forever, that it was simply another stage of existence.

And he did believe it. Hell, he didn't have to believe it, because it was Fact and that was Truth, and he'd spent hundreds of Saturday Holy Days at Church and didn't even have to think to know that Fact and Truth were what really mattered, and it was comforting and right.

But apparently it was Fact and Truth that ghosts were cold, too, and that made him wonder if the City was cold, and if the dead spent their time there milling around in angry silence the way they were in that attic.

A lamp flew past his head and hit the wall beside him with a heavy thud. He scooped it up and ran with it, dropping it on the "safe" side of the line. Same with a large book bound in moldy leather, and a rusty frying pan. There wasn't as much small stuff in the attic as he'd originally feared, but he kept circling the floor, scanning it, almost getting used to the sensation of being dipped in ice over and over again.

Something heavy slammed into his shoulder. He spun around to see a ghost raising another chair leg high over its head, preparing to bring it down again.

He reacted without thinking, grabbing hold of the leg and pulling, turning so he could put his back into it. Damn, that ghost was strong. The edges of the wood dug into his fingers, into his ribs when he tucked it under his arm to get a better grip and leaned forward.

The ghost still didn't let go. This was fucking ridiculous. What was he supposed to do, spend the entire time up here playing tug-of-war with a dead guy for a chair leg? While more of them wandered around, faster and faster, probably grabbing more weapons to beat him into a bloody pulp?

The thought energized him a bit. He pulled harder, pushing his entire body forward, and ended up taking five or six steps before he realized what was happening.

Maybe he could . . . ? Yeah, that would work, right? The ghost couldn't cross that salt line, but he could, and the chair leg could.

It made him feel a bit like a sled dog, for some bizarre reason, but he did it, towing the ghost toward the line, pushing through the mass of them. The cold almost started to feel good, it was so hot up there.

He stepped over the salt line. Crossed the few feet between it and the wall, and gave the leg one last tug. The second the ghost's hands touched the air over the salt line it let go.

Yes!

He ducked out of the way of a flying picture frame and headed back out. Through the translucent forms filling the attic he saw Chess, bending over slightly with her hand out. Trying to find the portal, he guessed. Or hoped.

Not for the first time the idea that he had only her word that she actually knew what she was doing crossed his mind, but he shoved it away just as quickly. If she didn't, it really didn't matter. He was in that attic and he wasn't getting out until either she managed to fix the problem or they both died, so no point in worrying about it.

Terrible shouted from below, and Chess shouted back again that they were fine.

A few simpering china babies sat on the floor by the wall. A ghost picked one up, started advancing toward him. Rick ducked away, realizing as he did so that he had an advantage Chess hadn't explained. He could walk through them. They couldn't walk through each other.

He twisted his body, sliding through a ghost raising a shard of glass— that could not be a good thing, was there more broken glass around?—and around a heavy desk. More stuff, that was what he needed, stuff to get on the other side of that—

The china baby smashing into the side of his head stunned him, knocked him on his ass. Literally. For a second his vision blurred and shook; when the world snapped back into focus he saw light hit the shard of glass as it started to descend.

Without thinking he grabbed at the spectral hand that held it. It was solid. Solid and cold and damp, with a sort of horrible give to it, the kind of give all living flesh possessed but just felt wrong when the flesh in question glowed bluish-white and froze his own.

The ghost's face leered above him, its lips stretching into a hideous grimace. His arms shook from trying to hold it off. The point of the glass came closer, a little closer, aiming straight for his heart.

"Chess! Chess!"

She didn't reply, but he heard her footsteps, heard her voice as she yelled more of those makeshift syllables and flung something at the ghost.

Dirt. It landed on him and he realized it was dirt, dirt with a particular pungent smell. He also realized the ghost had frozen in place, and he took advantage of it, snatching the glass from its hand and tossing it at the wall.

That was a mistake. Another ghost caught it. Fuck.

Chess glanced over. "I've found it. Get that glass to the other side of the line and come over to the corner. I might need your help."

Okay, this he could do. He thought. The ghost grinned, holding the glass up, but it was still close to the salt line and wasn't moving quickly.

And his mother had told him playing basketball after school wouldn't actually teach him any real skills.

He looked at the glass, at the hand holding it. Focused on it. And ran, his hands outstretched. Another china baby smashed against the floor where he'd been; an old book glanced off his back. He ignored them.

His hands closed around the ghost's, shoving it forward. The ghost immediately went transparent. The glass fell to the floor, and unfortunately Rick fell with it, and it drove itself into his thigh.

It took every bit of strength he could muster not to cry out in pain, but he managed it, remembering Chess's warning about showing emotions. Instead he forced himself to get back up. They'd smell his blood, yes, and that was a bad thing, but he couldn't really do anything about that. Instead he limped over to where Chess stood, shouting back down to Terrible that they were okay and had found whatever it was.

She turned to him when he drew up beside her. "Look."

It was a wreath. What?

As he watched, another ghost slid out of it. It was horrible to see, like witnessing the birth of a grotesque baby. It swung at him, at Chess, several times, its expression growing angrier and angrier, until finally it passed through them, no doubt to hunt for a weapon of some kind.

When it had gone he realized that the center of the wreath wasn't there, or rather, that he couldn't see the floor through it. Instead the air appeared wavery, shiny almost, and tiny lights glowed in that space, lights and more shapes that could have been people.

"It leads directly to the City," she said, ducking as a candlestick flew past. "Look. It's mistletoe."

"I thought that was illegal." The second the words were out of his mouth he regretted them. *Duh, asshole.*

She must have seen his thoughts reflected on his face, because she didn't point out his stupidity. "It opens the gate between here and the City, see? That's why. Especially in a mistletoe wreath. The Church destroyed every one they could find right after Haunted Week."

"Right." Another ghost was forming in the center of the wreath. "So what do we do? I mean, what do you do?"

"I think I can try banishing them all, just sending them right back through without a psychopomp. Then we burn the wreath."

He nodded, just as if he understood what she'd said, which he didn't. He knew the words, knew that a psychopomp was an animal that carried spirits from this world to the City and that banishing was the act of summoning a psychopomp to do that job. But he had no idea what it actually entailed. It wasn't exactly something people got to watch. "Just tell me what to do."

"Keep collecting debris," she said. "And tell Terrible to watch out. When I send them all back it will probably create a vacuum in here. So, um, when I give the word, grab on to something, okay?"

His stomach lurched. Was she serious?

Stupid question; he should stop asking it. Yes, she was serious, and yes, Terrible might kill him if the ghosts didn't manage it first, and yes, this whole thing was a big mistake, and yes, if he made it out of there alive he was going to punch his brother-in-law in the mouth.

She touched his arm, gave him a sort of soft quiet smile. "Don't worry. You'll be fine."

He nodded.

Over the sound of his own footsteps as he half-ran, half-limped around the attic collecting more potential weapons, he heard her voice, low and smooth like music playing in another room. The blood leaking from his thigh excited the ghosts, just as Chess had said it would. They swarmed him, followed him, spun around him in a dizzying pattern of light. The cold wouldn't go away, even for a second. The feeling of them passing through him, as if he were one of them, or as though he didn't really even exist, wasn't really there, grew more and more unpleasant.

But not as unpleasant as the sound of the wardrobe scraping across the floor again.

He looked in that direction. Not just a few ghosts behind it now. At least a dozen or so of them, pushing the heavy piece of furniture. Pushing it right toward Chess. They must have figured out what she was doing.

As they picked up speed, more ghosts joined them. Within seconds, it seemed, he stood almost alone, watching the wardrobe slide across the floor.

"Chess! Chess, look out!"

Instantly he heard Terrible roaring her name from below. No time to try to shout back, and Rick supposed it didn't matter anyway. With a feeling rather like jumping in front of a loaded gun, he ran to the corner where she was, trying to catch the wardrobe before it hit her.

He'd just reached her side when her voice rose. Not in fear; it wasn't a scream. It was simply her saying those words, those itchy-sounding, tumbly words.

Light flashed from the center of the wreath, a second of bright blue-white light, and then—the space grew. He didn't understand how it could happen, but the wreath widened until the doorway or portal or whatever stretched from floor to ceiling.

That was when his feet started sliding across the floor.

Grabbing the wardrobe was instinct. So was grabbing Chess's hand.

Ghosts flew back through the portal, slowly at first, then faster as the vacuum increased. They, too, tried to catch the wardrobe, to hold on to him and Chess, but they couldn't seem to solidify enough to do so.

Chess started walking toward him, going hand-over-hand up his arm, until she, too, could clutch the wardrobe. The vacuum sucked at him, sucked in some odd way he didn't really understand. It wasn't a physical pull—well, it was physical, obviously, but the sensation seemed to come from inside him rather than outside.

"It feels weird," he managed. Holding the wardrobe with both hands necessitated pressing Chess between himself and the wood, almost spooning against her. She didn't seem to mind, which was nice.

"It's your soul."

"What?" Damn it, there it was again.

"It's your soul. The portal is trying to pull spirits back into itself, and it can't differentiate very well between disembodied ones and living people. Just hang on. Do you see any more ghosts in here?"

He craned his neck to the left. Was that glow a ghost or—

He lost his grip on the wardrobe.

As if in slow motion he felt himself falling backward, his head hitting the floor with a painful thud. Felt the rough wood floor beneath him scraping his back as he slid across it.

Chess grabbed his feet. He managed to force his head off the ground long enough to see her feet hooked on the edge of the wardrobe.

And long enough to turn around and see the portal only inches from his face, to see the cold darkness within, the black silhouettes and torch flames. Faces appeared in it and then disappeared, greedy eyes focusing on him, bony fingers trying to reach out and grab him.

He could practically see saliva dripping from their dead lips as they waited for him, ready to steal his life, to try to feed on that power. He had no idea what exactly they would do to him, but he bet it would be painful.

Chess shifted her grip, crooking her elbow around his feet and reaching into her bag. A second or two later she threw something at the portal, shouted something that sounded like "Belium dishwasher!"

The portal closed.

HE DIDN'T THINK he'd ever been so grateful for a beer in his life. Beneath all of the bottles of water in the cooler were a dozen or so of them, chilled to perfection, and he wished he could suck every one back at once.

Not only did he think he deserved a damn drink, he thought it would help a bit with the pain as Chess dug the glass shard out of his thigh.

He was wrong about that one. He just barely managed to stay silent. But at least it didn't take long, and when her hands touched his skin as she applied butterfly closures and some kind of ointment, covering it all with a bandage . . . well, that was nice, even though he felt shaky and weak from the loss of adrenaline.

Terrible stood in the corner, watching the wreath reduce to ash. Rick looked at him for a second, then turned back to Chess.

"So, um . . . maybe you'd like to go out to dinner with me or something, sometime?"

Terrible snorted.

Chess smiled, the kind of smile Rick knew meant *no* even before she opened her mouth, and started cleaning his scraped fingers with a baby wipe. "Sorry. I'm with someone."

"Oh. Oh, um . . . is it serious?"

She squeezed more ointment onto the place where the splinters had been, slowly like she was trying to gather her thoughts. She glanced at Terrible, a quick little eye-dart before looking down again; Rick figured she didn't want him to overhear. "He's my family," she said finally. Quietly. "He's everything."

"Oh," he said again, rummaging in his tired mind for a new topic of conversation. "So that thing I saw through the portal, was that the City of Eternity? Like, for real?"

Chess smoothed a Band-Aid over his finger. "Not really. Well, it is, but it's actually more like a tunnel into the City."

He took his hand back, took another swallow of his beer.

"All burned out here," Terrible said.

Chess looked over at him. "Good. Can you scoop up the ashes? We'll dump them down the sink later."

"You can't just leave them here?" Rick asked.

She shrugged. "Probably. But I'd rather be safe. You never know what can happen with stuff like that. Mistletoe is very powerful—as you saw— and there are a couple of spells that use mistletoe ash, so . . . better to just dump them."

"Because whoever set that thing up might come back and try again?"

"What? No, nobody set that up. That was your fault."

He jerked upright. "My fault? How did I—"

A heavy hand slammed down on his shoulder. How the hell had Terrible gotten there so fast? Rick hadn't even heard his footsteps.

"Oh, calm down. Both of you. Nobody deliberately set that thing off. It was you being here that attracted them."

Rick must have looked confused, because she sighed. "Think of it this way. All these years that wreath has been up there, but the house was empty. There was no energy inside it, you know? No life. But then you guys came in here tonight, and your energy activated the mistletoe and made a portal."

Terrible let go of Rick, shifted his weight. "Shit."

"Yes, shit. This is why you're supposed to let me look through these places first, right? Please? Next time?"

Terrible nodded.

"Good." She slapped her palms down onto her thighs and stood up. "Okay, are we all ready to go now?"

"Aye, guessing so."

Rick stood up, too. "Hey, do you need me back tomorrow night? Or . . ."

Terrible's eyebrows rose. "You wanna come back?"

"Well . . ." Did he? No, not really. But he still needed the money, and he didn't think he'd actually earned anything yet.

Terrible reached into the heavy pack against the wall and pulled out a wad of cash. "Here. You take this, aye? An' you ain't needing to come back. Thinkin' you done enough."

He held out his hand. Or rather, he held out a bunch of money, what had to be at least three or four grand.

"Oh, hey, no, I mean, I hardly did anything, the floorboards aren't even up at all."

Terrible glanced at Chess, then back. "Take it."

"But I—"

"Take it."

So he did, shoving it into his pocket without counting it. At least he knew not to do *that*.

He slung his backpack over his still-sore shoulder, and the three of them clattered back down the stairs and out the front door.

Down the street a gang of kids were giggling and playing with fire-crackers. On the corner a couple of hookers leaned against the lamppost, their skin glistening with sweat. The sound of breaking glass echoed over the other noises, the car engines and shouts and music.

"Well, okay, I guess," Rick said. He held out his hand to Chess, who shook it, then he did the same with Terrible. "It was nice meeting you guys and everything."

"You, too," Chess replied. "Take care."

Terrible grunted.

"Oh, and thanks," she said. "You were a big help . . . you were really brave."

Brave. Was he? He didn't feel like he was, hadn't felt it at the time, but when he looked back at what he'd done . . . yeah, maybe he was. His chest inflated.

But he didn't let on how that made him feel. Instead he just said, "Bye," and walked to his car, aware of their eyes on him, aware of the dark sky above and the city of ghosts beneath the earth. He'd seen it. He'd actually seen the City, he'd actually seen ghosts, been injured by them and watched them be defeated.

He was Rick the Brave, Rick the ghost killer. Rick the guy any girl would want to be with, and he was four grand or so richer, and life was pretty damn good, after all.

Full-Scale Demolition

SUZANNE MCLEOD

"The client's got a pixie portal in her swimming pool?" I groaned and shot a frustrated look down at the four Warded cat carriers I'd tucked into the shade of Nelson's Column. There were two sleeping pixies in each and it had taken me since dawn to catch the little monsters. It was now mid-day. The last thing I wanted was another pixie job. "Toni, please, *ple-ease*, tell me this is one of your windups?"

Toni, our office manager, laughed in my phone's earpiece. "Sorry, not this time, Genny. And it's an emergency job—" The trilling of the other line interrupted her. "Hang on, hon," she said, and I heard her faint, "Spellcrackers.com, making magic safe, guaranteed. How may I help you?" before I tuned her out.

Catching pixies was *so* not my favorite job. It made me feel like the wicked faerie who didn't get invited to the christening, but who turned up anyway. And catching pixies in Trafalgar Square on Easter Saturday, in an early heat wave, with a full complement of tourists, schoolkids, and al fresco sandwich-snackers happily pointing their digital cameras and video phones my way . . .

Well, you get the picture.

I raked fingers through the ends of my hair where it stuck to my nape and contemplated the last pixie. It was squatting on the flank of one of the four bronze lions that guarded the base of Nelson's Column, swishing its barbed tail like an angry cat. Its blue-gray scales shimmered in the sunlight, and its lipless snout was stretched in a taunting grin. No way was it going to make this easy. Then, as if to hammer that thought home, the pixie flapped its vestigial batlike wings, cartwheeled along the lion's broad back, and jumped up to perch on the statue's huge head.

The impromptu audience gathered below laughed and clapped and whooped. The two heritage wardens, who were doing crowd control around the column's base, exchanged a long-suffering look. And in the background the ever-present rumble of traffic rose and fell like the murmur of the sea. Which was where the pixie was going back to after I'd caught it in my hot sticky fingers.

Despite the fascinated audience, pixies in Trafalgar Square were nothing new. The first one appeared back in 1845 as soon as they'd begun pumping water into the newly built fountains—the fountains had opened a portal straight to the Cornish sea—and the pixies had been slipping through ever since. A cautionary lesson to anyone thinking about digging a new garden pond. Get a witch to do a magical survey first, or you never know where you might be connecting to—or what might live there.

"Genny Taylor!"

At my shouted name, I looked down to find a petite girl of about my own age—twenty-four—at the front of the crowd. She had spiky black hair, a silver dumbbell through her left eyebrow, and a tattoo of red and black triangles on the side of her throat, and she was overdressed for the heat wave in Goth-style camo gear. She grinned, lifted the huge professional camera hanging round her neck, and snapped off a couple of shots. Damn, my persistent paparazzo was back. She'd been stalking me for a good couple of months (one of the joys of being the only sidhe fae in London), though only the gods knew why, as I sincerely doubted the media needed any more photos of me chasing pixies. YouTube already had half a dozen videos, from what I'd heard.

I shifted, giving her my back.

"Hi, hon." Toni's voice returned in my earpiece.

"What's the story with the swimming pool anyway?" I asked.

"The client's doing renovations," Toni said. "One of the builders put an iron spike through the Ground Ward and fritzed it, and then some idiot left a hose running."

"Great." Repairing a Ground Ward added another hour to the job.

"Oh, wait till you hear the rest," Toni said. "The husband's an antiquities dealer, so the house is full of statues. Very old and very expensive statues. Hubby's on a buying trip just now, and the client's having forty fits in case something ends up broken."

Pixies love statues. It's what makes them dangerous.

A few years ago, a pack of about thirty-odd pixies, high on candies filched from a coachload of schoolkids (sugar works wonders for amping up magic), managed to partially animate the exact same bronze lion I was looking at. The lion shook its head, roared, and snapped its jaws at the crowd for over an hour before the pixies' magic finally wore off. So the Greater London Authority declared the pixies a health hazard, and Spell-crackers.com had won the contract to keep the pixie numbers down to acceptable levels.

"Thing is," Toni said, breaking into my musings, "you'll need to do the job on your own; everyone else is either down at Old Scotland Yard—" She paused, and we shared a moment's silence about the tragedy, currently absorbing the media, of the two eleven-year-old boys who'd gone missing from an amusement arcade a week ago. Any witch with a touch of scrying ability was helping the police right now. So far no one had gotten lucky. "Or they're off to the Spring Fertility Rite," Toni finished. Easter is the witches' big jamboree.

"No probs. Does the client know I'm doing the job?" Some humans didn't want a fae in their home—either too scared or too bigoted—and while I can pass for human if I hide my catlike pupils, it's never good business to fool the clients. Of course, I get other job requests that have nothing to do with *cracking* magic and everything to do with some jerk's sexual fantasy, so I find it pays to check.

"She asked for our pixie specialist." Which was my "star billing" on the company website. "Plus I told her, but she's worried enough that the Wicked Witch of the West could turn up on her doorstep and it wouldn't be an issue."

"Love you, too, Toni," I said drily, digging the Pixnap—my favorite pixie-sedating cream—from my backpack.

She laughed. "Oh, and stay out of my stationery cupboard until you've gotten rid of all that pixie dust."

"Hey, that was an accident," I said in mock affront, rubbing the honey-scented cream into my hands and forearms. "And I tidied all your pens after they'd finished doing the tango."

"Pixing my face wasn't an accident." Toni didn't mean *her* face, but the Green Man plaque hanging behind our reception desk. I'd been experimenting with pixie dust, and animated him. Trouble was, he'd been carved from a dryad's tree, and the pixie magic was taking its time wearing off. "He still winks every time I walk by," she said in disgust.

"Sorry." I stifled a chuckle. "At least he's stopped telling everyone to come back tomorrow."

She huffed, told me that she'd e-mail me the client's details, and we said our good-byes.

I turned my attention back to the pixie, who was doing a furious jig on the lion's head, and hauled myself up onto the bronze lion. Its metal back was scorching from the sun, and gritty from all the pixie dust. It really was way too hot for this. My Lycra running shorts and bra top had seemed a good idea at dawn, but now the black material was absorbing heat like a vamp sucking up blood, while the yellow plastic of the Hi-Vis waistcoat had welded itself to my spine. I sighed and shimmied along the lion's back until I crouched on its shoulders.

"C'mon, little pixie," I murmured, sliding my cream-covered hand up the lion's metal mane. "Playtime's over. Time to go home."

The pixie's snout peeled back to showcase a row of chitinous teeth, and warning clicks issued from its throat as it maniacally shook its head. I don't speak pixie, but its meaning was pretty clear—

"Back off, my bite's nastier than yours."

"Yeah, don't I know it," I muttered.

And out the corner of my eye I saw Tavish's broad shoulders shake with mirth. He was standing, well, posing really, on the fountain's highest bowl, which put him about twenty feet up, so I could hardly miss him. And if that weren't enough, he'd bespelled the water so it cascaded over him like a cloak of sun-trapped diamonds, making him look like some gorgeous, hedonistic river god. But then he was a kelpie, so the look was apt, even if his black cargo shorts sort of ruined it. Still, at least he *was* wearing shorts, and was in his human shape, so I counted that as a win.

I glared over at him. He gave me a happy thumbs-up, and the beads threading his long dreads flashed from silver to a gleaming turquoise. I glared harder. Bad enough having an audience without being critiqued by another fae, however hot he was. Though to be fair, Tavish didn't work for Spellcrackers, but he'd still offered to help when he'd strolled into the square five minutes after I'd arrived. I almost hadn't been surprised. He'd been turning up more and more on my outside jobs. If he'd been human I'd have expected the date question—hell, I was more than interested enough that if he'd been human I wouldn't have waited for him to ask. But he was wylde fae, likely older than the last millennium, tricky, capricious, and dangerous. And while I might be sidhe fae, I'd spent the last ten years living with humans. It was always possible I'd got my attraction wires crossed, and I didn't want to end up Charm-struck at the bottom of the River Thames.

The crowd whooped, drawing my attention back to the pixie, who was now striking muscleman poses. I inched my hand closer. The pixie tensed, webbed feet gripping the hot metal as it unfurled its useless wings. I froze. I hadn't safely caught all its pals to have this last one do itself an injury because I'd spooked it. After a moment, its wings dropped, and, holding my breath, I made a grab for its nearest limb, relieved as my fingers closed around its scaly left leg. It let out an ear-piercing screech that almost drowned out the crowd's disappointed boos, then mercifully went quiet as it sniffed the honey in the Pixnap and sank its teeth into my forearm. Gritting my own teeth against the dull pain, and carefully cradling the suddenly dozy pixie, I slid off the bronze lion and tucked the pixie in with its pals.

Now for the cleanup.

I opened the metaphysical part of me that can *see* the magic and *looked*. Almost everything in the square, including some of the audience, lit up as if it had been scattered with multicolored sugar sprinkles: pixie dust. Some of the dust was old and faint, some brighter and more recent. Cleaning this up was one of the reasons why I'd gotten the job at Spellcrackers despite my lack of spell-*casting* ability. (The other was my dubious celebrity quality.) It would take a coven of witches a good four or five hours to *call* all the pixie dust and *neutralize* it. And they'd have to enclose Trafalgar Square in a circle to do it. Way too expensive. The other, quicker way would be to *crack* the dust, but *cracking* magic doesn't just destroy the spell, and pitted bronze lions, broken pavement, and exploding pixies weren't included in the contract. Whereas I could do my party trick: suck the dust up like a magical vacuum cleaner, and *neutralize* it back at the office.

I sat and made myself comfortable next to the cat carriers, then dug out a spell-crystal and some licorice torpedoes from my backpack. Chewing on the candy for a quick magical boost, I activated the Look-Away veil in the crystal . . .

And *called* the pixie dust.

It flew to me like iron filings to a magnet, clumping in colorful patches on my skin. The patches rustled and tickled like dry grass in a wind. Weird, but not entirely unpleasant. But then the not-so-fun part kicked in: the pixie-dust sprinkles twisted into tiny fishhooks that pierced my flesh painlessly and jerked my limbs around as if I were a disjointed marionette. To anyone who couldn't *see*, I probably looked like I was convulsing. The usual nausea roiled in my stomach, and I closed my eyes, concentrating on straightening the hooks and dropping them into the metaphysical bag inside me.

"Well now, doll, that's as fine a sight as any I've seen for a long while." Tavish's soft burr snapped my head up.

He was crouched next to me, appreciation in the solid pewter color of his eyes. Apart from his Roman-straight nose, his long, angular features weren't classically handsome, but he was striking, and captivating, and alluring. Though, caution warned me, a lot of his allure was probably down to his kelpie Charm.

I scowled and pushed my sweaty hair back from my face. "Tavish, I look like something the cat's dragged in after a fight with birthday cake."

He blinked, his eyes changing from pewter to a pale, translucent blue, and then he gave me a lingering head-to-toe assessment. "Aye, doll, so you do," he agreed prosaically, the delicate black-lace gills on either side of his neck fanning wide. "But that's nae but your shell; your soul is shining with magic like a sun-kissed rainbow brightening the cold depths of the sea."

Kelpies are soul-tasters; they taste the souls of those who are dying. Of course sometimes the souls aren't actually dying until after the kelpie has Charmed them into the water. But Tavish abides by River Lore—has done so for a couple of hundred years—so he no longer Charms humans into the Thames, and of those he finds in the river, he tastes only those who have killed or want to die.

"Great," I said, unsure whether to be pleased my soul looked pretty (although maybe that should be *tasty*), or irrationally annoyed because he'd admitted I didn't look so good. "Any chance of you helping this rainbow up? I've got the pixies to pack off back to Cornwall and another job to go to."

"Nae problem, doll." He grasped my hand and pulled me up hard enough that my nose ended up pressed against his neck. I sucked in a startled breath. Boy, did he smell good: like oranges and peat-mellowed whisky. And his pulse was thudding temptingly close under the hot smooth skin of his throat. I almost succumbed to an urge to lick it, but my sensible head took charge, and reluctantly I pushed him back. He gave me a satisfied look, as if he knew exactly what I'd been thinking, but as I narrowed my gaze, his forehead creased in concern and he said, "I heard a lassie shouting for you from the crowd, was there maybe some trouble or t'other I couldnae see?"

I shook my head. "Nah, just an annoying paparazzo."

"A photographer?" His concern sharpened as he scrutinized the square. "Is she still here?"

"No," I said, frowning. "Why?"

He was silent for a moment before turning back to me with a frustrated look. "Those newsy folk are nae but pests," he said, and then with a soft snort of dismissal he changed the subject. "So, this next job you're going to, will you be fancying a wee bit o' company?" He flashed me a grin. "I ken 'tis the witches' special night, and I wouldnae want you being lonely, doll."

Anticipation flared inside me, and I straightened my attraction wires: we weren't talking about him tasting my soul here, but other much more earthly pleasures. But having him tagging along on a job wasn't a good idea . . . he'd be way too distracting.

"Appreciate the offer, Tavish," I said, promising myself: another time . . . maybe, "but I'm good."

"Aye doll, I ken you are, but 'tis myself I'm worried about."

I blinked. "Come again?"

"Well, after you were for saving my life"—he placed a hand over his heart—"there's nary a day goes by that I dinna feel lost and rudderless if I'm nae by your side."

I shot him a quelling look. "Tavish, removing that death curse from you does *not* mean I saved your life. The guy that sicced it on you didn't die, so it hadn't taken hold."

The beads on his dreads clicked a denial. "Nae, doll, you've a responsibility for me after that."

"Pull the other one," I said drily. "You're not Chinese, and neither am I."

"Och, well." He threw out his arms and heaved a sad-sounding sigh, and I couldn't help notice how his muscles shifted nicely under his green-black skin, which of course, was what he intended. At least I wasn't drooling. Yet. He smiled, a mischievous glint in his eyes. "If you're nae agreeing with me over that, then maybe you'll be wanting to be irresponsible with me?" He leaned down and dropped a hard, hot, glorious kiss on my lips, and a delicious spiral of lust coiled deep inside me. "Call me."

THREE HOURS LATER, my taxi turned into Belgrave Square. I could still feel Tavish's kiss like a promise on my lips, but his *Call me* was reverberating through my mind to an indecisive beat. Should I? A big, *big* part of me wanted to, but he was still wylde fae, and I was pretty sure it wouldn't be long before I'd end up way out of my depth with him . . . I tucked his enticing voice away to deal with after the job, and scanned my surroundings.

Elegant, imposing, and über-expensive nineteenth-century town houses, many of them home to more foreign embassies and Important Places than I could count on two hands, lined all four sides of the square. The houses guarded a well-stocked, well-manicured, and private central garden. The place bristled with flags, diplomatic cars, and enough magical security that my skin felt as if it were trying to rip itself from my flesh and crawl away, which was maybe why the place was strangely devoid of people, even for a late Saturday afternoon.

Why was someone who lived here hiring Spellcrackers.com? Not that we're not the best, but hey, anyone who could afford to buy a house here could keep a whole coven of witches on retainer. It didn't make sense.

Toni had told me not to worry about *why* when I'd asked her, just to sort out the pixie problem the builders had caused. Which meant my destination was easy enough to spot, even without the address Toni had e-mailed to my phone. It was the only house with a yellow rubbish chute hanging from a fourth-floor window. A haze of dust clung to its smart front, and a large, new-looking skip was parked outside and hemmed in by temporary fencing. If that hadn't given it away, then the fancy sign advertising the builders' company would have. As I got out of the taxi I had an errant urge to write *Spellcrackers wuz here* across it. I resisted. Instead I stacked the half-dozen cat carriers I'd brought under the colonnaded portico with the cheerful help of the taxi driver, and, once she was gone, I straightened my black trouser suit and cased the joint . . . sorry, job.

The Ward, shimmering like a diaphanous lavender curtain over the front door, was a standard-issue "sucker" one, as it's called in the trade. Once invited in, then you could pass back and forth over the threshold until the invitation was rescinded, much like the vamps it was colloquially named for. (Of course, once you've freely given your blood to a vamp, then there's no rescinding that particular threshold invitation, which is why all the vamp clubs have to charge entrance fees by law.) The Ward seemed a bit low-key for such an expensive end of town, but with builders, and the rest of the square's defenses, it was adequate.

I hitched my backpack higher, dug out my ID, and rang the bell. The person who answered wasn't the butler/builder/security I expected, but she was familiar, from her spiky black hair, the red and black ink almost encircling her throat, right down to the huge professional camera still slung around her neck. The petite paparazzo, a.k.a. my stalker.

"Sorry, no offense," I said, hiding my irritation behind a neutral tone, "but if this is an expensive way of getting an exclusive, I'm not interested."

"Hey, I know all the gear looks suspicious," she grinned, "but I'm not a pap. I have enough problems with them myself." She stuck out her hand. "Theodora Christakis."

My inner radar automatically pegged her as straight human. But the Witches' Market in Covent Garden sells all sorts of spells, legal or otherwise, and skin-to-skin contact is an easy way to *tag* someone. I *looked* at her outstretched hand, but she was clean. I still didn't take it, and she dropped her own.

"So, if you're not a pap, Mrs. Christakis," I said, "why have you been stalking me?" Okay, maybe I wasn't hiding my irritation quite that much.

She laughed, and I caught a glimpse of the silver ball piercing her tongue. "I haven't actually been stalking you, Ms. Taylor, or not much anyway." She paused. "I design graphics for computer games; taking pictures helps"—she pointed her camera at me, but the frown on my face obviously deterred her from snapping—"and your bones are slightly longer, proportionally, than a human's, so they make for interesting lines."

It all sounded plausible enough, but my bullshit antenna was still twitching.

"Don't suppose you've got any interesting ID, Mrs. Christakis?" I said flatly.

She disappeared into the hallway for a moment, then thrust a passport, a computer game, and a glossy magazine at me. "Is this interesting enough?"

The magazine showed a bride and groom laughing against a backdrop of rocky beach and sparkling, aquamarine sea. He was dark-haired, dark-suited, and tall, or looked it since his bride was petite. She was draped in an off-the-shoulder Grecian-style dress of red and yellow silk, with red and yellow veils covering her short black hair. Both bride and groom wore delicate gold crowns joined by a twisted red and yellow ribbon, which echoed the faint red and black ink that snaked over the bride's bare shoulder. A silver dumbbell pierced her eyebrow. The magazine was dated three months ago, and the headline read: WORLD EXCLUSIVE: CYPRIOT HEIRESS THEODORA BELUS WEDS ANTIQUITIES EXPERT SPYRIDON CHRISTAKIS ON THE SUN-DRENCHED ISLAND OF APHRODITE.

"Check out page fifteen," Theodora said.

I did. It stated that Theodora was the owner of Herophile Futures, a blue-chip company producing computer games featuring modern-day wars between ancient Greek gods. The game she'd given me was Quest for the Aegis of Athena.

I also checked her passport. Other than the fact that her legal first name was Herophile (and who would want to be called that?), Theodora was who she said she was.

And it was a job.

I packed my paranoia into my backpack and handed her the things back. "Very colorful dress, Mrs. Christakis. Thank you."

She grimaced. "Not my choice, unfortunately, but you can't argue with the old traditions." She stood aside and motioned me in. "Or at least,

I can't. Oh, and call me Dora. 'Mrs. Christakis' reminds me too much of my mother-in-law."

"Sure," I said, and transferred my cat carriers inside.

The entrance hallway was high and wide, with double doors leading off either side and an ornate marble-and-iron staircase sweeping upward. The walls were bare of pictures, the black-and-white marble floor was partially covered by drop cloths, and the only lighting was a couple of dangling bulbs. Next to a door at the back of the hall was a crisscrossed stack of toolboxes, a pyramid of paint cans, and three huge sledgehammers lined up by height. The builders were either toddlers, or neat freaks. Unsurprisingly, the place smelled of paint and the nose-stinging reek of turpentine, and I had a brief, regretful thought that my best black suit was going to end up trashed.

The double doors to the left were open, and the room beyond snagged my attention. It was haphazardly peopled with life-size statues of muscled, naked men in various athletic poses, and half-dressed women cradling fruit or pouring water. Scattered among the statues were marble busts, plaques, stone animals, and half a dozen knee-high stacks of shining silver and copper platters. It was like looking into a museum's messy storeroom, or the White Queen's lair, if she'd been Greek. Not to mention that the room was obviously pixie heaven.

I *looked*. And everything lit up with the telltale colorful sprinkles of pixie dust, but most of it was faint and old, with only a few brighter, newer patches. My paranoia peeked out of my backpack.

"We're renovating the whole house"—Dora smiled and pointed up the stairs—"so we're camping out on the second floor just now, but if you'd like something to eat or drink before you start, then you're very welcome."

As if on cue, a gray-haired woman in a black head scarf, who looked as if she were a hundred and suffering from eczema going by her wrinkled, scaly face, leaned over the banisters above. She waved a ladle large enough it could be classified as a weapon and shouted something (which was all Greek to me) in a strident, demanding tone. Dora repeated her offer of hospitality in a dutiful-sounding voice. I told her no thanks, and she shouted back in the same language (obviously it was all Greek to her too, except she understood it). The woman threw her hands in the air in disgust or despair and disappeared.

"Malia, my aunt. She refuses to believe that women work outside the home"—Dora rolled her eyes—"and therefore you must be a guest, and I am shirking my responsibility by not letting her stuff you full of food."

The aunt's stereotypical Greek appearance had almost settled my paranoia, although I still had questions. "So," I said, "how long have you had your pixie problem?"

"With all the building work going on, I'm not sure when they first appeared." Dora's reply was a bit too casual. "I've seen them in Trafalgar Square, and thought they were cute." She stopped and gave me a rueful grimace. "Look, to be honest, I'm using them in a new game, so it was handy having them around. Only then one of my husband's more expensive statues got broken, and he's due back next week, so, well, it's time for the pixies to go."

Made sense, but— "What about the local witches? Have you consulted with them at all?"

"I did," she said, and frowned, "but the local coven wanted to use Stun spells and nets." (Which was another way of solving the problem—with a low survival rate for the pixies.) "But I want it done humanely"—she smoothed her hand over her camera—"which is the way Spellcrackers does it, isn't it?"

"It is, yes." Humane to the pixies anyway; my arms still itched from their bites. Not that I'd want to catch them any other way. And after all, like all fae, I'm fast-healing, a bonus of being virtually immortal. So Dora's answers meant I was good to go, other than my last niggle of unease: "Where are the pixies?" I asked her.

"Mostly up on the third floor," Dora said. "But your office mentioned you'd probably need to close the portal in the swimming pool first." I nodded. It was standard operating procedure: pointless rounding them up before you'd stopped more coming through. Dora led me to the door at the end of the hallway, "It's down here, in the basement," and then she added in a rush, "I'm not sure, but there might be a bit of a problem."

I bit back a sigh. I hated it when clients didn't tell you everything going in; it always made my job harder. But at least that explained where my last doubt was coming from.

I gave her my best professional smile. "Why don't you show me, then?"

She opened the door to reveal a modern glass-and-chrome stairway that clashed with the rest of the house and the half-finished mural of ancient ruins and olive trees that decorated the stairwell wall. As we descended, the sound of crashing waves assaulted my ears and the salty scent of open water cut with the rank smell of death slapped me in the face. Either Dora had a hell of a wave pool down here, or she was right, and there was definitely a problem.

We reached the bottom of the stairs, walked along a long opaque-glass corridor, and at the end she opened another door.

The sound of the sea intensified.

I walked through the door with a feeling of trepidation. I just knew this wasn't going to be good.

The room and the swimming pool were both bigger than I'd expected. The pool was fifty feet long, thirty feet wide, and eighteen feet at the deep end, going by the markings stenciled onto the very obvious white squares on the walls, which ruined the whole illusion of the painted panoramic vistas. And judging by the way the pool's edges wavered with magic, instead of the pixie portal being the usual, easily closed hole about the size of a dinner plate, this portal was the size of the pool. Which explained why the waves were rolling toward us like we were on a beach in the Mediterranean, why the expanse of sandy-colored terra-cotta tiles (which was almost as large at the pool) was littered with dead fish and seaweed, and why there were three shark fins cutting an ominous figure eight in the pool's sea-dark water.

I stared, stunned, then walked to the water's edge. "How long's it been like this?" I asked, pleased my voice came out calm.

"Maybe a week?" Dora pulled a face. "Bruno, the mural painter, has been off sick, so no one's been down here. I didn't realize it was like this myself until not long ago, otherwise I'd have said when I phoned. You can sort it, can't you?"

No way in hell. This was way out of my league, but—I forced my mouth back into my professional smile. "I'm going to need some help with this." I dug out my phone. This needed a coven, but they were all at the Spring Rites, or scrying for the missing boys . . .

But there was someone who could help. Someone who was in his element in water, and who'd told me to *call him*. Tavish. Okay, so this probably wasn't the sort of call he was expecting . . .

He answered on the first ring. *Keen.* "Hello, doll," he said in his soft burr.

"Hey," I said, brightly, "I've got a bit of a fishy problem here. A big one. Sharks."

"Dinna let them bite you, doll."

"Ha, ha," I said. "But seriously, Tavish, there are sharks here, and I'm not about to start reenacting *Jaws*."

" 'Tis nae the sharks I'm fussed about. Tell the lamia: ten minutes. And see if you can find out where the children are." The phone went dead.

I stared at it, my mind whirling. Why did Tavish sound like he knew what was going on? What children? And who was the lamia? I transferred my stare to Dora, who, though she had her eyes squeezed shut, had her camera up and was snapping pictures like her life depended on it, and the paranoia in my backpack jumped out and sucker-punched me. "What's going on, Dora?" I demanded.

"What did he say, girl?" the heavy accented voice came from behind me.

I jerked around to see Dora's Aunt Malia. The old woman was blocking the doorway in the opaque glass wall. Now that she was under the brighter lights of the pool room, I could see that it wasn't wrinkles and eczema causing her face to look disfigured and scaly, but actual scales. She had to be the lamia. Of course, the big tipoff came when I looked down. Flowing out from under her heavy black dress was the tree-trunk-thick, red-and-black body of a gigantic snake. I froze, and while the scared part of my mind was screaming *Run!* the rest was rifling through my mental "lamia" file for any useful information.

"Are you both lamias?" I asked, surprised my voice still came out calm.

"Yes," said Dora, hugging her camera like a security blanket. "Well, Auntie is, and I almost am." Her hand went to the tattoo at her throat.

My mental "lamia" file search hit pay dirt. The original lamia had a fling with Zeus, and Hera, Zeus's wife, was understandably none too happy. In revenge, Hera forced the lamia to devour their offspring. But, insane with grief, the lamia didn't stop at killing her own children, and went on a feeding frenzy. Zeus finally pacified her with the gift of prophecy whenever she removed her eyes. Which wasn't any sort of compensation to my mind, but hey, what do I know. But although Zeus had soothed the lamia's madness, he was too late to stop her from turning into a daemon: one whose existence was sustained by eating children. And Tavish had told me to *find the children*. I put that together with the recent media splash and looked horrified from Dora to her snaky aunt. "Fuck, are you the ones who snatched the two missing boys?"

Aunt Snaky's lips lifted in a long hiss. "How long will it be until the kelpie is arriving?" She had fangs. And going by her expression, she obviously expected me to dissolve into hysterics and tell her everything I knew. Which wasn't much. Yet. My horror turned to icy determination. I wished, and not for the first frustrated time, that I could *cast* my own spells and solve the situation with some sort of magic, but I couldn't. So instead I needed to find out where the kids were and, more important, work out how to save them.

"How long?" Aunt Snaky said impatiently.

"Ten minutes," I said, and then not really expecting an answer, I asked, "Where are the boys?"

"They're still alive. Just," Dora said, surprising me, her eyes darting momentarily toward the shark-infested pool.

They were in the pool? How was that possible? And was my impression that Dora wasn't happy about things right, or was that just my own wishful thinking? I narrowed my eyes at her. "What does 'just alive' mean?" When she shrugged, I hit her with the next question: "What do you want Tavish for?"

"The kelpie is to retrieve something," Aunt Snaky said. "If he will agree, you will not be harmed."

Yeah, and I'm the queen of the goblins. "Retrieve what?"

"Theodora, bring the girl." A dry rustle whispered under the sound of the pool's waves as she turned and slithered along the corridor toward the stairs.

So, I was Tavish's incentive. Not that it mattered, since no way was I going to let him swap me for two little kids. And what did they want him to retrieve? Although another look at the swimming pool gave me a clue: Tavish was in his element in the water; if the boys were—what? imprisoned, trapped, or maybe hiding?—in the pool, then more than likely it was them.

Dora gave me a rictuslike smile—with no fangs; maybe her *almost lamia* comment meant she still had to eat her first kid before she fully metamorphosed?—and indicated I should follow. As the only other way out was the portal in the pool, and the sharks didn't look any friendlier than Aunt Snaky, I followed.

"So, was the magazine story, the pixies and all this, just a scam to get me here?" I asked, belatedly wishing I'd listened to my paranoia.

"No, it's all true," Dora said, a flicker of misery crossing her face. "I really am an heiress, and I did just get married."

Was the misery real? "You know," I said in a low voice, "if your aunt's coercing you in some way, I can help you, and we can save the boys."

"You can't. I thought you could . . ." She looked down at her camera screen, her fingers convulsed, then she said accusingly, "But you can't even *cast* the simplest spell, can you?" She was right, but that didn't mean we couldn't try *something*. "No, I might not want this, but I've got no choice. I'm my aunt's heiress, and I'm not talking about money. I've got plenty of that."

"There are always choices," I said quietly.

"Yeah, like what?" she muttered derisively. "Oh, and don't be fooled by Auntie"—she gave the lamia's swaying back a defeated look—"she might move slow, but her skin's as tough as old boots and I've seen her kill a swamp dragon with one flick of her tail."

Swamp dragons are huge, the size of a double-decker bus.

"At least tell me where the boys are?" I asked urgently, hoping she couldn't see how rattled I was.

"I told you," she almost growled, "they're in the pool." She shoved past me, ignoring my question as to how they were in the pool, and stomped after her aunt.

By the time we reached the entrance hallway—lamias are apparently akin to snails when it comes to stairs—Tavish was shouting and banging his fists on the front door.

Dora hurried to open it.

I hung back and made a grab for the hefty sledgehammer I'd seen earlier—it was big enough to do damage to a mountain troll, so hopefully it would make a dent in a lamia—but before my fingers touched it, Auntie's scaly tail whipped out, clamped around my middle, and pinned my arms in place. Then I was suddenly lifted and plonked down on my butt about six feet back from the open front door. I struggled and kicked, but despite my efforts, I couldn't escape my snaky straitjacket.

"Be still, girl." Aunt Snaky squeezed me, and pain bloomed down my arms.

Worried she'd break bones, I stopped wriggling and cast a searching look around.

Dora was almost hiding behind the open front door, white-knuckled hands gripping her camera. No help there. Tavish was outside under the colonnaded porch. He was a dark shape against the deep purple haze of the early evening sky, his eyes swirling bright silver, and his dreads dripping with glittering water—no, I *looked*, not water, but power. And it wasn't the sky that was hazy, but the Ward; it wasn't the sucker one from earlier, but something much heftier. Crap, that wasn't going to be easy to *crack*.

"The missing boys are in the swimming pool," I shouted at Tavish, "and it's got a pixie portal in it."

"Quiet, girl." Aunt Snaky shook me.

"Oh, and there's *three* sharks," I gasped.

"Guid to know, doll." Tavish smiled, teeth white and sharp and equally sharklike against his green-black skin. "Tell me what you are wanting, Malia?"

"I will return this one to you," Aunt Snaky said, "if you agree to retrieve the children for me. One of the boys is a wizard; he has taken himself and his friend out of our reach."

So they are hiding in the pool, not trapped. Clever little wizard.

Tavish obviously thought so too, as he laughed and visibly relaxed. "Then we dinna have anything to bargain with, Malia. You are already shedding. 'Twill nae be much longer before you slip your skin, and you'll nae manage to hold this Ward, nor the one enclosing the square, once your madness comes upon you." He crossed his arms. "So, I'll be waiting until then to retrieve the children."

Sounded like a plan . . .

"Do you not worry for your sidhe?" she asked.

Tavish gave me a considering look. "She's nae a child, and her soul is too dark to serve as your food."

I've got a dark soul? Whatever happened to being a rainbow? Still, good to know Tavish wasn't going to fall for Auntie's ransom demands, and that I wasn't on Auntie's menu.

"Especially when your own blood is handy." Tavish waved at Dora, still huddling almost behind the door.

But Dora was? Pity whispered through me. No wonder she was miserable.

Oddly Dora lifted her camera, shut her eyes, and snapped a couple of shots of Tavish. "The boys will be dead before the ritual is completed," she said in a distant voice. "You will be too late to save them."

"Tell me, lass," he said softly.

The camera flashed again. "If you pass the threshold before the ritual starts, their future changes."

"What to?"

Her eyes snapped open as she lowered the camera and said with a touch of exasperation, "I can't *see* it until it changes; you know that."

I groaned in disbelief. "Tavish, she's lying to make you agree."

Tavish lifted his gaze to mine, and then his eyes flickered to Auntie behind me. "Now I ken why you're here, Malia, and why this time you risk all to take other than your own kin. Your lassie here has inherited the gift of prophecy given to you by Zeus."

"Yes." Auntie sounded both proud and regretful. "It is over a century since a sibyl was last born to my blood, and none before has ever had such easy use of His gift. The digital camera is a glorious invention; *seeing* through it is less painful than removing one's eyes."

"Tavish." I struggled against Auntie's constricting tail. "C'mon, they're trying to scam you."

"Nae, doll." He shook his head. "Sibyls have to speak of that which they *see*, nae matter even if the speaking will lead them to harm. If the lassie says the boys will die if I dinna come in, then that is their future." He pointed at me. "But before I do, Malia, you will let the sidhe go."

"Theodora," Auntie said, "do you have it?"

Dora moved to a small table and picked up a halter of golden rope, knocking off the computer game she'd shown me earlier as she did. She carefully put the game back on the table next to the glossy mag, her fingers gently lingering on her wedding picture as if she were reluctant to let it go. Then she held up the golden halter to show Tavish.

He gave a derisive snort. "I offer you my word, Malia. There is nae need to bind me to your servitude."

"You do not think I would trust your kelpie half to be compelled by your word alone?" She sounded like he must really think her stupid. "It is too wylde and easily lost to the lure of the water." Which was news to me. I hadn't realized Tavish's other shape wasn't just him in another form, but judging by the frustration in Tavish's eyes, she was right, and he'd been hoping she wouldn't know.

Tension thickened the air, and I thought we'd hit some sort of supernatural Mexican standoff—

The sudden sting of fangs in my throat startled me more than any actual pain. I yelped in surprise, and stupidly thought, *Damn, she's bitten me.*

"With my venom in her body, kelpie," Aunt Snaky said, "the girl will die before dawn, even with her sidhe blood. Agree, and I will give you the antidote."

Sick fear curdled my belly. I swallowed and pushed it away. I frowned down at Auntie's red-and-black scaly tail wrapped around me. She had the antidote, but to get it, Tavish had to let her bind him with the golden halter. But if he was bound, then Auntie would hold all the aces, and I'd bet all of Dora's fortune that that would end up with Tavish, me, and more horrifically, the boys dead. Because no way was Aunt Snaky going to say *Thank you* and wish us good health after her dinner.

"Die before dawn's a bit dramatic, isn't it?" I tilted my head back to look up at Auntie. Her hair had dropped out, and her features appeared to have melted, leaving her head doing a good impersonation of an egg, if eggs had red-and-black scales. Very attractive. "Don't s'pose you could be more specific about how much time I've got left?"

She frowned at me, then looked back at Tavish. "Do you agree, kelpie?"

In answer, Tavish screamed with rage and smacked his palms against the Ward. His magic rolled over me like the pressure wave after an explosion. My ears popped painfully, but the Ward didn't break, just flashed the vivid crimson of an anti-*crack* grid and absorbed all the juice he'd thrown at it.

"Kelpie, you cannot break the Ward by force." Aunt Snaky echoed my thoughts. "The more power you use against it, the stronger it becomes. And I would that you were at your best for the task I require of you."

He curled his hands into frustrated fists and dropped his arms. Then he smiled. It was his kelpie smile full of Charm, a predator's smile, but one that cajoled and tempted and beguiled. *A smile that pledged to take all my sorrow, all my loss, all my hurt and leave my soul light and pure and at peace, if I would only come to him, and join with him in the depths* . . . I clawed at the scaly tail that imprisoned me, fighting to go to him, to be with him—

"Theodora! Stop!"

Auntie's shout broke the Charm-net Tavish had caught me in, and I sagged in her hold, bereft and despairing as if I'd lost something precious. The sound of sobs made me look up, and I blinked at Dora. She was on her knees at the front door, grief-stricken tears streaming down her face, and the hand with the gold halter stretched out to Tavish, frozen with her fingers only millimeters away from the Ward. Damn, he'd almost gotten her to break it. But the Ward was still there— An idea burned bright as dragon's fire in my mind.

"You are also time wasting, kelpie," Aunt Snaky said sharply. "Do you agree?"

"Hey, Tavish," I called, "speaking of time wasting, I thought you said my soul looked like rainbows this morning?"

Tavish shook himself like a horse shedding water and sent me a puzzled look. "What, doll?"

Gods, give the kelpie a clue. He needed to get in, and the Ward needed to disappear. So I'd do my party trick. Simple. "Rainbows, and pixie dust, remember?" I said, pointedly.

His dark-pewter eyes showed a shocked rim of white as he caught on. "Nae, doll, you canna, 'tis too strong."

Two boys' lives were at stake. "We can but try," I muttered, and *focused* on the Ward . . .

I *called* it.

For a second, nothing happened, and my stomach clenched in desperation. Then the Ward glowed like hot embers. Auntie hissed and her tail tightened round me, compressing painfully. The Ward melted from the doorframe and flooded like molten lava across the tiled floor toward me. She hissed louder, but just as she started to jerk me away, the Ward streamed over my legs—

—heat blazed through my veins, seared the breath from my lungs, shriveled the flesh on my bones—

And I fell into a furnace of fiery flames.

I CLIMBED MY way back to consciousness and blinked as the blurred writing in front of my nose rearranged itself into something legible: *Round Wire Bright Nails, Steel–Self Color, 6.00 × 6 inch, 1-kg pack.* I blinked again, tried to ignore the spike of pain that felt like a dwarf was hammering one of the six-inch nails into my brain, and scanned around. Apart from the statues in the room off the hallway, I was alone.

Good news: I wasn't dead. Yet. My head was the only thing that was hurting. And the Ward on the front door was now bubbling away inside me like a malevolent spell in a black witch's cauldron.

Bad news: Sucking up the Ward had killed my phone, there were still two kids hiding out in Aunt Snaky's swimming pool, and there was no sign of the gold halter, so Tavish could be fishing the boys up for her dinner.

Good news: Tavish had said Aunt Snaky was near shedding her skin, and I'd gotten the impression that if she did it when the boys weren't around, they'd be safe. Tavish was tricky enough to play for time.

Bad news: If the boys weren't around, Auntie would eat Dora. And I wasn't sure if Dora wasn't as much victim as baddie in all this. And whether her camera was a sort of weird "sibyl accessory" or not, she'd obviously thought getting me involved was going to somehow save her.

But whether Dora needed saving or not, Tavish and the boys still might. I started to scramble up but promptly fell flat on my butt, and discovered why nothing but my head hurt. Aunt Snaky's venom evidently contained some sort of neurotoxin; my legs were paralyzed and the rest of me was about as coordinated as a goblin high on methane. I clamped down on the dread threatening to short-circuit my mind and forced myself to assess the situation.

I could lie here and wait to be rescued, or die (cheerful thought), whichever came first. Neither prospect filled me with anything like joy. Or I could do something. Oh, and if I needed any more motivation, I still owed Auntie for biting me, and for my trashed trouser suit. I needed something to fight with. Half a dozen Stun spells would come in extremely handy right now, but all I had in my backpack was another Look-Away crystal. I surveyed the hallway looking for anything else that could help. There was the army of statues, but even if I had enough pixie dust to animate them—which I didn't—they'd only end up damaging themselves. My eyes lit on the box of nails. And the sledgehammers lined up along the wall. Auntie was magical, and while her snaky skin might be as tough as old boots, nothing reacted well to having six inches of metal hammered into it. Using my arms to pull myself around on the smooth marble floor— thanking the gods it wasn't carpet—I gathered the hammer, the nails, the spell, and two of the platters, which I'd discovered were actually small arm shields, and bundled them all up inside a drop cloth.

By the time I was finished, sweat was stinging my eyes, my arms were shaking with strain, and my headache was holding a fireworks party inside my skull.

I started dragging my haul toward the door down to the swimming pool.

Luckily, the door was open, and thanks to the thunderous sound of the waves crashing in the pool, sneaking stealthily down the stairs was one thing I didn't have to worry about. Getting down them was. After much maneuvering I balanced the bundled drop cloth on the backs of my thighs, tucking an end into my waistband, and started crawling down headfirst. The numbing paralysis had crept up around my waist, which was a good thing: it meant I couldn't feel my hips bumping down the sharp-edged stairs. I was going to be bruised six ways to Sunday.

"Always hoping I get to see Sunday," I gasped, reaching the bottom.

I dragged myself along the opaque glass corridor, pushing snake scales the size of my palms out of the way, until I reached the open door to the pool room. I rested my forehead on the cool tile and went over my plan again, then sent a quick prayer to whatever gods might be listening.

I unpacked my loot from the drop cloth, my nervous fingers feeling like rubber sausages.

I propped the two shields—one copper, one shining silver—against the glass wall, activated the Look-Away crystal, and slid forward so I could peer into the pool room.

Hope and relief flooded into me as I searched for, but didn't find, any signs of the missing boys.

Or Tavish.

And the sharks were gone.

But unfortunately Aunt Snaky wasn't. She was swaying gently at the edge of the pool, staring out at the waves breaking its surface. She was fully snaked out, with a huge hood of black-and-red scales framing her head and shoulders. The rest of her was nude, if you discounted the dia-mond pattern of scales sweeping down her back and tapering into her coiled serpent's tail. And around her waist was a wide shawl of what looked like crinkled plastic. I frowned, mystified, until I realized it was her partly shed skin.

Next to her, Dora sat huddled on the tiles, staring down at her camera.

She was also nude; the same pattern of red-and-black scales marked down her back and arms, but hers was fainter, and her hair was still black spikes instead of a cobralike hood.

Showtime.

I crunched down on a mouthful of licorice torpedoes, grabbed a handful of the six-inch nails, and threw them out over the beachlike expanse so they landed between Auntie and me.

They chinked loudly as they scattered and bounced over the terra-cotta tiles.

Dora and Aunt Snaky both searched the pool room, looking for the source of the noise. In the wrong direction. Yay for Look-Away spells.

I threw more nails.

This time the spell failed, and they both turned my way.

Dora's eyes widened in surprise and possibly hope.

Auntie hissed, her snaky red eyes gleaming angrily in her much younger and much less wrinkled face. She started sidewinding slowly toward me, her tail making a sizzling sound like water on a hot plate.

I rolled the copper arm shield out in front of me, swallowing back panic as I realized the numbness was creeping up my chest and into my shoulders. I shouted a warning to Dora. She jerked in shock, then lifted her camera to her face instead of moving. Damn. Her choice, though.

I reached deep inside myself for the solid lump of pixie dust, and then, using my will, I blew half of it so it sprinkled over the nails, and prayed the pixie magic would do its stuff. The nails jumped to attention, sharp points spiking upward, and formed my own little defense of six-inch spears. Auntie slid right over them. Dora was right; her skin was as tough as old boots. They didn't slow her down much. But hopefully they'd done enough to persuade Dora to believe in me.

"Last chance, Dora," I shouted.

Relief swept over me as she leaped up and dived into the pool.

Auntie's huge tail whipped up and back—

I ducked down behind the arm shield I held and slapped the last of the pixie dust on the small bas-relief face carved on the shield's front.

—the tail hurtled down toward me, shedding sharp-edged red-and-black scales—

A tremor shivered through the shield and its carved face let out a furious screech.

—the scales flashed to gray, and Aunt Snaky's tail and the rest of her turned to stone.

I dropped my head to the cool floor and gave thanks.

The shield quivered against me, reminding me that I had one last thing to do. Clumsily, I rolled out the other shining silver shield in front of it. For a second I caught the reflection of the small, stylized Medusa head carved in the center of the copper shield, her lips drawn back in a fang-filled grin, tiny serpents writhing around her angry face, before she saw her own mirror image, and she too turned to stone.

The numbness crept into my fingers, both shields slipped from my hold, and unconsciousness rolled over me.

I CAME AROUND to the quiet slap of water and the strange taste of dark spiced blood in my mouth. Surprise and relief drifted through me that I was alive and could feel all my toes and fingers, and the rest of me, even if it felt like I'd been mugged by a horde of Beater goblins. How I was alive was another matter, but I was too exhausted to care, so I just lay there.

After a while a rhythmic sound pricked my ears, and I realized I'd fallen asleep. I opened my eyes. The water in the swimming pool was flat and peaceful; the waves had gone. But as I watched, a dark shape swam closer, spreading gentle ripples in its wake. It reached the edge and rose up out of the pool, water and blood dripping from its matted green-black coat, and I saw that it was the kelpie horse. The kelpie stood for a long moment, his broad chest heaving, and then he shuddered and flicked his tail over the bloody bite marks in his muscled flank, and picked his way through the rubble that littered the terra-cotta tiles like the aftermath of an explosion.

The kelpie whickered worriedly as it reached me. It lowered its head and blew a greeting of whisky-peat breath into my face. I lifted my hand and stroked the warm velvet of its muzzle, smiling as its chin whiskers tickled along my arm, and reached up to trail gentle fingers over the black-lace gills that fluttered under my touch.

"You're beautiful," I murmured.

The kelpie tossed its head, red beads clicking in the knotted dreads of its mane, and magic cascaded over the horse like multicolored jewels sparkling in the brightness of the lights . . .

And Tavish took his human shape.

He slid tiredly down next to me and pulled me into his lap, and I tucked my face into the smooth heat of his neck as he wrapped his arms around me.

"The boys are both safe and well, doll," he said in a rough burr. "They were in a circle at the bottom of the pool, and the wee wizard was just about done in *holding* it."

Good. "What about you? You're hurt."

"Och, the sharks were a mite bothersome"—he patted my shoulder—"but naught to worry about. So, did Malia take the lassie once she'd shed her skin?"

"No," I said, and told him what had happened.

"It was Dora," I finished, "or rather her game, Quest for the Aegis of Athena, that gave me the idea."

He picked up a lump of stone: it had scales etched on one side. "How did Malia end up like this?"

"Ahh, that wasn't me. Last I saw Auntie, she was all in one piece." Even if she'd had a bit of a stony expression going on. I pointed at the sledgehammer standing defiant in the middle of the rubble and said dead-pan, "Think Dora decided on a full-scale demolition."

"Aye, well," Tavish answered in an amused voice, "it tipped the scales in her favor."

I groaned. "*That* was bad."

He laughed. "Yours were nae any better, doll."

I stuck my tongue out at him, then asked the question that had been bugging me. "How did you know what was going on?"

"Hmm," Tavish snorted softly. "I'd seen the wee lassie's soul when she was following you, but she was still human enough that if she wasnae using her camera, I couldnae *see* the lamia's taint. And without *seeing* that, I couldnae tell what her shell looked like. Then after the children went missing, Malia phoned, wanting my help with something. Lamias mostly take their own blood when they shed to forestall any repercussions, but I caught on that Malia wasnae going to this time. So we were tiptoe-ing around a bargain, but I couldnae get close enough to find the children until she lured you here."

"So you used me as bait?"

"Something like that," he said quietly. "I'm sorry, doll."

The boys were saved, we were both alive, Dora had escaped and hopefully had a chance at a new life now she wasn't going to be a lamia, and in the end the only one dead and gone was Auntie. Which really wasn't such a loss. So there really wasn't anything to be angry about.

I tugged a couple of his dreads. "Next time you decide to set me up," I said, "tell me first."

"Aye," he murmured, "if you say so."

I licked my lips and tasted the dark spiced blood again. "Dora must have given me the antidote," I said, almost to myself.

Tavish didn't answer, and, happy just to be alive, I listened to the steady beat of his heart for a while, then traced a finger over his lean chest. "So, how about we do something a bit more irresponsible for our next *date . . .*"

He gave a soft laugh. "What sort o' thing have you in mind, doll?"

"When you think of it"—I smiled sleepily—"call me."

SIX WEEKS LATER I received a parcel at the office. Inside was a glossy celebrity magazine. The cover showed a smiling Dora standing in front of a huge poster depicting a pixie in a muscleman pose. The headline read: THEODORA CHRISTAKIS, OWNER OF HEROPHILE FUTURES, ENDS 40 DAYS OF MOURNING WITH THE ANNOUNCEMENT OF HER NEW VENTURE. Also in the parcel was a computer game; its brightly colored sleeve read: PIXIE PLANET ~ PROTECTING OUR FUTURE: HEROPHILE'S NEW LINE OF EDUCATIONAL GAMES FOR THE YOUNGER GENERATION ~ ALL PROFITS TO BE DONATED TO CHILDREN'S CHARITIES.

Good to know Dora was planning on helping kids now, instead of eating them.

I wished her good fortune.

It's All in the Rendering

SIMON R. GREEN

There is a House that stands on the border. Between here and there, between dreams and waking, between reality and fantasy. The House has been around for longer than anyone remembers, because it's necessary. Walk in through the front door, from the sane and everyday world, and everything you see will seem perfectly normal. Walk in through the back door, from any of the worlds of *if* and *maybe*, and a very different House will appear before you. The House stands on the border, linking two worlds, and providing Sanctuary for those who need it. A refuge, from everyone and everything. A safe place, from all the evils of all the worlds.

Needless to say, there are those who aren't too keen on this.

IT ALL STARTED in the kitchen, on a bright sunny day, just like any other day. Golden sunlight poured in through the open window, gleaming richly on the old-fashioned furniture and the modern fittings. Peter and Jubilee Caine, currently in charge of the House, were having breakfast together. At least, Peter was; Jubilee wasn't really a morning person. Jubilee would cheerfully throttle every last member of the dawn chorus in return for just another half-hour's lie-in.

Peter was busy making himself a full English breakfast: bacon and eggs, sausages and beans, and lots of fried bread. Of medium height and medium weight, Peter was a happy if vague sort, but a master of the frying pan—on the grounds that if you ever found something you couldn't cook in the pan, you could still use it to beat the animal to death. Peter moved happily back and forth, doing half a dozen difficult culinary things with calm and easy competence, while singing along to the Settlers' "Lightning Tree" on the radio.

Jubilee, tall and blond and almost impossibly graceful, usually, sat hunched at the kitchen table, clinging to a large mug of industrial-strength black coffee, like a shipwrecked mariner to a lifebelt. Her mug bore the legend *Worship Me Like the Goddess I Am or There Will Be Some Serious Smiting.* She glared darkly at Peter over the rim of her mug as though his every cheerful moment were a deliberate assault on her fragile early-morning nerves.

"It should be made illegal, to be that cheerful in the morning," she announced, to no one in particular. "It's not natural. And I can't believe you're still preparing that Death by Cholesterol fry-up every morning. Things like this should be spelled out in detail on the marriage license. I can hear your arteries curdling from here, just from proximity to that much unhealthiness in one place."

"Start the day with a challenge, that's what I always say," said Peter. "If I can survive this, I can survive anything. Will any of our current Guests be joining us for breakfast?"

"I doubt it. Lee only comes out at night, and Johnny is a teenager, which means he doesn't even know what this hour of the morning looks like. Look, can we please have something else from the radio? Something less . . . enthusiastic?"

The music broke off immediately. "I heard that!" said the radio. "Today is Sixties day! Because that's what I like. They had real music in those days—songs that would put hair on your chest, with tunes that stuck in your head whether you wanted them to or not. And no, I don't do Coldplay, so stop asking. Would you care to hear a Monkees medley?"

"Remember what happened to the toaster?" said Jubilee, dangerously.

There was a pause. "I do take requests," the radio said finally.

"Play something soothing," said Peter. "For those of us whose bodies might be up and about, but whose minds haven't officially joined in yet."

The radio played a selection from Grieg's *Peer Gynt*, while Peter cheerfully loaded up his plate with all manner of things that were bad for him. He laid it down carefully on the table and smiled over at Jubilee.

"You sure I can't tempt you to just a little of this yummy fried goodness, princess?"

Jubilee actually shuddered. "I'd rather inject hot fat directly into my veins. Get me some milk, sweetie."

Peter went over to the fridge. "Is this a full-fat or a semiskim day?"

"Give me the real deal. I've got a feeling it's going to be one of those days."

Peter opened the fridge door, and a long green warty arm came out, offering a bottle of milk. Peter accepted the bottle, while being very careful not to make contact with any of the lumpy bumpy fingers.

"Thank you, Walter," he said.

"Welcome, I'm sure," said a deep green warty voice from the back of the fridge. "You couldn't turn the thermostat down just a little more, could you?"

"Any lower, and you'll have icicles hanging off them," said Peter.

There was a rich green warty chuckle. "That's the way, uh-huh, uh-huh, I like it, uh-huh, uh-huh . . ."

"No Seventies!" shrieked the radio.

Peter shut the fridge door with great firmness and went back to join Jubilee at the kitchen table. He passed her the milk and sat down, and then he ate while she poured and then sipped, and the gentle strains of "Solveig's Song" wafted from the radio. It was all very civilized.

Peter glanced back at the fridge. "How long has Walter been staying here, princess?"

"He was here long before we arrived," said Jubilee. "According to the House records, Walter claims to be a refugee from the Martian Ice People, exiled to Earth for religious heresies and public unpleasantness. Hasn't left that fridge in years. Supposedly because he's afraid of global warming; I think he's just more than usually agoraphobic."

Two small hairy things exploded through the inner door and ran around and around the kitchen at speed, calling excitedly to each other in high-pitched voices as they chased a brightly colored bouncing ball. They shot under the kitchen table at such speed that Peter and Jubilee barely had time to get their feet out of the way; just two hairy little blurs.

"Hey!" said Jubilee, trying hard to sound annoyed but unable to keep the fondness out of her voice. "No running in the House! And no ball games in the kitchen."

The two small hairy things stopped abruptly, revealing themselves to be barely three feet in height, most of it fur. Two sets of wide eyes blinked guiltily from the head region, while the ball bounced up and down between them.

"I don't mind," said the ball. "Really. I'm quite enjoying it."

"Then go enjoy it somewhere else," said Peter. "I have a lot of breakfast to get through, and I don't want my concentration interrupted. My digestion is a finely balanced thing, and a wonder of nature."

"And stay out of the study," said Jubilee. "Remember, you break it, and your progenitors will pay for it."

"We'll be careful!" said a high piping voice from somewhere under one set of fur.

The brightly colored ball bounced off out of the kitchen, followed by excitedly shouting hairy things. A blessed peace descended on the kitchen as Peter and Jubilee breakfasted in their own accustomed ways and enjoyed each other's company. Outside the open window, birds were singing, the occasional traffic noise was comfortably far away, and all seemed well with the world. Eventually Peter decided he'd enjoyed about as much of his breakfast as he could stand, and got up to scrape the last vestiges off his plate and into the sink disposal. Which shouted, *"Feed me! Feed me, Seymour!"* until Peter threatened to shove another teaspoon down it. He washed his plate and cutlery with usual thoroughness, put them out to dry, and stretched unhurriedly.

"Big day ahead, princess," Peter said finally. "I have to fix the hot water system, clean out the guttering, make all the beds, and sort out the laundry."

"I have to redraw the protective wardings, recharge the enchantments in the night garden, clean up after the gargoyles, and refurbish the rainbow."

"I have to mow the lawns and rake the leaves."

"I have to clean out the moat."

Peter laughed. "All right, princess. You win. Want to swap?"

"Each to their own, sweetie. Be a dear and wash out my mug."

"What did your last slave die of?"

"Not washing out my mug properly. Be a dear; and there will be snuggles later."

"Ooh . . . Sweaty snuggles?"

"In this weather, almost certainly."

And that should have been it. Just another day begun, in the House on the border. But that . . . was when the front doorbell rang. A loud, ominous ring. Peter and Jubilee looked at each other.

"I'm not expecting anyone," said Jubilee. "Are you?"

"No," said Peter. "I'm not."

The doorbell rang again, very firmly. One of those *I'm not going to go away so there's no point hiding behind the furniture pretending to be out* kind of rings. Peter went to answer it. He opened the front door and immediately stepped outside, forcing the visitor to step back a few paces. Peter shut the door very firmly behind him and had a quick look around, just to make sure that everything was as it should be. In the real world, the House was just an ordinary detached residence, a bit old-fashioned-looking, set back a comfortable distance from the main road, with a neatly raked gravel path running between carefully maintained lawns. Flowers, here and there. The House was almost defiantly ordinary, with doors and windows in the right places, and in the right proportions, tiles on the roof, and guttering that worked as often as it didn't. Nothing to look at, keep moving, forgetting you already.

Standing before Peter was a rather uptight middle-aged person in a tight-fitting suit, whose largely undistinguished features held the kind of tight-arsed expression clearly designed to indicate that he was a man with an unpleasant duty to perform, which he intended to carry out with all the personal pleasure at his command.

"Is this number thirteen Daemon Street?" said the person, in the kind of voice used by people who already have the answer to their question, but are hoping you're going to be stupid enough to argue about it.

"Yes," said Peter firmly. He felt he was on safe enough ground there.

"I am Mister Cuthbert. I represent the local Council." He paused a moment, so that Peter could be properly impressed.

"Damn," said Peter. "The *move along nothing to see here* avoidance field must be on the blink."

"What?"

"Nothing!" said Peter. "Do carry on. The local Council, eh? How interesting. Is it an interesting job? Why are you here, Mister Cuthbert? I've been good. Mostly."

"It has come to our attention," said Mister Cuthbert, just a little doggedly, "that you have not been maintaining the proper amenities of this residence to the required standards."

"But . . . it's our house," said Peter. "Not the Council's."

"There are still standards! Standards have to be met! All parts and parcels of every house in the district must come up to the required criteria. Regulations apply to everyone; it's a matter of health and safety." And having unleashed that unstoppable trump card, Mister Cuthbert allowed himself a small smile. "I shall have to make . . . an inspection."

"What?" said Peter. "Now?"

"Yes, now! I have all the necessary paperwork with me . . ."

"I felt sure you would, Mister Cuthbert," said Peter. "You look the type. Well, you'd better come on in and take a look around. You'll have to take us as you find us, though."

WHILE PETER WAS having his close encounter with a supremely up-its-own-arse denizen of the local Council, there was a hard, heavy, and even aristocratic knock at the back door. Jubilee went to answer it, frowning thoughtfully. Visitors to the House were rare enough, from either world. Two at once were almost unheard of. The back door to the House was a massive slab of ancient oak, deeply carved with long lines of runes and sigils. Jubilee snapped her fingers at the door as she approached, and the heavy door swung smoothly open before her. She stepped forcefully out into the cool moonlight of late evening, and her visitor was forced to retreat a few steps, despite himself. The door slammed very firmly shut behind her. Jubilee ostentatiously ignored her visitor for a few moments, glancing quickly around her to reassure herself that everything on the night side of the House was where it should be.

Here, the House was a sprawling Gothic mansion, with grotesquely carved stone and woodwork, latticed windows, cupolas, garrets, leering gargoyles peering down from the roof, and a tangle of twisted chimneys. Set out before the House, a delicate wicker bridge crossed the dark and murky waters of the moat, leading to a small zoo of animal shapes in greenery, and deep purple lawns. Ancient trees with long gnarled branches like clutching fingers stood guard over a garden whose flowers were famously as ferocious as they were stunning. The night sky was full of stars, spinning like Catherine wheels, and the full moon was a promising shade of blue.

Jubilee finally deigned to notice the personage standing before her. He didn't need to announce he was an Elven Prince of the Unseeli Court. He couldn't have been anything else. Tall and supernaturally slender, in silver-filigreed brass armor, he had pale colorless skin, cat-pupiled eyes, and pointed ears. Inhumanly handsome, insufferably graceful, and almost unbearably arrogant. Not because he was a Prince, you understand; but because he was an Elf. He bowed to Jubilee.

"Don't," Jubilee said immediately. "Just . . . don't. What do you want here, Prince Airgedlamh?"

"I come on moonfleet heels, faster than the winter winds or summer tides, walking the hidden ways to bear you words of great import and urgency . . ."

"And you can cut that out, too; I don't have the patience," said Jubilee. "What do you want?"

"It has been made known to us," the Elven Prince said stiffly, "that many of the old magics, the pacts and agreements laid down when this House was first agreed on, are not being properly maintained, as required in that Place where all that matters is decided. I must make an inspection."

"Now?"

"Yes. I have the proper authority."

"Buttocks," said Jubilee, with more than ordinary force. "All right, you'd better come in. And wipe those armored boots properly. The floor gets very bad-tempered if you track mud over it."

PETER LED MISTER Cuthbert around the House. Because the man from the local Council had entered the House from the everyday world, that was the aspect of the House he should see. So it always had been, and so it must always be, in the House that links the worlds, if only because most people can't cope with more than one world at a time. Mister Cuthbert took his own sweet time looking around the kitchen, sniffing loudly to demonstrate his disapproval of absolutely everything, and then allowed Peter to lead him out into the main hall.

"How many rooms in this residence, Mister Caine?" Mister Cuthbert demanded, peering suspiciously about him.

Peter didn't like to say *It depends*, so he just guessed. "Nine?"

"Oh dear," Mister Cuthbert said smugly, shaking his head happily. "Oh dear, oh dear, Mister Caine . . . That doesn't agree with our information at all! I shall have to make a note."

And he got out a notepad and pen and took his own sweet time about making the note. Peter tried to lean in to see what he was writing, but Mister Cuthbert immediately turned away so he couldn't.

"I haven't been here that long," said Peter. "The wife and I only moved in three years ago."

"You haven't gotten around to counting the number of rooms in your house, in three years, Mister Caine?"

"I've had a lot on my plate," said Peter.

"So; you don't actually own this desirable residence?" said Mister Cuthbert.

"We hold it in trust," said Peter. "It's like the National Trust. Only more so. You'll find that all the proper paperwork was submitted to the Council long ago . . ."

Mister Cuthbert sniffed loudly, to indicate he didn't believe that for one moment but would let it go for now. He was so busy with this little performance that he didn't notice all the faces in the portraits on the walls turning to look at him. Disapprovingly. Mister Cuthbert wasn't supposed to notice anything of that nature, but with the avoidance spells malfunctioning, God alone knew what else might go wrong in the House . . .

Two small hairy things chased their ball down the hall and then slammed to an abrupt halt to stare at Mister Cuthbert.

"My niece and nephew," Peter said quickly. "They're visiting."

"What a charming young boy and girl," said Mister Cuthbert, just a bit vaguely. And to him, they probably were. Though given his expression, charming was probably pushing it a bit. He reached out to pat them on the head, but some last-minute self-preservation instinct made him realize this wasn't a good idea, and he pulled his hand back again. Peter hurried him past the hairy things and showed him the downstairs rooms. Mister Cuthbert was, if anything, even less impressed than before and made a number of notes in his little book. Finally, they went upstairs.

"We have two Guests staying with us at the moment," Peter said carefully. There were others, but none of them the kind that Mister Cuthbert could usefully be introduced to. "In the first room we have a young lady called Lee, visiting from the Isle of Man. Next door is Johnny, a young man just down from London, for a while. Do we really need to disturb them, this early in the day?"

"Early?" said Mister Cuthbert. "I myself have been up for hours. I am not the sort to let the day pass me by when there is important work to be done. Oh no; I must see everything, while I'm here. And everyone. My job requires it." He stopped suddenly and looked about him. "What the hell was *that*?"

"The hot water boiler, up in the attic," Peter said quickly. "It's temperamental. Though you'll have to bring your own ladder, if you want to inspect it. We don't go up there."

"The boiler can be inspected on a future visit," Mister Cuthbert conceded. "There must be something seriously wrong with it, if it can make noises like that. Sounded very much like something . . . growling."

"Oh you are such a wag, Mister Cuthbert," said Peter. "Such a sense of humor."

Mister Cuthbert headed for the Guest rooms. Peter glared up at the attic. "Keep a lid on it, Grandfather Grendel! We've got a visitor!"

He hurried after Mister Cuthbert, who had stopped outside the first Guest door. Peter moved quickly in and knocked very politely on the door.

"Lee? This is Peter. We have a caller from the local Council. Are you decent?"

"Close as I ever get, darling," said a rich sultry voice from inside the room. "Come on in, boys. The more the merrier, that's what I always say."

Peter swallowed hard, smiled meaninglessly at Mister Cuthbert, and put all his trust in the House's special nature. Fortunately, when he and Mister Cuthbert entered the room, it all seemed perfectly normal, if a bit gloomy. A slim and very pale teenage Goth girl was reclining on an unmade bed, dressed in dark jeans and a black T-shirt bearing the legend *I'm only wearing this till they come up with a darker color.* She also wore steel-studded black leather bracelets around her wrists and throat. Her unhealthily pale face boasted more dark eye makeup than a panda on the pull, and bloodred lips. The bedroom walls were covered with posters featuring The Cure, The Mission, and Fields Of the Nephilim. The girl rose unhurriedly to her feet, every movement smooth and elegant and just that little bit disturbing, and then she smiled slowly at Mister Cuthbert. Peter moved instinctively to put himself between Lee and the man from the Council.

"Just introducing Mister Cuthbert to the Guests, Lee," he said quickly. "He can't stay long. He has to get back. Because people might notice if he went missing."

Lee pouted. "I don't know why you keep going on about that. It was just the one time."

"Are you . . . comfortable here?" said Mister Cuthbert, apparently because he felt he should be saying something.

"Oh yes," said Lee. "Very comfortable." She smiled widely at Mister Cuthbert, and there was a flash of very sharp teeth behind the dark lips.

Peter quickly maneuvered Mister Cuthbert back out into the corridor. The man from the Council was flustered enough that he let Peter do it, even if he didn't quite understand why.

"Does she pay rent?" he said, vaguely.

"No," said Peter. "She's a Guest."

"I'll have to make a note," said Mister Cuthbert. And he did.

The next door along opened as they approached it, and out stepped a quiet, nervous young man, in a blank white T-shirt and distressed blue jeans. He was handsome enough, in an unfinished sort of way. He put his hands in his pockets, because he didn't know what else to do with them, and looked mournfully at Mister Cuthbert.

"Hello. You're not from the tabloids, are you?"

"No, Johnny," Peter said quickly. "He's from the local Council."

"Don't I know you from somewhere?" said Mister Cuthbert, doubtfully. "I'm almost sure I've seen you somewhere before . . ."

"I was on a television talent show," Johnny said reluctantly. "It all got a bit much, so I came here, to . . . get away from it all, for a while."

"Oh, I never watch those shows," Mister Cuthbert said immediately, in much the same kind of voice as one might say *I never watch bear-baiting.* He insisted on a good look around Johnny's room, found nothing of any interest whatsoever, made a note about that, and then trudged back down the stairs again. Peter hurried after him. Mister Cuthbert strode back through the House, into the kitchen, and then stopped abruptly at the front door. He gave Peter a stern look, the kind meant to indicate *I am a man to be reckoned with and don't you forget it.*

"I can see there are a great many things that will have to be dealt with to bring this property up to scratch, Mister Caine. I shall of course be sending in a full investigative team. Have all the floorboards up, to inspect the wiring. Might have to open up all the walls, rewire the entire House. And a residence this size, with guests, should have proper central heating; not just some noisy old boiler in the attic. That will definitely have to be replaced. I'm sure I saw rising damp, the whole of the outside needs rendering, and what I can see of your roof is a disgrace! We'll have to put up scaffolding all around the property." He smiled thinly, his eyes full of quiet satisfaction. "I'm afraid this is all going to prove rather expensive for you, Mister Caine; but regulations are regulations, and standards must be maintained. Good day to you. You'll be hearing from me again, very soon."

He left the house as importantly as he'd arrived, slamming the door behind him. Up in the attic, Grandfather Grendel made a very rude noise, and the House smelled briefly of rotting petunias.

JUBILEE LED THE Elven Prince Airgedlamh around the House, though of course he saw a very different establishment. He strolled arrogantly down the hall, refusing to be hurried, remarking loudly on the substandard nature of the ambience and the lack of proper protective magics. He did notice the portrait faces on the walls glaring at him with open disdain and met them all glare for glare. He was used to general disapproval. He was an Elf. Jubilee let him wander round the downstairs rooms, making haughty and occasionally downright rude remarks as the mood took him, before Jubilee was finally able to lead him upstairs to the Guest rooms. Grandfather Grendel made some more extremely rude noises.

"Be still, old creation," said the Elven Prince, without even looking up at the attic. "Don't make me have to come up there."

He pushed open the first door and strode right in, not giving Jubilee time to knock or even introduce him. Inside, the room was dark and clammy and subtly oppressive. The Elven Prince slammed to a halt in spite of himself, and Jubilee moved quickly in beside him. Lee might be just a teenage Goth in the day world, but here her true nature was unleashed. Leanan-Sidhe was a dark Muse from the Isle of Man, inspiration for artists of the macabre and the mysterious; those who dreamed of her often produced powerful and magnificent work, only to burn out fast and die young. Leanan-Sidhe was a harsh mistress and a debilitating Muse, and everyone knew what she fed on.

The Elven Prince bowed stiffly to her, again almost in spite of himself. The Muse's room was a dark cavern, with blood dripping slowly down the rough stone walls. Leanan-Sidhe reclined at her ease on the huge pulpy petals of a crimson rose, floating in a sea of tears. She was a dark presence of overwhelming demeanor, more shadow than substance. Her ashen face floated in the darkness like a malignant moon on a very dark night. She had no eyes, only deep dark eye sockets, and her mouth was the color of dried blood. She smiled sweetly on Prince Airgedlamh, revealing rows of very sharp teeth, like a shark.

"Come on in, sweet prince, my very dear, and I'll show you what dreams are made of."

The Elven Prince wavered but stood firm. "Tempt me not, dark Muse . . ."

"But darling," said Leanan-Sidhe, "that's what I do . . ."

She laughed richly, and the Elven Prince couldn't get out of the room fast enough. Jubilee smiled sweetly at Leanan-Sidhe, who dropped her a brief wink, and then she went back out into the hall. With the door safely shut again, Prince Airgedlamh quickly regained his composure and insisted on moving on to the next room. Jubilee nodded, and again Johnny was there waiting for them.

"Hello," he said sadly. "I'm Johnny Jay, the voice of the suffering masses. Pop prince of show tunes. Simon Callow says I'm a genius."

"I do not know you," said Prince Airgedlamh.

Johnny Jay actually brightened up a little. "Really? Oh, that's wonderful! Such a relief, to meet someone who doesn't want something from me. Even if it's only an autograph."

Prince Airgedlamh looked at Jubilee, who shrugged briefly. "Mortal stuff. He sings."

"Yes," said the Elven Prince. "I see the mark upon him. Send him to the Unseeli Court. The Fae have always had a fondness for human bards."

"I think he's got enough problems at the moment," said Jubilee.

But the Elven Prince had already lost interest and turned away. Johnny nodded glumly and went back into his room. Prince Airgedlamh stopped at the top of the stairs and looked up at the attic, where loud shifting noises suggested that something very large was trampling down its bedding.

"What *is* that? I can sense its age, but its true nature is hidden from me."

"Oh that's just Grandfather Grendel," said Jubilee. "He's been up in that attic for centuries, according to the House records. My husband and I inherited him when we moved in. As long as we throw him some raw meat once in a while, and a handful of sugar mice, he's happy enough. Every now and again he threatens to spin himself a cocoon and transmogrify into a whole new deity, but it hasn't happened yet. I think he's just bluffing. Of course, it could just be a plea for attention."

"Guests are supposed to be strictly temporary," said the Elven Prince. "That is the point of a Guest, is it not?"

"Nothing in the rules," Jubilee said blithely. "Besides, who knows what *temporary* means, with a life span like Grandfather Grendel's?"

They went back down the stairs and had only just reached the bottom when two small hairy things came running down the hall, pursued by the bouncing ball. They stopped abruptly to stare at the Elven Prince and then snarled loudly at him. Huge mouths full of jagged teeth appeared in their fur.

"Vermin," said Prince Airgedlamh. "I shall have to make a note."

"We are not in any way vermin!" snapped one of the hairy things. "We are scavengers! We keep the House free of pests. We're only supposed to eat small things . . ."

"But we are perfectly prepared to make an exception in your case!" finished the other. "No one bullies Jubilee while we're around."

"Want me to do something appalling to Prince Scumbag here?" said the ball, bouncing threateningly in place.

"Everything's under control, thank you," said Jubilee, in her best calm and soothing voice. "You boys run along."

They did so, reluctantly. The Elven Prince did his best to pretend nothing had just happened. He sniffed coldly and looked down his long nose at Jubilee.

"I can see there is much here that will have to be done to bring this

House into line with all the relevant agreements. The gargoyles must be neutered, the moat must be dredged, and many of the old magics have been allowed to fade around the edges. They will all have to be renewed, with the appropriate blood sacrifices. Your garden is a disgrace, and where have all the mushrooms gone? This House has fallen far from what it should be, and much work will have to be done to put things right. Appropriate payments will of course also have to be made."

He bowed quickly to Jubilee, before she could stop him, and then he strode back through the House and was out the back door and across the wicker bridge, heading off into the night. Jubilee closed the door thoughtfully after him and then walked back down the hall.

"All right! That's it! Everyone join me in the kitchen, right now! House meeting!"

IN THE KITCHEN, very soon afterward, Peter and Jubilee, Lee, and Johnny sat around the table and looked at each other glumly. The radio was being quiet, thinking hard, trying to be useful. The fridge door had been left open, just in case Walter felt like contributing something useful. Up in the attic, Grandfather Grendel was being ominously silent.

"We can't let this happen," Peter said finally. "We just can't! Scaffolding from the Council, blood sacrifices for the Unseeli Court; all kinds of interior work to satisfy both sides . . . there's bound to be an overlap! They couldn't help but interfere with each other and cause all kinds of conflicts. This House is supposed to link the two worlds, not bang their heads together."

"It could mean the end of the House as a refuge," said Jubilee. "If no one feels safe and secure here, if we can't guarantee anonymity . . . No more Sanctuary for anyone."

"I can't go back to the Isle of Man," Lee said firmly. "I have had it up to here with being a Muse. I do all the hard work and the artists take all the credit! I never even get a dedication . . . And they're such a *needy* bunch! So clingy . . . All those bloody poets hanging around, demanding inspiration . . . I haven't had a decent holiday in centuries! I never wanted to be dark and morbid anyway . . . I should have been a sylph, like Mother wanted . . ."

"I know what you mean," Johnny Jay said diffidently. "I won't go back to London. I just won't. Ever since I won that damned talent contest, the television people and the tabloids have been making my life a misery. I never wanted to be a national icon; I just wanted to sing, and make people happy. The tabloids have been doorstopping all my family and friends, and anyone who ever spoke to me, looking for *interesting* stories; and when they don't find any, they just make some up! I've never even been to Spearmint Rhino!"

"I am not leaving!" said Leanan-Sidhe. "I have claimed Sanctuary, and I know my rights! I demand that you protect me from this unwelcome outside interference!"

Peter looked at Jubilee. "The rules of the House say we have to give Guests Sanctuary. No one ever said we had to like them."

"We can still give them a good slap," said Jubilee.

"Can I watch?" said Johnny Jay, brightening up a little.

"We have to do something," said Peter. "If the nature of the House is compromised, if the two worlds can no longer be kept separate . . . Could that actually happen, princess?"

"I don't think the matter has ever arisen before," said Jubilee, frowning thoughtfully. "The House exists in a state of spiritual grace, of perfect balance between the two worlds of being. Shift that balance too far either way, and this House could cease to function. A new House would have to be created somewhere else, with new management. We would not be considered. We would have failed our duty. After all these centuries, we would be the first to fail the House . . ."

"It hasn't come to that yet, princess," said Peter, laying one hand comfortingly over hers. "Can the House really be threatened so easily? I thought the House was created and protected by Higher Powers."

"We're supposed to solve our own problems," said Jubilee. "That's the job."

"Cuthbert might not know what he's doing," said Lee, "but you can bet that bloody Elf does. He must understand the implications of what he's saying."

"Of course he does!" said Jubilee. "He knows exactly what he's doing. Our usual avoidance fields didn't just happen to fail, revealing us to the normal world, at exactly the same time the Unseeli Court decides to take an interest in us. This was planned. I think somebody targeted us, set this all in motion for a reason."

"To destroy the House?" said Lee.

"Who would want to do that?" said Johnny Jay.

"Or . . . are they doing this to get at someone who thought they were safe, inside the House?" Lee scowled, and something of her darker persona was briefly present in the kitchen with them. They all shuddered briefly. Lee politely pretended not to notice. "I thought anyone who claimed Sanctuary here was entitled to full privacy and protection? If any of those demanding little poets have followed me here to make trouble . . ."

"Your safety in all things is guaranteed, for as long as you care to stay here," Jubilee said coldly. "It isn't always about you, you know. I think . . . this is all about me, and Peter. It's all about us."

"Your family never was that keen on our marriage, princess," Peter said carefully.

"It wasn't their place to say anything," said Jubilee. "It's the tradition, that the House's management should be a married couple, one from each world. I was happy to marry you, and happy to come here; they should have been happy for me."

"I was never happier than when you joined your life to mine," said Peter. "You're everything I ever wanted. The House was just a wonderful bonus. But . . . if our marriage is threatening the House . . . I'm here because I wanted to be part of something greater, something important. I won't let that be threatened because of me. We can't let the House be destroyed because of us, princess. Not when it's in our power to save it."

"It's my family," Jubilee said grimly. "Has to be. My bloody family. They'd be perfectly ready to see this House destroyed, just to have me back where they think I belong. Because they can't bear to believe that they might be wrong about something. Maybe . . . If I were to go back, they might call this off . . . But no. No . . . I could leave this House to protect it, but I couldn't leave you, Peter. My love."

"And they'd never accept me," said Peter. "You know that. I'd have to agree to leave you before they'd take you back."

"Could you do that?" said Jubilee.

"The House is bigger than either of us," said Peter. "We've always known that, princess. I could not love thee half so much . . ."

". . . Loved I not honor more," said Jubilee. "We both love this House: what it represents, and the freedoms it preserves."

"That's why we got the job," said Peter. "Because we'd do anything to protect this place. And now that's being turned against us."

"I could leave," Lee said abruptly. "If I thought it would help. If only because you two clearly serve a Higher Power than me."

"Same here," said Johnny Jay.

"No!" Peter said flatly. "Either the House is Sanctuary for everyone, or it's Sanctuary for no one. You mustn't go, or everything we might do would be for nothing."

"And we can't go either!" Jubilee slammed her hands down flat on the tabletop, her eyes alight with sudden understanding. "Because that's what they want! They're depending on our sense of duty and responsibility to outweigh our love for each other. That we'd be ready to break up to preserve the House! I'm damned if I'll let my arrogant bloody family win! There has to be a way . . ."

"It's not as though we're defenseless," said Lee, her bloodred mouth stretching wide, revealing far too many teeth for one mouth. "Let us lure them in here, and I will teach them all the horror that lurks in the dark."

"Do you sing, oh muse of psychologically challenged poets?" said Johnny. "Because I'll wager good money that between us we could whip up a duet that would rattle the bones and trouble the soul of everyone who heard it, whatever world they came from."

"We will chase them, we will chase them, we will eat them up with spoons!" chanted the small furry things in the doorway, while the ball bounced excitedly up and down between them.

"I could throw things at people," Walter said diffidently from the fridge. "If they got close enough."

There was a low steady rumbling, from up in the attic, as Grandfather Grendel stirred. When he spoke, his words hammered on the air like storm clouds slamming together.

"Let all the worlds tremble, if I must come forth again. There have been many powers worse than Elves, and I have slaughtered and feasted on them all, in my time."

"No!" Jubilee said sharply. "This House was created by the Greatest of Powers to put an end to conflicts, to give hope and comfort to those who wanted only peace. If we defend the House with violence, we betray everything it stands for. There has to be another way."

"There is." Peter leaned forward across the table, taking both of Jubilee's hands in his. "The House exists . . . because it is necessary. It was brought into being, and is protected by, Powers far greater than your damned family, princess. Even your people wouldn't dare upset those Powers—so call their bluff! Tell them that if this House's function is destroyed because of them, we'll make sure everyone knows it's all their fault! Tell them; it's all about rendering unto Caesar. Let both sides perform whatever home improvements they feel necessary . . . as long as they don't interfere with each other, or the running of the House! Or else! Your family might have raised arrogance to an art form, but even they're not dumb enough to anger the Powers That Be."

"Peter, my love, you're brilliant!" said Jubilee. "I think this is why I love you most. Because you save me from my family."

"Any time, princess," said Peter.

THE NEXT DAY, bright and early, but not quite as early as the day before, there was a very polite knocking at the House's front door. When Peter went to open it, he found Mister Cuthbert standing there, looking very grim. He nodded stiffly to Peter—or at the very least, in Peter's direction.

"It seems . . . there may have been a misunderstanding," he said, reluctantly. "It has been decided in Council that this residence is exempt from all health and safety regulations and obligatory improvements. Because it is a Listed and Protected building. No changes can be made, without express permission from on high." Mister Cuthbert glared impotently at Peter. "I should have known the likes of you would have friends in high places!"

"Oh yes," said Peter. "Really. You have no idea."

And he shut the door politely but very firmly in Mister Cuthbert's face.

Meanwhile, at the back door, Jubilee was speaking with the Elven Prince Airgedlamh, of the Unseeli Court.

"So it was you," she said.

"Yes," said the Elven Prince. "All things have been put right; no improvements will be necessary. The Unseeli Court has withdrawn its interest in this place. The House shall endure as it always has; and so shall you, and so shall we."

"Go back to the family," said Jubilee. "Tell them I'm happy here."

"Of course. But there are those of us who do miss you at Court," said the Elven Prince. "Good-bye, princess."

In Brightest Day

TONI L. P. KELNER

I'd thought I'd have most of the day free for Internet surfing—a mixed blessing resulting from not having any clients in the offing—but the phone rang just as I was finishing the weekly lolcat roundup. I let it ring twice before answering, hoping that would demonstrate promptness without the betraying stench of desperation.

"Rebound Resurrections," I said in my best business voice. "How can I help you?"

"Dodie? It's Shelia Hopkins. Gottfried is dead."

"Well, yeah." He'd been dead for a couple of weeks.

"I mean he's dead again."

I could have corrected her once more—technically Gottfried was dead *still*, not dead *again*—but I figured it would go faster if I let her explain. The problem was that Gottfried was no longer moving or responding. That might be normal behavior for most dead people, but no matter what some of my fellow houngans might think, I'm pretty good at what I do.

I raise the dead for a living.

• • •

THIS PARTICULAR JOB had started out well enough. The work crew had nearly unearthed the coffin by the time I got to the cemetery the day before, so I just said hello-how's-it-going and let them keep digging. A foursome— two women and two men—showed up a few minutes later, and I voted the distinguished woman in a navy skirt suit and sensible heels most likely to be my client.

"Mrs. Hopkins?" I asked. "I'm Dodie Kilburn."

I know she was surprised—she and I had handled all the advance work via phone and e-mail—but she was too well bred to comment on the fact that I don't look much like a typical houngan.

As soon as I got my ring and license from the Order of Damballah— the houngan version of a professional organization—I'd dumped the wannabe voudou queen look: hair dyed jet-black, loose cotton skirts, low-cut peasant blouses, and a tan-in-a-can. That meant I was back to my natural strawberry-blond hair and freckles and was wearing jeans and a turtleneck sweater.

Mrs. Hopkins introduced the other three, and they all shook my hand somewhat reluctantly, but I didn't take it personally. A lot of people freak when they meet a houngan, and it's even worse when said houngan is about to raise a revenant. So it was no surprise that they stuck with weather-related chitchat while we waited. For the record, it was unseasonably cool for fall in Atlanta.

Once the workers got the coffin out of the ground and next to the open grave, they had me sign their paperwork and took off. Unlike Mrs. Hopkins and company, they weren't bothered about what I was about to do—they just wanted to get home in time to catch the Falcons game. They'd be back the next day to take the coffin to a storage shed and temporarily fill in the grave.

Once they were gone I said, "I'm ready to get started."

"Already?" asked Elizabeth Lautner, the other woman in the group. When Mrs. Hopkins had said she was the dead man's assistant, Elizabeth corrected her—she'd been his associate. Elizabeth's dark brown hair was in a short, asymmetric cut, and she was wearing more mascara than I use in a year. "I thought that you had to wait until midnight to raise a zombie."

"Number one, we don't like to call them zombies. *Revenant* is the PC word. And honestly, it doesn't matter what time of day it is. We only work nights because the cemetery managers don't want us working while they're trying to have funerals. Go figure. By the time a cemetery shuts down for the day and the crew gets the coffin out of the ground, it's usually close to midnight anyway. We just lucked out tonight." Not only was there the football game, but the man hadn't been buried very long, so the ground was fairly soft.

One of the men nervously asked, "Do you open the coffin now?" He was Welton Von Doesburg, and I think he'd picked his suit to live up to the name. He'd identified himself as Von Doesburg Realty, giving the impression that anyone in the known universe would know what that meant.

"I won't open it until I've brought Mr. Gottfried back," I said.

"Just Gottfried," Elizabeth said.

"Right, like Cher or Gallagher." I didn't get so much as a snicker in response. "Anyway, the coffin doesn't affect the ritual."

"I read about that," said C. W. Ford, a man with a solid build and worn jeans. "Loas can go right through a coffin." Mrs. Hopkins had said he was Gottfried's construction chief.

I said, "I don't really have much to do with the loas. I'm more of a force-of-will kind of gal. You know, like the Green Lantern—I've got the power ring and everything." I held up my right hand with the golden signet ring. The engraving was of an ornate cross, the vévé of Baron LaCroix, the Order's mascot. " 'In brightest day, in blackest night, no evil shall escape my sight.' "

I waited a second to see if anybody would finish the Green Lantern oath, but all I got were blank stares. "Green Lantern from the comic book?" I prompted. "Or the Ryan Reynolds movie?"

"We should let you get to work," Mrs. Hopkins said with a hint of impatience.

"You bet. If you folks wouldn't mind stepping back a bit . . ."

They did so, and I got my carton of Morton's salt out of my satchel and started walking around the coffin, pouring it as I went. "Be sure not to break this line."

"What happens if we do?" Von Doesburg asked.

"Nothing dire. I just won't be able to raise Gottfried. Now I'll need the sacrifice."

"I've got it," Mrs. Hopkins said, reaching into a leather briefcase.

"I read that houngans used to cut the throat of a rooster," C.W. said.

"They do still do in some parts of the world, but it doesn't work here. If sacrificing a chicken meant that you were going to go hungry for a week, that would be meaningful. But giving up a chicken isn't a big deal for you or me. We need a real sacrifice. It could be anything valuable, even just sentimental value, but it's handier to use something with a known price tag." If for no other reason than because it made it easier for the Order to set standard rates.

"Here you go," Mrs. Hopkins said, handing me a velvet pouch. I poured a quarter-carat diamond onto my hand, and even in the dim evening light, I could see the sparkle. I slipped it back into the pouch and then put it on top of the coffin.

Von Doesburg said, "What's to keep you—I mean, an unscrupulous houngan from pocketing the diamond when nobody is looking and then pretending that the loas took it?"

I wanted to tell him that if I'd pocketed a diamond every time I raised a body, I'd have a better car than my six-year-old Toyota, but he wasn't the first one to ask, so I restrained myself. "Tell you what, why don't you come over here next to the coffin? Just be sure to step over the salt line."

His eyes got wide, and I think he'd have made an excuse if C.W. hadn't snickered. That was when he stomped over. "Now what?"

"Hold out your hand."

He obeyed.

I reopened the pouch and let the diamond fall onto his palm. "Now make a fist and hold it over the coffin while I do the ritual. If that rock is still there when I'm done, you can keep it."

Papa Philippe, my sponsor at the Order, wouldn't have approved of my letting a civilian get involved, but I figured it was the best way to prove my point.

Once Von Doesburg was in place, I began the ritual, which really isn't that much to see unless you throw in the voudou special effects and dance numbers some of my fellow houngans favor. First I knocked on the coffin three times. With some jobs, I add a knock-knock joke at that point, but this didn't seem like the right crowd. Then I gathered my will and reached into the body of the man in the coffin, though to the onlookers it probably just looked like I had a real bad headache. That was pretty much it.

When I felt Gottfried stirring, I started unscrewing the fasteners holding the lid shut.

Von Doesburg stepped back in such a hurry that he broke the salt line, but I didn't need it anymore anyway. It would have been nice if he'd helped me get the lid open, but I managed on my own and looked inside. The mortician had done a good job with Gottfried. He looked fairly natural.

The revenant blinked up at me, and when I held my hand out toward him, he let me help him out of the coffin. His skin was cold to the touch, of course, but I'm used to that. Fortunately he was wearing a real suit, not one of those backless things. A dead man's ass isn't particularly appealing to me.

"Gottfried?" I said.

"Yes, I'm Gottfried," he said, showing the usual amount of new revenant confusion.

"Do you know where you are?"

"I'm . . ." He looked around the cemetery, then at the coffin he'd climbed out of. "Am I dead?"

"Yes, you are." Back when houngans first went public, it had been tricky to convince a fresh revenant that he was actually dead, but I'd never resurrected anybody who hadn't already known it could happen to them. That made it easier for everybody concerned. "I brought you back to finish your last job. Do you remember what that is?"

It's important for a revenant to know why he's back in this world. Houngans, at least licensed ones, don't just bring people back for fun. First off, we need the permission of the next of kin. Second, there has to be a compelling reason for us to take on a job. It was okay to bring back Grandma to tell the family where she'd hidden the Apple stock certificates, or Dr. Bigshot to finish a research project, but not to bring back Marilyn Monroe for a reality show. Third, the revenant has to be willing to take on that task. Once Gottfried's was done, he'd have to go back to the grave.

It's like Papa Philippe says: we just raise the dead, we can't bring 'em back to life.

Gottfried hesitated just long enough to worry me, but then said, "The house. I was renovating a house. I've never done a house before. It's special. It's going to be my famous house, like Frank Lloyd Wright had Fallingwater."

It wasn't the explanation I'd been expecting. According to Mrs. Hopkins, the house was special because after Gottfried fixed it up, it was going to be sold to raise money for the Stickler Syndrome Research Foundation, of which she was the chairman. But as long as it was important to him, the ritual would work.

"Are you willing to stay long enough to finish the house? Because if you're not, I'll lay you back to rest right now." I could tell Mrs. Hopkins didn't like it when I said that, but I'd explained to her that no houngan could make a revenant walk the earth if he didn't want to.

So we both relaxed when Gottfried said, "I want to finish the house."

"Awesome. Now do you remember these people?"

That was another test: to be sure Gottfried had come back with enough of his faculties to finish his work.

Gottfried focused on them, his reactions getting closer to normal every second. "Yes, of course. Hello, Shelia."

"I'm glad to see you, Gottfried," Mrs. Hopkins said, but she didn't come any closer. No surprise there. No matter how determined my clients are, they still tend to freak when they see a dead man walking.

Gottfried went on. "C.W. Elizabeth. Von Doesburg." He looked at me. "I don't know you, do I?"

"No, I haven't had the pleasure. I'm Dodie Kilburn. I'm going to help you get that house finished."

"Good. I want to finish the house."

Revenants aren't known for their conversational skills—once one has focused on a task, that's all he's interested in. Gottfried must have had a strong focus even while living to have already fixated on his.

I said, "Gottfried, I'm going to take you to a special hotel for the night."

"Because I can't go home anymore."

"That's right." We started down the path to the cemetery exit, and I said, "Mrs. Hopkins, I'll bring Gottfried to the work site tomorrow."

"That'll be fine."

"And Mr. Von Doesburg, you can open your hand now."

He did so, then stared at his empty palm. The diamond was long gone.

THERE WAS NO need for me to stick around once I'd checked Gottfried in at the Order's Revenant House. It was the job of the apprentice houngans working there to explain what he'd need to know about being a revenant: stuff like him not having to eat or go to the bathroom, though drinking water would help him speak; how his sense of touch wouldn't come back completely, which meant that he wouldn't feel much pain but would have to be careful to keep from damaging himself, since he couldn't heal anymore. Of course, he'd likely seen a revenant at some point, so he might remember how it worked, but it was different when you were the dead one.

I was walking back to the parking lot when I saw a shadowy figure waiting for me. I stopped, and a man dressed in a shabby top hat and a tailcoat worn over a bare chest sauntered toward me. He was carrying a cane with a silver skull for a knob, and there was a chicken foot sticking out of his hatband. His black skin gleamed as if it had been oiled, which it probably had been.

"Dude," I said.

He didn't respond.

I sighed, then said, "I see you, Papa Philippe."

"Dodie Kilburn," he said in a husky voice, "I hear you raised a man for no good reason."

"Says who?"

"The loa be telling me."

"Don't the loa have better things to do?"

"They do," Philippe said, dropping out of his voudou patois, "but Margery doesn't."

"I should have known." Margery, the woman who ran the office of the Order, knew the business of every houngan in the Atlanta area. "Then she should also have told you that I had an excellent reason to bring Gottfried back."

"Actually, I should have heard it from you, what with being your sponsor."

"Since when do I have to get approval for a job?"

"Since you took one that three other houngans turned down."

I had wondered about that—it wasn't like I had clients busting down my door. Most newer houngans get referrals from established ones, but most older houngans think I'm a flake. "I don't know what their problem was, but I did my homework. The next of kin signed off on it, and the job fits Order guidelines."

"Bringing back a world-famous architect to fix a house?"

"It's a special house, like one of Frank Lloyd Wright's houses."

He didn't look impressed.

"And it's for charity."

No response.

"Am I in trouble with the Council?"

"There's been some talk, which could have been avoided if I'd known ahead of time."

"I'm sorry—the client was in a hurry, and—"

"And you haven't had much work this month."

"No, not so much." I hadn't had much the month before, either. If things didn't improve, I was going to have to either go work with my father's insurance agency or go work for another houngan, which would probably mean doing the whole voudou queen thing, including trying to make Dodie sound appropriately exotic. If I'd had any dealings with the loa, I'd have sacrificed my autographed photo of the cast of *The Big Bang Theory* to get them to throw more work my way.

Philippe said, "Just give me the details."

I told him what Mrs. Hopkins had told me, that a supporter had left a dilapidated mansion to the Stickler Syndrome Research Foundation in his will, and how she'd gotten the idea of reimagining the place in order to sell it for mucho bucks. Somebody knew somebody who knew somebody who knew Gottfried the architect and talked him into taking on the job pro bono. Unfortunately, midway through the project, Gottfried fell down a flight of stairs at his condo and broke his neck, which left the project in limbo.

"Couldn't somebody else finish the job from his plans?" Philippe asked.

"Gottfried wasn't big on planning. They had some rough sketches, but Gottfried is famous for adding things as he goes, and without all those special touches, they won't be able to get nearly as much money. Not to mention the fact that Gottfried started the crew doing some things without telling them what he was aiming for, so there's all kinds of work half-finished. They really do need him."

"And he's willing to do the job? You asked him?"

"Duh!"

"Okay, I think I can spin it the right way. But if you get another job like this one, please run it past me first."

"You bet."

" 'Cause Papa Philippe think you make master houngan someday if even it kill you—if it do, he be bringing you back hisself."

THE APPRENTICES HAD Gottfried all ready to go when I got back to Revenant House the next morning, and they had found him a pair of khakis and a polo shirt to wear instead of his burying suit. Though he told me good morning when he got in, he didn't say anything else for most of the drive. I took that to mean that he was ready to hunker down and work.

The house he was working on was part of a gated community in Dunwoody, one of the pricier Atlanta suburbs, and the security guard didn't look impressed by my beat-up car. Then he saw Gottfried and did a double take before letting me drive into the Emerald Lake development.

The town houses and lawns looked nauseatingly perfect, and Gottfried must have agreed, because he blurted out, "Cookie-cutter crap." I saw several signs proudly proclaiming that Emerald Lake was a Von Doesburg development, which explained why the man had been at the cemetery the night before.

The mansion being renovated was at the end of a road, right on the lake, and obviously predated the cookie-cutter crap. It had three stories, wide white columns, a balcony on the second floor, and a veranda that stretched all across the front of the building. There were tarps and piles of supplies everywhere and a Dumpster in the middle of the front yard, but I could see it was going to be a showplace. No wonder Gottfried had been willing to come back to finish.

As soon as I parked, Gottfried got out and started walking toward a trailer parked on the edge of the lot, so I followed along. A sign on the door said CONSTRUCTION OFFICE, and when Gottfried opened it, we saw the four people from the previous night plus another guy.

"Good morning, Gottfried," Mrs. Hopkins said, but Gottfried went right past her to go to the desk and start flipping through papers.

"Well!" said the newcomer, a scrawny man with his nose hiked up in the air.

"Dodie," Mrs. Hopkins said, "this is Theo Scarpa, the president of the Emerald Lake Homeowners' Association."

I said pleased-to-meet-you.

"Mr. Scarpa has some questions about . . ." She glanced at Gottfried. "About your work."

Scarpa sniffed, and at first I thought it was a comment on me, but then realized he was checking to see if Gottfried stank of rotting flesh.

I said, "No, he doesn't smell. In fact, revenants smell better than most living people."

"I see," he said, as if suspecting a hidden insult. "Sorry, but this is my first experience with this kind of thing. Can you tell me how you expect him to be able to finish a renovation this complex? It's my understanding that a revenant has limited mental capacity."

"It's not that his capacity is limited—it's just very focused. Gottfried is just as capable of finishing this house as he was when he was alive. The difference is that he no longer has any interest in anything other than this task."

"But he's got to modify his plans to fit into our development," he said, waving a handful of papers at me. "How can he do that?"

"This house predates the development," Gottfried's assistant, Elizabeth, said. "You should be modifying those trashy houses to match his work."

The two of them started in on each other, ignoring Von Doesburg when he tried to calm them down. I said, "Mrs. Hopkins, if you want my advice, I'd say to let Gottfried get to work."

"That's an excellent idea," she said. "C.W., why don't you take him out to the house?"

The construction chief nodded and said, "Come on, boss, and I'll show you what we've done while you were gone."

"Gottfried, I'll be back this evening to take you back to Revenant House," I said, but he didn't even pause. As I'd told Scarpa, his attention was all on the house. I checked with Mrs. Hopkins to see what time I should pick him up, and left her to handle the bickering.

It was at about three thirty that afternoon when I got that panicked call about Gottfried being dead. Again.

FOR ONCE I was glad I didn't have any other jobs going so I could drive over there right away. A bunch of men wearing tool belts were standing around, and when I got out of my car, Elizabeth came running over to nearly drag me inside the house.

Just past the front door was a gorgeous set of stairs, the kind made for sweeping down in a ball gown. The image was spoiled by the sight of Gottfried's body at the bottom. And it was a body, not a revenant—he didn't even look a little bit alive anymore, and the smell of formaldehyde was strong. Mrs. Hopkins and C.W. were looking down at him.

"What happened?" I asked.

"Your damned spell wore off," Elizabeth snapped, "and he fell down the stairs."

"Wait. He died before falling? You saw that?"

"No, I didn't see it—I was in the trailer—but what else could have happened?"

I pushed past her and went up the stairs. The floor up there was covered with a sheet of sturdy paper that must have been taped down to protect the wood from the workers, and the tape at the very edge had peeled off, leaving a fat curl of paper.

Elizabeth had followed me up, so I had to push by her again to go look at Gottfried's shoes. Revenant House must not have had any shoes in his size because he was still wearing the black dress shoes he'd worn in his coffin, and I could see scuff marks on the toes.

"His original cause of death was from falling, right?" I asked.

Mrs. Hopkins nodded.

"Then this is what must have happened. He tripped on that paper up there—revenants don't have a lot of feeling in their extremities and tend to be clumsy. He could have survived the fall just fine—you can't really kill him, just damage him. But when he felt himself falling, he remembered the other fall, and let himself die. You could say it scared the life out of him." It was unusual, but not unheard of. Papa Philippe had once raised a drowning victim because she was needed to locate some important papers, but when the revenant saw she was going to have to go on a boat, she collapsed and he couldn't raise her again.

I was afraid I'd get some push back, but Mrs. Hopkins was nodding. "The contract did say something like this was possible. The question is, what do we do now?"

"You'll have to bring him back," Elizabeth said.

"According to our contract, you'd have to pay me again," I pointed out, "but since this is for a charity, I'll do it for free." Well, that and the fact that I was hoping that Mrs. Hopkins would mention my name to the wealthy friends her clothing choices implied she had. "But I need another sacrifice."

"This is outrageous!" Elizabeth said, but C.W. was pulling a ring off his finger. "Use this."

"Are you sure?" I asked, taking it. It was ugly, but it was gold and the sapphire looked real.

"Yeah, take it. My ex-wife gave it to me—I never did like it."

"Is it enough?" Mrs. Hopkins wanted to know.

I hefted it. "Yeah, it should be." I remembered Papa Philippe's warning from the night before, and said, "I should talk to my sponsor first."

"There's no time!" Mrs. Hopkins said. "Scarpa is coming back with an inspector. Gottfried has to be up and talking."

"How long do we have?"

"Von Doesburg is stalling him now. Twenty minutes, if we're lucky."

I should have called Papa Philippe anyway, but instead I sent Elizabeth out to my car to get a fresh carton of salt. I could have done it myself, but what was the fun of having a minion around if I didn't take advantage of her. Then I made a circle, put the sacrifice on the floor next to Gottfried's body, and did my thing. Five minutes later, I was explaining to Gottfried why I'd brought him back again, and with my fingers crossed, I asked if he was still willing to finish the house.

He agreed just in time for Von Doesburg to arrive with Scarpa and the inspector. I stayed around long enough to make sure Gottfried was compos mentis enough to hold his end of the conversation, then made myself scarce. I could have left entirely, but I was going to need to take Gottfried back to Revenant House in an hour or so anyway, and you can hardly get anywhere in the Atlanta area in that length of time. So I found where somebody had set up a bunch of folding chairs under a tree and swiped a bottle of water from a cooler that looked as if it was there for everybody.

C.W. came and got a bottle of his own after a while. "How're you doing?" he asked.

"Not bad. You?"

"Not your average day on the work site, that's for sure."

"You mean you don't work with revenants every week?"

"Not hardly," he said with a grin. "I guess it's old hat to you."

"I don't usually raise the dead on-site, but otherwise, same old, same old."

"Have you been doing this long?"

"Since college. I was an apprentice for five years, then got my license about a year and a half ago."

"You went to college for this?"

"Nope, I just happened to fall into it after a particularly wild Halloween party at one of the frat houses. Somebody had brought a stuffed black cat—the taxidermy kind, I mean—for decoration, and while I was drunk, I started patting it. Before I knew it, the thing was purring. We had to call a real houngan to put it back to rest, and he told me I should look into doing this as a career." I shrugged. "What can I say? It's a living."

It took him a minute, but he eventually got the joke and chuckled.

"I am sorry about your ring."

"Don't be. I only wore it because the ex-wife wanted it back in the divorce settlement. I was just afraid it wouldn't be enough of a sacrifice."

"Something valuable, something important. Either will work." We sipped for a few minutes, and then I asked, "So what's Scarpa's deal?"

C.W. made a face. "He hates this house being here because it makes the other houses look like slapped-together garbage, which is what they are. It pissed him off no end when Mrs. Hopkins brought us in to fix it up."

"Wow. He puts the *ass* in *homeowners' association*."

That got a snicker.

"Wait, didn't Von Doesburg slap together the garbage? Why is he helping you guys fend him off?"

"He says it's because having a Gottfried house here will increase the profile of the place, but I think he's trying to persuade Shelia to let him buy up some of the acreage around the lake so he can put in a country club. He's been trying to get hold of the land the house is on for years, but the owner wouldn't sell. Von Doesburg thought he'd get it cheap from the heirs, but that was before Shelia got involved."

He went on to tell me about the plans Gottfried had for the house. "When he died, I didn't know what we were going to do, but now that he's here, we're on track."

C.W. went back to work and I went back to killing time until construction shut down and Gottfried was ready to go. Again, conversation was spotty, though I did warn him again about poor sensation in his feet so he wouldn't have any more "fatal" falls. I stopped in at Revenant House just long enough to suggest they find him some sneakers so he'd have more traction.

Papa Philippe was waiting for me again.

"I was going to call you," I said before he could speak, "but there was no time. Then there were people around. Then I had Gottfried in the car, and I couldn't talk in front of him and it would have been dangerous to text while driving and—"

"And you was hoping the loa not be watching you this day." He shook his head. "The loa always be watching."

"The FBI really ought to have the loa working for them. Do you want to know what happened?"

"Not me, but Tante Ju-Ju be wanting to know."

"You're joking."

He just looked at me.

"When?"

His answer was to gesture toward a dimly lit path into the woods.

"Shit."

I didn't know how extensive the Order's grounds were. Revenant House and the office buildings were close to the road, but stretching behind were all kinds of paths and other buildings, most of which I avoided whenever possible.

Papa Philippe let me lead the way until we got to the hut from which Tante Ju-Ju held forth. Presumably she had a house somewhere with a TV, a microwave, and plumbing, but I'd never seen her anywhere outside Order grounds, and I didn't think anybody had ever seen her break character. She was either a true believer, or the best method actor ever.

Tante Ju-Ju was sitting outside her hut on a rickety stool, stirring a pot of something ominous over a fire. She was dressed like all the other voudou queens in the Order, but the skirt and the peasant blouse looked comfortable on her and her coloring was natural. Her tignon had seven points knotted into it, just like Marie Laveau's supposedly had, and mysteriously it never slipped, even though I'd never seen a bobby pin in her vicinity.

"I hear you raised the same man twice," she said without preamble. "Why he not stay moving after the first time?"

I explained how Gottfried had fallen, ending with, "He didn't want to feel himself die again."

"So why you bring him back?"

"His task wasn't finished yet."

"This task need doing that bad?"

"I think so."

"You only *think* so?"

"Okay, I'm sure," I said. "He's finishing a house to raise money for a foundation that studies a condition called Stickler syndrome."

"This syndrome, it be killing people?"

"No, but they have a lot of pain and sometimes they lose their sight and hearing. Isn't that enough of a reason?"

"That what I be asking you."

Okay, I was missing something. "If it were me, I'd want to come back for a task like this."

"Why I care what you think?"

"You asked—" I stopped and tried to figure out what she was getting at. "I brought Gottfried back because the task is important to him. He doesn't care about the charity, but he does care about leaving the legacy of the house."

Tante Ju-Ju nodded. "Then maybe you do the right thing. What do the loa tell you?"

"I don't talk to the loa."

Papa Philippe winced, but it was nothing I hadn't told him before.

"What if they be talking to you and you not be listening?" Tante Ju-Ju asked.

I didn't have an answer to that.

She waved me away. "You go on. I talk to the loa about you. When they tell me, I tell you."

I didn't need Papa Philippe's touch to tell me I'd been dismissed, but I was glad to have his company walking back down that path, even if neither of us spoke. If he hadn't been there, I'd have been tempted to run.

"Why in God's name did you tell her you don't talk to the loa?" he asked once we were at my car.

"Because I don't. Just because the first houngans were practitioners doesn't mean that everybody needs the loa to raise revenants. I do fine without them."

"Some people say the loa aren't happy with that, and that's why your revenant failed."

"That's not true!"

"I believe you, but would it hurt you to at least pretend to respect the loa?"

"I do respect the loa and voudou, but as a religion—it's not *my* religion. For me to wear a tignon wouldn't be showing them respect—it would be mocking them, just like it would be for me to wear a nun's habit or a yarmulke. And you know damn well that most houngans only pay lip service to the loa."

"There are plenty of us that believe."

"I know you believe, Papa Philippe, but you know I don't."

"Dodie, it's just clothes."

"If it's just clothes, then why can't I wear mine? Look, I don't tell the other houngans how to do their job, and all I want is for them to do the same for me. If that means I never make master, then so be it."

"I'm not talking about making master. I'm talking about you losing your license. I'm talking about you getting ejected from the Order."

"Because of blue jeans? I don't wear my zombie movie T-shirts to work anymore."

"It's not just that. It's everything, the attitude toward the loa, the jokes. And now you've not only brought back an architect to fix a house, you had to bring him back a second time. You need to tread carefully."

"Hey, I'm not the one falling down stairs."

He shook his head and sent me home, but I knew he was worried. Which got me worried. What if I was wrong about Gottfried? What if I hadn't done a good job bringing him back? What if he collapsed again? What kind of job could a former houngan get?

I didn't sleep very well.

I WAS HAPPY to see Gottfried in brand-new Converse sneakers when I picked him up the next day—plenty of tread on those babies. I was less happy to hear the apprentices whispering about me and looking at me in what they imagined was a subtle manner. One actually made devil horns at me, as if my being there could contaminate a house where dead people spent the night. I returned the greeting with a traditional one-finger salute.

"How are you today?" I asked Gottfried.

"Fine. I practiced walking last night—I won't trip again."

"Good. And the work is going well?"

He just smiled, which was enough of an answer.

C.W. was waiting for us on the porch of the house, but when he started to lead Gottfried in, I said, "If you don't mind, I'm going to stick around today. Just in case."

"If the boss doesn't care, I don't care."

"All I care about is the work," Gottfried said.

You have to admire that focus.

So I spent the day following him around, envying the fact that he didn't have to breathe in the ever-present dust. I'd expected a world-famous architect to spend most of the day in the trailer, but Gottfried was a hands-on kind of guy. We went up to the attic to check out the roofing, down to the basement to check on mold, outside to see if the shingles were being attached properly, back inside to approve of the fixtures in the master bathroom—and that was just in the first hour. He didn't actually sit down until nearly noon, and even then he preferred to work in the house's kitchen so he could keep an eye on things. That was when I ran out to the nearest McDonald's for a bag of grease, salt, and caffeine.

When I got back, Gottfried was in conference with Elizabeth. She'd managed to ignore my presence so far that day, and glared at me now. I would have stayed out of the way, but I realized Gottfried was signing his name.

"Gottfried, you know your signature isn't valid, right?" The courts had decided that for a dead man to sign anything was the same thing as forging, and the people at Revenant House were supposed to have told him that.

"It's just an order for supplies!" Elizabeth snapped.

But Gottfried was reading the paper in front of him. "This isn't about the house," he said. "I only want the papers about the job."

"But Gottfried—" Elizabeth started to say, but when I got close enough to snoop, she snatched it up. "Sorry, my mistake. This wasn't supposed to be in this stack."

The afternoon was the same as the morning. We went up, we went down, we went outside, we went inside, Gottfried climbed a ladder, I stood below and wondered if I could catch him if he fell again.

Never having been on a building site that didn't involve Legos or sand, I was surprised by the number of decisions that had to be made and the arguments that ensued. Who knew that using the wrong color of wood would totally destroy a house's aesthetic? I didn't even know that a house had an aesthetic.

By the time the living workers were ready to call it a day, I was exhausted. Back to Revenant House for Gottfried, and after making sure Papa Philippe wasn't poised to issue warnings, it was home to takeout Thai food for me.

The next day was mostly the same, except a little more contentious as the arguments from the previous day escalated—Gottfried ordered one man to completely replaster the ceiling in the dining room because it swirled the wrong way and told C.W. to send back a whole load of lumber because they weren't building an Emerald Lake shack. I tried to hide my grin when both Von Doesburg and Scarpa heard that latter comment, but I didn't do a very good job.

Once again, around midday Gottfried settled down in the kitchen for paperwork. After Elizabeth's attempted document-signing trick, I'd decided to hang around the whole day and had brought lunch with me. So while Gottfried pored over his notes and blueprints, I found a relatively dust-free spot at the counter to eat my ham sandwich and apple.

C.W. came to speak to Gottfried, got snarled at for not meeting code, and then grabbed a Coke out of the refrigerator, one of the few appliances in the house that was plugged in.

"You ready to change jobs and go into construction?" he asked me.

"I'm thinking not. You guys work too hard. And I'd probably never be able to keep to the code."

"The what?"

"I heard Gottfried saying something about keeping to the code."

He laughed. "He meant the building code. This house was built long before a lot of the regulations were established, but our renovations have to be up to code."

"So it's nothing to do with pirates?"

"Just Captain Bligh over there."

I lowered my voice. "Sorry Gottfried is giving you a hard time. Revenants aren't good at compromise."

"Gottfried was never good at compromise. He's actually easier to deal with now than when he was alive."

"Seriously? Why did you work with him?"

"Because when the job was done, I knew it was something that would last. That made it worthwhile."

He finished his Coke and headed off for code-meeting while Gottfried continued to bark orders at everybody in range. Since he didn't look as if he was going to be moving any time soon, I said, "Gottfried, I'm going to go visit the little houngan's room."

Since my bladder capacity didn't affect the task at hand, he didn't bother to respond.

The bathrooms were not in usable condition, which meant I had to brave a Porta-Potty. That was enough to make me go as fast as possible, even if I hadn't been on watchdog duty. But despite the added incentive, by the time I got back to the kitchen, Gottfried was gone.

I wasn't immediately alarmed—he hadn't promised to stay put, after all. So I spent a few minutes looking for him. When I had no luck, I started asking all the workmen I came across if they'd seen him. That was worse than useless because construction workers concentrating on their work don't pay attention to the clock, so I couldn't tell who'd seen him last.

I finally spotted him after I'd gone outside—C.W. thought Gottfried went to inspect some ongoing work on the foundation, but he was actually inside when I spotted him at the entrance to the second-floor balcony. As I watched, he stepped over the yellow caution tape that had been strung up to block the entrance.

I wanted to call up to warn him to be careful but was afraid to distract him. Instead all I could do was hold my breath as he bent over to examine the junction of the balcony with the house. I heard rather than saw the wood give way, and later decided that I must have screamed when he tried to grab for a handrail that splintered under his weight.

Even at that distance, I could still sense that Gottfried was aware, but a split second after he started to fall, I felt him give up the ghost. All that hit the ground was a body that had been dead for weeks.

PEOPLE CAME RUNNING from all directions, but the first to reach Gottfried was Elizabeth. She turned away when the smell got to her, her hand over her mouth. I thought she was going to cry, but then she saw me and she went from sad to furious in nothing flat.

"You incompetent moron! You let him die again!"

"I didn't do anything. He fell!"

"Yeah, right," she said. "A real houngan can keep a revenant alive for months, years. You can't even manage two days."

"He fell," I repeated. "The floor he was on broke. Go look!" But in looking at the faces around me, I could tell nobody really believed me, and nobody rushed up to examine the evidence, either. "Fine, I'll raise him again and we'll ask him what happened." I wasn't completely sure that Gottfried would care enough about the question to answer it, but if I framed his repeated "deaths" as a barrier to finishing the job, it might get his attention. "Get me a sacrifice and I'll get him up and moving again."

But Mrs. Hopkins was shaking her head. "No, we can't do it to him again. You said it yourself—a revenant has to want to stay long enough to finish the task. It's clear that Gottfried doesn't. We have to let him rest."

"He doesn't want to rest!" I protested.

"Obviously he does," Von Doesburg said. "It seems to me that if you'd done your job properly, you'd know that. I think the courts will agree with me."

"There's no need for that—I'm sure Dodie did her best," Mrs. Hopkins said kindly, "but it's over. I need to see about getting Gottfried back to his grave."

The people there didn't literally turn their backs on me, but they might as well have. Even C.W. just shook his head sadly when I looked at him.

"I'll mail your check back tomorrow," I said to nobody in particular, and walked away.

MY PHONE RANG as I walked in my front door, and the voice on the other end said only, "The council be wanting to see you at full dark." Then whoever it was hung up.

It was all I could do to keep from banging my head against the wall. Maybe there was something to the loa business—how else could they already know?

I knew Papa Philippe would want me to dress the part, so I took the time to rummage around and find my loose cotton skirt and blouse, the myriad strings of beads and amulets, and the curly black wig I'd worn as an apprentice. Then I fastened on my tignon of calico scarves knotted together, needing a dozen bobby pins to keep it on my head. It was while I was applying makeup six shades darker than my real complexion that I got a good look at myself in the mirror. And nearly laughed my ass off.

So when I arrived at the Order's compound, it was only after I'd washed my face, pulled the tignon from my head, dumped the jewelry onto the floor, and changed into blue jeans and my *Shaun of the Dead* T-shirt.

Screw 'em if they couldn't take a joke.

A pair of apprentices—one in tignon, one in top hat—was waiting for me at the head of the path leading to the council's gathering place with burning torches in hand. They didn't speak, but produced some excellent expressions of contempt when they saw my clothes. I just said, "Hey, fabulous outfits! Are those new looks for you?"

They led the way down the path until I could see a clearing with the roaring bonfire the council kept lit no matter what the weather was, then stopped. Obviously I was supposed to make the rest of the trip on my own.

"Tweet me!" I said to my exiting escorts as I followed the dusty path to the gathering place. The fire should have been comforting in the chill of a fall evening, but it really wasn't.

I stepped into the center of the clearing and waited. I knew there were people around me, but I couldn't see them until somebody struck a match. Then I could just barely make out the features of Papa Philippe as he walked around the edges of the clearing, stopping every few feet to light a candle in the hand of a council member. There were thirteen candles—the full council was there. It wasn't a good sign.

Then Papa Philippe came to stand beside me, which was a relief. At least he was still willing to act as my sponsor.

Tante Ju-Ju was standing in the middle of the row of council members. "I see you, Dodie Kilburn. I want you to tell me what you been doing since I talked to you before."

I did so, ending with my walking back toward my car after Gottfried's fall.

"And you just leave after that?"

"I thought about it, but no, I didn't leave. I turned around and went back."

There were murmurs from the rest of the council, but Tante Ju-Ju kept eyeing me. "What you waiting for? Keep on talking."

. . .

I REALLY HAD intended to drive off in ignominious defeat, stopping only at the nearest Publix to pick up a gallon of fudge ripple ice cream, but just before I got to the car, I turned around and stomped back to the people clustered around Gottfried's body.

Somebody had found a tarp to lay over him, and most of the workers had wandered away, but the key players were still there: Mrs. Hopkins, Elizabeth, C.W., Von Doesburg, and Scarpa.

"Hang on," I said, "something stinks here, and I'm not talking about Gottfried."

Elizabeth sputtered, but I didn't give her a chance to go into a righteous tirade.

"I spent all of yesterday with Gottfried and he was fine. I spent half of today with him and he was fine. But the second I leave him alone, he falls. Again. Don't you people think that's just a little bit suspicious?"

"What are you talking about?" Elizabeth said.

"I'm talking about murder." Well, technically it wasn't, since you can't murder a dead man, but it sure got their attention. "I know Gottfried's will was strong, so he didn't just die, and I don't believe he had two accidents. Somebody either pushed him, or set a trap. Both times."

"Who would have done that?" Mrs. Hopkins asked. "And why?"

"Why does anybody kill somebody else? Either the killer hated Gottfried or he—or she—benefited from his death."

I spent a second considering the possibility that Hopkins had been the one, mainly because of the way she'd refused to let me raise him a third time, but it didn't compute. She needed him to finish the job, and I hadn't picked up on the first hint of her having anything against him.

"This is ridiculous," Scarpa said, starting to inch away. "I'm not going to stand here and be accused of . . . Of whatever it is you're accusing me of."

"I haven't accused anybody yet. But you—and the rest of you, too—can stand here and listen, or I'll—"

"You'll what?" Von Doesburg scoffed. "Call the cops? There's been no crime committed."

"I won't call the cops. I'll call the loa." The disadvantage of being a houngan is that people think you can commit creepy acts. The advantage is that people think that you *will* commit them.

"What do you want from us?" Scarpa asked in a strangled tone.

"Answers. And the loa will know if you're lying." Of course, the loa wouldn't have told me squat, but they didn't know that. Having already tentatively eliminated Mrs. Hopkins from my list of suspects, I went on to Elizabeth. "Did you talk to Gottfried while I was in the bathroom?"

"How would I know when you were in the bathroom?"

"Okay, fine. Did you talk to him while I wasn't around?"

"No. I was in the trailer most of the day unsnarling purchase orders."

"Did anybody see you?"

"People came in and out, but nobody was with me constantly."

"Okay." I made as if to turn to somebody else, then jerked back to her—I'd seen the maneuver on TV. "What was that paper you tried to trick Gottfried into signing yesterday?"

"I wasn't trying to trick him!" she said. "It was something he'd promised to do before he died, but he never got a chance."

"What was it?"

"A recommendation letter. I'm applying to architecture schools. I figured I could get his signature and then fudge the date to make it look like he'd done it before he died."

C.W. said, "Gottfried told me that she was applying, if that helps any."

Actually, it did. Even if Elizabeth had wanted to kill Gottfried for some reason, she wouldn't have done so until he signed her paper. True, she could have forged it, but she could have done that anytime.

On to C.W. He'd been awfully nice to me—maybe he'd had an ulterior motive. "What about you?" I said to him. "If Gottfried was out of the way, you could have gone on to finish the renovation your way."

"My way? I don't have a way. I'm a builder, not a designer. You give me a blueprint or even something sketched on a napkin, I'll build it, but I wouldn't know where to start on a project like this."

I would have loved to have a loa with a lie detector standing by, but he sure sounded sincere to me. "Then tell me this. Did you see Gottfried any time today when I wasn't with him?"

"No, you were sticking to him like glue."

"All right then, Mr. Von Doesburg and Mr. Scarpa. Same question. Did you speak to Gottfried at any time today when I wasn't around?"

Scarpa shook his head vigorously, but Von Doesburg said, "Yes."

"You did?" I said, surprised that anybody had admitted it.

"I went looking for him, as a matter of fact, and found him on the second floor examining flooring. I assume it was after you left him."

"What did you want with him?"

He gave me a condescending smile. "I wanted his advice on a project I'm working on—it's fairly technical. I could explain it, but only another architect could understand."

"Did he help you?"

"We talked for a few minutes, but then he said he needed to check something on the balcony. I thanked him for his time and went into an empty room to call my office. Then I heard a scream and ran outside. I suppose somebody else could have been upstairs when we were and followed Gottfried, but I didn't see anyone."

I was about to make a stab at Scarpa when I realized what Von Doesburg had said. "Dude, you're so busted."

"I beg your pardon."

"Okay, all of you have interacted with Gottfried since I first got him back. Has he expressed any interest in anything other than finishing this house?"

There was a round of heads shaking.

"He wouldn't even sign Elizabeth's paper—something he'd promised to do—because it wasn't directly connected to his task. So why would he have given Von Doesburg advice about a different project?"

"I'm no expert in zombie behavior," Von Doesburg said, "so I can only tell you what happened."

"Bullshit," C.W. said. "The boss wouldn't have given Von Doesburg the time of day when he was alive. Everybody knows he thought the man's work was crap."

"I assure you that Gottfried respected me as a colleague," the developer said, but he was sweating.

"Let's find out for sure," I said. "Let's ask Gottfried."

SO YOU DONE raise him again?" Tante Ju-Ju asked.

I nodded. "I hope that's it, too—it gets harder every time. But Gottfried came back. His body is a bit banged up from the falls, but he's still willing to do the task. And when I worded the question the right way—asking him what work needed doing on the balcony—he told us that it was Von Doesburg who told him to check for termite damage. Which there was, only not in the place Von Doesburg told him to look. Von Doesburg set him up to fall, and probably pushed him down the stairs the other time, too."

"Why he want to get rid of a revenant so bad?"

"We're not absolutely sure because Von Doesburg has clammed up, but I started thinking about what Gottfried said about substandard building materials, and how he wasn't building an Emerald Lake house. I got C.W. to take a look at Mr. Scarpa's house, and apparently the place wasn't built to code. Fixing it will be expensive and Scarpa said he was going to sue Von Doesburg to recoup his costs. Chances are that all the houses in the development have the same code violations. The man's going to be bankrupt."

"You think that enough? Or are you gonna send the loa after him for messing with your revenant?" Tante Ju-Ju said, with an ironic twist to her lips.

"Actually, I suggested to Mrs. Hopkins that the police just might want to investigate Gottfried's real death a little more closely. After all, he must have discovered the problems with the Emerald Lake houses before he died, and from what I know about him, I don't think he'd have kept quiet."

"Where the revenant be now? You didn't bring him here."

"They've lost so much time these past couple of days that Gottfried insisted on working through the night, and you know how hard it is to argue with a revenant. With Von Doesburg out of the way, I figured he'd be safe enough there—C.W. and Elizabeth will keep an eye on him."

"I think Dodie done us proud," Papa Philippe said firmly. "If she not be bringing that man back, people start to think we can't keep a revenant up and doing his task."

"Maybe she did—maybe she didn't," Tante Ju-Ju said. "Tell me this. That third time you bring him back, where you get that sacrifice?"

I was so screwed. I'd been hoping nobody would ask that question, which was why I'd kept my hands behind me while I was talking. "I used my Order ring." I held out the hand with the white mark that showed where the ring had been.

There were audible gasps, and if looks could have killed, I'd have been

revenant material. I was afraid to look at Papa Philippe, who must have
been wishing he were anyplace on earth other than standing next to me.

"Why you sacrifice that ring?" Tante Ju-Ju asked. "You got nothing
else to give the loa?"

"What could I have given them? My car? My computer? None of that
is worth anything."

"But the ring be gold so that make it valuable?"

"No! Yeah, sure the gold is worth something, but that's not what made
it valuable. A sacrifice has to mean something, right? The ring was the
only important thing I had."

"Why it be so important?"

Was this a trick question? She knew what that ring symbolized. "Papa
Philippe gave me that ring when I became a houngan."

"You saying being a houngan is something special?"

"Are you serious?"

"You the one who never be serious about what you doing!"

"Sure, I make jokes. It's a funny job—people are funny, and dead
people even more so. That doesn't mean I don't take raising the dead seriously. I help people finish their life's work so they can rest easy. If that's
not special, then I don't know what is!"

She looked at me for what seemed like a year. The other council members were looking, too, and probably Papa Philippe, too. Then Tante Ju-Ju
smiled so wide it was almost scary.

"You come here."

I wasn't sure if I wanted to, but since Papa Philippe nudged me and I
was outnumbered, I went.

"Gimme your hand." When I held it out, she slipped a ring on my
finger, right where the other one had been. "The loa, they do like jokes.
They be wanting you to stay houngan."

"They aren't playing a joke on me, are they?" I asked.

Tante Ju-Ju said, "No, I think maybe they be playing a joke on the
rest of us houngans!" Then she actually laughed out loud, and the rest of
the council joined in. People started patting me on the back and kissing
both my cheeks, as if they'd been in on it from the beginning, but I didn't
think they had been. Papa Philippe was nearly as happy as I was.

It wasn't until I got back to my car that I took a good look at the ring

Tante Ju-Ju had given me. It wasn't the gold signet I'd expected. It was green plastic, and in place of the vévé of Baron LaCroix, it had a simple circle with two lines on either side.

"In brightest day, in blackest night," I said. She'd given me a Green Lantern power ring.

ABOUT THE AUTHORS

PATRICIA BRIGGS is the #1 *New York Times* bestselling author of the Mercy Thompson and Alpha and Omega books. She is grateful that although most adults who play all day with their imaginary friends get sent to the funny farm, authors get paid to do it. She currently lives in eastern Washington State with her family and a small herd of horses.

VICTOR GISCHLER's work has been nominated for the Edgar® and Anthony awards, and has been translated into Turkish, French, German, Italian, Spanish, Japanese, Portuguese, and Czech. His novel *Gun Monkeys* is being made into a film with Ryuhei Kitamura attached to direct. He has scripted such titles as *Punisher*, *Deadpool Corps*, *Death of Dracula*, and *X-Men* for Marvel Comics. He lives in Baton Rouge, Louisiana, with his wife, Jackie, and son, Emery. He loves his giant charcoal grill. His fantasy novel based on the characters he created for this anthology is in the works.

JAMES GRADY, author of *Six Days of the Condor* (adapted into a Robert Redford film), received Italy's 2004 Raymond Chandler Medal, France's 2001 Grand Prix du Roman Noir, and Japan's 2008 World Baka-Misu award. In 2008, London's *Daily Telegraph* named Grady as one of "50 crime writers to read before you die." Montana-born Grady's short stories have won numerous awards. He has written for film and TV, and is also a contributor to AOL's news site PoliticsDaily.com. He and his wife, writer Bonnie Goldstein, live inside D.C.'s Beltway.

New York Times and *USA Today* bestselling author **HEATHER GRAHAM** majored in theater arts at the University of South Florida. After a stint of several years in dinner theater, backup vocals, commercials, and, of course, bartending, she stayed home following the birth of her third child (of five) and began to write, working on fiction—horror, paranormal, historical, suspense, and romance. After some trial and error, she sold her first book, and since then she has published more than a hundred and fifty books in all genres. She wrote the launch books for Shadows and Mira, and has been published in more than twenty languages around the world. She loves all her associations—Romance Writers of America, Horror Writers Association, Mystery Writers of America, International Thriller Writers, and Sisters in Crime—and is pleased to have been honored with awards from Waldenbooks, B. Dalton, Georgia Romance Writers, *Affaire de Coeur*, *Romantic Times*, and more. She has been quoted, interviewed, or featured in such publications as *The Nation*, *Redbook*, *People*, and *USA Today*, and has appeared on many newscasts, including local television and *Entertainment Tonight*. Heather loves travel and anything to do with the water, and is a certified scuba diver. Her greatest love remains her family, but she also believes her career has been an incredible gift, and she is grateful every day to be doing something that she loves so very much for a living.

SIMON R. GREEN has hit middle age, and middle age is hitting back. He rides motorcycles, appears in open-air productions of Shakespeare, and once appeared naked in a production of *Tom Jones*. His series include the Forest Kingdom books; the Deathstalker books; the Nightside books; the Secret Histories starring Shaman Bond, the very secret agent; and his latest series, Ghost Finders. He really would like to take a little rest, sometime soon. He has lived most of his life in the small country town of Bradford-on-Avon, the last Celtic town to fall to the invading Saxons in A.D. 504. He has worked as a shop assistant, bicycle repair mechanic, journalist, actor, and Chippendale. One of those may be a lie.

CHARLAINE HARRIS, author of the Sookie Stackhouse and Harper Connelly novels, has won numerous awards, including the Anthony and the Romantic Times Lifetime Achievement Award. Her first book was published in 1981. She lives in southern Arkansas with a current count of four rescue dogs and one husband. Her three children are grown and more or less out of the house.

STACIA KANE is the author of the gritty dystopian urban fantasy Downside series starring Chess Putnam and featuring ghosts, human sacrifice, drugs, witchcraft, punk rock, and a badass '69 Chevelle. She bleaches her hair and wears a lot of black.

Award-winning author **TONI L. P. KELNER** writes the "Where Are They Now?" mysteries featuring Boston-based freelance entertainment reporter Tilda Harper. The latest is *Blast from the Past*. Her short stories have featured carnivals, vampires, pirates, private eyes, werewolves, and demonic obscene phone callers, but this is her first zombie story. She notes that while the Stickler Syndrome Research Foundation is fictional, Stickler syndrome is a real condition. Visit www.sticklers.org to find out more about it.

E. E. KNIGHT resides in Chicago with his family. He enjoys his short commute between reality and his imaginary worlds but still manages to get lost. He can be found online at eeknight.com.

ROCHELLE KRICH's debut novel, *Where's Mommy Now?*, won the Anthony Award and was filmed as *Perfect Alibi*. In addition to writing five stand-alone suspense novels and short stories, she is the author of the Jessie Drake and Molly Blume mystery series ("a sleuth worth her salt"—*The New York Times*). *Dead Air* won the Romantic Times Reviewers' Choice Award, and *Grave Endings*, a Molly Blume mystery, won the Mary Higgins Clark Award. Rochelle is currently at work on a stand-alone novel, *Mind Games*. Having recently survived a bathroom remodel, she is highly qualified to write about home improvement and "things that go bump in the night."

MELISSA MARR grew up believing in faeries, ghosts, and various other creatures. After teaching college literature for a decade, she applied her fascination with folklore to writing the *New York Times* and internationally bestselling Wicked Lovely series (a film of which is in development by Universal Pictures). She has also written a three-volume manga series (*Wicked Lovely: Desert Tales*), a number of short stories, and the adult novel *Graveminder*. All of her texts are rooted in her lifelong obsession with folklore and fantastic creatures. You can find her online at www.melissa-marr.com.

SEANAN MCGUIRE was born and raised in Northern California, explaining her love of redwoods and fear of weather. She majored in folklore at UCB, leaving her with one clear career path: fantasy novelist. Currently, she writes two urban fantasy series with DAW, October Daye and InCryptid, and writes science fiction thrillers as Mira Grant, with Orbit. She lives in a crumbling farmhouse with too many books and several abnormally large blue cats. When not writing, she attends conventions, watches television, and argues endlessly about the X-Men. Seanan is exactly as much of a geek as this bio makes her seem.

SUZANNE MCLEOD writes the Spellcrackers.com urban fantasy series about magic, mayhem, and murder—liberally spiced with hot guys, kick-ass chicks, and super-cool supes. There are currently six books planned in the series. Suzanne was born in London—her favorite city and the home of Spellcrackers .com—and now lives with her husband and geriatric rescue dog on England's (sometimes) sunny South Coast. In her nonwriting life she occasionally works at renovating property; luckily, she's yet to meet a client who is truly undead. "Full-Scale Demolition" takes place six months before the start of *The Sweet Scent of Blood*, the first Spellcrackers novel.

S. J. ROZAN, a lifelong New Yorker, is an Edgar®, Shamus, Anthony, Nero, and Macavity winner, as well as a recipient of the Japanese Maltese Falcon award. She's served on the boards of Mystery Writers of America and Sisters in Crime, and as president of Private Eye Writers of America. She leads writing workshops and lectures widely. Her latest book is *On the Line*. Find her online at www .sjrozan.com.